The White Night
of St. Petersburg

PRINCE MICHAEL OF GREECE

The White Night of St. Petersburg

Translated from the French by Franklin Philip

Atlantic Monthly Press
New York

Originally published in the French language under the title *La nuit blanche de
Saint-Pétersbourg* by XO Éditions, Paris.

Published simultaneously in Canada
Printed in the United States of America

FIRST EDITION

Library of Congress Cataloging-in-Publication Data
Michel, Prince of Greece, 1939–
[Nuit blanche de Saint-Pétersbourg, English]
The white night of St. Petersburg / Prince Michael of Greece ;
translated from the French by Franklin Philip
p. cm.
ISBN 0-87113-922-7
1. Nikolaæ Konstantinovich, Grand Duke of Russia, 1850–1918 — Fiction.
I. Title: White night of Saint Petersburg.   II. Philip, Franklin.   III. Title.

PQ2673.I238N7813 2004
843'.914 — dc22   2004050205

Atlantic Monthly Press
841 Broadway
New York, NY 10003

04 05 06 07 08   10 9 8 7 6 5 4 3 2 1

In memory of Talya

From M. to M.

The White Night
of St. Petersburg

1

One morning in July of 1998, all the Romanovs still living assembled in the lobby of the recently renovated Astoria Hotel in St. Petersburg. They were waiting to leave for the Peter and Paul Fortress in order to attend the solemn burial of Tsar Nicholas II, his wife, Alexandra, and their children, who were to be interred together with the men and women murdered along with them. Only the *tsarevitch*'s little dog, which had been shot at the same time as the family, did not qualify for this privilege.

They had arrived in St. Petersburg a day or two earlier, these survivors of the legendary dynasty that since the sixteenth century had ruled the largest empire in the world. They came from all over, chiefly America, and nearly every country in Western Europe. At least three generations: the elderly ones, noble in appearance and in mourning attire, of course, but elegantly groomed; and the youngest ones, with children of their own who had little grasp of their family's history. On the television set installed in the hotel's lobby, they followed the preparations for the ceremony, which was broadcast live.

A large air force plane had just landed from Yekaterinburg, where the imperial family had perished and where their bodies had miraculously been found a short while before. On the runway the honor guard stood at attention, swords drawn, and the military band played a funeral march. The soldiers in full dress uniform lowered the caskets from the plane one by one and bore them on their shoulders to the hearses.

All those assembled in the hotel lobby, their eyes glued to the little screen, bore the same name as the victims, the world-famous patronymic of the Romanovs, but their blood ties were distant or nonexistent. None was old enough to have known Nicholas II; the eldest barely remembered their parents or grandparents talking about him. During the revolution of 1917, more than twenty members of the imperial family had been murdered. Those who survived and their descendants had afterward been persona non grata in the Soviet Union. Penniless, most of them had had to adapt to new circumstances, to build a new life wherever they had been led by chance, to take their places in settings and gatherings other than their own. Since their homeland had severed any connection with them, the youngest ones had consigned it to a corner of their memories, covered with dust.

And then came the burial of the last tsar, not only spectacularly resoldering the connection, but also placing them in the spotlight in a Russia they did not know and in which, for the duration of a ceremony, they became again the first family. On the screen they saw the caskets stamped with the two-headed eagle, and the few among them who spoke Russian attempted to decipher the names inscribed in bronze on the lids: Olga Nicolayevna, Tatiana Nicolayevna, Maria Nicolayevna, Nicholas Alexandrovich, Alexandra Feodorovna . . . And, almost in spite of themselves, they felt a lump in their throats, and tears came to their eyes. For, reemerging from the past, the most horrifying, bloodiest tragedy in history, that of their own relatives, abruptly touched them and moved them deeply.

All of a sudden the door of the lobby opened with a racket and in walked a woman on crutches who was clearly elderly, tall, and imperious. In spite of her years and her crutches, she still had a queenly bearing. Her clothing was worn but in good taste, and she wore it with a natural elegance. Her gray hair was arranged in a careful upsweep; her nearly unlined face had the complexion of a girl. Her dazzling blue eyes sparkled. She glanced at the fifty men and women gathered in the vast, columned hall. Who was she? Her name was Natalya Androssov Iskander Romanov. *I had never heard of her* . . .

Prince Nicholas stepped forward. The head of the imperial family and the eldest of the Romanovs, he is a tall, imposing man whose word is law. He walked up to the intruder and bowed in greeting. At this gesture the others understood that she must be treated as a member of the family. Even so, they did not pay much attention to her.

Instinctively, they sensed that she was different from them and hence she was unwelcome. They had seen so many impostors parade by—phony Anastasias, phony *tsarevitches*, then phony sons or daughters of *tsarevitches*. . . . They no longer even protested when these self-styled relatives showed up here and there to claim a share of the illusory inheritance or simply to brush against the glory of the name. But they kept at a distance anyone who sought to get into their invisible but hermetically sealed circle. And so, although they didn't draw away from the intruder, they also did not approach her. Thus, imperceptibly, they isolated her.

Never since the fall of the Russian Empire more than seventy years earlier had the church of the Peter and Paul Fortress, the pantheon of the imperial family, housed such a prestigious ceremony. Hundreds of altar candles made the gold of the altar screen, the iconostasis, glitter. Clusters of prelates in ceremonial robes swung their censers. To the right, the imperial family. Elsewhere, the ambassadors, and the civilian and military authorities. In front of the caskets of Nicholas II and his family, Boris Yeltsin himself—he who not long ago had had the Ipatiev house in Yekaterinburg razed to the ground because it was becoming a place of pilgrimage—the very person who had authorized this solemn funeral. We could see the former communist bow his head before the remains of the last tsar, and then offer his condolences to Prince Nicholas, effusively shaking his hand. It was not the reconciliation of the past and the present; it was two pasts, imperial and communist, merging in a strange present.

The intruder, Natalya Androssov Iskander Romanov, ended up in the last row of the family. No one took her arm to help her walk. No one paid any attention to her. She cared nothing about that. She had come not for the living, but for the dead.

I myself had been invited to the funeral of Nicholas II because my grandmother, the grand duchess Olga, was a Romanov. She was not yet sixteen when she left her native country for Greece in order to marry George I. Warmly welcomed by the Greeks, she devoted herself to them without counting the cost. She not only established charitable institutions, hospitals, and orphanages, but took charge of them personally. She never mixed in politics. Of all her prerogatives, she retained only one—to be accessible to all, to listen to those who needed her, and to act upon the promptings of her limitless compassion.

Although she took care to hide it, she remained Russian at heart. And so it was that, after twenty-five years of marriage, when she was not expecting to have anymore children and yet gave birth to her last son, she had decided deep in her heart that he would be the Russian of the family. Each year she took him along for her lengthy stays in Russia, and she taught him Russian, which he spoke like a native. She often had him visit his numerous relatives and had him play with the children of Nicholas II, especially with Anastasia, who was the same age as he. She was delighted to discover a Slavic soul in him and a talent for music that came from that source. This youngest child of Queen Olga was my father, Christopher of Greece. He passed on to me his interest in everything having to do with Russia. In the end, the history of these diverse and lively tsars, strewn with sudden twists and with tragedies, resembling fiction, is merely a family affair!

The intruder, Natalya — Talya to her friends and relatives — intrigued me. During my stay in Moscow some years earlier, a Russian friend had offered to introduce me to one of my female cousins who had lived there forever. I confess I was doubtful about her authenticity and I didn't follow up. Now, destiny, on the occasion of these national funerals, had brought us together, and I wished to meet her. The same friend who had told me of her existence set up an appointment. I was not yet convinced, however, that she was genuine.

So I went to Moscow to meet this living enigma. For miles the car drove over the very wide Kutuzov Prospekt. We drove past the log hut where, on the eve of the battle of Moscow, Kutuzov made the heroic decision to give up Moscow to Napoleon. The countryside was filled with lush orchards; then we reached a sort of suburb where apartment houses under construction alternated with decrepit public housing projects. We stopped in front of the most dilapidated one, under the gaze of a learned gathering of

babushkas—elderly Russian women. Miraculously, the elevator still
worked.

Talya lived there in a tiny, cluttered two-room apartment.
Books, old newspapers, and cardboard boxes were scattered among
shelves sagging under cheap knickknacks. An ornamental tree took
up too much space. Vases stuffed with flowers were placed everywhere. Above the narrow bed were lined up yellowed photos and
popular icons.

Most of all I was struck by Talya's eyes. They flashed with
an almost unbearable brightness. The voice as well, strong, authoritarian, issuing its orders to the ravishingly beautiful journalist
attending her, to the bearded cousin who had brought me there,
and even to the dog Malesh, the only one who didn't listen to her
and who did exactly what he pleased. Eighty-two years old and
still in top form and stylish, her pale blouse, her navy blue slacks
testified that she still knew how to dress. In accord with traditional Russian hospitality, she had prepared a real feast; pâtés she
had taken three days to make, bottles of wine, and a cherry brandy
of her own making that could wake the dead and kill off the living. Too bad if it was only five o'clock, we had to eat and above
all drink our fill.

Since her door was never closed, children constantly came in,
curious to get a look at the visitor. They were the offspring of an
alcoholic neighbor, and Talya had become a grandmother of sorts.
She would give them small change so they could walk the dog
Malesh, when he was feeling disobedient. They spent it on candy.

Talya's appearance left no doubt: even in this wretched studio apartment, she reigned like a queen. Everything down to the
tiniest detail and slightest gesture announced it.

So I dared to ask the question that had preyed on me:

"How is it that a Romanov like yourself has managed not to
be arrested, imprisoned, tortured, or shot by the Soviets?"

"My mother remarried and, to protect me, my stepfather adopted me and gave me his name. My last name is still Androssov."

But it wasn't as simple as that.

"Everyone knew that I was part of the ancien régime. Apparently that could be seen a mile away! The KGB was aware of my real identity."

"Did they put pressure on you or make threats?"

"Not directly, but I sensed their presence constantly. . . . I was always under their surveillance; it was invisible, the worst kind of all."

"So you had to lead a completely hidden existence?"

"Not at all. Quite the reverse. I was a star!"

"A star! Of what?"

"The circus. I was a motorcycle acrobat!"

I hid my amazement so poorly that Talya was amused. After a short silence she satisfied my curiosity.

"When I finished high school, I found the universities were closed to me. At the time there was a law prohibiting members of the old aristocracy from getting a higher education. So I had to work and earn a living! I learned to make shoes, hats, belts, dresses. But I didn't see myself remaining a manual worker for the rest of my life. . . . I always loved exercise and sports. I'd ridden horses since childhood. Later on I learned to drive, I took part in auto competitions, and I even won some races! And then I loved danger. At the time there were in Gorky Park a couple of Germans who did an acrobatic routine on motorcycles. They vanished when the war was starting up. I don't know whether they were driven out or left of their own accord. They left all their equipment behind. A contest was announced to choose their successor. I applied for the job. One female candidate who had registered didn't show up; another one broke her leg. So I was the only one competing. I won, and soon I was hired by a well-known circus."

Talya picked up her crutches, arose, whirled around the apartment, jostled the people around her, pulled down a cardboard box half torn open, took out some snapshots, and threw them on the table. All of them showed her in the days of her glory: here with her hair tousled, astride her motorcycle; there a little tiddly, sailor's hat, cigarette butt at her lips, and wearing a man's suit; there again in profile in a pose worthy of famed portrait photographer Cecil Beaton. A matchless beauty!

"Were you ever in love, Cousin Talya?"

"Yes, with the circus wall that I had to leap on my motorcycle!"

"Have you been loved, Cousin Talya?"

She smiled enigmatically and refrained from answering me. She had no need to. I guessed that she had broken hearts and left behind a string of lovers.

Her appearance, her behavior, her style—everything about her disconcerted me. She put me in mind of the seventeenth-century *tsarinas*, capable of anything, particularly of excesses, and whom nothing had daunted. Under her impressive personality she was authentic, imperial, and unadulterated. But in the end, who on earth was she? For that indeed was the crucial question, the question for which I had come seeking an answer.

"I'm the granddaughter of the grand duke Nicholas Konstantinovich, your grandmother Olga's brother."

"Excuse me, Cousin Talya, but my grandmother had only three brothers: Constantine, the illustrious poet Dimitri, who was assassinated during the revolution, and Viaceslav, who died when he was young."

"She had a fourth one, the eldest, my grandfather."

As tactfully as I could, I tried to get her to admit that no Grand Duke Nicholas Konstantinovich appeared in any of the family portraits that I had looked at many times, to the point of knowing them by heart.

"That's true, Cousin Michael, he's no longer in them, but he was there. He was stricken from the imperial family as if he had never existed."

"Among the Romanovs, brothers poisoned their sisters, wives murdered their husbands, fathers tortured their sons, but no one was ever struck off the lists!"

"And yet, that's what happened to my grandfather. . . ."

It had been snowing nonstop in St. Petersburg since dawn. The thick flakes covered the gray-coated soldiers who, bayonets fixed, formed a line from the Winter Palace to the fortress, like strollers in close ranks. Another solemn funeral was going on in the church of the Peter and Paul Fortress, the funeral of the empress Alexandra Feodorovna. But this was a long time ago, in November of 1860.

The carriages of the royal court followed the immense catafalque crowned with black feathers, and dropped off their illustrious passengers in front of the sanctuary, opposite the cells of political prisoners, for the fortress was both an imperial pantheon and a state prison. The church's interior had been spruced up for the occasion. Veils of crepe that resembled lacework of golden bronze hung from the huge iconostasis; other veils, black mourning crepes, were wrapped around massive columns and covered the heavy coats of arms and the imperial crowns of gilded cardboard. Thousands of candles barely managed to warm the atmosphere. The church was packed.

Facing the "royal door" of the iconostasis, the casket of the deceased empress was set on a catafalque overloaded with altar candles, emblems, trophies, coats of arms, and flowers. Following the custom of the Orthodox Church, the casket was open. The hooked nose and bony face of the emperor's mother could clearly be seen. She was the daughter of the colorless Frederick William III of Prussia and the incomparable Queen Louise, the beauty who alone had dared to stand up to Napoleon. At her birth she had been named Charlotte, but upon her marriage she followed custom and russified herself into Alexandra Feodorovna.

Her husband, the emperor Nicholas I, had cheated on her without losing the deepest respect for her. She had been his supporter, his adviser. This inflexible tyrant had terrorized the whole empire, beginning with his own family, but not his wife. Without ever standing up to him, she had been able to defend herself. She had brought up her children faultlessly and they adored her. With as much firmness as sweetness, she had kept the court on a superb footing without tolerating the slightest disturbance. Her charity was proverbial and she was deeply missed.

The reigning emperor, Alexander II, was the chief mourner, clearly recognizable by his abundant sideburns that blended with a full mustache. By his side, his wife, the beautiful empress Maria Alexandrovna, with a melancholy gaze. A bit farther away, a short man with a pince-nez hanging from a cord of black silk, who is scarcely noticed because he is accompanied by the grand duchess Alexandra Joséphine, by far the most beautiful of all the ladies of the court.

Finally come the imperial children, including this boy of about ten, a bit skinny, with delicate features, watching his entourage with a sort of irony, surprising to say the least in this atmosphere of deep reverence.

Now came the funeral's most solemn moment. Emperor Alexander II made his way to the catafalque, a lighted altar candle in his hand. He knelt, bowed deeply before going up the velvet-carpeted steps, leaned over the casket, and gently kissed his mother's forehead. Then he stepped back, made the sign of the cross, and returned to his place under the canopy. In order of precedence, each member of the imperial family followed his example. Next, some employees of the court closed the casket's lid and nailed it shut, the hammer blows resounding harshly in the silence. To finish it off, a heavy gilded sheet embroidered with the deceased empress's coat of arms was thrown over the casket. Then, to signify that Alexandra had truly left this world, the emperor and his family, followed by all the courtiers, turned the candles they held in their hands upside down and extinguished them by crushing the wicks on the stone floor. The songs of the choir started up again while the prelates withdrew through the royal door behind the iconostasis.

Suddenly a flame ran up the crepe veil draped behind the imperial family. In a second, the erminelike rabbit fur that they wore caught fire, and soon the coats of arms were burning brightly! Already the fire was threatening the gilded cardboard crowns and the poles supporting the canopy. No one knew what to do. The formal respect inspired by the emperor, the fear of showing the slightest sign of panic, immobilized most.

Some officials, chamberlains, came up to the emperor to protect him from the fire spreading above his head. Alexander II did not lose his self-control. Without moving, without any visible emotion, he gave orders. The page boys rushed to the casket of the dowager empress and lifted it up to keep it safe from the flames.

The imperial family moved away a little from the flames, the soldiers tore away the half-burned draperies and trampled them underfoot, others with their swords brought down the coats of arms and the glowing crowns. The cautious clergy had not moved from behind the iconostasis and observed the scene through its openings. Soon the fire was brought under control. With the emperor in the lead, everyone went back to their place as if nothing had happened. The prelates, sparkling with gold and brocades, emerged from the iconostasis and the service resumed. All that remained was an abominable odor of burnt fabric that overpowered the scent of the incense.

In the carriage that had brought him, his imperial highness, the grand duke Nicholas Konstantinovich of Russia, Grand Cross of the Order of St. Andrew, of the Order of St. Anne, of the Order of St. Vladimir, of the Order of the White Eagle of Poland, colonel-in-chief of the Volynski Regiment, of the Ismailovsky Guards, head of the 4th Battalion of the Guards of the Imperial Family, commander of the 84th Regiment of the Shirvan Infantry, was thinking. He was ten years old, and he had been given these titles, decorations, and honors at his birth. He wondered what had impelled him to set fire to the crepe veiling with an altar candle, knowing full well that he was running the risk of dramatically interrupting his grandmother's funeral.

Even so, he had deeply loved the recently deceased woman. As far back as he could remember she had surrounded him with deep tenderness, had lavished presents on him, and above all she had always shown how much she valued his company. It was he whom she had chosen, with only three of her other grandsons, to accompany her five years earlier to the coronation of Alexander II. The journey in the imperial train, the solemn entry into Moscow in a coach, the halls of the Kremlin, the processions, the cheering crowds, the ceremonies where one had to remain standing for hours, the coronation banquet . . . ; of this emotional kaleidoscope, he still kept the image of his grandmother dressed in silver brocade and sparkling with enormous diamonds.

The previous winter, while she was staying on the Riviera in an attempt to treat a bronchial condition, she had asked for him to join her. She already was ill, and silence hung heavy over the great villa she had rented. Despite her weakness, she had made an effort to take him out for a walk to Cimiez. She endeavored to entertain him by calling in magicians, singers, musicians, and even the famous canary tamer, Miss Van der Meersch! For all this, little Nicholas had been profoundly grateful.

So why, during her funeral, did some irresistible impulse impel him to set fire to the crepe veil? He tried to persuade himself that it had been an accident, but deep inside he knew that he had done it on purpose. Might it have been through a taste for farce that he had wished to disrupt this overlong ceremony, to upset this starched world, to shake off the yoke he felt weighing on his shoulders? He loved being provocative, and nothing could stop him from doing whatever came into his head. But especially, as always, he had wanted to catch the attention of his mother.

His mother was seated next to him in the carriage. For Nicholas she was the most beautiful woman on earth. He could not conceive of there being someone more perfect and appealing. He could not stop looking at her large blue eyes, that straight slender nose, that tiny mouth, that dazzling complexion, that mass of auburn hair, that haughty attitude that made her even more attractive.

Nicholas preferred her on the evenings when there was a ball at court. As fashion demanded that she bare her shoulders and leave her bosom largely uncovered, he was fascinated by her satin-smooth skin and by those thrilling depths that brought out her slender waist and flared crinolines. Alexandra Joséphine covered herself with jewels, pearls, diamonds, sapphires, and emeralds, but even this glittering display did not compare to her own personal radiance.

No one was unaware that Nicholas was her favorite. Each time she saw him, she squeezed him to her as though he were an infant and, in the photos, she always has a possessive bearing toward him. She was proud of her son's beauty, proud of his progress in his schooling, for his teachers never ceased praising his intelligence and precociousness. Everyone thought she spoiled him too much, that she ought not excuse his whims and fads or favor him so conspicuously over his brothers and sisters. Nevertheless, Nicholas would have loved to see her more often.

At the time, children and their parents were separated by a boundless distance, and the grand duchess was much too conventional to break with established custom. So she saw Nicholas at only certain times of day, when the tutors and governesses brought her children to her. What's more, she was too wrapped up in herself. The beauty so admired by all the court and by her son required her continual attention. She slept in a corset to keep her slim-waisted, and she had cut out in ivory or silver the exquisite form of her slender foot to give as a present to her friends!

Another of her occupations was Anikova, that short, plump, and ruddy-faced woman.

Anikova attempted to be discreet, but she was everywhere. Nicholas saw his mother shut herself up with the woman every day for hours, and then there was no question of intruding on her. No sooner was she separated from Anikova than she was looking about for her or sending a footman to find her. She couldn't do without this woman, to the point that Nicholas was jealous of her. There were things that he didn't understand but which he felt or guessed. The guardsmen and women attending his parents—aides de camp, lady's companions—had the nerve to talk in front of him: "That Anikova, what a pain!" "She claims to be the daughter of the duke of Angoulême!" "She's crazy!" "Not at all, she's an adventuress who knows perfectly well what she's doing!"

He himself heard his mother say some things that were surprising:

"Queen Marie Antoinette told me through Anikova that I ought not to leave for Germany just now."

Wasn't Marie Antoinette that unfortunate monarch who, he had been told repeatedly, had been the close friend of his great-grandmother and whom the French revolutionaries guillotined? Thanks to Anikova, Marie Antoinette was at all the family lunches up to the day when Nicholas's father exploded:

"That's crap!"

"How dare you?" snapped the grand duchess Alexandra, flushed with rage.

Nicholas sensed his parents' disagreement. He hated Anikova, whom he held responsible for it. Spiritism was widespread at the Russian imperial court, séances were held for the emperor, for the empress—still, Alexandra was going too far! This Anikova completely dominated her. A daughter of the duke of Angoulême, just think! All the imperial entourage knew for a fact that the son of Charles X was impotent! Marie Antoinette advises her. . . . Marie Antoinette orders her. . . . The dowager empress, Alexandra's mother-in-law, hadn't dared intervene, but, sensing that her daughter-in-law was neglecting her children in favor of the adventuress, she had had them brought to her and had subtly tried to replace the absent mother. This was one of the reasons for her preference for her grandson Nicholas.

During the grand duchess's many trips, the children were left at the mercy of those who were supposed to educate them. Governesses, teachers, guardians—all Germans. The dynasty, despite its very Russian name, was of German origin. The wives of the emperors and the grand dukes were all German. The grand duchess Alexandra, also German, believed in her country's superiority. Constantine, Vera, Dimitri, Viaceslav, who were too little, were still under the care of women, but Nicholas and Olga, his younger sister, were subjected to a frightful program. Not a moment's rest or relaxation. Of course, they did not spend the whole day in the classroom, but the recesses, the walks under surveillance, were still moments of intensive training in various sports. Olga got out of it by being a downright poor pupil. Scoldings slid right over her unshakable sweetness. Nicholas himself proved brilliant in all subjects, but a certain person was never pleased.

That person was Mirbach, the German tutor who headed the

whole educational team. The better Nicholas did, the more Mirbach grumbled, demanded, criticized. Nicholas redoubled his efforts, but without success. He was exhausted, troubled, but Mirbach refused to take this into account. Scoldings and punishments rained down on the hyperintelligent child.

One day Nicholas, once again deprived of his mother, went into the office of his father, detained as he often was up in St. Petersburg, and took a miniature picture of the grand duchess. He had dozens of photos of her hanging in his bedroom, but this reproduction of the famous portrait by Winterhalter fascinated him.

Mirbach stopped short before the miniature sitting on his pupil's desk.

"How have you dared to steal this object belonging to your father?"

"I didn't steal it. I simply borrowed it while he was away."

Mirbach refused to hear anything of the sort. He grabbed hold of the whip he always had on him, forced Nicholas to take down his pants in front of the servants, and gave him a violent whipping. Not only on the buttocks, but also on the hips, where the pain was excruciating. Nicholas bit his lips so as not to scream, but he could not keep from groaning.

Passing by in the corridor, the countess von Keller, the grand duchess's lady-in-waiting, opened the door and witnessed the scene. This compassionate woman was indignant and scolded Mirbach for his excessive severity.

"As soon as the duchess gets back, I shall let her know about this incredible brutality!"

"You should know, countess, that I am carrying out the precise instructions of her imperial highness. It was she who decided in detail the program of education of her children, including what punishments they would undergo and for what misbehaviors."

"I can't believe that she authorized you to whip this unhappy child!"

"All you have to do is ask her when she gets back."

"Don't tell me you have previously inflicted this treatment on a boy of eleven?"

"I apply it each time the young grand duke deserves it."

Poor Nicholas took advantage of this to make his escape. He ran to curl up in his refuge, a shadowy cupboard under a service stairs. As usual, Saviolov, his father's former manservant, now in Nicholas's service, brought him the food he preferred, bread and tea. The child stuffed himself with them to the point that he was not hungry at lunchtime, and he refused to eat. No one paid him any attention.

No one ever forced him to eat healthier and more varied food. No one really looked after him.

2

Nicholas's father, the grand duke Constantine, had nothing impressive about him. Much shorter than the other grand dukes, he was extremely nearsighted, to the point of being unable to do without his pince-nez. Even so, his long beard divided in two gave him a certain presence. And, contrasting with his slim appearance, he had a stentorian voice with which he had fun startling those who met him.

Nicholas's parents had made a love match. When he was nineteen, during a trip to Germany, the grand duke Constantine had met Princess von Saxe Altenburg, then sixteen. "It will be she or no one else," he had declared, and her delighted parents had accepted.

Soon, however, his true inclinations landed him in politics. When he was twenty-five, and fighting in the Crimean War, he sent his father, Nicholas I, letters that the latter deemed the most lucid and pertinent reports on the situation. Then, after their father died, he had set himself up as the sincerest, most direct, most heeded adviser to his brother Alexander II. It was he who had encouraged him to halt the Crimean War as soon as possible and at any cost as it was getting nowhere. It was he who had promoted the emancipation of the serfs. And to set a good example, he had begun by freeing the serfs living on his huge estates.

Despite the generation gap, Constantine Nikolayevich was much more a friend than a teacher for his children. Except that he was never there! In the winter he and his wife often left on a long cruise to escape St. Petersburg's harsh climate, and several times he didn't hesitate to disrupt Nicholas's studies to take him along, on the specious pretext of "getting him used to the sea." Not a matter of seaborne habituation, these trips were merely a series of stays in the magical villas of Sicily, the palaces of Naples, the islands of Greece, and the hotels of Jerusalem, Beirut, and Cairo.

While traveling, the protocol was lightened. Nicholas had almost all his meals with his parents. His mother drew him to her and held him tight against her as she did at home, then shoved him away when something else came to occupy or distract her, and in the end he felt she was no longer there. It was also an opportunity for him to hear his father express himself more freely than usual. He railed against the backroom politics in Italy, the corruption in Egypt, the inertia of the Ottoman Empire. Politics, always politics . . . Away from Russia, the grand duke Constantine also enjoyed criticizing the Russian government. In thinly veiled words he denounced the obscurantism of Russian conservatives, the inefficiency of the imperial administration, the preposterous cruelties of the secret police, and the irresponsibility of the ruling classes. He criticized his emperor brother for being too conciliatory, and for being particularly feeble in his reforms. Constantine didn't conceal what he wished for Russia: a Western-style parliamentary government. The grand duchess kept mum, but her horrified expression made it clear to Nicholas that, here again, his parents didn't see eye to eye!

It was because of this liberalism that Alexander II, who was indifferent to the conservative opinions of his ministers and his parents, sent his brother Constantine to the hotbed of the empire, Poland, which was then under Russia's jurisdiction and always on the point of rebelling. The new viceroy took his whole family with him. They lived in Warsaw's uncomfortable and old-fashioned royal castle with its rows of daunting portraits of the past kings of Poland.

The beginnings were promising. His reputation preceded him and the grand duke Constantine was well received, but Nicholas noted that the crowd was rather sparse behind the rows of Russian soldiers. These soldiers, on the other hand, were omnipresent, so the grand duke confined the occupation army to the barracks to make it less visible. Many Polish nobles accepted the Russian viceroy's invitations, but were their flattering remarks really sincere? Constantine hastened to free nearly all the political prisoners. He wanted to win the Poles over to his brother the tsar. He made a show of having nothing to fear. Every day he went about in Warsaw unescorted.

One afternoon when he was going out for his walk, Constantine decided to take Nicholas and his sister Olga with him. The grand duchess, who had to preside over a charity committee and couldn't accompany them, protested. "You ought not to, Kostia, after all the warnings we've had lately!"

The grand duke swept these pleas aside. The more she insisted, the more he set his mind on going out anyway.

"At least leave the children in peace."

"On the contrary, Sannie, this will be an opportunity for them to visit Warsaw!"

The city's Russian governor stepped in:

"Let your imperial highness at least accept an escort."

Constantine sharply refused.

"We have, however, picked up some pieces of information that are precise and all in agreement. . . ." Constantine's only answer was to push the two children into the barouche. The group rode at a trotting pace through the principal avenues. Constantine gave the names of the aristocracy's palaces while Nicholas persisted in staring at the crowd, which was large for this promenade time of day. Everyone recognized the viceroy, the men raising their hats and the women venturing a little curtsy, but most of them looked away. The grand duke made a show of not noticing and continued to point out the important monuments to the children.

With his child's instinct, Nicholas understood that something was not right. He didn't know if there was any danger, but he sensed that the calm was merely apparent, and that behind it lay a growing unrest. Even his sister, who was generally a merry chatterbox, silently snuggled up to their father. Yet they completed the outing without incident and returned to the royal castle. The grand duchess was waiting for them on the front steps, beset with extreme anxiety.

"An assassination was planned. Did you know about it, Kostia?"

"As you can see, Sannie, there was no such attempt! Those were only rumors. Our ride couldn't have been more peaceful or more pleasant."

In spite of this steady tone, Nicholas straightaway noticed that his father's brow was furrowed as when he was greatly worried. There nearly had been an assassination attempt, as we later learned. That day, the Polish nationalists had planned to throw a bomb into the viceroy's open carriage, but the presence of Nicholas and Olga had stopped them at the last minute. "You don't assassinate children!" the plotters had declared. So no assassination attempt, but the tension was such that the explosion was inevitable. There was a rebellion.

Nicholas saw the fear in the faces of those around him. He heard the shots fired, the screams, he counted the cannons aligned in the palace's courtyards, pointing at the gates the rioters were attempting to force open. In the windows and on the roofs he saw the guards, their rifles aimed at the crowd. An escort, and what an escort — more numerous, more armed than ever — accompanied him and his family to the train station, for the grand duke had been called back. General Paskievich, who replaced him, suppressed the rebellion with cannon fire. With thousands of corpses on his conscience, he uttered that famous statement, "Order prevails in Warsaw!"

Alexander II didn't hold Constantine's failure against him. He didn't give up on his brother's counsels, as his brother didn't give up on his own liberalism. When Constantine had just returned, Alexander II sent him to the navy, which was greatly in need of modernization. There, Constantine applied himself with his customary energy and in a few years made the navy an ultramodern instrument of war. As a result, Alexander II named him head of the Empire Council, the state's highest authority.

For Nicholas, his father was his idol.

Following the custom for adolescents of the aristocracy, the young Maria von Keller had just been presented to the court. But she had known the imperial family since childhood. Her father was a close friend of the grand duke Constantine, and her mother was a lady-in-waiting to Nicholas's mother. So it was quite natural for her to be invited in that summer of 1865 to the Pavlovsk Palace, not far from the capital.

Intelligent and ambitious, Maria was delighted at the flattering opportunity. Three-quarters of an hour by train brought her to the village's little station. A court carriage was waiting for her and it soon entered the park. The carriage descended into a little valley where a river lazily flowed. Maria caught sight up on a hilltop of the majestic form of the yellow-and-white palace. The carriage veered left and followed a broad tree-lined driveway, from which she finally saw the splendid residence in all its façade, which stretched out in a semicircle from a central pavilion.

In fact, it was rather small—"small" being understood in the fashion of imperial Russia! Maria had already spent time in the other palaces, Tsarskoie Selo, Peterhof, Gatchina, whose buildings spread over acres. By comparison, Pavlovsk appeared tiny. The carriage came to a halt in front of a side pavilion. A lady-in-waiting sprang from a door, welcomed Maria, and brought her by a wide stairway to her apartment: a bedroom overlooking the rear of the park, an anteroom lined with closets, a bathroom. Two chamber-maids rushed to unpack her things. The lady-in-waiting waited for her while she freshened up and then took her to the second story and into the family's living room.

The grand duchess Alexandra and her children welcomed her with great affection, and Maria immediately felt at ease. She raised her eyes and looked around, noting everything. Quickly her gaze was concentrated on the eldest of the children, the grand duke Nicholas. The boy had filled out. Tall, both muscular and agile, with a refined face and noble features, downy hairs shaded his lips and emphasized their sensual curve. His long auburn hair was slightly wavy, and his large golden brown eyes with heavy eyelids steadily took the girl in.

Sensing the admiration he was eliciting, Nicholas soon became Maria's personal guide. Everything that money and good taste could create in the way of luxury, refinement, and the unique had been thought of for Pavlovsk. It was originally a present from Catherine the Great to her son, the future Paul I and his wife, Maria

Feodorovna. The two of them had made it the most precious center of art. The large apartments they lived in had been left as they were since their deaths, and, having been made into a museum, were practically no longer used. Nicholas showed off to Maria the paintings of great masters aligned on the flowered silks, the pieces of French furniture with delicate bronzes mixed with their even more excellent Russian copies.

They stopped before a set of Sèvres china.

"This was a present from Queen Marie Antoinette to her great friend, my great-grandmother the empress Maria Feodorovna, who loved to work with ivory."

And he showed her objects fashioned in this way by the late *tsarina*.

The grand duke's family lived in the wings of the palace. There, too, were masterpieces from the Spanish, Italian, and French schools of the eighteenth century, stunningly beautiful miniatures, chests of drawers by Riesener or Roentgen intermingled in accord with the taste of the time—represented by comfortable armchairs, green plants, nests of tables weighted down with knickknacks and placed in strategic spots so that the unwarned visitor banged into them, regiments of framed photographs . . . and a great deal of plush.

Nicholas spoke often of his great-grandfather the tsar Paul II, founder of Pavlovsk. "His mother, Catherine II, detested him, she could never be bothered with him! He was considered crazy, you know. . . . Nevertheless, he was extremely perceptive, to the point of being a forerunner. He wanted the good of everyone, the good of the empire, but no one understood him, his family less than anybody else. He did things that caused him to be misjudged. He was considered an abominable tyrant! In fact, he was never understood, a poorly loved man who never had a chance to display his true colors. He ended up assassinated in the most horrifying way, as you know. He is by far my favorite ancestor. It may be that I see myself in him . . . ," he added with an expression so grave that Maria shuddered. "I want to raise a statue to him here, before this marvel that he created, to make up somewhat for the injustice of which he was a victim."

Just as it was for all the other members of his family, Pavlovsk was Nicholas's favorite place. It thus became the same for Maria. They spent a good part of the day outdoors. They explored the gigantic park; they chose as the goal of their promenade the various follies scattered over it where sumptuous snacks awaited them. They got lost in the wild copses that stretched for miles in the beds of small valleys. They went boating on the river, they did some racing with large coaches called charabancs, they galloped in the alleys, they organized picnics. Maria became acquainted with the local mosquitoes, enormous insects that did not give their victims a second's respite but whose bites were not painful. A supreme favor: the grand duchess opened her private reserve, a rose garden dating from the eighteenth century that she lovingly looked after.

For Maria, Nicholas was gradually turning into an apostle of the forbidden. One day he convinced her to jump over the wall to leave the park. It was impossible to leave through one of the gateways, for the guard would immediately warn those concerned, so they clambered over the railing! Maria just had time to tear her skirt before finding herself on the other side.

"Here we are, free!" exclaimed Nicholas.

And he led her in front of the Vauxhall, the well-known restaurant of Pavlovsk where the most fashionable residents of the capital rubbed shoulders. They didn't dare venture inside, and both of them looked through the windows at the elegant couples whirling around to the sound of an orchestra that Johann Strauss himself was sometimes not averse to conducting! Maria, noticing some fruit-and-vegetable peddlers selling sweets, asked Nicholas to buy her some hard candy, her passion. Nicholas sadly shook his head: "I have no money. The little I get I spend on books."

Maria couldn't get over it.

"How is it, your imperial highness, that you are poor? And all this, then?" she said, pointing out the château and the park.

"Someday, Pavlovsk and many other things will be mine. . . . But, for the time being, I have a pension that is pathetic, just a few dozen rubles a month. But don't worry, you'll still have your candy!"

Before Maria could stop him, he darted over to the display and, without the peddler seeing him, pocketed a handful of hard candy. Then in a pirouette, he returned laughing to his friend.

"But that's stealing, imperial highness!"

"Everything's mine . . . Nothing's mine."

On the way back, a pensive Maria asked him:

"What kind of books do you buy with your pocket money?"

"Travel books. I dream of being an explorer, going off exploring the great deserts of Asia."

Even during vacations, the studies program of the imperial children was not completely suspended. The grand duchess proposed to Maria that she follow along with Nicholas and Olga the lessons in French literature overseen by Mr. Ricard, a teacher at the naval and commercial schools. Maria accepted eagerly, not so much for the charms of French literature as for those of Nicholas. She had discovered that he was a poet, and a musician as well, for he played the piano, the violin, and he sang with a magnificent voice! Maria heard him from her bedroom when he sang Russian songs, so grave and melancholy that each time she was overwhelmed.

Mr. Ricard's classes were held in the classroom on the château's third story. There they were, deep into the tragedies of Corneille and Racine. Nicholas learned with astounding speed; it was enough for him to read the monologue once or twice in order to learn it by heart and recite it with a passion, like a professional actor, backed up with gestures and comical expressions. Maria lived as if in a dream. She saw herself in Chimène, in Bérénice. Nicholas was Le Cid, Titus, Hippolyte. Maria imagined herself rescuing him from the clutches of Phèdre.

One morning Mr. Ricard proposed they do an exercise in versification on the theme: "The thoughts of a veteran present at the review of the horse guards in March." Then no one spoke. . . . The sun streamed through the open windows and the buzzing of insects, the songs of the birds, and the thousand evocative noises of nature could be heard.

Olga began writing the title of her poem, dipped her quill in the inkwell several times, looked at the blank page, reddened, and burst into tears. She rushed out of the classroom. Maria found it hard to concentrate. Her eyes never left Nicholas, who was seated next to her.

Bent over his sheet of paper, he wrote quickly. She heard his pen scratching the paper, then he stopped, stood up, and, with the verve of an actor in a boulevard comedy, set about declaiming. Maria was barely listening to him; she was in raptures. She could not keep her eyes off him; she found him wonderfully handsome. While reciting, he shot her insistent looks. She lowered her eyes and went back to her assignment. Nicholas went on intoning his poem, in French of course, more and more loudly to prevent Maria from concentrating.

> At my waist I shall not have
> My sharp and cutting sword
> And I shall no longer feast
> To the sound of cymbals and songs.
> No longer will I give hell
> To conscripts frozen at attention

And wearing this mufti jacket
They will treat me like a boor . . .

Nicholas stopped, Maria couldn't help rising, and, red with
excitement, her eyes sparkling, she brought the house down with
her applause. Mr. Ricard was similarly red, but from anger.

"How dare you, imperial highness!"

"Dare what, Mr. Ricard?"

"Your last two lines are an insult to the army, to the veterans."

That day, exceptionally, the grand duke Constantine was having lunch in the private dining room. In all summer simplicity. The
footmen had exchanged their heavy gold-braided livery for lighter
clothing. The china, glassware, and silverware were simplified,
bearing only the imperial coat of arms engraved in gold as well as
the monograms of the grand duke and his wife. There were fewer
courses than usual, for the weather was very hot. In midmeal the
grand duchess announced to her husband that Mr. Ricard had
submitted his resignation.

"Why?"

Because the teacher judged some lines in Nicholas's poem
insulting.

"So what are those lines?" inquired the grand duke.

Nicholas lowered his eyes, full of a false humility. It was Maria
who recited them:

"And wearing this mufti jacket/They will treat me like a boor."

The grand duke burst out laughing.

"Without any doubt Nicholas is a born military man!"

The grand duchess managed to persuade Mr. Ricard to withdraw his resignation, and the classes resumed as usual. However,
the exercises in versifying were dropped. Corneille and Racine were
also abandoned in favor of Victor Hugo, not the Hugo who was
bitterly opposed to the regime of Napoleon III, but the earlier Hugo,

the writer of tragedies that Mr. Ricard considered innocent, and yet . . . *Lucretia Borgia* was set aside because of its scandalous subject matter, but *Les Burgraves*, which takes place in the pure and pious Middle Ages, presented no risk. Now here it was that Nicholas in a monologue clung to these lines:

> Let us reign, we are brave,
> By the iron, by the fire
> Scoff at kings, governors!
> Governors, scorn God!

He wouldn't let go of this quatrain! From morning to evening, he bellowed it out, not only in the classroom but during lunch, dinner, at all the family gatherings!

> Scoff at kings, governors!
> Governors, scorn God!

Accustomed to his eccentricities, the family paid him no attention, but one of his aunts, a visiting grand duchess, was deeply offended by it. She admonished Alexandra.

"So who taught these rebellious verses to young Nicholas?"

"The good Mr. Ricard."

"What good Mr. Ricard? My dear Sannie, he must certainly be a Jacobin! You didn't realize! You shouldn't keep company with a man who teaches such blasphemous verses to your children!"

Maria was watching Nicholas while the teacher's fate hung in the balance. With a sardonic expression, Nicholas was looking by turns at the visiting grand duchess and at his mother. He realized that Maria was watching him, and he mischievously winked at her. She blushed. Mr. Ricard was dismissed that very day.

Maria was indignant and waited until the afternoon snack to say so. That snack was at the Roses Pavilion, a delicate construction built by Maria Feodorovna in celebration of the victory of her son Alexander I and the defeat of Napoleon. The others played in the nearby meadows speckled with flowers or fished in the nearby stream. Remaining alone with Nicholas, she had no eyes for the garlands of roses painted on the paneling.

"Why did you let Mr. Ricard be fired? You knew that that was an injustice!"

"In any case, no one would have listened to me, least of all my mother. As for my visiting aunt, the source of all the trouble, I was literally hypnotized by her stupidity."

"Could Mr. Ricard really be a Jacobin?"

"I'd admire him all the more for it. I'd find a way to send him some compensation."

"Why do you persist in reciting those lines? They could indeed seem blasphemous."

"That is just why I chose them! *And scoff at the kings,* Maria, *at all the kings!*"

"But your parents, your family, the emperor?"

"The emperor is a man like everyone else. I love him for what he is, I hate him for what he represents."

"But the empire, Nicholas?"

"Russia would be much better off as a republic!"

Maria was overcome, but she did not give in:

"But *scorn God,* Nicholas."

"Do you want me to believe in a God that permits an injustice as blatant and cruel as the firing of Mr. Ricard?"

Another morning, as Maria was getting ready for the day, brushing her hair, she heard beneath her windows ferocious barking and piteous bleating. She rushed over to the casement. Brandishing a whip, Nicholas was egging on three bulldogs to pounce on a lamb that he had tied to a tree.

Maria was transfixed. Initially paralyzed with surprise and horror, she got a grip on herself and ran to knock next door, that of Colonel Mirkovich, Nicholas's assistant tutor. The colonel had also noticed the scene but had not dared to intervene.

"Something has to be done. He must be stopped," ordered the young lady.

The colonel disappeared down the stairway. Maria went trembling back to the window. She thought she must be hallucinating. Below, no more dogs, no more lamb, no more Nicholas! It had all happened so quickly she wondered whether she hadn't dreamt it.

At breakfast she didn't utter a word. Then she went back to her apartment and heard strange noises coming from one of the closets of her anteroom. Surprised and a little apprehensive, she opened it. Out trotted the lamb she had seen that had been on the point of being devoured by the dogs. His frizzy hair adorned with ribbons, he set about licking her hand.

Shaking people up was the favorite pastime of the fifteen-year-old Nicholas.

For Nicholas was not "like the others," which made him only more attractive. Maria had heard that when he was eleven or twelve, at the emperor's palace in Tsarskoie Selo, he had violently banged his head while running down a staircase. There followed weeks and months of illness punctuated by terrible headaches, and since then Nicholas has had migraines, which might explain the behavior he sometimes exhibited with his family circle. His mother seemed to adore him, his father overlooked many small faults in him, and yet he appeared distant with his parents. As for his brothers and sisters, he often treated them harshly, even Olga, for whom he obviously had boundless love.

What puzzled Maria most was the relationship between Nicholas and his tutor. Nicholas was no longer a child, and the attitude of Mirbach bespoke the respect owed a grand duke who would soon be of age. But when Mirbach gazed at his pupil, his pout betrayed his skepticism—even a feeling of disgust. For his part, Nicholas behaved with him as if he didn't exist. He did not speak to him, didn't even seem to notice his presence, and when Mirbach spoke to him, he always responded with few words while looking at someone else. More than once Maria had surprised Nicholas's fugitive gaze falling on the German, and she had had the time to see hatred mixed with fear. She wondered what terrible secret—dormant but still active—had come between them.

In truth Nicholas was unlike any other member of the imperial family, and Maria had a chance to verify it when the grand duke heir, Alexander Alexandrovich, the son of Alexander II, came to lunch at Pavlovsk. He was a gruff giant of Herculean strength, capable of tearing a pack of cards between his hands or of bending a silver salver. Despite his youth, he had no grace, no charisma. And his powerfulness precisely made him unusually clumsy.

Right away Maria perceived the antipathy between the heir and his cousin Nicholas. What's more, Alexander took the liberty of attacking the liberal politics of his father the emperor, which—everyone knew this—was defended if not inspired by the grand duke Constantine, Nicholas's father. Constantine tried to keep calm in responding to his nephew, who made a gesture too abruptly and knocked over a glass of red wine on the embroidered tablecloth. The grand duke couldn't keep back a little sarcastic laugh:

"Just look at these bovines that St. Petersburg sends us!"

Nicholas guffawed. And Maria saw the heir's face turn crimson with rage.

3

Even though at birth he was named (honorary) colonel-in-chief of several regiments, the young grand duke Nicholas underwent training like any officer. He took part in maneuvers, on land in the infantry, on the Baltic Sea in the navy. An extraordinarily gifted officer cadet, he was the first one in his family to graduate from the most demanding Military Academy of the General Staff. He advanced quickly, to second lieutenant, lieutenant, and then captain. From then on he was old enough to take part in the annual ceremonies at the court, such as the first day of January, then the seventh day of the same month for the Water Festival, the Orthodox Easter, and the Emperor's Day celebration.

On his eighteenth birthday in 1868, Nicholas was given a privilege that enabled him to show his generosity. He gave large amounts of money to his servants and even to his teachers. To his elderly valet Saviolov, who had served at his birth as he had at that of his father, he gave a house and a garden in the Pavlovsk park. To commemorate his visit to a regiment, he allocated a grant for sending officers each year for instruction abroad.

At about the same time he was authorized to look after Pavlovsk, his preferred estate, which one day he would inherit. He had heating installed in the family's apartments, attended to the park, gave a new water pump to the town's firemen. And he finally realized his old dream by erecting at his own expense a statue of the tsar Paul I, his favorite ancestor, in front of the palace that bore his name.

He was prompted by marriages, baptisms, and funerals within the family to travel abroad. He was in Athens for the first confinement of his sister Olga. She had married a young naval officer, the son of the king of Denmark, who had been sent to Athens to occupy the throne. Nicholas scarcely remembered the Greek capital that he had visited with his parents. Since then, the city's population had increased more than fourfold. He was put up in the royal palace, an enormous and noisy barn of a place. He was assigned a huge bedroom with a high ceiling that overlooked a park covered with dense foliage of many different species of trees.

One evening, after one of the many banquets that marked his stay, he was overcome by an odd torpor. Perhaps it was the food that didn't agree with him, or perhaps he had drunk too much, for it was very hot. He tossed and tossed in his bed in pursuit of the sleep that eluded him. . . .

In the Winter Palace, the imperial residence, Nicholas's room was unquestionably the most enormous and magnificent. Located almost at the center of the building, decorated with giant gold trophies, it was used for the most formal ceremonies. Entering, surrounded by guards, Nicholas found it draped in black. A platform set up in the middle of the room was also draped in black, and the countless courtiers were dressed in black.

He crossed the room between two rows of soldiers from the Volynski Regiment, his favorite, who, as a sign of shame, held their guns upside down. The platform was surrounded by other soldiers who held their weapons at the ready. In the background stood the family, in deep mourning. He noticed that his uncle the emperor was ashen-faced. Nicholas was thrust onto the platform while his mother and the empress rushed to the feet of Alexander II, imploring his grace. He heard the emperor answer hoarsely: "I cannot, I cannot . . ." The emperor in turn mounted the platform and kissed him three times and said: "I commend you to God," before turning to the crowd and declaring, "As his uncle, I pardon him and love him; as the monarch, I am forced to condemn him."

The emperor stepped down from the platform, regained his place, ordered that the man be blindfolded and that his hands be tied together behind his back. "Fire!"

In his bedroom at the royal palace in Athens, Nicholas thrashed about violently and woke up covered in cold sweat. He ran to the window to take in a bit of air, but not a breath of wind ruffled the dark park. Thousands of crickets stridulated in the branches. He raised his eyes to the stars twinkling above him. Every detail of his nightmare came back to him. A horrible image. He had been condemned to death . . . but for what crime?

Back in St. Petersburg, Nicholas took up again the military training, the law classes, the court ceremonies. . . . However much the routine for a Russian grand duke differed from that of other men, it still remained a routine. Nicholas was bored and didn't accept it. He knew he was intelligent, clear-sighted, he saw through lies, illusion, and pretentiousness, he saw in a flash the truth of a human being or the reality of a situation.

He was not unaware that his future was laid out down to the most minor details, and he foresaw its shape without illusions. First the army — following orders and keeping his mouth shut . . . — marriage to a German princess whom he will not love, then children in whom he will take little interest, an honorary position where he will be advised to take no initiative, inaugurations, curtsies, trips to foreign courts, official receptions where he will meet thousands of people with whom he must never get beyond banalities — in short, a life all conformism and conventions, a hollow existence without feelings, without action, without love. However, it was not even conceivable to reject this future.

Whereas he is full of ideas, of energy, he feels capable of accomplishing great things, of undertaking much, of innovating, in other words, of getting off the beaten track, just what he was forbidden to do! Prisoner until death. And no one to understand him, no one to talk to, except those sheets of paper where he bared his heart, papers he hid at the bottom of some drawers.

At the same time, his horrendous headaches, the aftereffects of his childhood accident, wouldn't let go of him. For hours he lay gasping with the impression that his skull was going to split. The pain and the memory of the pain made his thoughts even blacker. Then, a single last resort, cynicism, a single satisfaction, provocation, a single pastime, debauchery.

In St. Petersburg the grand duke Constantine lived in the Marble Palace, an austere magnificence built by Catherine II for Orlov, her lover at the time. Next to the rococo halls that had remained intact since the eighteenth century, the family had settled in apartments recently decorated in the neo-Gothic style, with a winter garden in blossom all year round, a marvel! So many staircases and narrow corridors intersected in the palace that it was difficult to keep track of all the comings and goings. Especially what went on in the vicinity of a small door giving onto the quay.

There, every night, toward midnight, Saviolov, the faithful valet, paced up and down. In winter he attempted to warm himself up by this exercise, or he took shelter under the glass canopy while complaining about his master's whims. In the summer it was pleasanter, but even so he would have preferred to be in bed. But how could he say no to the master who had so generously presented him with the house and garden of his dreams?

A carriage drew up that Saviolov recognized. It stopped in front of him and he opened the door. Out stepped first Captain Vorpovsky, Nicholas's aide-de-camp and also his game beater in the hunt; Saviolov also helped a gypsy descend whom Vorpovsky had fetched from one of the specialized nightspots. Singer or dancer, no matter, she made her trinkets clink and rustled the silky folds of her very full skirt. Saviolov looked at her contemptuously and shot an ugly look at Vorpovsky, whom he detested, but the two newcomers had already disappeared inside the palace.

Following the aide-de-camp, the girl climbed the spiral staircase as far as a small landing. Vorpovsky opened a door and had her enter while asking her to wait; then he closed the door. Left alone, the girl looked around, dumbstruck, at the paintings, the porcelains, the statues, the many-colored floral patterns of the oriental rugs, but above all the weapons. Swords, daggers with hilts bejeweled with precious stones, revolvers inlaid in gold were displayed tastefully on the walls. She was surprised at the number of books everywhere, on shelves, on tables, and even in tall stacks on the floor.

A velvet door curtain rose and a young man appeared. The gypsy knew very well who he was; all the city's prostitutes spoke about him! Right away she noticed that Nicholas was drunk. Nevertheless, he greeted her politely and asked her a few courteous questions. Accustomed to being treated like an object, she couldn't get over it. They made love quickly, but attentively enough that

Nicholas proved himself an exceptional lover. Clearly in a hurry, he then led her to the bathroom of which her friends had spoken. She went into raptures over the marble bathtub as her feet trod the thick woolen rug. She could very well have lingered on the ottoman that held its arms out toward her, but she had time for only a fast washup before being shown out. On the landing she found herself face-to-face with one of her friends, whom Vorpovsky had just brought in. Next!

After starting by pinching, they said, the governess of his twelve- and thirteen-year-old sisters, Nicholas paid court to all his mother's maids of honor, achieving successes that would have astonished her, convinced as she was of the virtue of these young ladies. Gradually he was seized with a veritable addiction to the courtesans, who were all crazy about him! They found Nicholas handsome, generous, particularly gifted in bed, and the way he treated them filled them with wonder. Wasn't it said that he addressed them as if they were women of the world? Moreover, for their part, these women had eyes only for him. Many of them offered themselves to him more or less openly. He never refused. Baroness H . . . Countess Y . . . And even little Princess L.

Nearly all the women who passed through his apartments noticed that during their talks the grand duke stared for a long time at a heavily framed portrait. It pictured a haughty young woman, a blue-eyed blonde. "I love her, but she doesn't want me," he invariably murmured. Some of the guests attributed these words to drunkenness, others detected in them a deep sadness.

It was indeed a matter of sadness. For the grand duchess Alexandra had decided to marry off Nicholas, a classic way to settle down this impetuous young man who, in any case, had reached the marriageable age. His mother turned to Germany, a bottomless reservoir of wives for the imperial family, and her choice had settled on the exceptionally beautiful princess Frederika von Hannover.

An interview had been organized, according to the custom of the time, for two young royal personages who wish to meet without overcommitting themselves. The meeting had been brief but decisive. Nicholas had fallen madly in love with Frederika. The confirmed womanizer, the tireless Don Juan was transfigured!

Back in Russia, he had announced the good news to his parents, who were delighted, and, after receiving the emperor's amiable consent, he conveyed the official proposal of marriage, certain that it would be accepted. But the young princess did not want Nicholas. Wasn't he sufficiently titled, handsome, intelligent? Yes indeed, but Frederika had decided to never marry. Her parents had been as horrified by this as the parents of Nicholas were perplexed. Nothing could be done to sway the headstrong young princess.

This rejection had plunged Nicholas even more deeply in love. Frederika's portrait, which had been sent before her refusal, had been hung in his bedroom. The impossible love had turned into a passion exclusive of anyone else. To his mother he had explained the contradictory feelings that had taken hold of him. "I know that one day you'll have your way and impose on me the German woman you choose."

"In any case, Nicky, you'll have your own say in the matter. And don't German women make excellent wives?" answered the grand duchess with a wheedling smile.

"I hate the Germans."

"Are you forgetting that I'm German?"

"You're different."

How did Nicholas learn the news? First, by noticing that his father was absent more and more often. His responsibilities at the navy and at the Empire Council of Alexander II of course kept him far from his family, but more recently he was not to be seen on days and at times when his son had been accustomed to seeing him.

But it was his mother's distress that alerted him above all. That cheerful and lighthearted woman who loved parties now refused to go out. Her eyes were red, and Nicholas noticed that she often cried. He worried about her to the point of taking a step that was particularly hard for him. He questioned Mirbach, simply because his former torturer was his mother's confidant.

The tutor was only too pleased to satisfy him. "Your father has a mistress!"

A few more rumors and Nicholas was able to reconstruct what had happened.

Her name was Anna Vassilievna Kuznetsova, the illegitimate daughter of an actor and a ballerina. She herself would have liked to be an actress, but her guttural speaking voice had made that impossible and she had become a ballerina, a famous one. No longer a young girl, no one kept score of her intimate conquests; she had even been married.

The grand duke Constantine, hitherto the respectable husband and family man, having reached his fifties, fell in love with her like a schoolboy for a star, but the beauty had her peculiar ways. One does not give in so easily, even to a grand duke! And Constantine had become almost crazy as a result. He had run to his brother to ask for permission to divorce in order to marry Anna! The emperor refused, of course.

Since then, Constantine had showered Kuznetsova with gifts, bought her a house in the Crimea, had another one built for her in the very park of Pavlovsk while the lady was pregnant by him!

From time immemorial, emperors and grand dukes have had mistresses and illegitimate children, to the point where it has become something of an everyday affair, but Nicholas couldn't stand seeing his mother suffer. He, Nicholas, was not married; he could have all the girls he wanted. But his father? Openly cheating on his wife! Daring even for an instant to consider leaving her! Nicholas's idol had just fallen off its pedestal.

At that juncture the grand duchess withdrew alone and with dignity to Pavlovsk. Nicholas hastened to rejoin her there. He wanted to help and console her. But what was there to say to a mother who has been betrayed other than to express one's love for her? He encouraged her to seek diversions. It was not in her solitude at Pavlovsk that she would forget, that she would come to accept having the usurper around. She needed to come back to St. Petersburg and, instead of rejecting society life, she should plunge into it, if only to put an end to the spiteful gossip. Alexandra accepted. Nicholas thought he had won. Then his mother said to him, "It's you who are responsible for all this! If your life were a bit more settled and normal, your father wouldn't have committed such an indiscretion. It was your debauchery that inspired him; you're the one who set the example!"

This injustice so overwhelmed Nicholas that he could neither answer nor protest. He didn't understand that the grand duchess, in her humiliation, her suffering, had to find someone guilty to avoid acknowledging that she hadn't known how to hold on to the man she loved. She didn't entertain the thought that it was possible to resist her beauty, to which all her efforts were bent and which she believed irresistible. So she punished Nicholas. From then on, Alexandra openly showed her contempt for her once-favorite child. She no longer wished to see him. Nicholas had rejected his father, and now he was rejected by his mother.

Then he let himself sink into despair. He drank more and more. He drank anything—champagne, cognac, even vodka—and what made it worse was his capacity to hold his drink wonderfully well. Even though the amount he drank would have knocked out just about any seasoned drunkard, he remained standing and still clear-headed. But his disposition became increasingly demanding. One night he even had twelve women in a row brought to his bachelor pad. Twelve times, the loyal Saviolov had to open the little door of the Marble Palace. Whining and with quaking legs, he had to keep watch until dawn. Nicholas made love twelve times in a single night, and all St. Petersburg society spoke of it with shock and wonder! For Nicholas, who had hitherto been fairly discreet about his many sexual affairs, now wanted everyone to know the depth of his degradation. Alcohol and women—he could not escape their grip.

The next morning he got up early despite his late bedtime. He didn't have a hangover exactly, but this man, usually so agile and active, was having trouble moving and even thinking. His mind clouded, he let his gaze wander over the porcelains from China, the paintings from the Italian Renaissance, the Mayan statuettes and Aztec jades, for he had gone as far as taking an interest in pre-Columbian art, which was almost unknown at the time. An omnivorous reader, he felt incapable that morning of opening the slightest book, even of leafing through the rare editions, the volumes for book lovers, the great illustrated works all around him. Saviolov entered and announced that Dr. Havrowitz was asking to see the grand duke.

Dr. Havrowitz was the family physician. He had treated everyone in it, starting with the grand duke Constantine, who had given him two diamond rings that he wore with pride. To reward him for his good and faithful service, the emperor had named him private counselor. Although he was German, Nicholas had a liking for him.

Dr. Havrowitz came into the office, took off his greatcoat, which nearly reached the floor, and took off his top hat. Short and plump, he was always armed with a cane with a gold knob and always outfitted with his circular gold-rimmed glasses. Breathless from having climbed up the palace's steep steps, he was sufficiently at ease with the family to take a seat without being given leave to do so by the grand duke.

"To what favorable wind do I owe the pleasure of your visit, good doctor?"

"Not to the wind, imperial highness, but to the results of your recent medical analyses."

Nicholas was silent.

"The results are not good."

Nicholas gave the doctor a questioning look but still said nothing.

"Your imperial highness has contracted a venereal disease."

"I've got the pox?"

"How many times have I told you to take precautions. I've warned you! The way you have been carrying on and the partners you've been choosing, it was almost inevitable. Why did you not want to listen to me? It's as if you had done it on purpose."

"Who says that I didn't do it on purpose?"

Dr. Havrowitz didn't answer but tapped his ankle boots with the end of his cane. Nicholas then had a sense that he wasn't finished.

"Come, doctor, don't sulk like that! You'll run me through the usual treatments and it will go away. People don't die from the pox anymore."

"Yes, they do sometimes, imperial highness, when the illness is severe."

"Are you trying to say that I'm in danger of dying?"

"You're in a generally weakened state owing to your excesses. I did recommend tonics. You may have had this illness for longer than I can tell. You must immediately make a change in your life, start a radical treatment, and above all no more excesses and a lot of rest. Otherwise . . ."

"Otherwise, dear doctor?"

Dr. Havrowitz did not answer him.

"Otherwise, dear doctor, I won't be around for long!"

Instead of answering, Dr. Havrowitz stood up, bowed deeply, put on his top hat and coat, and, breathing noisily, made his way to the door and disappeared.

So he was condemned to die young. Nicholas assumed a strange smile. And just like any Russian in such circumstances, he murmured *"Nitchevo,"* it's nothing.

In a few days the grand duke Nicholas was going to reach his majority. In spite of the wrangling in the family, the event had to be celebrated as if nothing of the sort was taking place. His father, his mother, his brothers and sisters, his former teachers, and his friends hastily prepared their gifts. A party had been arranged. The Marble Palace was filled with happy excitement at the prospect of these festivities. What could be more joyous to celebrate than the birthday of this young man who had every talent and a fulfilling life in front of him.

The future hero of the day wrote in his diary:

> *Very soon I'll be twenty. Will I have more freedom? Still, this day of my majority is the great day of my life. It is time to review the path I have followed. It may seem a bit strange, but up to now I have lived only by thinking of the future, I was afraid to remember the past . . .*
>
> *My childhood was very sad. I recall certain happy days, but not with my parents. In all those years, the only happy times I spent were when I was staying with the emperor and empress.*
>
> *In fact I don't want to look back because I don't want to have on my mind that there can be happy children.*
>
> *I still don't understand why I am not loved, though those around me say that isn't true. Have I harmed anyone at all?*
>
> *Could it be that I am one of those creatures whose mere presence causes negative feelings in others? In imagining that this might be true, I feel the absolute poison of rage spreading in me. Where does*

*that come from, for children are not born with the burden of anger.
. . . The person who inculcated this horrible thought in me is guilty of
a grave sin. . . .*

*From that time I recall two or three good moments, a few good
ideas, but no good feelings. However, by nature, I had some in me,
surely, but they were buried by the German. From now on, I must
revive them, for it is impossible to live only in one's head.*

*Let's hope that this military academy changes me, that my best
qualities well up in my heart and that all the worst ones dry out and
die. I shall remember what I am writing today when I reach thirty, if
of course I don't burn this sheet of paper along with other documents,
the way I burned everything concerning Mirbach. Amen.*

27 December 1869

Nicholas could burn everything except the memories that tormented him.

They were all there around the table to celebrate his majority.
The whole family, all those who had surrounded him since he was
born. At least forty of them were in the great baroque hall of the
second floor, the most beautiful one in the palace. The marble of
the pilasters and the bas reliefs had the same pale coloring as the
icy water of the Neva outside and the landscape covered with snow.
Everyone seemed merry, even the servants in embroidered livery,
shorts, and silk stockings. Despite protocol, they had been in service at the palace for so many years that they were part of the family and smiled when the guests turned toward Nicholas and held
up their glasses to drink to his health.

Standing before his chair, Nicholas looked at them one after
the other without paying attention to them. With an absentminded
smile, he bowed slightly to respond to their toasts. He raised his
glass only in Mirbach's direction. . . . Mirbach whipping him, pull-
ing his ears, hitting his hands with an iron ruler. . . . Mirbach

subjecting him to icy showers, striking at him so violently that his head spun, Mirbach hounding him in childhood to the point of provoking his terrible headaches.

His father had too often been absent to detect this child-battering, which everybody around the boy knew about, his brothers, sisters, the servants, the governesses, but which no one dared to report for fear of retaliation. As for his mother, she didn't know the details, but as a principle she always approved of what Mirbach was doing. For a long time she had made a show of preferring Nicholas to her other children, and she had loved him so ineptly. . . .

"To your health, Nicholas, and may you live to a hundred!"

In answer, Nicholas only laughed sardonically. A hundred. While according to Dr. Havrowitz, he had only a few months left!

4

It was still early in the morning; the train had just left Berlin, which she found gloomy. She curled up in her first-class compartment and looked out the window at the stretches of land covered with snow.

Hattie Blackford, an American, was young and a devastating beauty. Sparkling eyes, a sensual mouth, long blond hair, exciting curves, every particle of her body contributed to her voluptuousness, and the men who saw her dreamt of only one thing, always the same. She knew it and decided to go with it, and even exploited it; she had made it her profession. Given her age, she was only at the start of her career, but her ambition was to surpass her great predecessors: La Castiglione, Lola Montez, and even Cora Pearl, her friend and "teacher." This, however, she did not confess in her diary, where with talent she recorded the days of her life.

For a long time she had wanted to visit Russia, and she had avidly read many books about it. She was fascinated by Peter the Great, who had become a carpenter and married a tramp; by the ice palaces built on the orders of the *tsarina* Anne; by the "wild splendors" of the great and cruel Catherine II. She imagined teams of spirited horses, icy hills on which people slid with vertiginous speed, nights with no darkness. Ever since she was a child she had repeated to her mother that it was there that she wanted to live when she grew up. Her mother had raised her arms to heaven. "But you could be frozen!" Nothing could discourage her. "When I go there, I'll be sure to wear furs" she said, although she was far from having any at the time.

The train slowed and stopped at a little station; she made out the name Wirballan. It was the Russian border, and everyone had to get off. First bad surprise, the customs agents went through her luggage and confiscated all her books. The imperial censorship was relentless. Second bad surprise, her passport was not properly stamped; it had to be sent to Königsberg and she was to wait for three days. Three days in this godforsaken spot? You can't get around the rules!

She protested so strongly that they ended up finding a room for her above the customs office. An iron bedstead, a white basin, not a drop of water. Hattie heard the bells signaling the train's departure, the whistle of the steam engine; through the window she saw the happy passengers hurrying onto the express train that would take them to Russia.

It was time for lunch. She went down to the waiting room and found her maid Joséphine holding in her arms her beloved Maltese cat, Lloyd, suffering from convulsions. It was too late and he died right before their eyes.

That afternoon, to relax, she tried looking at the countryside by leaning out the window, but the shutters were stuck closed with grime. She managed to open only a small transom, cold air streaming in. In the distance she spotted a blue dome strewn with golden stars. Certainly a pavilion? At last a little entertainment! She ran into the street and asked where the pavilion was: there was no pavilion, it was only a church. She walked over to it. On entering, she was charmed by the interior, glittering with gold and silver. "I have always been captivated by anything that shines." Her future was fully to prove it.

When she got back to the customs office, Hattie found the head customs officer in discussion with a civilian. She soon understood that the civilian was an agent of the secret police. These gentlemen asked if she had any acquaintances in Russia who could help her. She mentioned several of her old "customers." They pouted.

"Do you know General Trepov, madam?"

They were referring to the much-dreaded police chief of St. Petersburg.

Alas, Hattie had never had the pleasure of making his acquaintance. On the other hand, she knew Mr. Goodenough well.

"Madam, that is not a Russian name!"

"Really? He's very well known in the theater!"

The theater . . . The two men had a sudden inspiration. "Do you mean Stepan Ghedeonov, the head of His Majesty's Theater?"

"That's him. Indeed it is!"

Two smiles brightened these gentlemen's faces. "Are you an actress, madam?"

"Yes, I am." She in fact knew of only one theater, the world, where since her youth she had acted in only a single play, her life. The gentlemen obligingly supplied her with writing materials. She wrote a telegram addressed to Ghedeonov, and then went up to her room and peacefully to sleep.

At two in the morning there was a knock on her door, and she woke up with a start. The two gentlemen told her they had just received a telegram, from General Trepov, authorizing her to proceed with her journey.

Hattie's train drove on through the empire. Endless stretches of snow, trees leafless black as in shadow theater, here and there a log hut, in the stations clusters of peasants, longhaired and greasy, but Hattie was not saddened by this monotony. Finally the train reached the capital. At the terminal, called Warsaw Station, she spotted an agent of the Hôtel de France, where she was to stay. He found her a carriage that, to judge by its dilapidation, must have dated back to Catherine the Great!

They say you should see St. Petersburg first in winter. Through the half-icy window, Hattie glimpsed the colossal perspectives, colonnades as white as snow, baroque palaces, enormous cathedrals, frozen canals, imposing statues. In the streets the numerous passersby hurried past the stores. Her carriage encountered sleighs going as fast as the wind.

At the hotel she recovered from her ordeal, first by taking a hot, perfumed bath, then by wolfing down slices of Russian bread, the best she had ever eaten. Close to four in the afternoon and night had already fallen. She took her writing case and sent notes to all her male friends, starting with Ghedeonov, the famous theater manager. The only thing to do now was wait and see if her fishing had been productive.

The doorman at the hotel, who had sworn he knew the addresses of all these gentlemen, had in fact drawn a blank. "That fool just told me that he could find only one, whose reply he handed me," said Joséphine, passing the note to Hattie.

A short note from Prince Gagarine: "Make yourself as beautiful as possible and wait for me at your hotel at midnight."

At midnight, no one. She had abandoned hope when, suddenly, Prince Gagarine materialized—an old man, certainly, but attractive, ready to listen, also with a fine title and a considerable fortune. A coach promptly took them to the nearby Green Restaurant.

Hattie found herself in a huge hall full of uniforms. Men only, and all servicemen. From their age and appearance, she immediately nicknamed them "the club of the silver-plated elders." She was handed a glass of vodka, which she downed in one gulp. It was something new to her, and in her diary she was careful to note that the taste reminded her of a kind of corn whiskey. She was fascinated by the stripes, the aglets, the ornamental braiding, the decorations worn by these officers. She asked them a hundred questions on this subject. Soon she had as good a knowledge of the ranks and the regiments of the Russian army as the highest-ranking general!

She learned to down a drink in one gulp, Russian-style: you place your right arm under that of your neighbor, drink up, dab each other's mouth, and kiss each other three times, twice on the cheeks and the third time on the mouth. This sport especially pleased her and permitted her to display her talents. In short, the late supper lasted until seven in the morning. Gagarine proposed a ride in a troika to get some fresh air, and only much later did she get back to her room at the Hôtel de France, with the conviction of having spent a profitable night.

Hattie spent the mornings of the next few days carrying out the duties of the complete tourist—she viewed all the monuments of St. Petersburg—and spent her nights drinking with the silver-plated elders. But she had other aspirations.

It was then that an English colleague showed up. Mabel Grey had started as a clerk in a fashionable clothing store, where her beauty had soon been noticed. Hattie had heard of her in Paris; it was said that Mabel had been "on the closest possible terms" with one of the sons of Queen Victoria before being carried off by a Russian aristocrat. From then on, she was well off and respectable in Moscow.

Hattie's reputation had preceded her. Mabel was curious to meet her.

"You are as irresistible as I was told!"

That was her introduction, to which Hattie tactfully replied, "As for you, they really didn't do you justice."

Without seeming to, Mabel observed Hattie from every angle. "You have a quality that the ladies at the court don't have. You look after your appearance down to the tiniest detail, you leave nothing to chance."

Mabel had reached an age and a status that eliminated any kind of rivalry. The complicity of language and profession did the rest between this American woman and this Englishwoman lost in the heart of the tsarist empire.

The Englishwoman invited the American to give up "the silver-plated elders" for "the golden youth" and presented her to a great many spirited and polyglot princes, counts, and barons. Hattie kindled their enthusiasm by hesitantly expressing herself in the Russian that a student was teaching her several hours every day. They all drank huge quantities of champagne, then they piled into sleighs and rushed to the "gypsies," those fashionable cabarets proliferating on the islands neighboring the capital.

The sleighs slid silently along; the cold was sharp and cut through clothing and even the furs. They arrived at Dorrots, the chic spot at the time, and Hattie went from the North Pole to the tropics without transition. An oppressive heat pervaded this place, transformed into a winter garden with exotic plants, murmuring fountains, grottoes lined with cushions to encourage private tête-à-têtes. A swinging door opened and in came gypsies: some very young girls, others less young, rather handsome men with a fierce look. They started singing songs that were sometimes tearful, some-times jolly to the point of laughter. There followed wild and fren-zied dances.

Hattie was so taken by the show that she took off a diamond bracelet, a trophy from a defunct love affair, and tossed it to the dancers. The gypsies were enthusiastic! The enthusiasm of the golden youth who wouldn't let go of Hattie! The revelers proposed she accompany them on an excursion to Tsarskoie Selo, the village not far from St. Petersburg where the imperial Summer Palace stood. They took a train and even reserved a whole coach of it for their group. In three-quarters of an hour they reached the little sta-tion and found themselves in the beautiful villa of Prince Gagarine.

Some twenty men, young and dashing, and two women, Mabel and Hattie. The band of the prince's regiment arrived and played a serenade. Then they all drank themselves silly until a stunned Hattie saw the soldier-musicians seize their colonel, the prince, and toss him in the air, skillfully catching him. That was the greatest sign of affection that the Russians could bestow, it was explained to her. Was proof of this affection not to be bestowed on Hattie as well?

Immediately she felt herself seized by forty hands, tossed in the air, with just time to think that these were her last moments before she was caught gently and set down on the floor. She had behaved so magnificently that her admirers repeated the stunt sev-eral times before drinking everyone's health and declaring her a hero amongst heroes.

Then they set off again by sleigh and went into the park of the imperial palace. In the moonlight the sleighs slid along the snow-covered paths while their riders bawled out songs and drank straight from bottles of champagne and vodka. They ended up at the home of another colonel, also a prince. They began making music again, dancing until dawn, without stopping drinking for an instant. They even decided to go on by horseback to visit a nearby menagerie, but Hattie couldn't take it anymore. Pleading that her riding habit was too tight, she collapsed on the first handy sofa and fell deeply asleep while the others, who were tireless, jumped into the saddle and vanished.

After three weeks of this way of life, Hattie was half dead with fatigue. Despite Mabel's help, Hattie's "fishing," although not fruitless, did not yield sufficient quality. . . . The silver-plated elders gladly paid, but became rare; given their age, their excesses had to be less frequent. As for the golden youth, it was more eager, more present, but less golden than it appeared. The rich parents had tightened the purse strings of their sons.

That evening, a weary Hattie decided not to go out. Although she had received several invitations, she preferred to remain in her suite at the Hôtel de France. At eight o'clock, after a light supper, she went to bed, hoping that ten hours of sleep would help her get back to normal.

But at midnight she woke up. She picked up a book and leafed through it, waiting for sleep to return. Some time passed, she had no desire to sleep, and the book bored her. Hattie rose and wandered about in her dressing gown. Going by her desk, her eye was caught by an invitation for that very evening to the formal ball at the opera. Mabel Grey had discouraged her. "The affair has lost all its glamour. It used to be that the grand dukes and even the tsar showed up for it, but now there are only middle-class people!"

Hattie turned the invitation over repeatedly in her hand. Giving way to an impulse, she decided to go there at once. Going alone was impossible. She woke up her faithful chambermaid and asked her to accompany her. Joséphine allowed herself to be persuaded, but not without grumbling. She helped her mistress put on her finery. In every circumstance, Hattie dressed with the greatest care. As Mabel had remarked, she left no detail of her clothing to chance.

That evening she chose a light and flowing dress of white silk that went together well with her black silk domino and her mask adorned with lace. Joséphine put up her blond hair in a chignon of curls that she embellished with a long string of pearls that, in Mabel's opinion, gave her a kind of Slavic elegance.

The two women left in a carriage. Before entering, they adjusted their masks. The gold-and-white hall was brilliantly lit by enormous chandeliers. The orchestra seats had been removed to make room for the dancers. The boxes reserved for the late supper were decorated with flowers, but there were very few people. It was either too late or the ball was not a great success.

"This is a real waste of time," sighed Joséphine.

"Be quiet and sit in the corner while you wait for me."

Hattie, who wasn't easily discouraged, went to have a look around.

She noticed a detachment of golden youth surrounding a man a bit younger than the others, very tall and extraordinarily handsome. Though she had never seen him before, his good looks acted on her like a magnet. She approached. Despite her mask, her friends recognized her, and one after another offered her his arm.

"No, gentlemen, this evening I don't want any of you! I will take the arm of that beautiful boy whom I don't know. . . ."

The young man graciously bowed, offered his arm, and left with Hattie to go to the brilliantly lit corridors around the boxes. He was so tall that he had to bend over to say to her, "Excuse me, but I don't know a lot of English. . . ."

"That doesn't matter, I also speak French!"

The young man threw questions at her thick and fast. Had she been in Russia long? Had she seen the emperor yet? The grand dukes? The court? Hattie was sorry to have to answer in the negative; like all American women, she was fascinated by royalty, and her dearest wish was still to meet the imperial family.

"Do you know who I am?" asked the young man, abruptly using the familiar *"tu"* form of the second-person pronoun.

"No," Hattie replied, using the familiar pronoun. "I don't know anything about you except that you're young, handsome, a captain in the horse guards, and you are an aide-de-camp of the emperor."

The young man was flabbergasted by Hattie's knowledge, not knowing that the "silver-plated elders" had coached her in recognizing uniforms of every rank. He explained that he was indeed an aide-de-camp of the emperor who, in appointing him, wanted thus to thank his father, a rich storekeeper in Moscow, for the considerable wealth he had spent on the Crimean War.

"As for me, I am poor, for I squandered my whole fortune on pretty women!"

He examined Hattie, trying to guess her features under the mask. "What's your name, beautiful mask?"

"Fanny Lear, if it pleases you," ventured Hattie on an inspiration.

"Fanny Lear! I've heard that name before. Isn't it from a comedy by Meilhac and Halévy that was such a hit in Paris?"

Hattie congratulated him on his culture.

"I even recall the plot," he went on. "Isn't it about a seaman's daughter who comes into a large inheritance and goes to Paris to buy herself a marquis as a husband, then makes herself a place in the aristocracy?"

"I would like that to be my story. I wasn't born with the virtues of the poor, but with those of the rich."

"Then, Fanny Lear, you will be rich!"

With these introductions, she huddled up against the young man and set about telling him the thousand follies that went through her head, her impressions of Russia, of St. Petersburg, of the imperial government, of the arbitrary treatment she had experienced, beginning with the incident at the border.

The young man suggested she sit down. She was dying to, and headed for one of the red velvet banquettes lined up against the walls.

"Not here," the young man exclaimed. "I have a box. We'll be much better off there."

She followed him until he halted before a door. A braid-trimmed footman opened it. She saw a small sitting room stretched with red and gold damask on which were embroidered the imperial coats of arms with the two-headed eagle. The door was closed; Fanny was alone with the young man, who gently guided her to a sofa. From his pocket he drew a gold cigarette case on which Fanny noticed the imperial coat of arms once again. She stared at him in astonishment.

"Well, well, Mademoiselle Fanny Lear, so you've never seen a grand duke of Russia before!" he mockingly exclaimed, and he asked her to take off her mask.

She refused to do so. Then he eagerly questioned her about the beauties her mask and costume were concealing. What did she look like? Was her figure as perfect as the hand and foot he'd glimpsed. Silence.

"Are you pretty?" he asked, almost anxiously.

"Judge for yourself, your highness." And Fanny took off her mask.

Each one stared at the other. As an expert, he took stock of her astonished eyes, dark yet so sparkling that they looked light, her voluptuous mouth, her neck well exposed by the chignon, the décolleté full of promise, the slender waist, the extraordinary sensuality of the whole.

Fanny saw that he was magnificently built, wide shoulders, a willowy figure, a slim waist. A blending of strength and grace. She was attracted by his large, muscular hands, hands that she wanted to feel on her body. She noted the oval face, the very white skin, the broad forehead, sign of a keen intelligence, the thick black eyebrows, the straight nose, "voluptuous, like those of the ancient statues of Venus and Apollo." His eyes surprised her: very deep-set, she had thought they were brown, but they were rather green with golden highlights. She read irony in them, but their expression was continually changing, at one moment dreamy and tender, at another clouded by sadness. It was his mouth that drove Fanny wild with desire. Rather large, with red lips whose curve cast a spell over her, a smile now caressing, now ardent. She wanted to cry out to him: "Kiss me, and to feel your lips on mine, I would gladly die at once."

However, he went on gazing at her lovingly.

"Have you looked at me enough, are you satisfied?" she asked him.

"Not half enough. I don't think one could ever gaze at you sufficiently."

She then launched herself into a helter-skelter speech, speaking to hide her embarrassment and to prevent him from moving too close. He took her hand.

"You call that a hand? It's a little bird's foot."

"Don't laugh at it, for I could be tempted to show you that it is hard to deflect."

He took her into his arms, holding her tight. She tried to escape.

"Would it be possible to accompany you to your place for a late supper?" he asked her.

"Why not! But at this time of night the personnel at the hotel will have gone to bed."

Never mind, he would send his aide-de-camp to find some food.

At the moment of leaving, Fanny remembered her chambermaid, the good Joséphine, whom she found on her banquette, still waiting. At the exit of the opera, a host of valets surrounded them.

"Karpish!" cried the grand duke.

A dwarf immediately appeared at their sides, clothed in red from head to toe, down to the tiny boots, with a coat carelessly thrown over his shoulders that was edged with fur and floated in the night air. He opened the door of a magnificent carriage, whose driver was a giant. Fanny then saw a soldier already seated inside.

"Captain Vorpovsky, my aide-de-camp."

The man, who had dark hair and dark skin, was rather handsome. He was smiling. He knew how to look at women, he had seen so many of them with his master. . . .

When they entered Fanny's sitting room at the Hôtel de France, Nicholas Konstantinovich looked with curiosity at each element of the setting. He paused before the window box. Instead of flowers, it held only bulbs.

"This is both my decoration and my salad, your highness. I eat only onions and bread."

Nicholas burst out laughing.

At this moment his aide-de-camp came back with what he could find in the hotel's kitchens, a basketful of fowl, fruit, and salad. For drinking, Fanny's tooth glass would have to do. With no place settings, they were reduced to eating with their fingers.

Vorpovsky's presence discommoded Fanny. Nicholas guessed this and enjoined the latter to withdraw.

"I have something to speak to you about, Fanny."

"It's six o'clock in the morning, your highness. I need some sleep."

"You can sleep right away if you make me a promise on your word of honor."

"I'm too bohemian to have a word of honor!"

Nicholas sat down at Fanny's desk and scribbled a few lines on a sheet of paper with the hotel's letterhead. "Sign it, you must."

And Fanny read it. "I swear by everything I hold most sacred in the world not to speak to anyone, not to see anyone, ever, anywhere without the permission of my august master. I make the commitment to abide by this oath as an honorable American woman and I declare myself the slave, body and soul, of the grand duke Nicholas Konstantinovich of Russia."

Fanny couldn't believe her eyes. Was this a joke? But Nicholas's magnetic gaze was at this point so powerful that her resistance melted away. Like a robot, she took a pen and signed "Fanny Lear."

Nicholas took her in his arms and kissed her. "You are henceforth mine." Then this curious confidence. "I once loved a beautiful princess, and she didn't want me. But my honor was at stake and I would never marry anyone else. You see, you've just signed a contract for life!"

Then they gave themselves to pleasure. She with all the art that her profession gave her, he with the passion given him by nature. Right away she felt that he'd had many experiences, but he must have been dealing with women who were insufficiently skilled or with low-class trollops. She taught him slowness, progression, and refinement. She taught him how to explore the most secret recesses of her woman's body. She had him reach peaks of ecstasy that he didn't expect, making a consummate art of her sensuality. In one night she attached him to herself forever.

Perhaps this is the moment to make a few corrections to Fanny's diary, which has been respected faithfully since the moment of her arrival in Russia. According to her, she decided to go to the ball on a last-minute impulse, and thus mere chance was responsible for her meeting the grand duke Nicholas, whose identity, moreover, she didn't initially know. We could just as well imagine that, having drawn up the list of possible targets with the indispensable Mabel, the latter had steered her to the decisive encounter, knowing the grand duke had to be there. Carefully informed, Fanny would recognize him without too much trouble. She had only to place herself in his way and let him win her over. Fanny

could be satisfied; she had finally caught the big fish she was an-
gling for in Russia.

The next morning, remaining alone, Fanny felt, according to her
own confession, "like the princess of my dreams," but as five o'clock
approached, the time at which Nicholas had promised to pay her a
visit, she had a sense of being the one "who had been given a white
elephant and who doesn't know what to do with this present . . ."

When her lover showed up, her apprehension vanished. He
took a bracelet from his pocket, a thick gold chain whose clasp was
a turquoise heart, put it around Fanny's wrist, closed the heart, and
hooked the little gold key to her charms.

"You are too generous, my lord!"

He told her to stop using "my lord" and the "*vous*" form of
address. That evening he was to have dinner with his father, the
grand duke Constantine, but Nicholas sent him some excuse or
other and spent a second night at the Hôtel de France.

Three days later, a note from Nicholas let Fanny know someone would come to fetch her at seven o'clock to take her to dine
with him at his place. At that hour there was a knock on her door.
Fanny hastened to open it. His imperial highness's representative
was the dwarf Karpish, who began speaking Russian to her with
such garrulousness that Fanny didn't understand a word of it. She
followed him to the carriage driven by the giant, whose white beard
came down to his belt.

Once at the Marble Palace, they didn't enter at the main steps,
but at the side entrance that so many streetwalkers and women of
the world knew so well. The faithful Saviolov was waiting for the
visitor and led her up a flight. Entering Nicholas's private apartments, Fanny went into ecstasies over two paintings by Greuze, two
ravishing women, a shade too innocent. Then she paused before a
portrait of a young woman who was tall, blond, wearing court dress.
A beauty.

"Who is that?" she asked innocently.

"Princess Frederika, of course."

Fanny gazed at the image with keen curiosity. Nicholas broke the silence. "Isn't her resemblance to you surprising?"

Fanny didn't dare agree. Nicholas became impatient.

"Okay, say it—what do you think of all that?" His irritation showed in his tone.

"If I can be for you in any way what she would have been, I will be . . ."

She didn't turn around. She knew he was contemplating the portrait of this beloved woman who had refused him, and she didn't want to see the expression on his face.

"Dinner is served," announced Karpish, who had come in without knocking.

Fanny welcomed this distraction gladly. Nicholas led her to a table set in a corner for a light and intimate meal. The almost inedible dinner surprised her; she wondered how, with an army of French chefs, gastronomy could be so lacking in an imperial palace. On the other hand, the wine proved to be of the highest quality, in particular a Tokay, "a personal present of the emperor of Austria," Nicholas announced.

Saviolov, while providing the service, continually looked at Fanny and whispered in Nicholas's ear comments in Russian that were obviously about her.

After that late supper, Nicholas introduced Fanny to Turkish coffee and the water pipe. It took a couple of trials: she spit, she coughed before correctly inhaling the sweet-smelling smoke. Once again she paused before the two paintings by Greuze.

"These women represent the curse and the remorse," explained Nicholas.

"Why such sinister titles?"

Without answering, her lover led her to the bathroom. Noticing the ottoman, she sat there in a most lascivious pose.

This time the eroticism was spiced with an exquisite apprehension, for the true master of the place, the grand duke Constantine, could suddenly materialize at any instant. This thought, this fear, made Nicholas and Fanny all the more passionate. A tiger and a tigress wild with sensuality, intoxicated with amorous pleasure, they grappled with each other for long hours, then remained exhausted on the rug with the bold floral pattern. Fanny spent the rest of the night in Nicholas's apartments, and then the morning. Right in the middle of the makeshift lunch, Saviolov suddenly appeared in the library and, panic-stricken, announced the coming of the grand duke Constantine.

Looking around, Fanny wanted to hurl herself into a closet, but spotted her hat and her veil on the bed. She pounced on the bed and pulled the brocade curtains around her shut. This piece of furniture had been Nicholas's latest acquisition, a very large and very deep Renaissance bed that originally accommodated a whole family. Four sculpted columns held up a gilded canopy.

But it was precisely this curiosity that the grand duke Constantine had come to admire! He walked around the bed to look over its details, followed by his trembling son, then abruptly he parted the curtains. Fanny only had time to stick her head under the pillow.

"Who is this woman?"

"It's someone who came to collect money for a charitable organization. When she heard you coming, she lost her head and hid."

"Is she pretty?"

"No, she is old and ugly."

Nicholas's father burst out laughing.

"Then I won't bother looking at her."

He left the apartment.

Barely had he closed the door behind him than he opened it again, and Fanny heard him say, "I'm sure you're lying to me, Nicholas. I think it must be that American woman, and I want to see her, for they say she's very pretty."

"It's not possible, papa; she's shaking with fear and doesn't want to show herself."

The father dropped it . . . and Nicholas pulled a trembling Fanny out of her hiding place.

"So the whole family knows . . . about you, about me, about us . . ."

"Not only my family, but the entire city, and I'm delighted! For I'm proud to have you as a mistress."

In an era when almost insuperable barriers came between generations, Fanny was happily surprised by the companionship, even complicity, that she detected between the father and the son. She would have loved to see the father again, to which the son responded with a categorical *nyet:* "Too many things divide him and me."

Fanny hugged the walls as she left the Marble Palace.

5

Nicholas had made an appointment with her for five o'clock that afternoon at the Hôtel de France. No sooner had he arrived than he
directed her to throw some things in a bag, for he was taking her
away within the hour. Where? To Pavlovsk.

Fanny jumped, for that was the home of Nicholas's mother,
the fearsome grand duchess Alexandra. Nicholas swept aside
Fanny's objections and had her get into the troika in which the
omnipresent Vorpovsky, his aide-de-camp, was already seated.
Soon they reached the gates of the town and went into the open
countryside. The night was so dark that Fanny could make nothing out apart from the snowbanks that looked like enormous white
mountains. If little could be seen, the cold on the other hand was
frightful; the wind was biting and brought tears to her eyes.

She would have liked her two companions to look after her, but they had gone to sleep. She feared that they would die frozen, and she woke them a bit abruptly, which put both of them in a very bad mood but didn't stop them from going right back to sleep. The troika went rushing through the dark and glacial night. Fanny was besieged by drowsiness, fatigue, the cold, and even boredom. Finally she saw a light and then very soon a carriage entrance.

A guard emerged from a sentry box and presented arms. A bell announced the visitors' arrival. Fanny could see nothing of the palace.

In the ill-lit vestibule, she took off her snow-covered outer garments. Nicholas pushed her into a hallway, a door opened, and she found herself in a magnificent hall, brightly illuminated, marvelously heated, filled with masterpieces. Nicholas went off to greet his mother and would soon come back.

Fanny thought of herself as an accomplished courtesan, self-educated, impelled by real artistic curiosity. So, looking around, she easily identified the portrait of Catherine II by Lampi, that of Peter the Great by Nattier, and she judged the proper value of the porphyry table, the Chinese silks embroidered with large songbirds, the eighteenth-century bronze clocks that joyously rang, uncoordinated, at various times.

Nicholas had returned. Fanny noticed his inscrutable face, his sad expression. He answered her questions wearily.

"My mother scolded me about you. Each time I come to see her, I have to hear a litany of criticisms."

"But everyone says you're her favorite."

"Does she even love me?"

They sat down at the table. Despite the somber mood, Fanny noticed that for once the imperial food was exquisite. One glass of champagne followed another. Nicholas was drinking more than usual.

"I hope you can come back often to this estate of Pavlovsk, to which I am deeply attached."

Then, taking up his guitar, he began to sing in his deep, baritone voice. Fanny was deeply moved by his melancholy and that of the song. At length, on the pretext of having her visit the bedroom, he led her there for the night.

The next morning, the breakfast was rather simple. Only tea and bread, that famous Russian bread that she so much appreciated. Gone was the veil of sadness that had cast a shadow over the evening before. Nicholas behaved like a kid full of pranks on vacation. To visit the palace, he had Fanny cross-dress so that neither the grand duchess Alexandra nor the servants suspected her identity. With wild laughter, he had her put on a man's vest, hid her face with a thick scarf, and covered her head with one of his own hats. The long coat covered her skirts. In this outfit he walked with her to his aviary and his zoological park. But the birds and the deer, discouraged by the cold, refused to show up.

The visit to the great apartments was punctuated by light touching, furtive caresses, quick fondling, stolen kisses in the doorways. Nicholas took pride in the statue of Paul I that he had had erected. Fanny listened to him praise this grandfather of his. He had been naturally good, frank, and loyal, he had been proud and let himself be attracted only by the true, the noble, and the just. He had perhaps too short a temper and was prone to outbursts of anger, but they didn't last long. His mother had completely spoiled him as a child. Later she had surrounded him with spies, untrustworthy creatures who set traps for him, with the result that people had built up the most dreadful idea of him.

Listening to Nicholas, Fanny wondered several times if he were drawing a portrait of his great-grandfather or of himself. He expressed himself with the restraint and emotion characteristic of a person divulging something personal. Do people normally have tears in their eyes when talking about an ancestor?

Seeing an emperor up close, in the flesh, was the dearest wish of an American woman. So Fanny had a whim; she wanted to meet Alexander II.

She knew that Nicholas couldn't present a courtesan to his uncle. But she also knew, as did all of St. Petersburg, that every afternoon the emperor took a walk in the Summer Garden. So Fanny went to this attractive park that stretched from the Old Michael Palace to the Neva. She passed through the elegant iron gate, walked over the little bridge spanning a canal, and began strolling in the paths strewn with copses and statues of mythological figures.

At two o'clock on the dot, she saw a sleigh loom up drawn by two magnificent horses and led by an imposing driver. An officer descended. Two members of the secret police materialized and took his fur coat. Fanny noticed that he was not so young, but very handsome, that he was wearing the uniform of the knights of the guard with the white cap bearing red stripes.

Before beginning his walk, Tsar Alexander II looked around. His gaze scanned Fanny and seemed to transfix her; his eyes were a magnificent light blue, but their expression was severe and almost hostile. Fanny didn't know how to respond; should she curtsy or appear not to notice the insistency of this gaze?

Alexander II headed for her. She was trembling with excitement. After a grand duke, why not an emperor? He was a ladies' man, she had learned, and what a catch! The biggest one of all. The absolute master of life and death of 100 million subjects. The possessor of unlimited riches. The world's leading collector of jewels and precious stones.

His favorite black spaniel was following him. Perhaps Fanny was discreetly summoning the animal. In any case, the dog came to sniff at her, let himself be stroked, licked her hand. "Milord!" The emperor, irritated, called off the dog, which obeyed him. Alexander II turned off on a path and walked away. The opportunity had been missed. And Fanny, a good sport, ecstatically repeated to herself the Russian proverb, "God has his subjects, but the tsar has his faithful."

She told Nicholas of her adventure, for she knew how he worshiped his uncle. "If ever some misfortune befalls me, the emperor will be the only one to take pity on me," he often repeated. Then this immediate reservation: "I would have myself killed for him, but I would like to destroy his government!"

Every day Fanny was confronted with her lover's contradictions, with that ambiguity he cultivated, a prince down to his fingertips who dreamt only of being a free, creative man. Little by little she was taken into his confidence. "My father has only two passions, politics and his dancer." As for his mother, the grand duchess, he never talked about her. Fanny knew by instinct that this subject was off-limits. She was surprised to see this man, who had everything that one could desire, including the most expert and loving of mistresses, fall into the blackest of moods.

"I think, Fanny, that I am stamped with the seal of misfortune and was born under an unlucky star."

The frightened Fanny didn't know how to respond. Lost in his thoughts, Nicholas went on. "It seems to me that someday I shall commit a terrible and degrading action."

What nonsense! Where did this crazy idea come from? From a frightening dream that had come back every night for some time now. The same one he had had three years earlier when he was in Athens for the birth of Olga's first child. And then he told Fanny about his nightmare, in which he saw himself executed for some crime: "And I woke up with a start bathed in a cold sweat." Fanny's laugh rang false.

"Dreams lie."

A courtesan's profession demands that she be calculating. Now Fanny saw that she was increasingly disregarding this creed, so much did Nicholas disconcert and thereby disarm her. Precisely in connection with money. That very afternoon, while walking arm in arm along the Nevsky Prospekt, the capital's main commercial street, she stopped before the window of a cake store. She never could resist sweets. She asked her lover to buy her a meringue, a mountain of cream topped with irresistibly appealing green angelica. Nicholas abruptly refused. "It's much too expensive."

"What, too expensive? Barely a few rubles!"

But Nicholas was already dragging her away, almost by force, the same Nicholas who the day before had given her a bracelet worth several thousand rubles, a gold circle set with two big cabochons of emeralds. How could he make a scene over a few rubles after proving so generous and spending galore for her without batting an eye? She had forgotten that members of the imperial family never carried cash. When they went into a store, it was enough for them to sign their initials at the foot of the bill, which was sent to the palace and immediately settled.

The grand duke's education had only complicated his relationship with money. Up to the age of twenty, he had been allocated the ridiculously low sum of ten rubles a month; then, on the day of his majority, in one stroke, he was allocated by the imperial privileges two hundred thousand rubles each month.

Every day, in the course of their conversations, Fanny learned something more about Nicholas's childhood and adolescence. On the one hand, people were extremely severe with him; on the other hand, he was allowed to do whatever he wanted, principally as regarding his diet. He could have as much of his favorite foods — bread and tea — as he wished. His whims were overlooked, but on the other hand . . .

Fanny had noticed curious marks on his hips, whitish striations. One morning when both were resting after a night of love, she caressed him and her hand lingered on these marks.

"Are these birthmarks?"

Nicholas shook his head. She questioned him, he didn't want to answer, and she was surprised to see him take on the expression of a frightened child. It took her a long time to get him to confess the truth.

"I was often beaten as a child. These marks were left by my tutor's whip."

More moved than she'd wanted to be, Fanny suddenly glimpsed a past of solitude and suffering. She herself had not had a rich and fulfilling childhood, but at least she had been happy. She decided to help him and set herself up as his governess: no more alcohol, a healthy diet, eggs, butter, red wine, chops. At first Nicholas angrily refused to obey, then he yielded, and soon it did him good. He looked better, he got stronger. "What a pity, Fanny Lear, that you weren't my tutor!" Fanny felt a surge of a real maternal instinct rise up in her, one that brought her much closer to him than sentimental or physical ties.

After Fanny and Nicholas had been together for five months, he could no longer leave her, even for a short break, and when he was forced to do so, it was for an absolute necessity. The philosophical Fanny realized that all her previous lovers had proved just as demanding. During their affairs, whether short or long, they had adored her without giving her a second to breathe.

But with Nicholas it was different, for she had become his accomplice. His numerous prostitutes, despite their sincerity and good intentions, had only rather limited resources out of bed. As for socially respectable women who threw themselves at him, they were all motivated by ambition, greed, or stupid romanticism. Fanny was new. Familiar with high society, its stars, its palaces, its manners, this American woman, standing on the solid base of her native country's democratic republic, kept an amused eye, a detached judgment, on the world of monarchy. Her thoughts about the courtiers she had met, the palaces she had visited, the relatives of whom Nicholas had spoken enchanted him and made him see his obligations from a new angle that allowed for a greater distance. Fanny was not far from considering the Russian court a circus, and Nicholas saw it as a prison; they were made to get along! Fanny liberated Nicholas; at the least she opened up a new path for him.

Nevertheless, even if he were in love, Nicholas couldn't remain faithful. His temperament prevented him that. And his family obligations offered him enough pretexts to hide his furtive encounters. It was the perfumes that alerted Fanny. Barely was she reunited with her lover than she immediately detected a foreign element on his clothes, on his skin. It was easy for her to recognize a cheap cologne or a scent imported from Paris, depending on whether Nicholas had just left the arms of a gypsy girl or a countess.

"Quick, bring me some water to wash away this abominable odor!" she cried out.

Nicholas smiled; she forced herself to laugh as well, as she knew that with him it was better to avoid seeming affected or displaying the slightest weakness, for he would take advantage. Reassured by her apparent calm, he repeated to her what other women had said about her. He even showed her their letters full of slander mixed with declarations of love and indecent offers. One night at the opera, when Fanny saw these great ladies look her up and down, she consoled herself by recalling their shameless confessions of passion.

However, Nicholas's infidelities, even devoid of consequences, affected her. Then she sought refuge at the home of her friend

Mabel Grey, who consoled her, calmed her down, and on the basis of her years of experience lavished her with shrewd advice. That day, it was a particularly exasperated Fanny who burst into Mabel's boudoir.

"I won't tolerate him anymore! He gave as an excuse a dinner at his Aunt Helen's in order to go to that Pahlen. You know, Mabel, that nasty-looking, tall, and skinny woman. I believe he's become infatuated with her. In any case, I can't take it anymore."

In her anger Fanny hadn't noticed that someone else was in the boudoir, up to then sunk in an armchair, unmoving and silent. When he stood up, Fanny found an adolescent whose face seemed barely out of childhood, a cherub all arms and legs, but whose eyes and smile betrayed a sensuality, almost a perversity, powerfully attractive.

With a mocking smile, Mabel presented him. "This is Nicholas, Count Nicholas Savine. And believe me, he'll go far!"

Not only was Mabel well off and respectable, from then on she was rich, concluded Fanny. So rich that she no longer needed to be kept and could afford the luxury of keeping very handsome young men like this Savine.

Quite naturally, this young man joined in the conversation, which centered on Nicholas. "No man of the world is deserving of making such gentle eyes cry."

The young lad expressed himself like an old veteran at making gallant remarks. Fanny asked him commonplace questions, simply for the pleasure of gazing at him. He was not very tall, his hair curly brown, almond-shaped blue eyes, extremely fair skin, a slightly hooked nose. He appeared frail, but that could be misleading.

"And what do you plan to do in life, Count?"

"To join the Volynski Regiment."

"But that's the one that Nicholas commands! Would you take orders from that wicked man?"

"Certainly, since there's a chance he'll become emperor."

"That's Savine's obsession," interrupted Mabel. "He's convinced that your escort will ascend to the throne."

"But come on, that's impossible!"

"It is possible, for his father, the grand duke Constantine, was the son of an emperor."

"Just like the present sovereign Alexander II."

"No, for Alexander was born before his father Nicholas I had ascended the throne.

These judicial and genealogical subtleties were over Fanny's head, but she had not so quickly given up the idea of having a potential emperor for a lover. Savine felt that he was winning the argument.

"The grand duke Constantine is much more intelligent and above all much more scheming than his older brother. He is very popular, and it wouldn't take much for him to take the place of Alexander II."

"And who would succeed him one day?" insinuated Mabel.

"Nicholas," whispered a stunned Fanny. And she was very pensive as she took her leave.

"I hope we see each other again, Count Savine."

"I have no doubt we will."

The ice was melting away, the snow had disappeared, and spring had come back, bringing Easter, the Eastern Orthodox Church's most important holiday, Fanny's first Russian Easter.

Virginally dressed in white, a cross at her neck, a candle in hand, she went to the church next door to the hotel. The sanctuary, like the city, was plunged into almost total darkness, but the church was full. Prayers followed one another in a murmur, and then Fanny sensed that the congregation was becoming excited, the time was drawing near. The voices of the priests grew stronger and the murmur rose in volume in the congregation.

The bell tolls midnight. A candle in hand, the bishop comes out of the iconostasis and with a resounding voice announces in Russian, "Christ is risen!" In unison, the whole congregation answers him with joyous fervor, "Indeed, He is risen!" Then all the congregation lights their candles, sparks flying, and in a few minutes the church is revealed in soft light. In the distance the cannon booms to proclaim the event, and all the bells begin ringing.

Soon everybody goes back home, taking care not to let their candles go out. The streets are full of men, women, and children whose faces are illuminated by the flickering flames. All of them are hurrying to their homes to sit down to the Easter banquet.

Nicholas stayed at the palace, where the night of the Resurrection was celebrated with extraordinary glitter. Having returned to the Hôtel de France, Fanny had no intention of staying cooped up in solitude. She had invited to her suite a few merry guys she had met on her arrival in St. Petersburg, and she made for them an eggnog whose ingredients she had selected: a hot mixture of eggs beaten in sugar and whisky. The eggnog was a tremendous success! The evening wore on very late, with increasingly heavy drinking. Poor prince L. drank so much eggnog, he passed out right on the living room rug!

He was still there the morning of the next day when the hotel staff and Nicholas's servants came to wish Fanny a happy Easter, bringing her the customary flowers and fruit. To thank them, she gave each one a porcelain egg filled with coins. Nicholas arrived just after they left. From the many bits of evidence scattered on the floor, he estimated the success of the party of the night before and his rage was as sudden as it was irrational. He insulted Fanny so much that, outraged, she gave him a light slap.

"What gives you the right to hit a grand duke?"

"For me you are not a grand duke but my lover. And when you forget to be a gentleman, I have the right to remind you of it!"

Red with anger, Nicholas left the room, slamming the door, only to reopen it a few seconds later and set down on the table the present he had brought, a little gold Easter egg with Fanny's monogram in tiny colored precious stones.

Summer had come. St. Petersburg became intolerably hot and emptied out. The grand duke Constantine and his family were spending the holidays at Pavlovsk. Nicholas rented a beautiful dacha next door to the estate, where he set up Fanny. She was delighted with the house and the garden, whose flowers filled the air with a lovely fragrance. The lovers strolled in the great park open to the public, slipped into dense copses, whispered words of love, far from everything, letting the insects buzz around them.

They were brought back to reality one day when the wife of a colonel approached Nicholas and, after a deep curtsy, said, "How can your imperial highness compromise himself with a woman like that?"

"Alas, madam, I see I am forced to deprive myself of the pleasure of speaking with you."

The woman reddened and vanished, but the damage was done. She had touched a nerve. . . . Fanny and Nicholas were forced to admit what they had avoided recognizing: their affair was severely condemned. Their love confined them to a strange solitude, for everyone was against them.

Every year at the end of July, military maneuvers were held at Krasnoye Selo, presided over by the emperor. The entire court moved there for several weeks, crowded together in huge wooden villas that resembled Swiss chalets. The women were in the party, the imperial theater as well, which gave performances in a wooden theater. Ballerinas and actresses mingled with grand duchesses. Sixty thousand soldiers camped out in the surrounding area and took part in daily exercises that were observed by the emperor and the imperial family from the top of a little artificial hill where enormous tents made it possible to shade themselves from the sun and have something to eat at lavish buffets.

One chalet, which bore the name Constantine, was assigned to Nicholas. He brought Fanny there disguised as a valet and wearing her lover's livery. So she made the short trip between Pavlovsk and Krasnoye Selo on the upper level of Nicholas's carriage.

Nicholas took part in the maneuvers at the head of his Volynski Regiment. It was Fanny who sounded the wake-up call, or rather it was she who heard the cannon announcing that it was time to get up. She forced her lover to get out of bed and helped him put on his uniform in next to no time. She prepared his breakfast, which he wolfed down at top speed, and, hidden behind the shutters, she saw him go by at the head of his regiment.

One morning, Fanny had just put on her livery when there was a loud banging on the door.

"Nicholas, are you there?"

She looked through the crack of the shutter and almost fainted: it was Alexander II in the flesh! Without losing her head, she opened the door and bowed deeply. "His imperial highness has already left with his regiment."

The tsar inspected the valet and frowned, clearly intrigued. "You're not from here, are you?"

"I am German, to serve your imperial majesty."

"*Vielleicht.*" Perhaps, he said in German.

The tsar hesitated, then went away. Fanny was so frightened that, once the door was closed, she had a child's reaction: she ran up to the attic and hid in a corner. That evening she told Nicholas the story.

"You're a fairy, Fanny Lear; you're always making me admire some new quality of yours."

The maneuver left lots of leisure time, which enabled Nicholas to help Fanny discover the imperial palaces thereabouts. He took her to Peterhof, where, at his order, they turned on the magnificent fountains with statues of golden bronze spitting their water in thousands of ways. Nicholas rang a bell, and immediately carp that were more than a hundred years old rose to the surface of the water to get the large hunks of bread that Fanny had fun throwing to them. At Gatchina, a combination of château and barracks built by Paul I, there was a bloody shirt that he had been wearing at the time of his assassination, and Fanny swore she had felt his ghost. In the same way she was certain she'd seen traces of tsar Peter III's blood at Ropsha, where he had been assassinated at the order of his wife, Catherine II. Never mind if the most reliable historians claimed that he was strangled or smothered.

Nicholas took her to Strelna several times. It was the second vacation spot of the grand duke Constantine, an immense building in baroque style erected on a hill and overlooking a classical park that stretched out in pools and flower beds all the way to the Baltic Sea. About Strelna, Fanny retained mainly the memory of the old and very pious mother of Bobesh, one of Nicholas's loyal manservants. Fanny had hesitated to go on this visit, for she distrusted Russian hygiene: "Cleanliness is not always next to godliness," she often said.

But she had had to recognize that she had been wrong, for the log hut painted white, with windows decorated with flowers, was the picture of cleanliness. The old woman had received them in her one room, immediately bringing out white bread, butter, cheese, tea, sugar, chocolate, candy, cigarettes, and, most important, a bottle of good Madeira obviously from the grand duke's wine cellars. Nicholas had asked her son Bobesh to play the accordion. Intoxicated by her master's visit and also by one or two glasses of Madeira, the mother began dancing in the most comical fashion. She was not ridiculous, she was touching, and Fanny had tears in her eyes when, upon leaving her, the old woman ardently kissed her hands.

Between the maneuvers, the excursions, and the love, the days could have followed one another delightfully. Alas, Nicholas fell ill. Although the doctors studied his case and offered various explanations for his fever, Fanny, with her woman's instinct, held responsible the fragility of his nervous system. She did not know its causes, but she did know that this came from far back, deeply rooted in his childhood.

Rather than the potions, she felt the most effective remedy would be her presence. So she didn't leave him, occupying his mind by reading to him the most entertaining books. She also believed in the laying on of hands. She kept her fingers on his forehead for hours. And he got better, indisputably.

"Fanny Lear, you saved my life and I shall never leave you."

Nevertheless, those days when she had constantly kept watch over Nicholas had been rather trying. Barely moving from his bedside, from time to time she saw soldiers and officers who passed by the window. Did she perhaps recognize Savine, that wicked cherub, enlisted as he had wished in the Volynski Regiment? And had she seen him, she would certainly have given some sign of recognition. The fact was that Nicholas, just recovered, became inexplicably suspicious of her. He was back on his feet again, just in time to witness the great finale of the maneuvers, an inspection followed by a torchlight procession.

After seeing him leave, Fanny donned her disguise and returned to the staging grounds for the maneuvers. There wasn't a breath of air. It hadn't rained for weeks and the horses' hooves kicked up clouds of so much dust that soon nothing could be seen. Nicholas looked for his beloved in the middle of the shadows moving in the reddish fog. He didn't find her and was convinced she hadn't come. Still not well, psychologically fragile, his unreasoning jealousy took hold of him again: Fanny had certainly taken advantage of the maneuvers to find one of those all-too-attractive officers swarming around!

Beside himself with rage, he came back to the Constantine villa and fell upon Fanny, who had arrived a few minutes before him. He harshly shouted at her and criticized her for her absence. Fanny tried to stem the tide, to explain the truth to him. He didn't want to hear anything and pelted her with insults. She herself felt rage overcoming her and grabbed one of her ivory hairbrushes and broke it over his head. He rushed over to the other brush, made the gesture of throwing it at Fanny, then threw it out the window. He left, locking the door. Fanny was a prisoner.

Outside, she heard the lively music of the regiments and the pounding of hooves. Too bad for Nicholas; she didn't want to miss the show! Through the windows she caught sight of a young groom, called out to him, and in her best Russian, aided by gestures, asked him to throw her one of the keys to the house. Miraculously, the boy understood and freed her. Still wearing the livery, she took the sole means of locomotion left at her disposal, a carriage drawn by ponies. She applied the whip and off they galloped.

When she got to the field of maneuvers, the torchlight procession had just ended. The regiments, the bands in the lead, returned to their billets while a splendid carriage preceded by horse guards passed by in front of her. It was the grand duchess Alexandra, who was making her way back home with her son Nicholas. Fanny met his gaze for a second and saw him go pale as if he were about to faint. Fanny's carriage was immobilized along with a hundred others by the cortege of the imperial family. She saw them all parade by, with Alexander II at the rear on a magnificent chestnut horse that accompanied the empress in her four-horse carriage.

When Fanny, stamping her feet with impatience and apprehensiveness, could finally make an about-turn, she made haste to get back to the villa Constantine. She found the house upside down, the panic-stricken servants running all over the place.

The grand duke had had an attack; his blood had gone up to his head. The doctors had to be called! Without panicking, she had a basin of hot water brought in and forced Nicholas to have a foot-bath. She applied poultices to his calves and poured ice water on his head. "I looked after him like a child," she related in her diary. And it was a child who asked for her forgiveness.

"My dear Fanny, I thought you had left me. If such a misfortune happened to me, I think I would go mad, that I would die."

"First, I have no intention of abandoning you, and in any case, if I did, that would not prevent you from living!" she rather coolly replied.

She knew that if she followed Nicholas in the twists and turns of his contradictions, she would get lost. He was short-tempered, a hothead, but his relentless intelligence combined with insight revealed people's deepest nature. He was also a man who was good, loving, and protective of the weak. As for his political opinions, sometimes he idolized the emperor, sometimes he gave vent to the most acerbic criticisms of the government and the imperial system.

Here at Krasnoye he had been happy while among his fellow officers and his soldiers, but sometimes he felt revulsion for the army.

"I don't want to get bogged down in it!"

"But then what do you want to do?"

"Great things in great spaces. I think I am capable of them provided I'm given the possibility."

The strangest thing was that Fanny believed him.

The next day, the Krasnoye Selo camp made tracks, and Nicholas and Fanny returned to Pavlovsk. They separated at the entrance to the estate. Nicholas went to greet his mother, and Fanny returned to their dacha.

Scarcely had she entered than she was stupefied. Everything that had made for the charm of the place—the paintings, the knick-knacks, the flowers, the vases, the photos, the books, down to the counterpane on the bed—had been taken away! Fanny was becoming used to this sort of thing. Fanny ordered the doors and windows to be locked, and to be opened for no one at all. Unearthing two shawls that had been overlooked in the plundering, she used them as blankets for sleeping on the bare mattress.

Just as she was going to sleep, she heard the bell ringing, fists knocking on the doors, on the shutters, insistently, with fury. At first she refused to move, then she went to open the door. It was Nicholas, breathless. Coolly, she asked him for an explanation. Rather embarrassed, he confessed that when he had seen her the day before driving his ponies at the end of the torchlight retreat, he thought she was leaving him. So he telegraphed Pavlovsk to remove all these familiar objects. Later, he had forgotten . . . and his people had plainly worked with great zeal to totally empty out the house!

Despite herself, Fanny discarded her severe expression and burst out laughing. "As your imperial highness can observe, there's no counterpane! If he deigns to accept half of my bed, I'll exchange it for half of his cloak."

In a few instants there was no longer any need of a cloak or a counterpane, for in the gentle summer night their two bodies ignited each other, and once again voluptuous pleasure burst into flame.

The next day Fanny got back her paintings, knickknacks, books, and photos, with a bonus—a very long necklace of very large pearls. She looked at them for a long time, let them run through her hands, and had no pleasure in doing so. She had succeeded in making herself adored by a grand duke of Russia, handsome, rich, and yet she was overcome by weariness to the point of having it leech all her energy, all her desire to struggle. Nicholas's mood swings, his endless histrionics, certainly were responsible in part, but she was wondering above all about the future of their affair. There was no question of marriage; the emperor's nephew couldn't marry an American courtesan. She loved him enough to remain only his mistress, but how long would he be attached to her?

Russia had ended up discouraging her, this magnificent but unpredictable country, deeply moving but uncertain: the soil on which she would have loved to build a fortune and a position re-mained as unstable as the marshes on which St. Petersburg had been constructed.

6

It was then that Nicholas decided to take Fanny on a long trip. He asked for a leave of several months to restore his fragile health, as had been prescribed for him by Dr. Havrowitz, the very man who had diagnosed the seriousness of his syphilis. Nicholas had to begin the trip, however, by accompanying his mother, who also was going to Western Europe. So he left St. Petersburg in a special train that was followed soon after by the express train bearing Fanny.

They met up in Warsaw, which Fanny detested right off. They went through Dresden and arrived in Vienna. To enjoy a good rest, they settled in Gritzing, a rustic suburb, with stylish villas, opulent orchards, welcoming and rather popular inns where the whole Viennese society came to drink the little local white wine.

After the walks in the countryside, it was nice to sit at a table under the arbors. People pretended not to see those nearby, but Fanny, who recognized some archdukes at nearby tables, was the object of their insistent and expressive gazes. Similarly, Nicholas was the target of all the ladies. Gritzing welcomed pell-mell all social classes, "including the one I belong to," confided Fanny, that most highly valued of courtesans.

That day she went for a walk alone. Soon leaving the paths taken by the illustrious strollers, she went into a copse. There, without being noticed, she came upon a couple. From the back she recognized the woman, a Hungarian of easy virtue, very beautiful, very sensual, and, as Fanny had noticed, slovenly. She was holding the hand of a man hidden by a tree trunk, but even at a distance Fanny recognized the hand, which was that of Nicholas.

The couple was engaged in the most intimate conversation. Fanny drew closer, still without being seen. She had a poor understanding of the German they were speaking, but it was nonetheless sufficient to catch an address, a time, a meeting place given by the Hungarian woman to her companion. Her heart broken, Fanny managed to slip away.

She returned to the villa in Gritzing, and when Nicholas arrived he confronted a fury spewing reproaches. To his astonishment, she told him of the scene she had just witnessed. For a response Nicholas flared up, accusing her of being a spy, and he declared offhandedly that people who listen at keyholes always hear things that are disagreeable.

Then Fanny reminded him of everything she'd done for him since they'd met, her devotion, her self-denial, her faithfulness, her love. She was so much in the right that, following custom, he reacted arrogantly and slapped her. Moreover, he was leaving, he announced, and would never come back. Good-bye Fanny and long live freedom! Remaining alone, Fanny wept bitter tears, wrote him ten, twelve, fifteen letters that she tore up one after the other.

The faithful, loyal Joséphine knocked on the door and announced Prince Gagarine, the most prominent representative of the silver-plated elders, who had welcomed Fanny on her arrival in St. Petersburg. For a long time he had courted her, hitherto unsuccessfully. Fanny had him ushered in and straight out told him what had just happened. He of course did not let this golden opportunity slip through his fingers. He deplored the inexcusable attitude of his imperial highness; he was not a worthy prince but a boor! If Fanny wanted at last to fulfill his wishes and follow him, he promised her an ideal existence, the exact opposite of the hell she had gone through.

Fanny accepted with no hesitation. In a few minutes, the luggage was readied. Like a robot she let herself be taken to Gritzing's small train station, but just at the moment of boarding the train for Vienna, she hesitated.

"No, I could never make up my mind to do this. I don't want to leave him."

Prince Gagarine took her arm gently but firmly and forced her to climb into the compartment.

"It's the grand duke I love, not you!" she screamed as the train slowly pulled away.

"I couldn't care less. For more than a year I've loved you, I've finally had the chance to hold you, and I'll not let you go."

Once in Vienna, Gagarine took a magnificent suite with Fanny in the Sacher Hotel. And he locked her away there.

The next morning she overheard a conversation in German between him and his manservant. She understood that Nicholas had come to the hotel and asked for her, that he had even insistently demanded to see her but was told that she wasn't staying there. She wrote him a letter again, then two, which she disguised, addressing them to the embassy of the United States and that of Russia. Prince Gagarine was very careful to not mail them, just as he had "forgotten" to give her several missives from Nicholas that had reached the hotel. He announced to Fanny that that very evening they would be leaving for Kraków and from there to Russia. They left the hotel by some service stairs and got into a carriage with closed curtains.

During the trip to the station, Fanny frantically kissed the charms, the rings, and the bracelets that Nicholas had given her. Gagarine shrugged his shoulders.

"I never saw a spirited woman moan this way and cry so over a lover who left her!"

At Kraków, where they stayed for a week, Fanny calmed down. Or pretended to calm down. She seemed so submissive that the prince relaxed his surveillance. But she wasn't just pretending; she found this new companion rather sweet, affable, charming, highly intelligent, and, as she confided in her diary, she had "a great fondness" for him. They even reached an agreement: Fanny would go to Paris to put her affairs in order, later to rejoin him in Russia, where she would devote herself to him for good.

The prince accompanied her as far as Dresden and then she proceeded alone to France.

Paris, September 1872. The city had greatly changed since Fanny had left it; she barely remembered the dreadful wounds of the Franco-Prussian War and of the Commune, and yet its beauty and power to captivate were intact. Like a child recovering its toys after a long absence, Fanny avidly sought out the restaurants, the stores, the nightspots she had known; she visited "comrades," former lovers. She relaxed and had a wildly delightful time. She loved Paris more than she had loved any man. She forgot Nicholas,

Prince Gagarine, Russia—she especially wanted to forget that she had to go there in a few weeks.

One day there was a knock at the door of her apartment. A Russian-speaking voice asked to be admitted. She imagined that it was a messenger of Prince Gagarine and opened the door. It was Vorpovsky, Nicholas's aide-de-camp. He handed her a fat envelope closed with a seal. She had only to glance at it to recognize the NK surmounted by the imperial crown. She took the envelope but didn't open it. Vorpovsky began: "In the name of heaven, follow me."

"But that's impossible!"

"I beg you to read this letter. He is very ill and if you don't come back, you'll be the cause of his death."

Fanny broke the seal and read the long letter. Nicholas admitted to every possible wrongdoing, and yet he loved Fanny with all his might, all his soul. He adored her, so much that he was almost ashamed of this feeling and wanted to hide it. He begged her to give him at least the chance to see her one more time. After having held her in his arms, after having been able to utter "Fanny Lear" one last time, then he could die in peace. Let her not refuse him this final prayer.

Fanny was persuaded and ready to set off again. But she didn't want to show it to Vorpovsky right away. The latter mistook her silence and launched into an impassioned plea in favor of his master.

While listening, Fanny observed him. He's not bad, this young officer! Less handsome, less attractive than Nicholas, but even so very charming, especially after old Gagarine. Fanny also noticed that while defending Nicholas, Vorpovsky was staring hungrily at her. With her experience, she felt that it would take only a little for this man to fall in love with her, but that, held back by his loyalty, he would never dare confess it. So it was with an irresistible smile and one of the most provocative expressions that Fanny announced, "Okay. I give in to your arguments. I'll follow you."

Mad with joy, Vorpovsky hastened to send a telegram announcing the success of his mission. For her part, Fanny remained shaken by her prior unhappiness; afraid of making a mistake, she didn't know what to believe. In the express train taking her to Vienna, she met by chance Prince Esterhazy, who belonged to the richest and most illustrious family in Hungary. In her dismay, she confided in him. He tried to calm her down and succeeded so well that she went to sleep.

The train stopped, and she awoke abruptly. They were in Vienna. When Fanny saw the porters take her luggage and put it on the platform, she panicked, spinning around the compartment and uttering incoherent words. She even lowered the window with the intention of throwing herself outside! Prince Esterhazy took her arm. "Hold on to your presence of mind. You are loved and you shouldn't be afraid of anything." Then he whispered in her ear, "The grand duke is there on the platform."

Fanny didn't dare move. Esterhazy raised her up and guided her down the steps of the coach. Before her stood Nicholas. He took her in his arms and led her away. Fanny didn't even have the strength to thank the prince.

Nicholas was as upset as she was. He made confused gestures, mumbled incomprehensible words. He had even lost the number of the carriage he had rented, and if the cabman hadn't seen him from afar, they would have had to get back by foot.

When they were both in the carriage, Fanny regained some of her composure. "Now that was a fine way to make me welcome!"

She immediately felt herself held so tightly as to be smothered, covered with passionate kisses.

"You will never leave me again, isn't that so, you will never leave me again. Say it, Fanny."

"I'm expecting to stay only three days in Vienna."

"We'll see about that. I'd kill you rather than lose you."

Nicholas had reserved a suite at the Archduke Charles Hotel. They had barely entered their room when they threw themselves at each other. They didn't leave their suite for several days.

Even so, Fanny felt some remorse in connection with Prince Gagarine. She didn't want to confess the truth to him just now, not to make a complete break with him. Did one ever know with Nicholas? So she sent to Paris letters that would be mailed from there telling him her return would be delayed.

At the end of a few days, Nicholas and Fanny came out of their bliss to attend a performance of *La Traviata*. During the last act, Fanny saw tears running down Nicholas's cheeks. He was in the grip of so strong a fit of nerves that he had to get up and withdraw to the tiny sitting room behind the box. Fanny remained in her seat, thinking it was only a passing weakness. After a quarter of an hour, he still hadn't come back.

She found him on the floor in the little sitting room, racked with spasms. He gasped, "I sense, I foresee that we will be separated once again, and that's what is causing my pain."

She managed to calm him down and get him back to the hotel.

"It's pointless to see misfortunes so far ahead," she told him, and for the rest of the night she tried to prove to him that only the present counted.

With harmony restored, the real journey Nicholas had promised Fanny could finally begin.

However, a grand duke of Russia cannot travel with only his beloved. Accompanying them were Dr. Havrowitz, that fat German, whom Fanny instinctively distrusted, and Victor Vorpovsky, who had crafted their reconciliation, henceforth the slave of Fanny, who distrusted him slightly as well. Saviolov, the loyal servant, could not be missing from the group as well as the manservants, the indispensable Joséphine, and forty-nine trunks in addition to two dogs named Bologna and Venice, in memory of the cities where they had been purchased.

In Rome, Fanny accompanied Nicholas to the antique dealers, where he spent a fortune. In Bari she joined him in performing his devotions before the remains of St. Nicholas, his patron saint and that of Russia. In Brindisi they boarded the steamship *Amerigo Vespucci.*

The next day, when they went up quite early on the bridge, the ship had just anchored in Corfu. The pale blue of the sea merged with that of the sky, the rays of dawn brightening the colors of the eternally green island, and the mountains of Albania could be made out on the horizon.

Soon a frigate flying a Russian flag came close to the *Amerigo Vespucci.* The presence of a member of the imperial family could not go unnoticed! Nicholas and Fanny could see among the Russian officers, in full dress, George I, Nicholas's brother-in-law, king of Greece. Fanny needed to disappear and headed belowdecks with Nicholas, who went down the stairs four at a time to put on his uniform.

He came back up just as quickly while Fanny remained enclosed below without, however, missing a bit of the show. The Russian officials and the king of Greece came on board while the grand duke's personal flag was run up the mainmast of the *Amerigo Vespucci.*

When everyone was leaving the ship, Fanny heard the salvos of honor shot by the warships of Russia, England, France, Italy, and Turkey that filled the bay. The launch into which her lover had descended pulled up alongside the quay. A feminine form threw herself in his arms; Fanny identified her as Nicholas's sister, Queen Olga. Soldiers and women in veils and parasols got into the carriages, and the retinue left in double-quick time for Monrepos, the holiday resort of the Greek sovereigns. She learned later that Nicholas had refused to stay there in order to rejoin her each night on the *Amerigo Vespucci*. That was, however, an end to her dream of peaceful tourism with her lover. She must hence-forth fill her days all by herself. She rented a carriage and took long rides over the island's winding, narrow roads. The olive trees, the bay laurels, the lavender, the rosemary created a symphony of scents and colors that no one could resist, but could Fanny appreciate this enchanting nature without Nicholas?

One morning Nicholas told her that she would be presented to his sister. Vorpovsky would take her there. The presentation would not take place at Monrepos, where the royal family was staying, but in Corfu Town, at the Palace of St. George and St. Michael, which was reserved for official ceremonies. Knowing that elegance goes hand in hand with simplicity, Fanny chose for the occasion a modest blue dress fringed in white.

When she crossed the vast white-columned hall, she experi-enced a certain apprehensiveness. Queen Olga was the first mem-ber of Nicholas's family she was to meet, and Fanny was aware of the hostility she stirred up. A lady-in-waiting, very short and dark, led her down vast resounding corridors.

The palace looked to her more or less empty. The Greek court was far less rich than that of Russia. Fanny was shown into a cor-ner room, not very large but filled with light. Olga acknowledged her curtsy. The queen wore a dress of ecru linen embellished with lace. She didn't look at all like Nicholas; her face was rather round, brightened by large blue eyes.

Fanny instantly fell under the spell of this beautiful and sweet young woman with an innocent gaze, who seemed to be unaware of the existence of evil and who saw only the good in other crea-tures. She knew, she felt, that the queen idolized Nicholas and that he in turn had the most sincere affection for her, the deepest

confidence in that sister whose goodness, generosity, and humanity he never stopped praising.

Olga spoke to Fanny as to a very important visitor. She asked
her a hundred questions about her journey and the places she had
visited. She suggested places for her to visit on foot and monuments
to discover. She led her to the window from which they saw Corfu's
admirable bay that had inspired so many paintings and watercolors.
The conversation went on in English, which the famously polyglot
queen spoke to perfection as she did five other languages. Fanny
felt so at ease with her that it seemed she had always known the
sovereign. She detected in her none of the reticence that the queen
might have felt toward a courtesan, but, on the contrary, all the
warmth, all the fellow feeling of one woman toward another.

Not once did Nicholas's name come up in the conversation,
but by her attitude the queen gave her to understand that she believed in the sincerity of his feelings about her. Moreover, at the
moment of leaving, Fanny heard Olga murmur, "Take care of him."

Fanny left so delighted with her encounter that she had no
desire to go back aboard the ship right away. So she proposed to
Vorpovsky that they go for a walk in town.

Everything looked charming to her, the arcaded houses, luxu-
riant small gardens, the irregular squares where the marble fountains murmured, the churches with Byzantine cupolas. She felt like
a schoolgirl on vacation. She confided to Vorpovsky the impression that Queen Olga had made on her and enlarged on the deep
and beautiful ties that brought the brother and sister together.

The aide-de-camp seized the opportunity: "You can imagine the
queen's joy when her brother is seated on the throne of Russia!"

"What? Do you too keep up that pipe dream?" replied Fanny,
who well recalled the words spoken by the young and charming
Count Savine the day she met him at Mabel's place.

"What pipe dream? The grand duke Constantine has much better rights to the throne than his elder brother. And besides, he would make a better emperor. As for his son and successor, he alone can transform our empire, our Russia, into a modern country! Many Russians like me know it, for his imperial highness has many supporters, in the army, the civil service, the intelligentsia, and even among the revolutionaries."

"My Nicholas will be emperor . . ." Fanny crooned softly, without fully realizing what words she was pronouncing.

The next morning Fanny had a cold shower. Nicholas was still in their cabin when Dr. Havrowitz arrived and began his lecture. Fanny's presence has become too awkward; everyone knows that she is hiding on board and that the grand duke returns to her every night. The Greeks were mortally offended that the brother of their queen had rejected their hospitality in order to sleep with his mistress! The visiting Russian fleet was horrified at this appalling behavior; the foreigners had a good laugh about it. It was a question of the dignity of the imperial family!

Nicholas was going to protest, but Fanny stopped him with a gesture of her hand. She proposed to go away; she would leave that very day for Brindisi and wait there until Nicholas had finished with his family obligations.

Once in Italy, she watched impatiently for the ship that would bring her lover to her. She didn't have long to wait, and the two of them were finally able to resume their travel.

At Amalfi, the great entertainment was to seat themselves like anonymous tourists at a communal table for all guests at the hotel. In Sorrento the spectacle of the tarantella did not suit them, for the famous national dance was performed by hideous old women. At Capri, to climb from the port to the little village, they were lifted onto two young donkeys. So small was Nicholas's that his feet dragged on the ground! Stifling laughter, Fanny nicknamed it "Don Quixote" and he named hers "Dulcinea," lady love.

In Naples they went around the antique dealers, from whom Nicholas purchased a great many objects in alabaster or porphyry. Since both of them were interested in contemporary art, they visited the studio of the sculptor Solari, whose numerous catalogs they had thumbed through. The artist, who rented the top floor of an aristocrat's palace, had constructed a studio there without asking anyone's permission. He specialized in representing the human body. Gazing at all those female nudes, a delighted Nicholas exclaimed, "Very beautiful bodies, maestro, but you haven't seen the most beautiful one."

And he tranquilly set about undressing Fanny. She didn't protest. Carried away by the voluptuousness of the moment, Solari didn't say a word, didn't move, so hypnotized was he. When Fanny was completely naked, he slowly examined her. Is it the man or the artist who's observing me? Fanny wondered. Probably both.

"Imperial highness, this beauty must be immortalized at any cost!"

"That's just what I had in mind."

Because Fanny could not pose, since they had to set off again, the sculptor asked for permission to make a mold. It was a terrible ordeal, a torture that was hard to imagine and that Fanny was ready to advise any woman against! The finished masterpiece would be sent to Russia. Meanwhile, the lovers left for Rome, Florence, Genoa, Milan, Venice, and eventually Trieste. There, they obtained the authorization to visit the nearby château of Miramare, the unfinished residence of the unfortunate Emperor Maximilian of Mexico. Despite its incredible sumptuousness, Fanny found it as sinister as a funerary monument. She couldn't stop thinking of the sovereign's widow, Charlotte, about whom close to nothing is known except that she was cloistered, owing to insanity, in a château in Belgium. The trip ended on this melancholy note.

The lovers returned to Vienna, where they had almost broken up forever and where they were now closer than ever. As the express train slowly came into the Warsaw station, the strains of military music were heard. The Volynski, Nicholas's regiment garrisoned in Poland, had come to welcome them. The soldiers were impeccably lined up on the platform and the officers with swords drawn presented arms while the majestic strains of the Russian imperial anthem resounded.

Through the window of their coach, Fanny saw Nicholas step down and salute his men. Once again she was seduced by that mixture of innate nobility, grace, elegance, and kindness. She felt proud of him.

7

On returning to St. Petersburg, Nicholas was summoned by his uncle the emperor. He went to the Winter Palace, entering through the portal reserved for the imperial family. Recognizing him, the guards stood at attention. When he appeared in his uncle's anteroom, the aide-de-camp on duty rose from his desk, went to knock on a door, opened it, and stepped back for him to enter.

Nicholas was very familiar with Alexander II's office as he had often been summoned there, mostly for reprimands. Above a huge desk hung the marvelous Winterhalter portrait of the empress Maria Alexandrovna dressed in white silk and covered with pearls. Framing it were the paintings of the emperor's parents, Nicholas I and Alexandra Feodorovna, then came pictures representing battle scenes or uniforms of various regiments. Few seats, but tables and desks of all sizes overflowing with files.

Alexander II was wearing the uniform of his favorite regiment, a bottle-green jacket frogged with silver, pants braided in black. He was not alone. Next to him stood his brother Constantine.

The two men subjected Nicholas to a flood of reproaches, accusations, orders, with this leitmotif in every sentence: Fanny . . . Fanny . . .

The lovers had not imagined, had they, that their affair would go unnoticed, especially in the way they were conducting it! What's more, Nicholas, with his innate taste for provocation, had obviously taken advantage, using Fanny as the ultimate defiance of his career! His family disgraced, his country mortified, an unprecedented scandal, an American, a courtesan . . . A single conclusion: he must break it off immediately.

Nicholas ended the tirade by turning to his father and sharply retorting, "I am not so much to blame; it's in my blood!"

And he named Peter the Great, the *tsarinas* Anne, Elizabeth, and Catherine II, Paul I, Alexander I . . .

"Incidentally, Papa, excuse me for having forgotten to congratulate you!"

"For what, Nicholas?"

"On the birth of your son!"

That was to say, the latest of the illegitimate children he had fathered by his mistress. The grand duke Constantine could only blush to the roots of his hair.

When Nicholas told her of this scene, Fanny threw oil on the fire, for she said she'd heard some shameful things about his father's miserliness.

"Listen to this, Nicholas, la Kuznetsova must beg him to give her a few kopecks, so she can buy lemons for his tea, and if he has finally given her a villa, that's because it's located in the Pavlovsk park and didn't cost him anything!"

As for the emperor himself, he is no more virtuous than his brother Constantine, or his father and ancestors.

"Katia?" Fanny interjected. "You didn't bring up Katia when he summoned you to admonish you?"

Katia was Katerina Michailovna Dolgoruki, whom Alexander II, already in his fifties, had met some years previously while she was only a slip of a girl. She cast such a spell over him that, for her, he neglected the sweet empress, who was already suffering from consumption. He set Katia up as his official mistress, bought her a beautiful little palace in town, and fathered two fine little bastards by her. . . .

"It's she," Fanny continued, "who makes and unmakes the ministers. She leads your uncle around by the tip of his nose. That you dare not tell him when he blames you for loving me!"

There was something else Nicholas wouldn't dare. He would not reveal to Fanny that the secret police had prepared reports on her that the emperor hurled at him during the stormy scene at the palace.

That was how Nicholas had learned about her past, and first of all her real name, Hattie Ely. She had been born in Philadelphia, the daughter of a clergyman who came from a long line of uncompromising puritans. He had several daughters from a first marriage to a well-born young lady. Late in life he had married a beautiful, much younger, and less suitable woman with whom he had had Hattie. She had grown up with the frustration of not belonging to the best society of her half sisters and of not having the wealth of her classmates. At sixteen, while traveling by train with her mother, she had met a stranger named Calvin Blackford. She ran away with him and married him before discovering he was a drunkard and tubercular to boot. She had had a child, a little girl, who died after a few months. Hattie had then left her husband, who a short time later also died. Many rumors were spread about this death. The most plausible one was that the abandoned husband had committed suicide.

Having returned to Philadelphia, she began working at the federal mint before yielding to the advances of George Madison, a rich Texan. She would have liked to get married, but the Texan proved reluctant despite Hattie's efforts: "You are the most scandalous man in the city, I am the most scandalous woman. We were made to be married." Since he refused to comply, she had had the idea that only one lover was not enough for her. Many men had the practice of visiting her, so she had moved to a much larger house in the fashionable neighborhood of Rittenhouse Square. With these gentlemen as clients she had opened a real casino. She kept, it was said, a large silver bowl filled with one-dollar coins that the unlucky gamblers could draw on at will provided they paid her back for their losses. Dating from this time, Fanny had decided to educate herself. While her lovers were playing cards, she studied English literature or French poetry. French poets! Good heavens . . . It was this last feature that had most horrified the godfearing and ultrapuritanical society of Philadelphia. Ladies whom no one ever wanted to court let gentlemen know that it looked very bad to frequent the courtesan's house. The gentlemen deserted, and the courtesan felt she urgently needed a change of air.

With the money she had saved up, she left for Paris. Very quickly she became the close friend of Cora Pearl, who was also American. It was Cora who advised her to take a "nom de guerre," a pseudonym. Good-bye Hattie Blackford, it was Fanny Lear who then launched an attack on Parisian society, particularly targeting the most titled and well-to-do men. Having learned her lesson in Philadelphia, she henceforth planned methodically.

She became famous following her affair with the prince of Wales, the future Edward VII. She then landed a serious patron, the duke of Bodenbach. He was faithful for a certain time and extremely generous. When he left her, he told her that his name was also a pseudonym and that behind Bodenbach was hiding an authentic title from one of the innumerable German dynasties. He left her the present of a considerable sum, which Fanny devoted to the purchase of a small residence on the Boulevard Malesherbes. There she welcomed everybody who counted in the arts and literature, such as Alexandre Dumas, a regular at the house. The war of 1870 interrupted this promising existence. No more empire, no more dukes, no more festivities! Fanny, however, did not want to leave Paris right away for she had become enamored of the city, nor did she want to leave the French to whom she was grateful. She had her meals at the Rendezvous of the Cannonballs Restaurant and had to choose between "rat pâté" and "dog consommé à la Bismarck" while the Prussians were laying siege to the French capital.

However, she could see that she couldn't stay forever under conditions so disastrous for her profession. Go back to America? Out of the question. Her friend Cora Pearl had spoken to her of Russia. The gentlemen there had, she said, "grateful wallets" and a propensity to love loose women. It sounded ideal to Fanny, who left for St. Petersburg determined to land the big prize. And the big prize, the fool who let himself be caught in her net, it was he, Nicholas! concluded the emperor.

The blow was hard for Nicholas, who took some days to get over it. Once calmed down, he proposed a diversion to his mistress: a great military expedition was getting ready to colonize Central Asia and conquer the city of Khiva, whose khan was scoffing at Russia. He wanted to enlist in it. He was already dreaming of victories in this fabulous East; he imagined his triumphant return, with medals for bravery pinned on his chest.

"With such achievements, I won't be treated like a child, but like a man! And they will let me love you in peace."

Fanny remembered that several times during her trip with Nicholas, Dr. Havrowitz had spoken of this expedition and suggested that the grand duke take part in it in order to gather his laurels. Right away she understood this move. Since the grand duke refused to break off with her, despite the pressure they were putting on him, the only solution was to draw him away from her by attracting him with some oriental mirage, to the point that he would forget her—an old method that had for centuries proved itself in the great families.

"Don't tell me stories, Nicholas. That idea didn't come from you, but from Havrowitz!"

Nicholas had to admit that his father and the emperor had suggested to him that he enlist.

"Of course," Fanny insisted, "but it is Havrowitz who's behind this plan."

So Nicholas gave it all up. The very day of their return to St. Petersburg, the good doctor rushed to the palace and, having obtained an audience with the emperor, threw himself at his feet begging him to put an end to the spectacle of Nicholas's affair with Fanny. But beforehand, he had made a point, during their travels, to send several reports to Alexander II advising him to send Nicholas to Khiva.

"You see," concluded Fanny bitterly, "how right I was to distrust him." She was unaware that Nicholas's entourage was speculating about the reasons for his attachment to Fanny. A young man so fickle clinging to an American courtesan! They were convinced that if he persisted, it was only because of the pressure she put on him. Therefore, they had gradually shifted their thinking to put all their weight behind the Khiva plan, the more so as they understood that the idea attracted him. Others at court considered it rather well thought out to send off to the devil—that is, Central Asia—a grand duke who expressed ideas that were far too advanced. He could talk at his leisure of reforms before savages with slanting eyes.

Fanny then felt she was not up to struggling, not only against the imperial family and the court united against her, but above all against Nicholas's desire to take part in this expedition in order to break out of his life of idle luxury. Since he was burning to put himself to the test, there was nothing else to do but bow to his wishes.

"You'll see that they'll manage to separate us," she grumbled.

Nicholas immediately hurried to his father but, before enlisting, demanded all possible guarantees concerning Fanny: no one would touch her, no one would try to break off their affair. His father, too pleased to see his son committed to something, promised everything he wished. Similarly, the emperor, to whom Nicholas had the audacity to say, "My life is at your majesty's orders, but there is one limit where the grand duke stops, and a man's heart begins."

Alexander II understood his dear nephew and would respect his wish.

Nicholas's departure was approaching. The days went by too quickly, in sadness. Christmas came. On the morning of December 24, Nicholas unexpectedly came to fetch Fanny at the Hôtel de France, where she was still living. He seemed very excited. He took her to the square stretching before the vast Michael Palace, had her go up three flights of a modern apartment house, and pulled a key from his pocket. They entered a spacious and sunny apartment whose windows overlooked the square. The rooms were elegantly and tastefully furnished.

"It's for you," Nicholas announced. "It's so that you have a home while you wait for me to come back."

A Christmas tree had been set up in a corner and, next to it, a table filled with presents, books, knickknacks, pictures, china, and also caskets of small jewels. Nicholas wanted to have her try the bed immediately. They flung themselves on it and left only for a Christmas Eve supper.

The next morning, Nicholas drew her to the window. Down below waited a new surprise, a sleigh covered with bearskins harnessed to two magnificent black horses with a coach driver named Vladimir at his mistress's order. It was time to announce the bad news: he had to accompany his mother, who couldn't stand the Russian winter, to help her settle in Nice. And this just before his own departure.

One more punishment, Fanny said to herself.

Unresigned to being separated from Nicholas, she was eager to be present at his departure for the Riviera. She went to the terminal called Warsaw Station and concealed herself behind other travelers. A special train had been reserved whose locomotive had been heating up for hours.

Although the grand duchess was traveling incognito, Fanny saw, getting on the train *Baron Boye,* the marshal of her court, two ladies-in-waiting, her personal doctor, her masseuse, her hairdresser, the keeper of her jewels carrying the large case of simple traveling jewelry, two footmen, a woman for the wardrobe, and four chambermaids. Of course, all of them had their own servants and chambermaids, fifteen servants altogether, plus Dr. Havrowitz, and lastly the luggage. Several dozen huge chests were hoisted into the baggage cars, and then, at the end, the duchess's piano, which had been dismantled for the occasion. Her imperial highness could play only on her personal instrument, which accompanied her on her trips along with the pianist responsible for tuning it. The agents of the secret police were swarming around, whom Fanny had learned to recognize since they followed Nicholas's every step. Uniformed guards forbade entry into the court's waiting room, whose curtains were drawn.

Suddenly the locomotive whistled, the soldiers stood at attention, the door of the waiting room opened, and the grand duchess appeared on Nicholas's arm. She was swathed in sable, and a sapphire fastener held the veil of her hat. She went by, fine looking and majestic, graciously bowing her head in response to the curtsies of the women and the bows of the men. Nicholas smiled distractedly until his eyes met those of Fanny. Immediately his smile froze. He went by, but he turned around, seeking to see her again. She had already gone away. The doors were shut on the coaches stamped with the two-headed eagle and, upon a final whistling of the locomotive, the train slowly pulled out.

Nicholas stayed only a few hours in Nice. Enough, however, to write Fanny several letters that left by special messenger. They were full of their coming separation: "When I think that in a few days I shall give you a final kiss, my heart is about to break. I feel that the blood runs less fast in my unhappy body—it's horrible!" Which didn't prevent him from going to Monte Carlo and trying his chances on the green baize. He won several times, and with some of his winnings he bought a Turkish blanket in crimson velvet with heavy embroidery that he hastened to offer Fanny upon his return, as well as several rolls of fifty gold louis also bearing the casino's seal, to which was added a more personal gift, a diamond bracelet.

Fanny smiled. She thanked him but was sad, for these presents did not undo the inevitable. Nicholas went to the barracks to say good-bye to his regiment. "I expressed my regrets about leaving them. I told them I had been devoted to them as to a family. As I was speaking I noticed tears in the eyes of many soldiers, and basically that touched me much more than the present, an icon, that the officers gave me. Frankly, I have loved the privates much more than the officers, and that explains a lot. . . ."

The day before his departure, he had to go take his leave of the different members of the family. Fanny received a note with an appointment in the church of the Peter and Paul Fortress where, according to custom, he would go to pay his respects at the tomb of his ancestors. She got into the sleigh he had given her. It was barely half past two in the afternoon and already it was getting dark. The snow had stopped falling, but the sky was heavily overcast.

Shivering, she found Nicholas in the freezing sanctuary. Her lover clasped her in his arms to warm her up. They stopped before the tombs of Paul I, his hero, Tsar Nicholas, his grandfather, and finally before that of the most illustrious of the Romanovs, Peter the Great. From his pocket Nicholas took out a small gold cross covered with cabochons of precious stones.

"When I was a child my parents gave me this cross in this very place. I give it to you so that you never forget me."

Fanny burst into sobs.

Back in her apartment, Nicholas rather coolly gave her precise instructions about the conduct she was to adopt and whom to see or not to see in his absence. He cut off a lock of her hair and put it into a locket with a chain that he slipped over his head. Fanny handed him one of her photographs, which he refused. "Having your portrait in front of me would affect me really too much."

The hour drew near. He took Fanny in his arms and put his cheek next to hers. She felt the tears running and she couldn't restrain herself any longer: she begged him not to abandon her. In his gaze she saw the temptation to give in, but he pulled himself together.

The clock struck six. He had to go to the Marble Palace to have dinner with his father before going directly to the station to catch the express train for Moscow.

They parted without a word, without a kiss.

Scarcely had he left than he began bombarding Fanny with telegrams and letters.

"Hold on," he demanded of her from the Kremlin in Moscow, where he had stopped off for a few hours.

"Despite long separation, am sure it is not the end," he telegraphed her from Saratov, the town where the train stopped and the real expedition began.

"I'm madly in love with you," he assured her as, sailing on the Volga, his boat arrived at its destination.

"I feel I could not stand an eternal good-bye with you. It's stronger than I am. . . . The horses are waiting. I must leave for Orenburg, where I will be in two or three days."

He reached that city located over a thousand miles from Moscow. The journey had worn him out. Night and day the sleigh had slid on the snow, the road was awful, but he drew consolation from the enthusiasm with which he was welcomed everywhere. True, he was the first member of the imperial family to venture so far east, so in every town, every village, there had been receptions, presentations, guards of honor, cheers, and applause.

Nicholas was not vain and didn't claim this popularity for himself, but he got drunk "on the power of the emperor of Russia, on this adoration that people have for his person and for everything around him." A fit of nationalism, highly excusable in his position and at his age, blinded him to the truth of the ferocious Russian imperialism. Peter the Great had had a good understanding of this two centuries earlier: the empire could not expand to the west, where Europe stood guard. In the east, it had already reached the Pacific. On the other hand, in the southeast it had much to gain! Except that a majority of those boundless territories that stretched between Russia, China, Afghanistan, and Iran were inhospitable and desertlike, albeit incalculably rich in resources. Moreover, a Russian presence was indispensable to counter the underhanded advance of the British from their base in India.

Peter the Great had sent, precisely to Khiva, a task force that was massacred down to the last man, from which arose a lust for revenge still burning two centuries later. His successors had acted more methodically, nibbling one after another at the sultanates that divided up the region and had remained in the Middle Ages. Bukhara, Sarmarkand, Kokand, and Tashkent were incorporated into the bosom of Russia in the guise of alliance treaties with the local potentates that were merely thinly disguised acts of annexation. There remained only the khan of Khiva to stand up to the Russian Empire.

This little king could hardly think he could vanquish the troops of the tsar with his pathetic little army, but he knew that the desert was providentially on his side. To get at him, you had to travel thousands of kilometers in one of the world's most daunting and deadly regions. No army had ever succeeded in overcoming this barrier, which allowed the khan, astride the heights of his mud palace, to scorn the overwhelming power of Russia.

"I imagine in advance the feelings I am going to have for the first time in my life seeing in the distance, in the middle of the limitless steppes, a gang of bandits on horses," Nicholas wrote. "All my blood boils when I think of that. . . . Another thought makes it also boil, more strongly, when I see a ravishingly beautiful blonde in oriental attire, her arms behind her head, with a rather occidental-looking man. It's Fanny Lear, my charming idol! I adore you. I belong to you completely, like a child. Like a slave. Yours forever . . ."

Leaving Orenburg, the army reached Orsk, where Europe ends and so does the telegraph service. He sent a final telegram. "Am in Asia, good-bye Europe. Good-bye dear Pavlovsk, good-bye Fanny Lear, good-bye my love, good-bye dear homeland. Bye for the last time . . ."

Heading south, they made quick work of hundreds of miles before stopping at Irghiz, a simple village on a river. Nicholas couldn't telegraph, but he still wrote, without knowing whether his letters would reach his beloved.

"I have a fever as I did in the past. My thoughts are a torment. But no, no, I tell myself it is impossible for my little Fanny Lear to be unfaithful. . . . For a few hours I become calmer. From time to time I imagine you leaving with someone else and never returning.

When I am more sensible, I regain confidence in you. I know that you love me and love me a lot, for you proved it when I fell ill last year, and at the camp when I was unbearable. . . ."

For her part, Fanny believed she would never get news and thought that their enemies had won. This time, she had lost Nicholas! In her despair she didn't want to just sit and wait, and on an impulse she returned to Paris, her favorite city.

Nicholas, who could not know any of this, still wrote her at the address on the square of the Michael Palace in St. Petersburg. Nevertheless, the gloomy, colorless steppes of Asia made him introspective.

> *When I turned twenty, I felt I had no family. The Marble Palace repelled me. Then I said to myself: I shall find a family somewhere else. I found a princess, I wanted to marry her—that plan failed. I went on looking among all the women in St. Petersburg. Soon I was punished and disillusioned. . . . Finally I met the pretty little blonde (I can love only blondes) Fanny Lear, who was witty and, more important, fond of me. That did it! The poor treatment I had received, the disappointments, and the endless stratagems I deployed for making myself loved meant that I wasted a whole year. As we could have been happy during that time, I was triply foolish. And yet it will soon be a year and a half that we have been together. May fate come to our aid and prolong our happiness. . . .*

The army reached Kazalinsk, the last vaguely civilized spot. The columns were to regroup there and wait for winter to end and get ready for the spring campaign. Nicholas was delighted because he was given responsibility for having a fort built that could house some three hundred soldiers. He was also promised the command of the vanguard. He was in charge of finding mounts, indigenous horses, which were small and ugly but very robust, that could go for several days without eating. Nicholas rounded up the camels to be loaded with luggage. He observed the nomads, representing so many races at the same time: the Kirghiz, the Turkomans, the Uzbeks, and the Karakalpaks. All these Asians thought only of seeing the humiliation and subjugation of Khiva, the detested and envied city, that city of bandits and plunderers.

His higher officers appreciated him, his comrades admired him. The only fly in the ointment was cousin George, the duke of Leuchtenberg, a distant relative. Nicholas judged him stupid, ingratiating, and a flatterer; his presence annoyed him. Nicholas's diversion lay in telling Fanny about his daily life, a pretext for thinking of her. "My little grand duchess of all the Russias . . . In this terrible desert, I am so longing for news of you. For a whole month now, I have seen only sand, yellow or red, tortoises, snakes, and all kinds of insects, more or less dangerous. You are my well-loved woman, my wife, my other half. I love you so much more than I would have been able to love my real wife, the princess. I smother you in my arms, I crush you with my legs, I kiss you everywhere and I fall at your feet. . . ." The distance only increased his passion.

At the end of March the army set off and entered into the unknown. That desert, imagined to be ablaze, was a world of ice. Everyone suffered from the cold in the tents and from the struggle to advance in the sandy steppes, where even the horses and camels used to the terrain were exhausted. Storms, which blew five days at a stretch, made matters worse. The temperature fell further; men were shivering. After crossing the frozen Syr Darya on foot, the troops encountered torrential rains. And the army of the khan of Khiva was still nowhere to be seen.

Then one fine day, spies announced five thousand mounted soldiers at a march of three days. Nicholas was thrilled! Finally the baptism of fire for this young man of twenty-three who was spoiling for a fight. But between them and the enemy stretched the Kyzyl Kum, "the red sands," the most dreaded desert in the world.

The rains had become infrequent and, on the khan's orders, the wells had been poisoned. The cold was replaced by stifling heat and there was almost no potable water. An infernal wind blew uninterruptedly. It stirred up the red dust that prickled, blinded, and penetrated everywhere, into clothing, tents, into luggage, into the eyes. At the same time the sun burned the pale Nordic skins. They were frightfully sunburned on their faces, necks, and hands. With the sand in their eyes and the glaring sun, they could scarcely see anything.

Every day the temperature rose a bit higher. Toward noon it reached 120 degrees Fahrenheit. The men were stretched to the limit. Every day dozens of them collapsed on the reddish soil. The expedition arrived at Adam Krylghan, a mere point on a map but well named, for in the local dialect it meant "the death of man."

Nicholas tolerated the ambient conditions better than the others. Despite a nervous, rather fragile temperament, he had a strong and resistant constitution. What's more, he knew that all eyes were on him and that he must set an example. The dust, heat, fatigue, hunger, and thirst must have no hold over the nephew of the emperor! His men adored him, for he was always in a good mood; he mingled with them and was always there to restore their courage when they lacked it.

Drawing near the Amu Darya River, his dream was finally realized: "Yesterday was the great day, we waged battle." More than three hundred thousand cavalrymen wearing black bearskin hats surrounded the Russians, charging on all sides, screeching and firing at random.

When night fell, the two armies camped facing each other. The next morning the enemy forces threw themselves on the Russian infantrymen with ferocious shouts, the boldest approaching to within forty paces to get better aim. Although the Russians were badly outnumbered, their weaponry and the fifty cannons of General Kaufman worked wonders: the enemy was routed; the Russians took over their camp and pursued them. Nicholas saw cavalrymen jump into the water and drown rather than surrender: "I frankly admit that my heart pounded when the bullets were whistling all around me. Fortunately, the enemy were poor marksmen and we had few losses. In general, it was a terribly moving day."

What he did not say was that everyone, from the commander in chief to the last of the privates, had noticed his calm, his courage, and his energy. Many had supposed that he was only, like his cousin Leuchtenberg, a ceremonial officer sent on a military tour. They would have taken great care not to expose him to dangers that he would choose to avoid. A member of the imperial family is not supposed to come under enemy fire. Whereas, in one battle, Nicholas earned his stripes. He was a warrior, a leader of men. He was a hero!

They were now not very far from Khiva. Nicholas thought the city would fall in a few days, but the enemy had further strength in reserve. When the army reached the Amu Darya River, the khan's artillery, massed on the other bank, attacked. A first cannonball landed not far from Nicholas; a second one came closer, raising an enormous cloud of dust. The cannonballs came in rapid succession, and two of his horses were killed before the Russian artillery counterattacked and the enemy was put to flight.

Then, with indescribable happiness, the Russians caught sight of the clear blue water of the Amu Darya. Without listening to orders, the soldiers, shouting with joy, threw themselves into the river. They knew they were the victors; they had won the wager; the enemy had no further defense. Indeed, the khan had fled and the city surrendered on May 29, 1873.

Nicholas was not present at the surrender, which he considered a formality. He had asked for a furlough, which his commander had granted him without consulting St. Petersburg, and he had by then already left the army behind.

On return to civilization and the telegraph, his first concern was to make an appointment with Fanny: "I will wait for you on July 6 in Samara, I leave this minute, I burn with impatience!"

This telegram, which had been sent to St. Petersburg, was relayed to Paris. Receiving it, Fanny rushed to an atlas in search of the city of Samara. It was very far in the Urals, several hundred miles east of Orenburg. Without waiting for a second — Joséphine was to follow with the luggage — Fanny went alone on the Nord-Express.

She only glimpsed Berlin, then Warsaw . . . Crossing the Russian plain made her seethe with impatience. In a hurry to be reunited with her lover, she found the landscape monotonous, boring. It was still night when the express came to a halt in Moscow. She had the whole day in front of her before she could continue her journey. She took advantage of this forced leisure to visit the Kremlin and the churches before boarding the express train for Nizhniy Novgorod. On reaching her destination, she just had time to climb aboard a steamboat that was going down the Volga.

The boat was jam-packed, no more single first-class cabins, and no second-class ones. Fanny shuddered at the idea of being cooped up in third class with the peasants, but the gentlemanly captain let her have his own cabin. The trip was hard, the heat frightful. Day and night, Fanny was eaten alive by the flies and mosquitoes. The travelers had brought their own provisions and picnicked just about everywhere. Her eyes fell on an unfortunate man afflicted with tuberculosis who was going south because fermented mare's milk, koumiss, had been recommended for his health, one of Nicholas's favorite beverages that she herself found revolting. The peasants were penned in like beasts, and Fanny was disgusted when she had to go through a teeming crowd of them on her way up to the bridge.

The boat reached Kazan. Fanny stayed at the Kommengo Hotel, which had been recommended. No sign of Nicholas. No telegram, no message. The heat that didn't let up prevented her from sleeping and cut her appetite. What's more, there was not a single book in the whole city written in anything but Russian. In short, Kazan's resources were so limited that the only entertainment Fanny found was a funeral she had come upon by chance.

The days went by, increasing her exasperation. Still no news of Nicholas. Finally she set off again for the north. She retook the steamboat, but this time she was provided with excellent comfort and charming company. Her cabin overlooked the bridge and fresh air came in through the half-open Persian blinds. Leaning on the rail, she gazed at the green twists and turns of the Volga. She ran into a messenger who was going to St. Petersburg to announce the storming of Khiva to the tsar.

Fanny caught her fellow travelers giving her curious looks. She was sure they knew her identity but were pretending not to. For tea, for dinner, she found herself next to an old lady who appeared to be a regular. The two women felt a growing liking for each other, and soon the old lady was telling her life story. Voyages on the Volga, that's all she knew. She was very rich and was so afraid her nephews were poisoning her in order to inherit that she spent the winter on the train between Moscow and Saratov, and the summer on the Volga, going down and then back up the river. "Even if the food is often inedible on these public conveyances, at least one doesn't run the risk of dying from poison!" Fanny nicknamed her "the queen of the Volga" and they became inseparable. On arriving in Nizhniy Novgorod, they threw themselves into each other's arms. Then the old lady looked into Fanny's eyes and in a quavering voice murmured, "May God soon return your prince to you, and may you be happy with him."

At the end of four days of waiting, Fanny decided to go back to St. Petersburg. She had scarcely got home when she received a telegram from Nicholas, sent from Orsk. He gave her a new rendezvous in Samara. Since love is stronger than fatigue, Fanny made the same trip, but this time in the opposite direction: St. Petersburg, Moscow, Nizhniy Novgorod, the Volga, Kazan . . . From there, a day of boating would take her to her destination.

The arrival in Samara was expected for five in the morning. At four o'clock Fanny was dressed, made up, and combed. Finding curling irons and managing to do her hair in the small cabin of a steamboat going down the Volga represented a real achievement! She eagerly scanned the sky that was giving way to dawn and saw on the quay not Nicholas but two of his friends, who handed her a letter: "At last after five months I'm going to see you again. . . . It already seemed to me that I was buried and everything was over, and here I am coming back to life. . . . I am persuaded that you were indeed right, here I am as you said, having become a man. . . ."

He asked her to follow his friends to the best hotel in town and there to get room 16, for that would be next to his. She arrived at the hotel and went up to her room. The floor boy who accompanied her left by the connecting door and locked it.

In her impatience Fanny redid her makeup a hundred times, did her hair again, took up a book that she was incapable of reading. She walked back and forth; she went to the balcony, but there was nothing. Suddenly she heard frenzied cheers in the street, and in the distance she recognized Nicholas from his height and his gait. An enthusiastic crowd, whom he graciously saluted, surrounded him and didn't want to let him go. For a secret rendezvous . . .

He entered the hotel, and soon she heard the door of the adjacent room open; she recognized his footsteps. She was quivering with excitement. The crowd massed in front of the hotel demanding "the conqueror of Khiva." He appeared on the balcony, saluted, and the crowd applauded him. She heard the window close and steps approach the connecting door, she saw the handle turn, but the door didn't open!

"Fanny, open the door!" His tone was both amused and impatient.

"But I can't, the floor boy locked it and took the key."

They had to look for the boy, wait for him to turn the key in the lock, and then Nicholas was standing before her. She was so upset that she half hid herself behind a curtain. He looked at her as though he were going to devour her, and she noticed his eyes filled with tears. He crossed the room to take her in his arms.

Holding each other tightly, they kissed, unable to utter a word. Then Fanny pulled away a little and stared at him. He was so tanned his skin was nearly black, and he was frighteningly thin. He looked so tired . . . She knew how to find the words to tell him how proud she was of him. Without any doubt he would receive the much-coveted medal, the Cross of St. George, whose jeweled pin she had bought before his departure, to fix to his chest at the proper time.

They both felt desire stirring in them, but Nicholas wasn't free. He had to be present at a luncheon that the municipality was giving, then review the city's firemen! Moreover, they couldn't linger in Samara, for Nicholas's father had sent a telegram asking for him. At least they would have this first night of getting together again all to themselves in room number 16.

The next day they embarked on the steamship, but they didn't have the right to appear in public together. Fanny got on board very early so as not to attract attention. Later Nicholas arrived, surrounded by authorities and a crowd of admirers. At the boat's every stop, an official reception awaited the conqueror of Khiva: speeches, triumphal arches, ovations, and drumrolls.

At night, the towns and villages they passed through were lit up, and Nicholas constantly had to salute, offer thanks, make a little speech, shake hands, kiss cheeks, and come up with compliments. Finally, in a moment of calm, he could hurry to Fanny's cabin. He was so exhausted that he put his face on her knees and fell asleep.

A triumphal reception was waiting for him in Moscow. More than the official luncheon at the governor's, it was the people's enthusiasm that touched him, because of its spontaneity and sincerity. The Russian people, like Fanny, were proud of Nicholas.

8

Fanny and Nicholas came back to Pavlovsk on July 12 and settled in the young woman's dacha. It was bliss, but they had only three days to take advantage of it, for once again the grand duke Constantine imperatively called his son to Warsaw to pay his respects to the emperor, who was residing in his kingdom of Poland. It was arranged that Alexander II, recognizing the merits of his nephew, would award him a medal on this occasion.

Immediately Nicholas got onto a train. Fanny was to follow him in a few days. She was getting ready to leave when a dispatch notified her that the rendezvous had been moved to Vilna, where the emperor was going. Blasé now and increasingly submissive, Fanny followed the instructions. She arrived in the Lithuanian capital in a violent storm. Waiting for her at the station was Vorpovsky, the aide-de-camp, who took her to the best hotel in the city. There, she ordered dinner, which arrived in her suite at just the moment when she was brought a note from Nicholas asking her to go at once to the palace of the former grand dukes of Lithuania: "You will enter through the garden door where the sentinel won't dare to hold you back." In the middle of the night and in a torrential rain, Fanny found she was obliged to go out again. She found a carriage that took her to her destination, but she was quivering with apprehension. Would they let her through? Fortunately the dwarf Karpish materialized, who took her by a service door to the second floor and left her in a large sitting room covered in yellow damask. It was in this very room that Tsar Alexander I had decided to retreat toward Moscow and that, the next day, Napoleon had begun his attack by spreading his maps on this round table covered in malachite where Fanny was drinking her tea.

Nicholas was taking a long time. He was at an official banquet in progress some rooms away. At last he came to her. Fanny rushed into his arms.

"So did you have the Cross of St. George?"

Nicholas had a sad smile: "Look for yourself."

Fanny recognized on her lover's chest the Cross of St. Vladimir, a second-class "honor." But there was worse to come. For it was his cousin, that moron Leuchtenberg, who, by flattering the right people despite his mediocre military performance, had received the Cross of St. George.

"But you were the conqueror of Khiva, acclaimed by all Russia!"

She felt deeply wounded, but at the same time she had a feeling he was keeping something from her. She questioned him, sought an explanation. Finally Nicholas confessed: having carried out his duty, and with the city of Khiva about to surrender, he felt in such a hurry to find his Fanny again that he had left the theater of operations without leave or, rather, he had been content to ask his commanding officer for it. Whereas, before his departure, the emperor and his father had made him swear to not come back without their express authorization. They were obviously counting on holding the rebellious young man in Central Asia long enough for him to forget his American woman. So he had disobeyed, and the outraged emperor had refused to bestow the much-desired cross on him.

"You see, Fanny, I had planned to take advantage of this occasion, where I would be congratulated and decorated, to ask the emperor for my finest reward, the authorization to marry you."

Nearly stunned by this revelation, Fanny fell into a stiff and uncomfortable armchair, both transported and overwhelmed. Although he had called her "my grand duchess," "my wife," she knew that it was as much joking as it was love, and she would never have imagined that he would dare to go against all the taboos for her. Little Hattie Ely Blackford of Philadelphia, the kid whose mother had lived from hand-to-mouth, the youngest child, scorned by her half sisters and ignored by her peers, the courtesan held up to ridicule by respectable people, the pariah, would become part of the imperial family as niece of the tsar of all the Russias! It was impossible.

"But, Nicholas, a grand duke can't marry a whore!"

Nicholas made an irritated gesture. "Forget your old profession once and for all. We love each other, and that's enough. I've had enough of the hypocrisy of others, of that of my own father, who keeps his dancer under my mother's nose, of that of the emperor who forces the empress to put up with his Katia. . . ."

"By marrying me, you'd lose all your privileges. . . ."

"On the contrary, I'd win freedom!"

Fanny was still too much under the shock of surprise to reflect. Distractedly she looked around the pompous, badly lit, and cold room whose heavy Empire furniture was lined up against the walls. Modesty prevented her, during a long silence, from posing the question she was dying to ask, and she murmured, "What was the emperor's verdict about his nephew's request?"

"He didn't let me speak. Right away he violently reproached me for having abandoned the Khiva campaign without his authorization."

Whereupon the grand duke heir had appeared, Alexander Alexandrovich, the giant with a reputation of being narrow-minded and vicious. He couldn't stand his elegant cousin, the darling of the ladies. He never missed a chance, taking advantage of his own position, to thwart Nicholas or humiliate him. Joining the fray, he had thrown back in Nicholas's face the opinions he had expressed and the company he frequented. He had more or less accused Nicholas of mutiny. The interview had gone so badly that Nicholas had given up his plan to ask for permission to marry Fanny.

Her head bowed, Fanny nervously wrung her hands. "The emperor will never grant it to you and . . ."

"Of no importance," Nicholas interrupted. "We'll go to Vienna to get married incognito." His voice suddenly turned stentorian. "Into my arms, Fanny, my little wife!"

He literally swept her up from her seat and, putting his arms around her, did a short dance. She joined in, and there they were, spinning around in the silence of the vast room surrounded by the night.

The next morning they left Vilna after taking some precautions. Fanny, followed by the faithful Joséphine, settled in a first-class coach while Nicholas ceremoniously got into his private coach attached at the end of the express train. As the train set off and picked up speed, each of the lovers could see Russian policemen racing along the platform trying to stop the locomotive — proof that the emperor was not pleased by their departure. They were nearly held back, but from then on they were not threatened.

Fanny tranquilly rejoined Nicholas in his coach. They were making love when the train stopped at the border between Russia and Austria. For Nicholas there was of course no problem, but poor Joséphine, remaining in the first-class coach, had trouble with the customs officers for she didn't have any papers. She was actually traveling on Fanny's passport. And there was no Fanny. "Where is she?" asked the customs officers. Joséphine couldn't tell them that she was in the grand duke's coach! The suspicious customs officers began frantically looking for the absent woman. Meanwhile, Joséphine managed to get the attention of one of the grand duke's servants, who immediately informed the lovers. Fanny descended from Nicholas's coach on the wrong side, went along the rails between two trains that had stopped, and returned to her coach. When the customs officers came back empty-handed, they were astonished to see the missing person at her seat as if nothing had happened! They stamped her passport without understanding how she had reappeared. The lovers were still laughing as the train reached Vienna.

Scarcely had they settled in the Archduke Charles Hotel when they hurried to the International Exposition. Fanny was particularly attracted by the jewels on display, for the sparkle of the precious stones had an almost sensual fascination for her. She stopped short before a diamond bracelet that had belonged to the French empress Eugenie, and a set of diamonds, sumptuous jewels of incomparable elegance, also worn by the former empress. When the Second Empire fell, the French Republic hastened to sell the crown jewels (not very skillfully for that matter).

The lovers, however, were not there for tourism. Nicholas had actually decided on a secret marriage. Fanny weighed all that that implied. At best she would have to remain in the shadows without ever appearing at his side. At the worst, if they managed to stay out of prison, it would bring permanent exile for Nicholas, the loss of his rank, his honors, and above all his fortune. Fanny cared nothing about that. The courtesan had given way to an amorous young woman filled with apprehension.

"Listen. I read in the newspaper that your parents are very nearby, in Munich. They might hear about our being in Vienna and about our plans."

"Don't worry! My mother has dug up a Bavarian healing woman who flatters her and has thereby gained enormous influence—my mother can no longer do without her. My father doesn't let that woman out of his sight; he watches her every move, tries to limit the damage. So they are preoccupied with other things, not us."

Nicholas went at once to find the Russian ambassador's priest to force him to marry them. The holy man, who was merely a kind of civil servant, raised his arms to heaven and protested that his career would be smashed, his freedom threatened, and his future ruined forever.

Hence, no religious marriage, but there remained a civil marriage ceremony, concluded Nicholas, who fell back on the municipal authorities. He had a representative of the Vienna mayoralty come at once and asked him to prepare the necessary documents. He pretended to be the count Herder. The civil servant, who was suspicious, asked to see the birth certificates of the future spouses. Nicholas, obviously, couldn't produce them, but he proposed funds by way of compensation and brandished a well-filled purse under the nose of the honest Austrian worthy. The latter nimbly made the purse vanish and left, promising to come back the next day with the necessary documents.

In twenty-four hours, Nicholas and Fanny will be husband and wife in the eyes of the law, if not in the eyes of God.

At that moment the door of their sitting room suddenly opened and the grand duke Constantine stood before them! He greeted Fanny amiably, as if she were an old acquaintance, and proceeded to lambaste his son with a speech he had prepared. Nicholas had been truly naive to imagine for an instant that his tricks would succeed. The Austrian police informed the Russian secret police, which reported to the emperor and the grand duke just about every movement made by the couple! The embassy priest had been warned in advance, and the representative of the Vienna mayoralty had given back the money-filled purse. In other words, no hope in any direction; every precaution had been taken to prevent a secret marriage.

On the other hand, if Nicholas agreed to calm down and show discretion and submission for a certain amount of time, then maybe the emperor would let him marry Fanny. Only a few months to wait.

"You mean, Papa, until Maria's marriage."

The grand duchess Maria Alexandrovna, the beloved only daughter of the emperor Alexander II, was soon to be married to Alfred, the duke of Edinburgh, one of the sons of Queen Victoria. Before this union, a morganatic marriage or other scandal in the imperial family must be avoided at any cost.

"Come back to Russia with me, and after Maria's marriage, we'll see."

"Do I at least have the right to bring Fanny back?"

With a sigh the grand duke approved and withdrew.

"At least my family has understood that it is pointless to try to separate us," Nicholas explained. And he immediately weighed the pros and cons. Rejecting the grand duke's proposal held the possibility of being married as soon as possible, for if Austria refused to cooperate, a more liberal country would do so, but that was to condemn themselves to live forever as outlaws. Accepting the proposal might bring the emperor's blessing, but it was also to throw themselves between the lion's jaws.

Nicholas chose to believe in his uncle's promise and in his father's sincerity. Fanny was careful not to give her opinion.

Returning to St. Petersburg, Nicholas had the pleasant surprise of learning that a new expedition in Central Asia was being
proposed, this time more scientific than military, to explore the Amu
Darya.

His parents, not satisfied with the result of his participation
in the Khiva campaign—which had merely strengthened his love
for Fanny—had a hand in this new project. The general staff, impressed by Nicholas's capabilities, offered him another chance to
make use of them.

The young man was enthusiastic. Central Asia proved unfor-
gettable and had an irresistible attraction. He sometimes had the
impalpable impression his destiny awaited him there. But the organization of this expedition was only beginning; one had to wait.

The grand duke Constantine took advantage of this to inform
him of a much more immediate intention. He had decided, in accord with the grand duchess, to give him his independence, to settle
him in his own residence, which would be their gift. Money didn't
count; he was free to choose the palace of his dreams!

"That is to say, they've decided for you to get married," remarked Fanny.

" Me, marry, yes, to you!"

"Because you imagine that your parents are offering you a
palace so that you can set me up in it as your wife . . ."

Nicholas's distress did not escape Fanny, and she didn't insist.

Immediately, Nicholas went in quest of a residence. There was
at the edges of St. Petersburg society a very old trollop, the daughter of peasants who, through her beauty and a string of cleverly cal-
culated marriages, had acquired a fortune and even the title of
princess. One of her husbands had allowed her to acquire a splendid
palace; another one had bankrupted her, which forced her to sell it.
Nicholas visited the palace, fell in love with it, and instantly bought
it. He forbade Fanny to set foot inside, for first he wanted to rid his

new residence of all the old things piled up there. He wished to re-decorate his new home from top to bottom, to furnish and fill it with his collections so the place would be worthy of his beloved.

But the beloved was unhappy, for Nicholas hadn't for an instant thought about what would happen to her if he left once again for Central Asia. And he'd bought this house without consulting her. Moreover, he was neglecting her for his new toy. He talked only about his palace and the work he would have done on it. He spent more and more time on it, to the point of disregarding her. He who hitherto was always in a great hurry to see her now arrived very late at their rendezvous on occasion. In short, Fanny was jealous, jealous of a house.

That day, Nicholas had made a luncheon date with her at the fashionable Aurora Restaurant near the Kazan Cathedral, right off the Nevsky Prospekt. Held back by the painters, the carpenters, the upholsterers, he showed up more than an hour late.

Only Fanny was no longer alone at the table. Nicholas saw with surprise a very young officer of his Volynski Regiment, the artilleryman Savine. He knew him, of course, since they rubbed elbows every day at the barracks, but he had never paid much attention to him.

Very calmly, Fanny explained that Count Savine, dining in the restaurant and seeing her alone, came over to her table, introduced himself, and proposed to keep her company while waiting for his commander to arrive so that she would not be defenseless against curious stares.

Nicholas of course asked the young Savine, who was on the verge of leaving, to stay and have lunch with them. They were young and hungry and wolfed down their food. Sauterne, Vouvray, Chambertin, and champagne followed one after the other.

How did the conversation get around to politics? Probably Savine imperceptibly steered it in that direction, and Nicholas, who had not forgotten the emperor's injustice after Khiva nor the way his family treated his love for Fanny, gave vent to his resentment in the form of violent criticisms.

Not only did Savine approve, he added to them. It was no longer the system, the court, or the government that they blamed, but the imperial family itself. Everything that Nicholas had endured since childhood because of his authoritarian and narrow-minded uncles, and his arrogant and brutal cousins, came out. They outdid one another in bluntly denouncing the vices of the grand dukes, their lack of patriotism, their laziness, their inhumanity, in fact their uselessness . . . and thus they cast doubt on the very legitimacy of the dynasty! It was merely one step further to conclude that the monarchy had to be overthrown.

Fanny, who was silent, was content to look from one to the other with a sometimes shocked amusement and a surprise tinged with tenderness.

Nicholas took a notebook out of his pocket and scribbled some bad verse.

I cannot be a coward, while my crowned parents,
Despots, tyrants, and impostors, cruel tsars
Steal the freedom and happiness of the poor Russian
　　people.
Let the power of the tsars fall from the throne, fruit of
　　our labor
And if my efforts and my plans collapse
It was the will of God who did not hear my appeal.

Always provocative, Nicholas recited it much too loudly not to be heard at the tables nearby.

"Will you leave it at poetry, imperial highness?" whispered Savine.

"Soldier, listen carefully. This country can make progress only by democratic means."

And he quoted the dyed-in-the-wool liberals, the knowledgeable democrats whom he frequented, whose names just by themselves would startle the court conservatives.

"On the present path," commented Savine, "and with such doddery old men, Russia will not make any progress in a thousand years! If your imperial highness wishes it, I shall have you meet my friends; they advocate faster, more radical methods."

"Do you mean you associate with revolutionaries, nihilists, and other terrorists?"

Savine sensed that Nicholas's interest had been piqued. With his own special intensity, Nicholas peppered him with questions about his friends and their plan of action.

"They can explain it to you better than I can."

Lunch over, the two young people separated, the best friends in the world. Nicholas hastened to get some information about Savine. This character could be summed up in three words: gambling, debts, women. His blood carried the gambler's vice. And he was losing. Having no personal fortune, he was kept by women. He had acquired an incomparable gift and attained peaks in debauchery as in fraud that made him out of the ordinary. He knew how to get money from moneylenders as well as from his mistresses. When the one grumbled, he turned to the others, and vice versa. His favorite victim was the richest, the toughest pawnbroker in the city, Rudolf Erholz. He owed him colossal sums, and yet he managed to obtain new loans by taking advantage of the moneylender's snobbishness, but especially by outrageous bragging. To sum up, he was a hothead who would venture anything because he had nothing to lose!

The grand duke was also a hothead, but had everything to lose. Still, he was attracted to the soldier, not only because of his political opinions but also because of his character, which fascinated him.

❊   ❊   ❊

Finally the day arrived when Nicholas invited Fanny to his place, his palace on Gatchina Street. She didn't want to go, she grumbled, she was in a bad mood. Without realizing it, she dressed in black.

Nicholas received her in the entrance hall. She made an effort to display a smile. They went up a pink marble staircase decorated with splendid vases, crossed a huge white-and-gold ballroom, a Louis XIV sitting room, and then, after seeing the gallery suspended above the great staircase, they reached a Moorish smoking room followed by a Louis XV sitting room that Fanny criticized, for its tapestries were faded. There followed a Pompadour boudoir covered in red lace and pink silk.

On a whim, Nicholas asked Fanny to sit on the sofa and imitate the pose of the former owner. He himself played the young suitors of the very old courtesan and ended up declaring to Fanny that his room would henceforth be "her small bedroom."

"Thanks very much, but first, you must have this sofa recovered; it has witnessed some of the old woman's erotic frolicking!"

They went into Nicholas's bedroom—covered in a gray cross-weave fabric and medieval furniture—and they visited the dining room lit by stained-glass windows. Fanny discovered next the theater and the half-neglected chapel before they came back into the private apartments and sat down together at a table.

They drank a great deal to each other's health, to the palace's health, and to the happiness they would have within its walls. Then Nicholas rose and went to open a little door that Fanny hadn't noticed. She cried out with wonder, for she had the feeling she was entering the cave of Ali Baba.

Two statues of women framed the door, one holding a glass of champagne, the other with a finger on her mouth. "Have as much fun as you want, but once you leave, keep quiet" they seemed to

insinuate. The fireplace, worthy of a medieval castle, could hold
several people. In front of walls covered in Cordoba leather were
spread china, majolica, crystal ware from Venice, chinoiseries, and
porcelains from Saxe, Berlin, and Vienna. Chairs made at the beginning of the seventeenth century were upholstered with the same
leather from Cordoba. Marble sculptures and Chinese vases stood
on a stone balustrade. The table of sculpted wood came from the
collections of Mr. Thiers. Several display windows were packed
with watches, snuffboxes, precious objects, medals.

Fanny had time to notice a small crystal jug bearing gold and
precious stones that had belonged to Peter the Great. She would
have liked to examine these treasures at leisure, but Nicholas was
in a hurry to describe the work he was planning for the place.

"You'll have your whole life to complete this palace, why are
you in such a rush?"

"I want everyone to be able to admire it before my departure."

"But when you get back, you won't have anything to do."

"Yes I will. I'll sell the objects that displease me, and buy others!"

And he told her his dream of a gallery of paintings. He would
buy Greuzes, Rubenses, Wouwermans, and other Flemish or Dutch
artists. He could not wait, everything must materialize right away
and the pictures appear as if by miracle.

"A collection cannot be made in a week," Fanny interrupted.
"It takes years to put together a fine set."

"You're nice, but you'd be even more so if you allowed me my
dear whims and minded your own business."

As it happened, in the entrance hall they came upon a dealer
in secondhand goods who had under his arm a Rubens for sale. A
Rubens, from that scalawag! Fanny burst out laughing. Nicholas
got angry. Fanny advised him to ask the dealer for a certificate of
authenticity. The latter obviously couldn't come up with one. Disappointed, Nicholas let him go off with his Rubens.

Fanny had won, but this incident left her pensive.

Her lover had fun filling up his palace as if she didn't count, didn't exist. Who would be the mistress of the house? Nicholas seemed to have guessed her question and said to her, "From now on this residence is yours."

As a guarantee, he handed her a silver key that opened the main door.

Fanny had a melancholy premonition and began crying. "This house is my rival and I'm jealous of it."

"It's true, I love my palace, but I much prefer my beautiful Fanny."

Nevertheless, Fanny was puzzled and vaguely uneasy. She wondered about this new mania. Certainly he had always been a shrewd connoisseur, an impassioned collector, but this sudden voracious appetite for art objects was disconcerting. In it she detected a kind of frustration. He was bored by his army service, the expedition to Central Asia seemed ever further off, so to pass the time he collected, but his rage to buy and sell could not be fulfilling for long.

9

"*Will you leave it at poetry,* imperial highness?" Nicholas couldn't get this question of Savine's out of his head — so much so that he spoke about it to Fanny, who herself informed the artilleryman. The latter had to be especially well connected, for the Central Committee of the Revolution agreed to delegate one of its most eminent members to meet the tsar's nephew.

The appointment was to take place late in the afternoon in Fanny's apartment. Nicholas arrived shortly before the agreed-upon time, all the same rather nervous at the prospect of meeting one of those indomitable fanatics who, knife between his teeth, dreamed morning and night of killing the whole family, including himself.

At seven in the evening, the doorbell rang.

"The music teacher," announced Joséphine.

There appeared a young woman, or rather a girl, pale and thin. Her simple gray, white-collared dress indicated she was not interested in elegance or fashion, and her dust-covered shoes gave evidence of a long walk on foot.

Nicholas, as an expert, noted the fineness of her features, the rather round face, the broad forehead, and her childlike mouth with pressed lips—she was afraid of letting loose some superfluous words, he thought. When she raised her long eyelashes that she kept lowered, he was struck by the resoluteness in her blue-gray eyes. He identified her by her hair; she had her hair cut short like a boy, as the liberals liked to do. So this fragile intellectual was the promised terrorist! Savine, whom she greeted as an acquaintance, but rather coldly, was content to introduce her by her first name, Sophia. Keeping her distance, she nodded slightly in Nicholas's direction and, smiling, warmly shook Fanny's hand, thanking her for receiving her in a few sentences pronounced in perfect English.

"You speak our language amazingly well," remarked Fanny. "Have you ever been to the United States?"

"No, madam, but I hope one day to see that paradise of liberty and equality, and study that democracy, which is a model."

She had spoken with a resounding tone that led them to imagine an extraordinary strength of purpose.

Fanny asked her to sit down and had tea served while Savine and especially Nicholas curiously stood back.

Fanny spoke: "You are absolutely right, young lady. Liberty and equality have made the United States a great nation, and will someday make it the first country in the world."

"We would like very much to follow your example," the visitor replied, "but that is not so easy. It is extremely hard to start a revolution here in this country of fanaticism and slavery."

All of a sudden the intellectual who had been withdrawn came to life and became so heated that her face turned red.

"We must fight not only the usurpers who sit on the throne, but also the people and their ignorance. The Russian people's stupidity has made them blind. They don't understand that their worst enemy, their master and their thief, are the tsar and his regime. Quite the opposite, they see the tsar as their protector and benefactor. What blindness!"

Nicholas stepped in. He was not irritated, but sincere. "Don't talk that way, young lady. Alexander II has done a lot for the people. He freed them from serfdom, from what you call slavery."

"Freed the Russian people from serfdom! What mistaken reasoning, what hypocrisy! They freed some landowners, they picked up their scourges and gave them to bureaucratic torturers, to law enforcement on the take, to crooked priests, to cowardly judges, to brutish police! Alexander abolished serfdom only to invent a new slavery even worse than the old one and even more immoral because it's hidden by false good intentions!"

In the passion of her speech, Sophia became almost beautiful; she lost that dull enveloping grayness and took on the shimmering colors of a gorgeous sorceress.

Fanny no longer knew what to say. Savine was observing the scene attentively.

Nicholas, both vehement and fascinated, questioned the revolutionary. "What are you waiting for? What do you want?"

"We're waiting for nothing, and we want everything! First of all, to overthrow the monarchy and set up a republic. Next, to throw open the prison doors, establish an egalitarian vote, freedom of the press . . ."

She became garrulous, expressing all the great principles that meant so much to her, principles that have become commonplace but at the time were energizing ideals, unbelievably daring plans, extreme and magnificent concepts. Nicholas shared a good many of them with her, but remained skeptical when it came to concrete steps.

"Up to now, you and your friends are rather content with endless talking."

Sophia tightened her lips and her pale eyes transfixed Nicholas. "Just so. The time for discussions is past. Remember what I say to you. The time for action has come!"

She had been talking to the three of them with impressive determination.

"What are you waiting for to act?" asked Nicholas.

"We are ready, but we need money." Sophia uttered this last sentence in an almost inaudible voice. She had lost her animation and was again becoming the shy intellectual of the start of their discussion. Savine broke in. "Money is the motor of everything. It is the driving force of war! And what is a revolution if it isn't a war! How much do you need to begin?"

Sophia's voice was no more than a murmur. "A million rubles."

Savine drew nearer, planted himself in front of Nicholas, and looked him straight in the eye without saying a word. Nicholas made a nervous little laugh.

"I would very much like to give it to you, this million, but I don't have it. The prerogative service would never grant me such an advance! Rather it is you, my dear Savine, who could lay his hands on this million. You know every moneylender in the city and you brag that you can get out of them anything you want! Why don't you go ask for this sum from that Erholz you keep harping on and on about."

"Because, despite all the credit you give me for my skills of persuasion, Erholz will never entrust me with so much money. He would advance a million rubles, or even much more, only to you. He told me that several times. He even said he would charge five percent per month, half of the usual rate. Of course, he would demand security of the sort that only you can provide . . ."

Savine broke off. Everyone was silent, frozen as if time had stopped. The silence continued while the evening shadows overran the room. No one thought to light the kerosene lamps. It was in a half darkness that a deep sigh was heard, then the clear voice of Nicholas. "That's it. You will have your million, I promise you."

He had been speaking at the same time to the young revolutionary, to Savine, and to Fanny. Sophia picked up her bag with an abrupt gesture, rose clumsily, and, almost without saying goodbye, vanished.

The winter had become more bitter when Nicholas proposed a wolf hunt to Fanny. She grumbled because she had reserved a box at the opera for the evening of the hunt, but she wanted to please her lover. The day before the hunt she put on men's clothing exactly like Nicholas's. She wore boots that were very high and much too tight, which put her in a very bad mood. She protested, although she was beginning to enjoy the adventure.

At what was known as the Moscow Station, Fanny for the first time went into the waiting room reserved for the court. The staff took this beardless teenager, cigar at his lips, for a young English prince who'd come to attend the imminent marriage of the grand duchess Maria. They saluted her militarily and she did the same. At two o'clock in the morning the two lovers reached a little country train station. They got into a sleigh that rushed off at great speed in the snow-covered night.

In the distance Fanny made out the lights of a village and heard peasants joyfully singing, for it was Candlemas Day. They stopped in a thatched cottage to spend the rest of the night. A servant had already set up a narrow camp bed on which they immediately flung themselves. Not for long, as they had to be ready at six o'clock.

They borrowed a sleeper, a huge sleigh used for crossing the steppe. After arriving at the meeting place of the hunt, they continued on foot. Fanny slipped, fell, and sank into the snow, in up to her waist! She was happy, for she had always loved winter, and the beauty of the surrounding countryside, the pink-and-gray light of dawn, then the orange light of the rising sun brought her luck.

Suddenly the peasants pointed out the tracks of a lynx. They followed it for more than an hour, without difficulty but not without danger, for these felines have a habit of hiding in trees and falling on the reckless hunter and biting his throat. With a certain apprehension Fanny raised her eyes to the branches overhanging her. Suddenly she spotted a sort of ball of tawny fur out of which emerged two sparkling pupils. She nudged Nicholas, who aimed and fired. The feline, its claws stuck into the trunk of the tree, didn't move. A second bullet brought it down.

They got into a troika and traveled for three hours through the countryside as far as Pavlovsk, where the real hunt began. Scouts had pointed out five wolves, and a hundred peasants worked as beaters. Nicholas came alongside Fanny in a blind close to the trail. At a given signal, the peasants began shouting and beating their bushes.

Then an enormous wolf pounced on the right. Nicholas managed only to wound it and the beast continued running, leaving behind a trail of blood. Some seconds later a second wolf came so close to Fanny that she started with terror. Three others followed, which Nicholas killed one after the other. They then took off in pursuit of the wounded wolf to which Nicholas gave the deathblow. Only one wild beast got away.

The beater collected the four corpses and threw them at the grand duke's feet. He broke off a branch of fir and presented it to

Fanny, who placed this hunter's mark on the dead wolves' bodies. The beaters cheered frenetically, took hold of Fanny, threw her in the air, and caught her with great skill. She had only a single fear, which was that her hat would fall and that her long blond hair would be exposed, revealing her identity.

Without taking a breather, they left just in time to catch the evening train for St. Petersburg. Two hours later, Fanny, in a low-cut dress, wearing all her jewels, beautifully made up and hairstyled, entered her box at the opera. This day seemed to be an interlude as radiant as was the beginning of her affair with Nicholas.

Fanny resided in her quarters at the palace on Gatchina Street, but she held on to the apartment on the square of the Michael Palace. She spent several hours a day there when Nicholas was detained by some function at the court or by his army duties. She even stayed the night when he warned her he would be returning too late.

Nearly every day they had lunch and dinner together, went riding in a sleigh, played billiards, and sipped their tea while reading, but Nicholas constantly left her to keep an eye on further improvements to the palace or to meet dealers in antiques and secondhand goods. For him, nothing appeared too beautiful for his residence. He had fountains constructed, grottoes, a miniature lake he stocked with fish, and an aviary he filled with songbirds.

The art objects arrived at the palace at such a pace that he didn't have time to unpack them. Others disappeared just as quickly—given away, sold, or exchanged. He bought at distinctly excessive prices, he sold at prices that were much too low. Fanny protested when, for a ridiculous sum, he wanted to get rid of an extraordinary collection of gold medals depicting the great characters and great moments of the dynasty.

"Three thousand rubles was all they offered you? That's robbery, Nicky!"

"You're right as always, Fanny Lear. I'm not going to sell them, I'll put them in hock."

One day Nicholas left her to go to a family meeting.

Was it a luncheon with his father at the Marble Palace? Was it an audience with the emperor at the Winter Palace? Whatever the case, the meeting was called off at the last minute. He decided to go to Fanny's place and pay her a surprise visit.

It was still early afternoon, but in winter night was already falling when Nicholas arrived in front of the apartment building. He rang, a manservant opened the door, and he saw the amazement in the face of the maid Joséphine.

He opened the door of Fanny's boudoir and . . . found them. The two of them were entwined on the sofa, Fanny in a moiré negligee under which she was plainly wearing nothing, he bare-chested.

"He" was Savine. There was no fear in his expression, just surprise and even a sort of amusement. He saluted Nicholas army-style while presenting himself as he did every day at the barracks. "Artilleryman Nicholas Ierassimovich Savine, at your highness's orders." Despite his partial undress, he put so much grace and courtesy in his salute that it didn't appear ridiculous. Fanny didn't move and was content to lower her eyes.

Rage made Nicholas turn red. But it still took him a few seconds before reacting further. Then he clenched his fists and his breath became short. He had murder in his eyes, he wanted to break something, he wanted to kill! He took a slight step toward the young man. Fanny stepped in and, in a languid voice, pleaded, "Stop, your highness, and listen to me before you do something silly."

Quite surprised by his mistress's composure and audacity, Nicholas looked at her and paused. Still languishing on the sofa and in a gentle voice, she explained. Nicholas had cheated on her many times, had he not, and probably was going on doing so, for that was his temperament. She was saddened by it, indeed angry, she had even suffered as a result, but good Lord! how pointless it was . . . So she

had ended up taking the situation philosophically, and since the opportunity presented itself, why not give herself some nonconjugal
pleasure as the grand duke had done so often? Let his highness reassure himself, she had had no other lover, Savine was the first! He
had declared his love for her with so much conviction that she couldn't
refuse. To allow this young man a few liberties didn't mean she had
fallen in love with him. She loved and would go on loving only one
man, you, your highness. So, instead of making a scene and slamming the door as you were clearly tempted to do, you should stay.
Three people can do a lot of nice things! Two men and one woman is
the ideal combination. How can your highness not know that! Then
let him allow his little Fanny teach him, to guide him . . .

Nicholas's mouth was stretched in an odd smile.

"So come, your highness, don't be afraid. Sit down next to me,
to my right of course, are you not the master of this place, of my
life, of myself? And you, Savine, sit here on my left. . . .

Fanny took Nicholas's large, muscular hand and slipped it into
her half-open negligee and placed it on one of her breasts. At this
contact, the grand duke shivered, his whole body electrified. Then
Fanny took Savine's hand and placed it on her other breast. . . .

When they separated at suppertime, they were all three aglow
from the experience, and without saying so promised to repeat it at
the first opportunity.

Thanks to the good offices of Fanny, the opportunity was not long in
presenting itself. Once again the experience, imagination, and sensuality of these three beautiful and perverse creatures set off erotic
fireworks. Now they could no longer do without their triangular
frolicking.

Nicholas was going through a period of uncertainty, confusion,
and torment, as his hastily scribbled notes testify:

I don't know what's happening to me. My head's on fire. My thoughts are all confusion. I want something, but I don't even know what it is. My blood boils so and I feel so much strength in me. . . . I am probably like one of those officers in Napoleon's army, I could be on a horse galloping sixty miles a day and remember, down to the tiniest detail, everything I saw on the way. Unfortunately, this is only my mental game.

I feel very excited and while I am in this state I can accomplish a great deal, but suddenly it's over, all my strength leaves me and my brain no longer works. My thoughts follow each other in disorder. For example, I am seated at a table preparing my next expedition to Amu Darya. I ought to leave all else aside. But no . . . I have to think about the vase from China, of the hunt, of the deer, of the work at Pavlovsk, of the different plans for the winter gardens, of antiques for the bedrooms.

At eight o'clock I am still in bed. It's the time I get up and take a cold shower, then straight to the Marble Palace to say hello to Papa. Next, I come back home. Glazunov is already there with the accounts, Toniolati with the antiques in the billiards room, the tailor with the new suits in the dressing room, Saviolov with some household business in my bedroom, while the officers and my comrades from the Khiva expedition are waiting for me in the living room. Also waiting for me is Vorpovsky, but in the Gobelins room. Architects are waiting for me with their plans in the gardens. At two in the afternoon I go out on horseback. At four o'clock I am in the little apartment on the square of the Michael Palace. At six o'clock, dinner with the family. At seven o'clock I don't recall what happened. . . .

For her part, Fanny—who, curiously, was not mentioned in these pages—each day succumbed a bit more to the charm of Savine, almost without realizing it, and right under Nicholas's eyes. Still, the latter was not jealous, for his mistress's weakness for the young soldier did not cast doubt on the ties between them. The two of them let themselves be simultaneously seduced by the inventive and sensual cherub.

Between Savine and Nicholas there was quickly established a kind of competition, a subtle game to win the favors of their mistress. It was about which of the two men would offer her the most attention, the most pleasure, the most presents. First it was Savine, who put in her hands an eighteenth-century pocket watch. The gold clasp hid an erotic scene in which three tiny automata, two men and a woman, played complicated games. The allusion made them smile.

"But how did you do it, you who doesn't have a penny?" asked Fanny.

"Once again I hoodwinked my friend Rudolf Erholz!" He related his discussion with the old moneylender, imitating his heavy accent and making Fanny laugh until tears came to her eyes.

For his turn, Nicholas offered his mistress a jewel box. It contained a brooch in the form of a clover—each of its four leaves was composed of an enormous pearl of a different color, white, pink, gray, and golden, surrounded by diamonds.

Although the value of Nicholas's present was ten times that of Savine's, Fanny pouted. All the grand duke had to do was go into the first jeweler to come along, choose what was most expensive, and have the bill sent to the palace! The soldier had had to cross swords with the moneylender who had control over him in order to offer his lady a present worthy of her. Stung, Nicholas promised to do much better than Savine.

Although his affair with the beautiful Katia was known throughout the empire, the emperor Alexander II kept up appearances, even if he did so more and more offhandedly. His relatives went on getting together for family dinners in the apartment of the empress, Maria Alexandrovna, the deserted wife. Not all the family was invited, for that would have meant using the palace's large dining room, but simply the favorites, and among them always the "Constantines," as the emperor's beloved brother and his family were called.

They gathered in the empress's red-and-gold boudoir, chatted, went to the sitting room next door, entered and left without ceremony, dined in the small dining room overlooking an inner courtyard. They came back to the boudoir to drink a glass of liqueur, but they didn't stay late, as the empress's deteriorating health prohibited it. Indeed, her consumption was rapidly worsening. And then the emperor and his brother Constantine were impatient to rejoin their second families, the one his Katia, the other his Kuznetzova.

At the end of one of these dinners, the empress, after taking leave of her family, went to her writing table and noticed the disappearance of a seal cut in a single topaz that she distinctly recalled having seen in its place before dinner. Disconcerted, she called her husband, who had not yet gone off. Alexander II's surprise was as great as hers, but being in a hurry, he didn't pay much attention to the incident.

However, the next day, the disappearance came back to him and he told his brother Constantine. The two of them got lost in conjectures, for the object could have been spirited away only by one of the family members who had been at the dinner.

"It was George Leuchtenberg," asserted Grand Duke Constantine finally.

The duke of Leuchtenberg was the cousin who had accompanied Nicholas on the Khiva expedition and obtained the Cross of St. George, an exasperating injustice for Nicholas but just as much for his father, who didn't forgive Leuchtenberg and moreover distrusted him.

"It's George Leuchtenberg," he repeated to his wife as he told her about the mystery of the disappearance of the seal.

"It's Nicholas!" exclaimed the grand duchess Alexandra.

Constantine exploded. How dare she make such an accusation? Had she gone crazy? Of course he's a little odd, he's a rebellious, undisciplined child, but because of that, to swipe an object on the empress's desk! Besides, his mother spoiled him too much. And with this accusation, Constantine left the room, furious.

During this time, Nicholas was putting in Fanny's hands the seal of topaz with the empress's coat of arms. The lady was delighted, his rival admiring. A contented Nicholas recounted his heroic deed.

Before dinner he had spotted the object he was counting on taking. The whole difficulty was to approach the empress's worktable without being noticed. He bent over the table as if to admire one of the many photographs cluttering the surface, seized the seal, and slipped it into his pocket. His heart was beating as if it were ready to burst. Afterward he had managed to remain completely natural while chatting calmly with the dinner guests.

Nicholas told the story with gusto and wit; his listeners were filled with wonder. After all, he concluded, stealing an object from one of the best-guarded places in the world, the boudoir of the empress of Russia, is more of an achievement than hoodwinking a moneylender who is used to letting himself be swindled!

It was Savine's turn to vaunt his abilities. He hurried to Erholz and managed to get out of him a sum even larger than the last time, one that immediately vanished with the purchase of a new jewel for Fanny.

In the oriental smoking room of the Marble Palace among the valuable rarities was an eighteenth-century porcelain cup and saucer of Chinese design of the highest quality, marked A. R.— Augustus Rex, that is, ordered for the elector Augustus the Strong. One fine day the grand duke Constantine noticed their disappearance. People were questioned right and left without too much pressure. One member of the grand duke's court, Baron Taube, said he had seen the cup in Nicholas's hands just after one of the palace luncheons at which the latter was regularly present.

A few days later a servant named Zerdinien came to the grand duke Constantine and, looking embarrassed, told him what follows. The previous evening he had been standing in a small room adjacent to the family's sitting room when the grand duke, the grand duchess, and their children had gone into the dining room next door. He, Zerdinien, had seen Nicholas remain behind, bend over his father's desk, take a gold pencil with rubies at the tip, and put it in his pocket. Constantine knitted his brow. He went to his desk and examined the small silver tray. The precious pencil was gone.

"Might as well be hung for a sheep as a lamb, " said Nicholas, handing over the Chinese cup and saucer and the gold pencil to Fanny.

If someone had told him to his face that he was a thief, he would have protested. He felt he was being perfectly honest and, although he thought himself everyone's equal, his origins put him above the laws of the common run of people. A grand duke could permit himself a few modest deviations from morality. But above all it was Fanny's enthusiasm when he set on her knees these doubly precious objects—precious first through their intrinsic value and precious again because they had been "pinched" from his family—that gave him the self-confidence that everyone had tried to take away from him, his mother most of all. As he himself summarized it: "I did my duty, I fought like a soldier, and was scorned. I steal, I'm admired."

The competition between Nicholas and Savine grew more intense. Each day they offered their lady increasingly sumptuous gifts, the fruits of swindling in one case, of petty theft in the other, with each of them boasting of his heroic deeds to Fanny's applause.

Nicholas gained the lead when he described his confrontation with his father. The latter had summoned him and man-to-man threw the accusation of petty theft straight in his face. He simply denied the whole thing. "I remained very calm, I was not at all nervous." And Fanny gave him the tender look that one gives to a child who has just passed an exam. For their reward, the young woman offered herself and her new creations that added spice to their erotic games.

And yet the trio's dynamic, by now well established, had a few setbacks. Nicholas began to have trouble putting up with this perverse three-way arrangement; he sometimes even wanted to send Fanny off to his rival:

"Madam, in the name of everything that you still hold sacred, I appeal to you leave the imperial residence, which blushes for your behavior. Go to the house that received you so well this morning. . . . Only try to give less occasion for embarrassment there, or greater occasion for honor, as you wish, than you have given me. I hope that you will not refuse me my final prayer. The blood that has rushed to my head alone prevents me from coming to beg you personally and to kiss your hand. Your servant."

10

In the midst of these events began the marriage festivities of the grand duchess Maria. Russia had not married an emperor's daughter for decades, so St. Petersburg was buzzing with excitement.

Nicholas of course didn't have a minute to spare. He was asked to welcome the foreign princes at the train station, to work as a guide for the august guests, to attend banquets, performances at the opera, and other evening events. He got a ticket for Fanny so she could witness the ceremony.

That morning the winter turned milder; the sun no longer sparkled on the ice, and the weather was gray and humid. Fanny's carriage was part of a long procession headed for the Winter Palace. There were so many carriages that they moved at a walking pace.

The soldiers strung together on either side opened a way in the middle of the very dense crowd.

Finally, Fanny reached the courtyard of the palace. She showed her ticket, and a valet took her to an aide-de-camp, who gave her instructions. She climbed the staircase of honor, called "the Jordan stairway," with its columns of green marble and gilded stucco. She crossed several already packed sitting rooms and reached a colossal hall. Right and left were raised galleries erected for spectators like her, many bourgeois people and notables, but no merchants or storekeepers that she knew of—the court didn't admit them. The guests had made an effort at grooming and dress. Fanny noticed gleaming jewelry, ribbons of various colors, and fans that seemed to her like magic butterflies. She also recognized several actors and particularly actresses, who belonged less to the theater than to their own category, the class of high chivalry.

Below, in the actual hall, the members of the court took their seats. The men in uniforms of all colors—blue, white, black, red, adorned with gold and silver—glittered with their large sashes and decorations. The women were wearing the traditional fashion, an embroidered low-cut dress, a long velvet train (whose color depended on the woman's position), a Russian diadem known as *kokochnik*, and a long lace veil. All the women were streaming with pearls, diamonds, and other gems. But all this elegance, Fanny noted, was accompanied by yellow features, wrinkled faces, powdered noses, painted cheeks. From time to time a fresh and rosy beauty raised the level a little.

The hall was so noisy it resembled an aviary gone mad. People were chatting, gossiping, observing, laughing a bit too loudly, turning left and right, and leaning over. Suddenly the great double door opened and there appeared the minister of the imperial court who, with his long white staff, struck the marble floor three times. Silence immediately fell. The ladies of the court formed two lines of velvet and jewels. Behind them, a wall of uniforms. Everyone stood at attention. The emperor and empress appeared, and immediately the ladies went into a deep curtsy while the men bowed their heads.

The emperor looked drawn. He appeared to have been crying. In town it was said that he was as sorry as could be to part with his only daughter, his favorite among his children by far. The gaunt empress was frighteningly pale. She was wearing a gown of cream-colored satin edged with sable and a very high diadem of diamonds in the middle of which sparkled a large pink diamond. Other diamonds adorned her ears, neck, arms, her bodice, and even her train, so much that Fanny wondered how she could stand their weight. At the cost of tremendous effort, the empress graciously nodded right and left, but the tension in her features revealed her suffering.

Behind the imperial couple came the heirs to the thrones of Russia, England, Denmark, and Prussia with their wives. The most beautiful of course was the princess of Wales, the ugliest in Fanny's eyes the princess of Prussia, the daughter of Queen Victoria, a short fat woman who appeared the foil of her neighbors. Beside her, the sister of the princess of Wales, the grand duchess heiress of Russia looked both fresh and majestic. Despite her short stature, people saw only her. She was at ease wearing a gown and jewels of unimaginable magnificence.

Finally, the bride and groom came up the aisle. He, Alfred, the duke of Edinburgh and Queen Victoria's second son, stuffed into the uniform of a Russian admiral, looked rather surly. His blue eyes had a disagreeable expression and he was not smiling. The grand duchess Maria had donned the outfit of all the brides of the imperial family, a gown of silver broadcloth, a train of crimson velvet edged with ermine so long and heavy that four chamberlains were barely enough to carry it. At her neck were three rows of huge diamonds; her diamond earrings were so heavy that they stretched her earlobes. On her head a ravishing, light crown of diamonds that looked like a ball of fire. Maria was young and quite pretty. Fanny noticed, however, that the lower part of her face was a bit thick and that she looked grumpy. It was rumored that she was not at all pleased to be leaving her family and Russia.

There followed all the members of the imperial family. Fanny recognized Nicholas's father by his short stature as he passed, and his mother, of impressive bearing, wearing more emeralds and sapphires than all the other grand duchesses combined.

But Fanny had eyes only for Nicholas. His stature outclassed all the other grand dukes, of whom he was certainly the handsomest. He had an arrogant look and a mocking smile, for he basically detested these sorts of ceremonies. He combined the noblest attitude with the agility of an athlete. His uniform, crossed with the pale blue sash of the Order of St. Andrew, suited him beautifully.

Back home, exhausted, Fanny found a message from Nicholas. He was too tired to come to see her now before the marriage ball, but he would send her one of his servants with a pass for her to attend it.

Fanny wouldn't have missed the show for anything in the world! So, at the specified time, she followed her guide through a service door into the Winter Palace. They went up a rather narrow staircase and passed the larder. Through the half-open door Fanny saw an army of gold-embroidered, liveried footmen bustling about the round tables prepared for the supper. The plates were of Sèvres china, the crystal ware gold-engraved, and every one of the huge chandeliers was a masterpiece of silversmithing. Fanny entered St. Nicholas Hall, one of the largest in the palace.

Immediately the tables were brought in and the guests seated themselves in the prescribed order. Above them, on a platform, the imperial family had taken their places around a semicircular table. Facing the emperor and empress sat the bishop of St. Petersburg, who said the Orthodox grace.

Every gastronomical delicacy had been served on the occasion of this marriage, from mountains of caviar to fresh fruit, cherries, and strawberries delivered by a special train from the Riviera. Fanny was not among the privileged guests, but among the observers of the supper. Nevertheless, a valet brought her a plate with ice cream, cakes, and orange segments as well as a fistful of candy and a glass of wine, all owing to Nicholas's thoughtfulness.

Toasts were drunk, no less than five of them, a military band played the national anthems, and finally the greatest diva of the time, Adelina Patti, as it happened seated not far from Fanny, rose and sang several arias. Then an army of footmen removed the tables in no time and the ball proper could begin.

The emperor began it on the arm of his daughter the bride, then the empress took the arm of the groom to the accompaniment of a solemn and ancient polonaise. This was followed by slightly more modern dances—polkas, waltzes, and quadrilles. From afar, Fanny could scarcely catch sight of Nicholas lost in the crowd, for there were more than a thousand guests. At least she would be able to say that she had attended a ball at the court of Russia, the dream of all American and even European women.

When the jewels taken out for her niece's marriage were being put back in their case, the grand duchess Alexandra discovered that her emerald earrings were missing. For her, the guilty party could only be Nicholas. So strong was her conviction that she declared to her entourage that she would speak to him the first chance she had. However, Nicholas had fallen ill; he was shut up in his palace, snug in bed, suffering from an intestinal disorder. He was too weak for visitors, even his mother. . . .

Not so weak, nevertheless, that he couldn't bear the presence of Fanny and the soldier Savine. He nonchalantly tossed on the counterpane the pair of earrings, which his mistress seized delightedly. Two round emeralds surrounded by diamonds supported two

other uncut emeralds, pear-shaped and a marvelous green, also surrounded by diamonds. Fanny clapped her hands like a child and
tried the jewels on her ears. Alas, she could wear them only in her
lover's presence, for they would be instantly recognized in public.

Ever the provocateur, Savine interrupted the scene. "It's not
by pawning these trinkets that we would get the million that your
imperial highness promised the cause of the revolution!"

"I could sell my gold medals," replied Nicholas abstractedly,
"the very ones that my dear Fanny Lear prevented me from selling
at a cut-rate price."

He sent Savine and Fanny to look for them in his little room
of interesting and unusual things, where they were laid out on a
piece of furniture. They came back empty-handed; the medals had
vanished.

"Then I must have pawned them, but I don't remember doing
that."

He promised to look for them the first chance he got.

"What are they worth?" asked Savine. "At the most three
hundred thousand rubles? That's far from a million!"

"And where do you want me to find that sum?" retorted Nicholas. "My father has millions in the stock market, state bonds, de-
bentures, but that fortune is deposited in the bank. My mother has
other millions in jewels but she would never give them to me. It's
possible she won't make a big scene over a 'lost' pair of emeralds,
but I can't filch her set of large diamonds, for heaven's sake!"

Fanny took on her most mischievous look. "What would you
give me, Nicky, if I found the necessary guarantees to get a loan of a
million from old Erholz?" And the beautiful American explained herself. During certain religious holidays, the private chapel at the
Marble Palace was open to the public, who could come and worship
in it. Hence the moneylender had more than once gone there to snoop.
Not only was he keen about everything concerning the imperial fam-

ily, but he was an experienced connoisseur. In addition, like so many converted Jews, he was in love with religious objects. So in the recesses of the chapel he had noticed many icons of very great antiquity, some of them still bearing their covering of precious metal blackened by the centuries, set with large, tarnished cabochons, uncut jewels of little intrinsic value but artistically priceless.

"Do you mean," remarked Nicholas, "those old things? We don't even know where they came from." For, like members of his family and the aristocracy in general, Nicholas preferred recently made icons painted with that realism inspired by Italy, with precious overlays engraved by the fashionable gold- and silversmiths, Fabergé and others, sparkling with newly cut stones. Though he appeared a fine connoisseur in every branch of art and a fierce collector, this freethinker was still indifferent to the old icons.

"Erholz has stopped dead in his tracks before those old things, as you call them," repeated Fanny. "He thinks only of them. . . ."

"So, he is ready to let go an enormous sum in order to have them," continued Savine.

"Nothing easier," Nicholas replied. "No one pays any attention to them. No one'll notice their disappearance."

Snatching those "old things" proved very easy. Barely restored to health, Nicholas had only to go to dinner at the Marble Palace and wait until the night was sufficiently advanced for him to go down to the chapel, take down the icons, and go back up with them to his apartment. Actually, there were so many pious images of all sizes, all kinds, all values, hung in no particular order just about everywhere in this sanctuary, that the purloining of some twenty or thirty from among them, especially those less in the place of honor, the less gilded, couldn't be noticed.

Conveying them out of the palace was distinctly more difficult. Nicholas himself had to pack the icons in crates, which, with Saviolov, he took down and put in his carriage. Next they were unloaded and taken up to the apartment in Michael Palace Square. As the crates were being stacked up in Fanny's living room, her feminine curiosity got the better of her. She wanted to gaze at the treasures to which she was offering hospitality. The crates were opened, the icons taken out, and Fanny went into raptures as much over their beauty, for she had excellent artistic taste, as over their value, for she had an equally developed taste for money.

A few days later Savine made Fanny and Nicholas laugh telling about the delivery of the icons to the moneylender. He arrived in the middle of the night at a low house with narrow windows fitted with thick bars, equipped with a single door lined with iron, as in a prison. Indeed, he had the impression of being in a prison. He was scrutinized at length by an enormous doorman and several manservants who seemed to swagger. Erholz was waiting for him in his study amidst a weird shambles. The old man was letting a long and respectable white beard grow, but his nose was the purplish red of an alcoholic. Most of the time he kept his small, glassy, bluish eyes lowered. He wore an old coat of very dirty velvet and wool slippers "embroidered by Rivka," his wife Rebecca.

"So what is there in these crates?" he had asked.

"I don't know, Herr Erholz, it was his imperial highness who entrusted me with them."

Savine was doing a perfect imitation of the moneylender's expressions and accent. He surpassed himself copying the old man's delight and greed when he saw the icons he had so long coveted.

"They're worth ten times this amount, Herr Erholz, but we are asking only a million, and just for three months."

The moneylender screeched, "A million! That's an outrageous sum! I've never had so much money on me, and it will take quite some time to get this million together."

Iimmediately the bargaining began, lasting a good part of the night. The 5 percent interest promised by Erholz was raised to

6 percent owing to the speed required. . . . It would also mean deducting the twenty thousand rubles he owed him. Savine ended up getting a bit more than nine hundred thousand rubles and, that amount in his pocket, he hastened to give it to Sophia. The promised million had finally fallen into the coffers of the revolution!

During Holy Week, the daily services — at least five hours at a stretch — were held for the family of the grand duke Constantine and those close to him in the chapel of the Marble Palace. According to the odd custom of the Russian imperial palaces, it was on the highest floor. Rather than a sanctuary, it resembled a sitting room with its bright gildings, its glittering gold iconostasis, and its flood of light.

In the Russian Orthodox tradition, Holy Thursday was reserved for the Holy Communion. Each person approached the iconostasis to receive from the archbishop the piece of blessed bread and to drink from the gold and diamond chalice. Although the sanctity of the place and the moment was supposed to have absorbed them entirely, several elderly ladies-in-waiting and ancient aides-de-camp noticed that several of the icons were missing. After the service, those who had attended were in the family sitting room around a Lenten buffet, neither meat nor fish, but caviar by the ladle. With pomposity and the zeal so characteristic of their age and standing, the elderly courtiers reported the disappearance of the holy images. While continuing to eat and drink, they commented, questioned each other, and questioned the servants, who were all but members of the family.

"Might it have been his imperial highness Nicholas Konstantinovich who borrowed those objects?" speculated the footman Sarytchev. "He loves antiques so much, he may have wanted to study them close up or have them copied the way he usually does."

The grand duchess Alexandra took offense at this. How dare a mere servant suspect her son!

Those "old things" didn't interest anyone, as Nicholas had claimed, but their disappearance did interest his father. It was no longer a matter of a little knickknack in places as private and inaccessible as the empress's boudoir or his own office, but of several objects taken away from a holy place. Wanting to find out the truth, the grand duke Constantine summoned Trepov, chief of the St. Petersburg police. He informed him of the theft and put him in charge of the investigation, for it was an ordinary criminal matter, no doubt the work of a small-time thief. The theft was easy, but accepting responsibility for it was difficult. Nicholas went over and over the problem obsessively. He was getting on less and less well with his parents, with his milieu, and the pressures to separate him from Fanny were becoming ever more intense. He found himself torn between his duty, his military obligations, and his desire to be with her. Finally, not for an instant did he forget the certainty that he would die soon, as the doctor Havrowitz had warned him.

They had just finished their dinner, Fanny, Savine, and he, and were, like every night, in Nicholas's study. The light was soft, here and there lending a sparkle to a crystal object, the gold of a bronze, and the emblazoned binding of a book. The aroma of spirits given off by the open bottles joined with the incense smoldering in the precious incense burners, with Fanny's heady perfume, and with the smell of cigars the two men were smoking. All three were lost in their thoughts that, without their realizing it, were going in the same direction, which Fanny summarized in an unexpected question.

"And now, gentlemen?"

"Now you and I are leaving for Paris," Nicholas snapped.

Fanny was stunned. "And your expedition to Central Asia. Are you abandoning it?"

"You won't see me committing myself to service for the tsar when I've just given a million rubles to overthrow him."

"Are you sacrificing your future this way?" Fanny persisted.

"What future? They might let me take part in some expeditions in unexplored deserts, but nothing more than that. They'll never allow me to do what I want, starting with marrying you. And I want to marry you, Fanny Lear."

"Wouldn't it be better to wait a bit longer, since the emperor promised to give you his consent after the marriage of your cousin?"

"Just a deception, my poor Fanny. . . . So it's decided, in a week the three of us will leave for Paris. There we'll get married without asking for anyone's permission, as I didn't manage to do in Vienna. . . . This time we'll succeed. France is a republic and has always protected lovers."

Nicholas didn't see the anguished look that Fanny gave to Savine, who didn't move, didn't open his mouth, and seemed to withdraw into himself.

"How are you going to go abroad this way?" she persisted. "I thought that when grand dukes get organized to move, it takes countless steps."

"I've already taken them. As custom requires, I've already asked the emperor's permission to travel to France or England for two or three months. He was quite willing to grant it. And as usual, I applied to the privileges service for a large sum for my expenses. I've just been given it. So I'm taking enough money to allow us to live comfortably for a while.

"And Savine?" Fanny couldn't help asking this question.

"He'll catch up with us the first chance he gets," Nicholas off-handedly concluded.

Fanny was strangely quiet but he didn't understand why. Savine visibly strained to add: "The future will smile on you."

"If God wishes to lengthen my life . . . If not, my widow Fanny will marry you, the artilleryman, and you will love each other in memory of me."

That evening they abstained from their erotic games; none of the three had any desire.

General Trepov, chief of the St. Petersburg police, had informers all over, particularly among the great and the rich, for he knew that the latter considered their servants pieces of furniture, so they acted and spoke in front of them as if they didn't exist, hiding nothing from them.

It was in this way that Trepov heard spoken of a certain Katya, for she was the second chambermaid at the apartment of Mrs. Hattie Blackford, known as Fanny Lear, American. Katya told her friends, who were also in service of other "big shots," that she had helped her mistress and her friends open some crates and remove large icons from them. To make herself more important, she described, one after another, the richness of the pious images. Now Katya had a boyfriend, a certain Andrei, on file with the police for having subversive political opinions.

It was not hard for Trepov to get Katya to talk, for she was already terrified owing to the summons from the police. A gentle blackmail of her "fiancé," who ran the risk of prison, if not worse, did the rest. She told everything they wanted and named Erholz, whose name Savine had mentioned several times in her presence.

Immediately, Trepov went to the moneylender's home. There too it was easy for him to get the icons handed over. Tightfisted as Erholz was, he knew where his interest lay, and he preferred losing nine hundred thousand rubles to risking an indictment and his ruin.

When the grand duke Constantine returned to the Marble Palace, he found General Trepov waiting for him in his office. He was a man whose face bore a sunken look and a dark, thick, and very long mustache. The grand duke Constantine had always distrusted this too respectful, too mild conservative who always smiled with an aggrieved look.

"We have recovered the icons of the chapel of your imperial highness."

"Where are they?"

"My officers have already put them back in their places."

"Who's the thief?"

"We haven't found the thieves for the good and simple reason that there was no theft. No theft, no thief!"

The grand duke allowed himself some sarcasm. "No thief! Did the icons fly out through the chapel windows? Would it be a miracle?"

"No miracle, imperial highness, but no theft, either."

"Excuse me, General, but I absolutely do not understand. Please be good enough to explain to me how those icons vanished."

"I beg you imperial highness to relieve me of the obligation of answering! Consider me the loyal and sincere servant of his imperial majesty, your brother the emperor. There was no theft, there was simply frivolity."

The grand duke thought he understood and turned pale.

"That means the stunt was pulled off by my son Nicholas!"

"As painful as it is for me to break a father's heart, I'm forced to confirm your suspicions. Yes, it was he."

"I imagine he must have pawned the icons at some money-lender's and given the money to his American lady friend for her mad expenses!"

Trepov saw the moment of his triumph come. He detested Constantine and Nicholas for their liberal ideas. At least the revolutionaries were declared enemies, while these cheap democrats did much more evil without seeming to. "The grand duke did not give the money to Mrs. Fanny Lear. He gave it to those madmen who give themselves the title of the Friends of the People and who are promoting a revolution."

Grasping the attack, the grand duke Constantine again turned icy. "But did you catch these people, General, and did you lock them up in the Peter and Paul Fortress?"

"That's not yet necessary. We know the identity of these visionaries. We keep them under close watch, particularly Sophia

Perovskaïa, who was the liaison to your son. Of course, they're dangerous, for they're capable of anything. But they are also reckless, and don't take any precautions. We prefer to let them remain free in order to know their accomplices, their offshoots, and their plans. We will intervene and neutralize them when that becomes indispensable, that is, when they're about to commit some serious crime."

While Trepov was speaking, the grand duke Constantine was thinking. He saw the trap being set. Since his son was financing the revolutionaries, his son would be seen as guilty. A liberal, come on now! We can expect anything from these irresponsible people! The conservatives would triumph and the plan of reform that, with all his might, he had been urging the emperor to adopt would fall through.

"I imagine, General, that you're straightaway going to make your report to his majesty."

"You're mistaken, imperial highness. I have much more esteem for you than you think. I don't want to besmirch your family's name. I repeat what I said: only frivolity inspired the theft of your icons. So, better to overlook what happened . . . this time. The perpetrator of the theft and the destination of its loot will remain a secret between you and me."

The grand duke Constantine understood that Trepov relinquished destroying him now in order to have a weapon against him that he would use when the time was right. It would be easy at any moment for him to claim before the emperor that he had come across new evidence in connection with the theft of the icons, incriminating Nicholas. Henceforth he was holding the sword of Damocles above the heads of the father and the son. Let the father behave himself, let him not go too far in his liberalism, let him refrain from spurring on his brother into excessive reforms, or else the son will be accused and the father irretrievably compromised.

Meanwhile, the grand duke played for time. He got up from his armchair and ended the interview with curtness and finality: "Thank you for your zeal. The most important thing is that the icons were recovered."

Constantine said nothing to his wife: she repeated everything. Nor to his son; he didn't feel up to it. The affair was thus hushed up . . . for the time being.

11

Nothing very striking happened on April 7, 1874. A nocturnal calm prevailed over St. Petersburg, disturbed only by late-night revelers. The palace of the grand duke Nicholas Konstantinovich seemed sound asleep. Nevertheless, the three accomplices, gathered in the room that Nicholas called "Fanny's small room," were very much awake.

Nicholas had had to attend a family dinner at the Winter Palace. To get revenge for the chore, he took advantage of the meal to commit a new theft. He stole another seal from the *tsarina*'s desk, her favorite, cut out of a single gigantic amethyst.

This prank, however, did not cheer them up like the earlier ones. They were drinking heavily, much more than usual. They were sad, for in a few days Nicholas and Fanny were heading west and would be leaving Russia for a long time, possibly for good. And secondarily, the three of them were to break up, at the very least temporarily.

With the hour growing late and the drinks of cognac numerous, Nicholas's mood was growing gloomy. All this was the fault of his family, the regime, the environment he'd come to hate. It was his parents who were forcing him into exile, who were preventing him from acting, from accomplishing anything worthy of him.

To counter her lover's glumness, Fanny let it be understood that the time had come for them to indulge in their usual games. . . .

"Straight to the Marble Palace!" Nicholas suddenly shouted.

He wanted to have the orgy at his parents' place, precisely to wreak his vengeance on them in order to soil the family residence with their frolicking and there to leave the scent of their immorality.

The coast was clear; his parents, right after the family dinner at the Winter Palace, had gone by special train directly to Pavlovsk. Like schoolchildren, they were suddenly in a hurry to perform this enormous stunt. They put on their coats, left Nicholas's residence without being seen, stopped a horse-drawn carriage, and had themselves driven not far from the Marble Palace. They continued on foot along the embankment; the sentinels guarding the main door were on the other side of the building. With his key Nicholas opened the little door, they climbed the narrow stairway, and arrived in Nicholas's third-floor apartment.

They resumed drinking, for bottles were all over the grand duke's residence.

It was three o'clock in the morning. Total silence reigned in the vast palace and there was no risk of coming upon a servant on some late errand. They started walking, trying to make as little noise as possible, but they were drunk, banged into the furniture, made the doors creak. They stifled their giggles . . . no one was there to hear them. They reached the grand duchess Alexandra's antechamber.

It was Nicholas who opened the door of his mother's bedroom. The curtains had not been drawn and the night's pale luminosity barely lit the room. The grand duchess's particular perfume, a mixture of roses and tuberoses, that floated in the room gave her son the impression that she was asleep in her bed, the bed on which they flung themselves to give way to all the caprices of their eroticism, more unrestrained than ever. When their bodies were satiated, they remained naked on the lacy counterpane, their eyes wide open. Above them were lined up Alexandra's most precious icons, images of Christ, the virgin, and saints, surfaces set with precious stones that shone faintly in the flickering light of the gold and silver nightlights.

They could not take their eyes off of these multicolored and evanescent lights. Having violated his mother's bedroom, having made love on her bed, Nicholas reveled in the sacrilege. He got up with difficulty as his head was spinning. Standing, still naked, wobbly, his finger pointed to the icon hanging in the center of the wall, just above the bed, a large Virgin covered with gold, studded with diamonds. "This one's my mother's favorite. It's the one my grandfather Nicholas I gave her on her wedding day."

With this, he seemed to spin around and then collapsed on the rug, passed out.

When he came back to, it was already late in the morning. He found himself in his own bed, in the bedroom of his palace. Half stretched out beside him, Fanny, dressed to go out, gazed at him with love. He remembered nothing.

She refreshed his memory. Quite a job to bring him back here! Neither she nor Savine knew how to leave the Marble Palace, especially in the darkness. After making several mistakes, they had managed after all to find the narrow stairway again that they had used before. They got Nicholas standing and dragged him along. At each step he threatened to crash down. They had to almost carry him the length of the embankment until they found a carriage. They didn't know how to get inside Nicholas's palace and didn't want to wake the personnel there by ringing. They had leaned him against the wall and were wondering what to do when the faithful Saviolov appeared in a window. He never went to sleep before his master. With signs, Fanny and Savine asked him to come down and help them. It was Saviolov who, despite his age, had carried his master up to his room. That was two days ago.

It was exactly eleven o'clock on the morning of April 10. An offering of thanks, on the occasion of the birthday of grand duke Vladimir, the emperor's second son, had just ended in the chapel of the Winter Palace. The whole imperial family was gathered. The grand duke Constantine, his wife, and their children had specially come back from Pavlovsk that very morning and traveled directly from the station to the Winter Palace.

Although he had received the usual notification signed by the minister of the imperial court, Nicholas had completely forgotten this birthday, as he had forgotten that his parents must return to the city to attend the ceremony. It was to be followed by an English-style breakfast before the party broke up.

On her arrival in the Marble Palace, the grand duchess Alexandra went up to her apartments followed by her lady-in-waiting, the countess von Keller. She went into her bedroom intending to take off her ceremonial clothes and put on a lighter dress. Immediately she noticed something strange. Above her bed, the halo in precious stones of one of her icons had been removed and placed over the star in diamonds of another icon, the most precious one of all as it was a keepsake given her by her father-in-law, Nicholas I. She hoisted herself up to remove the unseemly placed halo and discovered that the precious stones set on the star had been torn off.

She was as astonished as she was horrified by this sacrilege. Her screech was so frightening that her lady-in-waiting was startled and trembled with terror. The grand duchess thought first of calming this faithful friend. "I had to scream to free myself, to remove all the horror of my discovery, for it is Nicholas, it's my Nicky who committed this crime!"

Then the grand duchess had a burst of motherly love. No one must know what had happened. She will leave the halo over the star to conceal the theft. With all her heart, the countess von Keller encouraged her in this decision.

But they had forgotten about the chambermaids. They had followed the grand duchess to help her change and they saw everything; panic-stricken, they feared they would be blamed for the theft. The grand duchess and the lady-in-waiting tried to reassure them, but without success.

Nicholas was quite surprised to be summoned by his father. He didn't know that he had come back to the city. My God! Cousin Vladimir's birthday! It had completely slipped his mind, and his hangover had not helped him recall it.

The grand duke Constantine's office did not have that magnificent view of the Neva that graced so many rooms in the Marble Palace. He had chosen a large, rather dark room that overlooked a gloomy street, perhaps because it was situated in the part of the palace farthest from his wife's apartments. To his surprise, Nicholas found both his mother and father there.

As always when he entered the room, his gaze was attracted by the splendid portrait of the young grand duchess. Winterhalter had painted it when she had just turned twenty, a radiant beauty with long brown curls and a provocative décolleté, decked out in blue silk, lace, and pearls. Since then she had changed a great deal. She was still beautiful, but her nose had become much more aquiline and the charming look had been replaced by a regal bearing. She was intimidating; she knew it and took advantage of it.

Nicholas perceived a certain embarrassment behind the cordiality with which his father greeted him.

"Mama came to tell me that the diamonds on the icon given her by Nicholas I have been stolen."

Nicholas was sincerely stunned, and the grand duke Constantine continued with what his brother had confided in him. "At the palace this morning, the emperor told me that another one of the empress's seals has disappeared from her table, you know, the one with the big amethyst. It's the second time in a few months that an incident like this has happened, and both times after a family dinner."

Nicholas managed to display the greatest surprise. "But the diamonds in Mama's icon, when did they disappear? When did Mama notice it?"

The father provided the little information he had. He and Nicholas speculated about it until the son exclaimed, "It's like what happened at my place. My collection of gold coins disappeared!"

"You must tell the police, Nicky, right now."

Nicholas promised to do so as soon as he got home.

He had just left the room when the grand duchess emerged from her silence. "It's he, for the diamond star, I'm certain!"

"But no, Sannie, his surprise was absolutely not feigned. Our son is not a thief, I've been repeating that from the start!"

Both of them stuck to their positions. The grand duke Constantine was infuriated at his wife's insistence. All the more so as his conviction of Nicholas's innocence, which had already been shaken by the disappearance of objects belonging to the empress and even to himself, had been crushed by the revelation of General Trepov.

If his son were a thief and especially if that became publicly known, then the fragile dam would not hold and the flood would upset everything, the guilty one, his family, and all the efforts to liberalize Russia. No one must know, above all not the emperor! So Constantine was to conduct his own investigation. And if Nicholas really proved guilty, the father would decide on a punishment worthy of the crime. While waiting, not a word.

"In any case, Sannie, I ask you to keep it an absolute secret."

"On one condition, Kostia."

The grand duke raised his head, screwed up his eyes, and stared at her behind the lenses of his pince-nez.

The grand duchess shot her magnificent blue eyes at her husband. "On the condition that you swear to give up the other one forever!"

"The other one," Constantine understood, was his unofficial wife Kuznetsova. His wife's blackmail tore him apart. She had spoiled Nicholas for so long; now he at this point was trying to protect him and spare him shame. And he could do so only by parting forever from the woman he loved and the children she had given him.

The short man seated in the huge armchair before the table overflowing with papers, and the woman—standing, imposing, beautiful, and humiliated for so long—looked each other up and down. In the end the grand duke murmured, "I don't have the strength to give her up."

Without saying a word, his wife turned around and left the room.

The grand duchess Alexandra had to leave that very evening for Germany. In the late afternoon she had a visit from her brother-in-law the emperor, who'd come to wish her a bon voyage. Unable to utter a word, she took him by the hand, led him to her bedroom, and showed him the icon whose gold facing had been deformed and the black holes marking where the diamonds had been snatched away. Alexander II was indignant and promised to summon General Trepov as soon as he got back to the palace and put him in charge of the investigation of this unspeakable theft.

The grand duchess received other members of the family with whom she proved less discreet, particularly with her favorite niece, the grand duchess heiress Maria Feodorovna — Mini to the family. The wife of Sasha the Bear, whom no one really liked, this Danish-born woman — vivacious, charming, spontaneous, and affection-ate — had won over all the in-laws. With her, Aunt Sannie could open her heart. "I suppose, my poor Mini, that everyone in the family is going to suspect Nicholas!"

Mini didn't reply, but the tears formed in her eyes, and Alexandra took her silence for agreement.

Then Alexandra could leave for Germany in peace. She had begun to recount the theft of which she had been the victim, under the seal of secrecy, but to anyone who wanted to hear it. She had used Nicholas's bad reputation to focus the family's suspicions on him. She had spread the story so that the grand duke Constantine would not be able to cover it up. In condemning her son, she was taking revenge on her husband.

Back home, Nicholas told Fanny about the theft of the dia-monds on his mother's favorite icon. She was startled, she looked panic-stricken, she was short of breath, like someone drowning, and then she fell into a kind of listlessness. He didn't insist and yet he was dying to ask if she and Savine were responsible. It had occurred to him.

All the same, Nicholas was feeling the need to question Savine and sent someone to look for him. The artilleryman was not at home, and his servant announced that he didn't know where he was. A message was left for Savine to rush as soon as possible to the grand duke's palace, but still no sign of him. Fanny sent him several notes as well, begging him to meet up with her. The notes went unanswered.

Nicholas and Fanny spent the next few days in a strange state. As if their minds had been anesthetized, they were unable to act. They led a life that was more or less normal, but they made no plans, decided nothing. He withdrew into himself and she seemed like a robot.

When Nicholas returned to the Marble Palace, his father asked him if he had told the police about the theft of his gold medals. Nicholas had forgotten to do so, but once back home he hastened to send Vorpovsky to the neighborhood police station to report the disappearance of his treasure. He had added an inventory and exact descriptions of the medals. Several times later, his father asked him if he had recovered them. Nicholas could only answer in the negative.

Alexander II assigned the investigation of the theft of the diamonds to Trepov. The St. Petersburg police chief deserved the emperor's confidence. He knew that in an affair as delicate as a theft committed in an imperial residence, action had to be taken with the greatest possible discretion. He had already demonstrated this in how he handled the theft of the icons.

No question of sending policemen to overrun the Marble Palace and interrogate the people living there. The repercussions of such a move would be disastrous.

So his investigation began at the other end of the maze. His policemen were assigned to interrogate all of the capital's money-lenders. Two days were enough to achieve their goal. One of the pawnbrokers readily recounted that an officer had come with unset diamonds, small but of marvelous quality. What day did the officer come? On the evening of April 8, that is, five days earlier. But the moneylender had been closing the store and sent him away, especially as he immediately suspected that the provenance of the stones had to be shady.

Nevertheless, the officer with the diamonds had come again the next day as the store opened. As a result, the moneylender proposed a derisory sum for the precious stones, certain that the other man would reject it. To his surprise, the man was content with it, pocketed the rubles, and gave him the stones. The moneylender took out of his safe the sheepskin bag that held them and showed them to the policeman who, in possession of an inventory and a description, immediately recognized them.

The policeman bombarded the moneylender with questions about the officer, but the latter had never seen him previously and had no way to identify him. Another soldier happened to be there and joined in the interview. He was a regular whom the moneylender knew well. He had been there that day when the diamonds had been brought in. He couldn't put a name to the suspect officer, but on the other hand he was certain he had seen him before. Where? The policeman pressed him. The soldier redoubled his efforts to delve into his memory. "I remember now. I met the man you're looking for in the company of the children of his imperial highness the grand duke Constantine Nikolayevich.

The soldier couldn't remember any other detail.

The policeman returned to make his report to General Trepov. Immediately, Trepov sent some more experienced men to interrogate the moneylender and the soldier who had been found in his shop. The moneylender had nothing to add, so the policemen concentrated on the soldier. Did he remember any details that might make it possible to identify the suspect officer? For example, what uniform was he wearing? The soldier remembered it only vaguely as he tried to reenact the scene. The officer had been standing next to the moneylender's counter, waiting his turn. Then he opened a little sheepskin bag: the diamonds rolled out onto the table and the moneylender pursed his lips. At that instant the officer had leaned over to point out a particularly beautiful stone and the soldier had noticed, it is true, one of his epaulets, his eye attracted by two tiny crossed cannons embroidered in gold thread. He gave a most exact description of them.

Two crossed gold cannons? Trepov made inquiries and soon identified the artillery regiment whose officers wore this emblem. Only this regiment didn't belong to any of the many corps commanded by the grand duke Constantine or his son, and no one from their house served in it.

Trepov's perplexity was complete. The man couldn't have been mistaken; it was indeed two crossed gold cannons that he had seen on the suspect's epaulets.

"And yet no one in the grand duke's entourage wore the uniform of that damned regiment," he concluded before his general staff.

"Your excellency is mistaken," intervened one of the oldest sleuths in the house. "One man does serve in this regiment. Captain Victor Vorpovsky."

"What's his job?"

"Aide-de-camp to his imperial highness the grand duke Nicholas Konstantinovich."

The next day, April 14, Nicholas was still in bed when a messenger from his father summoned him to the palace. Fanny was awakened and helped him dress. He left with a completely empty mind.

He found the grand duke Constantine in company with General Trepov.

"Nicky, I had you come because what the general has told me concerns you."

Nicholas shuddered. Trepov went to open the door. Vorpovsky appeared, flanked by two policemen. Nicholas couldn't believe his eyes.

Trepov asked the aide-de-camp if he had indeed pawned some diamonds stolen from an icon of the grand duchess Alexandra as well as some gold medals that had disappeared at her son's place; Vorpovsky vehemently denied it.

"You were, however, recognized by your epaulets."

"Many officers wear ones just like them!"

The interrogation went on without any progress. Trepov ended up shrugging his shoulders.

"You may leave, Captain Vorpovsky, you're a free man."

With Trepov present, the grand duke Constantine questioned Nicholas about his aide-de-camp. Would he act as surety for him? Could Vorpovsky have committed an act of dishonesty? Did he need money? With all his might, Nicholas defended the man he considered his friend. Vorpovsky a thief? It's completely out of the question!

But he in turn was in a hurry to question Vorpovsky. He found him in the palace's huge entrance hall. The aide-de-camp seemed terrified, but at the same time he had a sly expression that Nicholas had never seen before. "Why are they accusing you?" Nicholas asked him. Did he know that moneylender? It didn't take long before Vorpovsky confessed. Yes he knew the moneylender; yes, he had pawned the diamonds.

Nicholas remained perfectly in control of himself. "Sit down and tell me exactly what happened."

They sat on a marble bench; before them came and went ranking servants, hurried soldiers, and palace regulars, who respectfully nodded at them. Vorpovsky began his story, speaking softly.

The other morning, an old, poorly dressed woman appeared at the palace on Gatchina Street. Despite her tattered clothes, it was evident that she belonged to the best society and that she had seen better days. She asked to see his imperial highness. Vorpovsky, who was used to warding off stray visitors, had told her that the grand duke was unavailable but that she could confide in him why she had come. She had then taken some diamonds out of her purse. It was, she confided, a family property, the last one she had. She was forced to sell them, and knowing that the grand duke was a collector, she had come to propose that he buy them.

Vorpovsky had been sure that this "treasure" would not interest his master. On the other hand, he hadn't wanted to disappoint the old lady, so, taking money out of his pocket, he had bought the diamonds himself. Only, not having many rubles on him, he had paid her a very small price that still had been enough to make her happy. Not knowing what to do next with his purchase, he had proposed it to the first moneylender to come along, and for it he had obtained a sum slightly higher than the one he had paid.

"But why didn't you tell all this to Trepov?"

"He made me too afraid."

Nicholas didn't want to look into the truth of this story to which he clung as if his life depended on it. He immediately went back to his father to relate the story. The diamonds had been recovered, Vorpovsky's involvement had been explained, the matter was closed!

Upon leaving the Marble Palace, Trepov went to the Winter Palace to give his report to the emperor. The grand duchess Alexandra could be satisfied, the diamonds stolen from her favorite icon had been recovered! Captain Vorpovsky, the aide-de-camp of the grand duke Nicholas, had pawned them at a moneylender's — this Trepov did not doubt despite the denials of the man concerned — but, he added, it could in no case be he who had stolen them. Very few people had access to the grand duchess's bedroom — chambermaids, ladies-in-waiting . . .

". . . and the family," added Alexander II. "It's like the knickknacks that disappeared from the empress's boudoir."

He began pacing back and forth in his office, his head bowed, lost in his thoughts, then in a commanding tone he dismissed Trepov. "I congratulate you, General, for your excellent work and for your diligence, but as you can understand, from now on, this affair is no longer your responsibility."

Alexander II thought about the incomprehensible disappearance of some precious objects, and now these diamonds that could have been stolen only by a member of the family. And his sister-in-law who made such a fuss about it . . . And the other members of the family who had been informed! As a result, the whole court must know about it. Too late to hush it up and impossible, seeing the potential accusations, to treat this offense as a petty crime. The investigation had to go on since the theft had not been cleared up, but from here on the secret police would handle it. They reported only to the emperor and their conclusions were exempt from the law. The emperor straightaway summoned their chief, Count Shuvalov, gave him the information assembled by Trepov, and charged him with taking over the case.

Besides being intelligent and courteous, Count Shuvalov was subtle and conciliatory, which enabled him to occupy the highest offices of the state and become particularly famous representing Russia at the Congress of Berlin. With Shuvalov in charge, the emperor was certain that the investigation would proceed with the required discretion. He was unaware, however, of how much his brother Constantine and Shuvalov detested each other. He knew they were opposed on very many points, for example, the Baltic states. Shuvalov advocated a certain linguistic and cultural autonomy while the grand duke Constantine had become an advocate for total Russianization. The two men had been violently opposed on this point at the recent meeting of the Council of Europe. Constantine had spoken much too sharply, to which Shuvalov, held back by respect, was unable to reply. So, upon leaving his interview with the emperor, he was rubbing his hands.

After Shuvalov, the emperor summoned his brother Constantine and announced to him that he had shifted the affair to the secret police.

"But before they get involved in it, I want to ask you solemnly whether or not you want the investigation of the theft of the diamonds to be pursued or halted. It's up to you to decide, and I shall respect your decision, whichever it is."

Constantine asked to think about it, but promised to give his answer before the day's end.

Back at the Marble Palace, he had his eldest son summoned. At exactly six in the evening, Nicholas entered his father's office. Constantine brought him up to date about his latest interview with Alexander II.

"The emperor left up to me the decision whether to pursue or stop the investigation of the robbery of the diamonds. Now I turn to you. Do you want the investigation to go on or to be ended? I'll tell the emperor whichever you choose."

"I insist, Papa, that the investigation proceed most energetically and quickly, and that they get to the bottom of the affair, but it shouldn't be only the secret police who are involved. I wish that the public investigation undertaken by the municipal police be resumed until justice is done!"

"Is that your final word?"

"Please understand, Papa, that I am as curious as you are to find out the thief of Mama's diamonds."

Profoundly relieved, the grand duke Constantine right away had the emperor informed of his answer. He and his son Nicholas were agreed that the investigation should be pursued whatever the cost and whatever the result.

Back home, Nicholas found Fanny in her "small room." She was wearing a black velvet skirt flounced with lace and a short white jacket adorned with a pink bow.

"How come you're so beautiful? Did you go out?"

Fanny made a gesture of distress. "I'm afraid, Nicholas. I have the feeling that a great misfortune is in store for me."

"What madness! You're simply a little nervous. . . . What misfortune could happen to you?"

Fanny questioned him anxiously about his interview with his father. He told her about the choice his father had offered him and the decision he had made.

In a plaintive voice she asked him, "Why do you want so much to find out who's behind the robbery?"

"Quite simply because there's a mystery . . ." Then, after a silence, he asked, "Have you had news of Savine?"

Fanny didn't answer right away, but seemed so broken that Nicholas could hardly recognize the laughing, teasing, indomitable beauty of her earlier days. Finally she confessed: "Actually, I did go out this afternoon. I wanted to find out the truth and had myself driven to Savine's place, where in fact I had never been before. I found all the doors open and the apartment deserted, altogether empty. A neighbor told me that he had vanished a few days before and that all his things had been taken away."

Nicholas didn't notice that she was on the verge of tears.

"After all this," he said to her, "maybe it was he who stole my mother's diamonds!"

"Did your father also talk to you about the theft of the icons in the chapel?"

"Not a word. Either there was no investigation, or it wasn't pursued. As I predicted, no one paid any attention to it." Then he abruptly added: "And you, do you know who stole the diamonds?"

For an answer, Fanny threw herself in his arms, sobbing, "Let's leave, right away!"

Surprised and pitying, Nicholas stroked her hair and told her gently, "We can't right away, we'll have to wait two or three days." Then he frowned and jokingly took on a severe look. "The other day when I announced we were leaving for Paris to get married, you didn't seem at all enthusiastic! And now you seem in a great hurry to leave here and marry me. . . ."

12

The Peter and Paul Fortress richly deserved its sinister reputation. Opposite the church that was a pantheon for the dynasty and behind the barracks was a line of low buildings containing the cells of political prisoners. These were situated just above the Neva's water level lapping against the walls. During heavy rains, water flooded into the cells, drowning one or two prisoners who'd been left there, perhaps intentionally. A humid chill prevailed in the place, winter and summer.

Captain Vorpovsky had been arrested in the early afternoon, in fact shortly after the emperor put Count Shuvalov in charge of the investigation. Despite his courage, his heart was in his boots. He had been locked up in one of the cells, completely undressed, and attached to a bench, and for hours he was interrogated by the secret police.

Twenty times, a hundred times, the same questions had been asked him about the grand duchess's diamonds. Who had handed them over to him?

Vorpovsky sometimes got his answers muddled. He begged to be untied for a moment, to be given a cigarette, a glass of vodka. All the answer he got was to have one of the henchmen grab his hair, violently pull his head back, and shout, "Let's go back from the start!" Vorpovsky couldn't help vomiting.

"Clear up that mess," ordered a voice from the dark. Vorpovsky tried to make out who had given this order. A field officer in full uniform emerged from the dark and came up to him. "Young man, since you're in police custody, you'll not be surprised that you're put in handcuffs."

The field officer made a gesture and the prisoner ended up with his hands chained to a roaring stove, his feet tied to the bench, and his body arched. His head hung down and he was unable to lift it up. Very soon his blood went to his head, heating it. The officer made another gesture, and the henchmen left the room. From then on Vorpovsky was alone with just the field officer.

The latter opened the stove door and a wave of heat rose to him. Using some tongs, he stirred the glowing embers. He took out one that he seemed to gaze at attentively, then put it back in the stove, which he left open.

"Captain, this is a very disagreeable business. Nevertheless, I think that you have important things to tell us. Despite the friendships you may enjoy with one or two distinguished people, in fact you are nothing. . . . No one can protect you or defend you! We have reason to suspect that your loyalty to your few high-up friends interferes with your patriotic duty to the tsar. After the little session we're going to have, you can protest as much as you like, if, however, you're able to do so, and no one will listen to you. I give you fifteen minutes to talk."

The field officer was peacefully sitting next to him and lit a cigar. The heat from the open stove made the two men sweat in large drops. The officer broke the silence only to say, "I've made clear to you that we could reasonably bring this business to an end. Don't you think so, Captain?"

Vorpovsky made an effort to turn his head toward the clock on the wall of the cell. The gazes of the two men met, the colonel made a gesture as though reluctant to do so, slowly got up, went to the stove, and, using some tongs, took out a glowing ember. He spit on it and the ember hissed, and he carefully put the ember back in the stove and took out another one. Vorpovsky, who already felt the heat near his crotch, twisted desperately.

A yell, an odor of burning flesh; the aide-de-camp twisted his body so violently at the excruciating pain that his head hit the stone floor. The colonel went to the door and opened it. "A glass of water. I think that the captain is ready to listen to reason!"

Delicately, the field officer poured cold water on Vorpovsky's inert face. He waited until the latter got a grip on himself, and murmured in his ear, "Captain, I put the ember back in the stove. In a minute or two I will take out another one. . . ."

"I'll talk. But untie me!"

"Talk first, tell me the whole story, and above all hurry up, we have only a little time."

On the evening of the interrogation, the grand duke Constantine went to the theater. He was in his box when the aide-de-camp on duty introduced an emissary from Count Shuvalov. The count urgently wished to see him and was already waiting for him at the Marble Palace. Constantine suspected he knew what it was about and, leaving the theater to return home, he made a detour to Gatchina Street to warn Nicholas. Only he was out of luck. Then he burst out in front of Saviolov, "Still with that American woman!" The servant, not at all impressed by the irascible grand duke, calmly explained that Nicholas and Fanny had gone to dine at a restaurant.

"Look for him everywhere and bring him to me as quickly as possible!"

He found the chief of the secret police in his office. The mere sight of the very tall, very thin man with long graying sideburns exasperated the grand duke, who had a complex about his short stature. Shuvalov respectfully bowed. With all possible solicitude he confided to him that the conclusion of the men under him proved that the person guilty of the theft of the diamonds could well be his son Nicholas. And he immediately added, "In the interest of the empire and the dynasty, the affair must be buried as soon as possible. I have consulted with Trepov, who began the investigation, and with his approval I took the necessary precautions. I already found a man who, for a considerable sum, is ready to confess to the crime. I'm holding him at your disposal. Imperial highness, I beg you, trust me and help me avoid a public scandal."

In an instant, all of Constantine's antipathy toward Shuvalov came back. His adversary had asserted that his son was a thief; this Constantine could not admit! His anger burst out. "Shut up, Count, you have made all this up to slander my son because you want to bring him into disrepute and in this way wound me! I asked Nicholas to come at once; I challenge you to repeat in his presence what you've just told me!"

And, full of rage, he began pacing back and forth in his office.

Shuvalov was also in the grip of anger, but he knew how to keep it to himself. He remained standing, impassive. The grand duke had not offered him a seat, so he refrained from taking one.

Nicholas showed up and apologized for being late. Shuvalov couldn't help admiring his style, his ease, the disdainful expression, the hard stare. Nicholas gazed at him as if he were an intruder of the worst kind. Shuvalov was infuriated.

"Your imperial highness, I accuse you of having stolen the diamonds of your mother, the grand duchess."

"You surely have evidence against me to make such an absurd accusation!"

"Your aide-de-camp, Captain Vorpovsky, admitted that you had handed over the diamonds to be pawned at a moneylender."

"I imagine that to get him to spit out such an outrageous lie, you used the techniques that have made you and your agency famous."

"Scoffing will get you nowhere, imperial highness; you stole those diamonds and had them pawned by Vorpovsky."

"I assure you that's false! Accusing someone who is innocent without proof, all the more so a member of the imperial family, is a very serious mistake."

"I shall have you confront Vorpovsky."

"Do so. Even under torture Vorpovsky wouldn't have lied."

The discussion at cross-purposes continued.

Faced with his son's assurance, his father became more and more contemptuous of Shuvalov, almost insulting. As for Nicholas, he remained polite but scornful. The chief of the secret police did not let go for all that. He questioned Nicholas continuously, looking for an inconsistency. How did Vorpovsky come into the possession of the diamonds he took to the moneylender? Nicholas repeated the story told by his aide-de-camp: an old, poor woman came to offer him the chance to buy them; Vorpovsky received her and gave alms to pay her for the precious stones; then, not knowing what to do, he pawned them. Shuvalov and even the grand duke Constantine both realized the absurdity of this explanation. Which one of the two had made it up, Vorpovsky or Nicholas?

Shuvalov sensed that the grand duke Constantine was shaken. So he gave up his interrogator's tone and spoke to Nicholas with great gentleness. "Imperial highness, I appeal to your sense of honor, to your heart as well, to your love of your mother. Confess . . ."

Constantine stepped in. "Nicky, if you're hiding something from us, say so!"

All of a sudden Nicholas lost his haughtiness. In turn he realized Vorpovsky's tale didn't make sense. But if his aide-de-camp had lied, what then had happened? He was seized with anxiety. He repeated that he knew nothing, he had not stolen the diamonds, and that if the story about the old woman was false, he didn't know how the diamonds came into the captain's hands. . . .

Father and son were increasingly disconcerted. Shuvalov profited from his advantage to go on asking questions in a honeyed tone.

Weakened, forced to the wall, Nicholas asked Shuvalov the crucial question. "After all, did Vorpovsky categorically confess that I in person had handed him the diamonds?"

"I never said that, imperial highness. Vorpovsky said that Mrs. Fanny Lear had handed him these diamonds on your behalf. Now, your ties to this woman are known and, moreover, you alone had access to your mother the grand duchess's bedroom."

The truth hit Nicholas like lightning. He suddenly realized that Shuvalov hadn't made anything up and that Vorpovsky hadn't been lying. Fanny? The thief? How would she have done it? Of course . . . the night they had gone into the grand duchess's bedroom . . . At dawn he wasn't conscious. That was the moment when Fanny . . . But she wasn't alone, there was Savine!

He had the feeling that his brain was splitting, that he was being stabbed by a dreadful pain. The truth was that Fanny was in love with Savine. The love, the friendship, the complicity they had paraded before him was only an illusion.

Nicholas wanted to cry out their names to denounce them. They'll be arrested, imprisoned, much good may it do them! Maybe tortured? No, the secret police would never lay a finger on Fanny; she's a foreigner, they'll be content to deport her.

And the whole world will know that little Fanny Lear is only a thief? Never! He doesn't want her to suffer. He loves her. She's betrayed him, now she implicates him in a crime, but he still loves her. As for accusing Savine, that would be accusing Fanny. Then . . .

He felt his whole life depending on what he was going to say.

His father and Shuvalov saw on his face the storm of emotions taking hold of him. They waited without speaking. Nicholas looked at them each in turn for a long time. "I am guilty."

The grand duke Constantine was appalled. "And you don't have a word of regret! But don't you have any conscience?"

Nicholas turned toward Shuvalov. "From the start, you wanted like the others . . . like my . . . to find that I am guilty. Well, be satisfied, I am!"

"You're only bitter, my son. What, not a tear . . ."

His victory assured, Shuvalov assumed an air of indulgence. "Your imperial highness may go back home."

Nicholas almost forgot to say good-bye to his father on leaving. He didn't see the aide-de-camp who stood up at his passing nor the servants who lined up against the wall. He tripped several times going down the large marble staircase that his ancestor Catherine II had so often climbed to meet her lover Orlov. Coming out of the doorway, he didn't return the salute of the sentinels who presented arms.

Nor did he react to Karpish, the dwarf who opened the door to his carriage. He threw himself into it and let himself be taken away.

After their dinner was interrupted at the restaurant, Fanny had gone back to Nicholas's place to wait for him. The hours went by, long enough for her to get worried.

Not wanting to go to bed, she paced back and forth in their bedroom, sitting down, getting up, going to the window to watch for him. She didn't hear him arrive, but saw him come into the bedroom. To her he appeared taller and thinner than usual, and so pale that he looked drained of blood. He stood up very straight and could hardly move forward.

Fanny ran up to him, full of questions. He didn't answer her. She wanted to fling herself in his arms, but he found the strength to push her away. "Don't wear yourself out, Fanny, I know it all."

"What do you mean, Nicky?"

He told her in a few chopped, angry sentences.

Fanny felt her face turning crimson at the same time as an icy cold went all the way down her back. She was petrified. Then, without his having asked for it, she began telling it all. This she earnestly desired, for holding back the truth was choking her.

She had let herself be bewitched by Savine. Barely had she met him at her friend Mabel's than he began courting her. It was at a time when she was exasperated by Nicholas's infidelities, and she had succumbed. For a while she had shared him with Mabel, for he didn't want to give Mabel up as she provided his subsistence. "Then Mabel found a new lover . . ."

". . . and Savine found himself without an income," Nicholas cut in. "Why didn't you support him?"

"I couldn't. He was too greedy."

"Still, love made you do everything and anything!"

It wasn't love, protested Fanny, but a diabolical possession! Savine is a manipulator, he was the brains behind the whole affair. He knew that Fanny wasn't a gold mine, but she could lead him to Nicholas. It was Savine who'd had the idea of making him a kleptomaniac. He knew that eventually Nicholas would be caught red-handed. It was necessary that he be singled out.

Savine had had her steal the icons of the Marble Palace chapel, supposedly to pay for the revolution but actually to set a trap for Nicholas. Other "filching" of this magnitude was envisioned for later on. The whole scaffolding had collapsed when Nicholas announced that he was leaving for Paris with Fanny in order to marry her. No more Russia, no more fortune, no more affair either, for marriage would have broken up their trio. She and Savine had decided to flee . . . while keeping Nicholas back in Russia.

"And to keep me back, you stole the diamonds?"

"It wasn't premeditated!"

The night when he passed out from drunkenness, Nicholas had fallen and lain there unconscious on the rug. Savine had gone on gazing at the icons. Then he had an idea: to steal the most precious object in sight so that the crime would be discovered the very day the grand duke and duchess returned, which was expected to be in a week. In the meantime he and Fanny would put some thousand miles between themselves and Nicholas. But the unexpected return of Nicholas's parents had upset everything. That day, Savine, probably forewarned, had vanished. . . .

"And Vorpovsky?"

"I gave him the diamonds on your behalf to pawn them at the moneylender's."

"You're lying! He knew that you'd stolen them and that I didn't know, since he told me that bedtime story about the old woman. . . . Was Vorpovsky your accomplice?"

"He's been in love with me ever since you sent him to fetch me in Paris."

"And he betrayed me, like Savine! Like you!"

Then Nicholas asked the ultimate question, the one that had been obsessing him since the start of the discussion. "And the million gotten out of the stolen icons, the revolutionaries haven't seen a penny of it. . . . Of course Savine kept it for himself?"

"On my honor, on my love, on my God, I don't know."

"Honor you don't have, love you don't know what it is, and your God is in fact the devil. . . ."

"Believe me, Nicky, Savine never told me what he did with the million!"

They fell silent.

Nicholas looked around. A few kerosene lamps spread a weak golden light in the huge room. His eyes scanned his favorite paintings, the knickknacks that Fanny had given him; then he looked at her and found her wild, with bulging eyes, as if he were gazing at some creature from hell. She shuddered. "Are you going to drive me away?"

"It's too late. Both of us are in the lion's den and, in spite of everything, I can't do without you. You will be the only one in my life. You will have been both my salvation and my destruction."

"In spite of everything, Nicholas, you're the only one I love."

They remained for a long time locked in a tender embrace, cheek to cheek. Fanny could sleep under any circumstances, but Nicholas had insomnias filled with nightmares.

Both of them woke up late, tired and anxious. They didn't want to get up, as if the bed were providing them with an impregnable refuge. The audacious American adventuress and the Russian grand duke full of effrontery were no more than two frightened children.

The day passed both interminably and too fast. At one moment they were turned in upon themselves; in the next they embraced, whispering.

"Will you still love me if I am arrested, if we are separated?" asked Nicholas passionately.

She kissed him fervently. "I owe you my freedom, maybe my life."

He hugged her very tightly.

"I don't know what's going to happen to me, but I beg you, my dearest, to forgive me for any word or act that could have hurt you."

"It's I," she protested, "who has always proved impatient, hot-tempered, demanding."

"No, it's I," Nicholas insisted. "Promise me you'll never forget me . . . I love you, Fanny, heart and soul, more than life."

He went to fetch a small jewelry box, opened it, and brought out a plain gold wedding ring. "I ordered this for you last year in Vilna. I had my name engraved on it, along with the date our affair began. Today's the anniversary of our meeting. I want you to wear it always."

He took Fanny's left hand and put the wedding ring on her ring finger. He had that ironic, exasperating smile that made him so seductive. "Thus I marry you, my morganatic wife, the only beloved spouse I shall ever have!"

The two of them momentarily forgot their troubles and let their too-long-suppressed sensuality take flight.

Nicholas fell back on the bed, beset by one of his frightful migraine headaches. Fanny left the bedroom to look for his medications and came back alarmed.

"In the hall there's a colonel in uniform, Prince Utomsky. He says he's your father's aide-de-camp and that your father asked him to stand guard here and not to let you out of his sight."

Nicholas immediately reacted. He told her to pack up the jewels he had given her and her most valuable things as soon as possible and to keep them safe at the United States embassy. Fanny hesitated. Why such urgency? Nicholas insisted so much that she gave in. He went himself to fetch the cardboard boxes to put everything in and added two sheets of paper to them. "Well, here is my will. You'll see that you haven't been forgotten. And this is an order to transfer to your name a hundred thousand rubles; use it only if you need to."

He wanted her to also take the precaution of stopping by the apartment on the square of the Michael Palace.

"Lord, Nicky, I've forgotten that I left them in a hiding place! The knickknacks that . . . you understand me! The seals, the cup, and the gold pencil—should I also store them at the embassy?"

"Leave them, Fanny; *finita la commedia* . . . Or, rather, bring them back here."

"But if they come to arrest you and make a search, they'll find them."

"Exactly. I want them to find evidence of my petty thefts. I'll be stigmatized but the shame of it will fall back on all the members of my family, and that will be my sweetest revenge."

Nevertheless, Nicholas was worried about her.

"They'll lay the blame on everyone who has anything—near or far—to do with me. Savine clearly understood this and vanished right away. If they come to your place to search, listen to me carefully. Without even waiting for any deportation order, take everything you can and leave Russia as soon as possible, otherwise you'd run the risk of ending up in Siberia! I could do nothing for you there, and that idea is killing me."

"But how? That's impossible! I can't be sent to Siberia like that!"

He shrugged his shoulders. "They will hide compromising papers at your place, they'll pretend to believe that you had entered into a plot against the regime. . . ."

"I would never commit such an abomination!" Fanny shouted.

Nicholas answered her calmly. "They are capable of anything."

Persuaded, Fanny went, with her boxes, to the American embassy to again meet the American ambassador, whose acquaintance she had already made. He was a friend, or rather an admirer, by the fated name of Jewell. He declared himself ready to do anything for her, beginning with carefully keeping her cardboard boxes.

Night was falling when she came back to Nicholas's place in a state of indescribable apprehension. He ordered her to calm down. It was especially important to show nothing and, on the contrary, to put them off the track. On that point, the opera *La Périchole* was being performed in Russian and he had reserved a box for her. She definitely had to show up there in all her splendor, with all her diamonds, the very ones she had just dropped off at the American embassy and that she would have to take back there after the performance. They would later meet up in the apartment of the Michael Palace square. Nicholas himself was going to dine at the Marble Palace; Prince Utomsky had brought him an invitation that amounted to an order.

Fanny worried. What was his father going to say? How were they going to behave? Were they going to insult him, mistreat him? Nicholas burst out in bitter laughter. "The usual hypocrisy in the imperial and royal families has it that nothing is said. It is possible that my father will avoid looking me in the eye and will speak to me as little as possible. But the resident members of his family, who are perhaps somewhat informed, even my brothers, will say nothing. Fortunately, my mother is in Germany. We shall only exchange banalities."

Fanny walked to the door with him and helped him put on his uniform.

"Be brave and strong, my love. If nothing out of the ordinary happens to me, I'll come to your place at midnight."

So Fanny returned to the United States embassy, where the obliging and loving Mr. Jewell returned her diamonds. She decked herself out with particular care, choosing a silver moiré dress of a traditional style that brought out her jewels. Putting them around her neck, her arms, and on her ears, she had a sense of dressing for some *danse macabre*. More dazzling than ever, she entered her box at the Alexander Theater displaying her most carefree look, smiling right and left as she greeted her acquaintances.

As the curtain fell, she hurried to the exit, ordering her coach driver to go back to her place at top speed. She burst into her apartment, took off her evening coat, and set about waiting.

Midnight came, no Nicholas . . . An hour went by, then a second one; Fanny paced back and forth with increasing tension and anxiety. She didn't know what to do. She listened constantly, and would recognize among a thousand others the clatter of his carriage and his steps on the stairway. Now and then she heard the sound of a barouche in the street, but it was not his. Then the silence of the night settled in again.

At four o'clock she raised the curtain, the dawn vaguely starting to break. She could bear it no longer and decided to go to his place. Perhaps he had changed his mind and gone back to his palace.

She put on her hat and coat, took her key, and went out. The city appeared totally uninhabited. She was not to encounter a single soul, did not come across a single carriage. She went along the Moïka Canal, and when she reached the Oaks Bridge, a ray of sunlight appeared above the apartment buildings and struck the bridge's gilded sculptures, making them shimmer.

She reached Gatchina Street and found the portal open. She crossed the empty entrance hall and followed the marble gallery to the Renaissance hall, where Nicholas liked to be. She turned the doorknob; the door was locked from the inside. She tried other doors; all the private apartments had been locked. Normally, under other circumstances, Fanny would have cried out, unconcerned with waking anyone.

That one night, however, she preferred to do an about-face and, tiptoeing like an intruder, she made her way back whence she had come.

This time the entrance hall was not deserted. Saviolov, old and faithful Saviolov, was standing at the bottom of the stairs. Large tears were running down to his white mustache. Fanny ran to question him. He could hardly answer, mumbling so that she had difficulty understanding his words.

This had happened barely a half hour earlier; "they" had come to arrest his imperial highness. Who? The grand duke Constantine's aides-de-camp and the henchmen of the secret police. But why, what had been the reason for such a decision?

During dinner at the Marble Palace, a frightening scene had taken place between father and son. It began at the table. They got up so suddenly that their chairs fell over, and they shut themselves away in the father's office. Despite the closed doors, they shouted so loudly that the aides-de-camp and servants heard everything. In the last violent exchange, the father reproached Nicholas for his crime, and especially his lack of regret and remorse. . . . Nicholas retorted that someday the truth might come out. The father then told him straight to his face that he lacked heart, that he was a cynic. He had insulted Nicholas so much that Nicholas exploded.

He in turn reproached his father, but also his mother, his teachers, for everything he had suffered in his childhood, the ill treatment he had endured, the indifference in which he had been left to rot, the lack of tenderness that were all responsible for what he had done.

"Was it the grand duke who ordered his son's arrest?"

Saviolov knew nothing about it, except that the father had sent a note to his brother the emperor.

When "they" had arrived at Gatchina Street, "they" had woken up the whole household. As his imperial highness didn't wish to open up to them, "they" had broken down the door of his bedroom. Nicholas had defended himself like the very devil, he had shouted insults, broken objects, overturned furniture! Finally "they" got the

better of him . . . not the father's aides-de-camp, who seemed horrified, paralyzed, but the henchmen of the secret police. To lay a
hand on a member of the imperial family did not disturb them any
more than arresting a mere peasant! And then, suddenly, Nicholas
calmed down and even fell into a kind of apathy before he allowed
himself to be taken away without resistance.

Where had they taken him? To the Marble Palace, and Saviolov
thought he understood that Nicholas would remain there, under
arrest in his own apartment.

"I'm going to tidy up the mess 'they' made. . . ."

The elderly valet trod heavily on the steps of the stairway.

When Fanny got back home, walking like a somnambulist, it
was broad daylight. Joséphine, opening the curtains of her bedroom, handed her a note that had arrived in the middle of the night,
just after she had left. It was from Mabel.

"Savine was arrested at my place. The poor thing, he'd found
irresistible arguments for me to give him a refuge and hide him. . . .
But why was he arrested? Because of his debts? Or because of another woman whose existence neither you nor I know about? I
immediately alerted the girls, our companions. They all know your
grand duke and Savine and they are better informed than the police informers! The rumor is going around among them that our
darling was accused of stealing diamonds. Now, you know as well
as I do that he is capable of the worst, but not robbery! Besides, if
he were sought for a crime of common law, the city police would
have been told to pursue him. But the men who came to arrest him
belonged to the secret police. For pity's sake, put me in the picture
if you can!"

Fanny stretched out on her bed. Exhaustion overcame her
despair and she drifted off to sleep in the midst of her sobs.

13

On the morning of the next day, the dwarf Karpish brought a note that Nicholas had managed to send to her. For paper he had had to tear a page out of a book on which he had scribbled.

"I'm a prisoner, I'm suffering horribly, but I am patient and I hope that things will soon get better. I love you. Nicholas"

Fanny calmly got up and had her morning tea. Lord, she had forgotten that appointment with her dressmaker! She dare not send her away. The dressmaker entered, opened her cardboard boxes, and had her try on the new dress she'd ordered. She avoided look-ing Fanny in the eye, seemed embarrassed, pressed for time. Fanny understood that the news was public knowledge and that every-one knew about Nicholas's arrest.

The interminable hours went by. Around three that afternoon Karpish brought a second note from Nicholas.

"Don't be frightened, don't fear anything, my *dushka,* they're going to conduct a search at your place. But you can stay calm, don't lose heart! Your unfortunate wretch. Nicholas."

A search, here? Luckily her diamonds were at the American embassy, but even so! She was afraid.

"*Excuse me, imperial highness,* if I've taken the liberty of disturbing you, but I have something important to say to you."

Dr. Havrowitz walked with a heavy step into the office of the grand duke Constantine. The grand duke, generally so lively, seemed lifeless. With a vague gesture he indicated to the old practitioner that he should have a seat. All of the Marble Palace was aware not only of the theft of the diamonds, but also of Nicholas's arrest.

Havrowitz had reflected on this affair. Here is a man who steals stones that are certainly precious, but there was no comparison with his fabulous fortune! Yet those diamonds are of incalculable worth because of their sentimental value for the family, and it was a member of the family who stole them. What's more, he didn't hesitate to commit the sacrilege of damaging a holy image. Finally, he pawned these jewels at a moneylender's, getting only a ridiculously small sum, which he gave to his mistress, who absolutely didn't need the money. . . .

All of that, concluded the doctor Havrowitz, made no sense. Recalling several characteristics that he had observed in Grand Duke Nicholas ever since his adolescence, and remembering certain incidents that happened during the Khiva campaign, reported by the officers who were with the grand duke, and taking into account other, much more recent episodes:

"My conclusion, which I've come to announce to your imperial highness, is that the grand duke Nicholas is suffering from grave nervous disorders. I suggest he be examined by specialists, particularly Professor Bablinski."

The grand duke Constantine gave a start. "The psychiatrist!"

At five o'clock, Fanny awoke to someone knocking. Dispatched by Nicholas, Saviolov had come to give her his instructions. A few instants later, someone was violently ringing the entrance bell. Joséphine went to open the door and some fifteen policemen — some in uniform, others not — overran the apartment.

Fanny protested this intrusion. A redhead who had the look of a cheap Don Juan seemed to be in charge, and he told her he was there at the emperor's command — and at that of Count Shuvalov, she mentally added to herself. She was frightened because, with the chief of the secret police, everything was to be feared. She was not wrong, for when she asked them to withdraw so she could put on a robe, the policemen did not move out of the way but on the contrary surrounded her while Joséphine handed her her stockings, slippers, and dressing gown.

The redhead announced that they were going to search the house, and thereupon they rushed into all the rooms at once.

Fanny and Joséphine ran to keep watch over them and prevent them from stealing anything, for the secret police's reputation was well known. The two women let them have keys so that they wouldn't break open the drawers. They obviously didn't find anything since it all had been dropped off at the American embassy. She overheard their surprise at this; they didn't know she spoke Russian. What? No jewels, no papers, no letters? Going into Joséphine's bedroom, they swiped the cakes, which they gobbled down, helped themselves to several glasses of wine, and lit cigarettes.

Fanny went to find their boss, the redhead with the red eyes and the insatiable look. "I allow only my equals to smoke in my presence!"

She threatened to denounce them to Count Shuvalov. One brief order and the henchmen put out their cigarettes. Still, Fanny's heart was in her throat, for she had forgotten some rather compromising papers in a secret drawer in the big red table in the living room. Fortunately, the men were so stupid that they wouldn't discover them, as they didn't see Joséphine, who, almost under their noses and at a gesture from Fanny, was burning letters and telegrams from Nicholas.

An important matter for them, they found seven thousand rubles in a drawer in Joséphine's bedroom. They accused her of having stolen them from her mistress. Fanny had all the trouble in the world getting them to understand that the money was the faithful chambermaid's savings. The henchmen were irritated, increasingly manhandling Fanny's furniture while their boss made eyes at her; he thought she was irresistible.

"We're going to take you along," said the redhead, throwing her coat at her.

She protested, but she let it happen.

"We're going to take you to General Trepov," announced the redhead.

But she thought they had been sent by Shuvalov! She immediately suspected a police war. All the same, Trepov was better. The chief of the St. Petersburg police was an honest, discreet man; things could be worked out with him.

Going out on the street flanked by two cops, Fanny thought without meaning to of all those unfortunates arrested this way, taken to God knows where, and never seen again.

When the carriage left them off in front of the somber police building, she shuddered. The stairway was so dark that she tripped on one of the steps. She felt she was truly in danger, what with so many sinister stories about the imperial police! She was pushed into a room and locked in. Up to then Fanny hadn't wanted to show her emotions, but there, alone, and locked in, she burst into sobs. She cried so loudly that the jailers heard her. They unlocked the door, entered, and asked her what the matter was.

Regaining her calm, she ordered them to fetch for her some roast beef, tea, bread, butter, and champagne. Dumbfounded, they went out again. Fanny couldn't help smiling at her little joke. Of course she wouldn't get anything! To her great surprise, the jailers brought her everything she'd asked for! She didn't doubt for an instant that it was on the personal orders of General Trepov.

Although she hadn't eaten anything for the previous twenty-four hours, she barely touched the food. While she was nibbling, a good old babushka entered the cell, spoke to her in a motherly way, embraced her, held her in her arms, consoled her, and also from time to time asked her questions. She was a "stool pigeon." No harm in chatting, thought Fanny! The old woman sweetly led her to a sofa and helped her lie down on it. The springs made it hard as wood. The old woman spread over her the coat she had brought, then sat in an armchair, obviously planning to remain there until dawn. Fanny turned toward the wall and let the tears silently flow. Her despair belonged only to her.

The next morning, as he did every day, the minister of war, his excellence Miliutin, went to the Winter Palace and entered the emperor's office to make his report. That day, Alexander II barely listened and seemed absent. The minister didn't insist and fell silent.

Finally the emperor admitted to him what was happening. His nephew Nicholas had been found guilty of theft. This wasn't the first attempt by this very bad boy. For some time he had engaged

in actions that were fraudulent, swiping things right and left . . .
he'd just stolen some jewels from his mother's favorite icon. The
police had also found at his place a number of precious knickknacks
that had disappeared.

"When I returned the seals he had taken to the empress, she
declared she'd have preferred to have lost them. As for my brother,
when I handed over the gold objects that his own son had taken,
he didn't even want to touch them!"

The emperor enlarged at length on this affair, which was
unique in the annals of the imperial family. It had known debauchery, incompetence, insanity, murderers, even half-wits, but never
a thief. The shame reflected on everyone, beginning with himself,
the tsar. "I intend to expel him from the army and lock him up in
a fortress. What do you think, Miliutin? Must there be a trial?"

"May your imperial majesty allow me to advise him not to rush
his decision and above all not to spread news of this affair. . . ."

But the sovereign and his minister both knew very well that the
rumor was already spreading throughout the city. And that was indeed the problem! Once the scandal was nicely packaged and passed
around furiously, it would be impossible to keep it a secret. . . . It was
necessary to act ruthlessly to stop it. To strip the guilty man of his
rank was proclaiming the emperor's love of justice and his impar-
tiality concerning his family. But this measure would not spare the
Romanovs, who would forever be stamped with the shameful mark
of thieves. The emperor and his family could not accept that.

Two days went by and Fanny was still locked up in the buildings of
the St. Petersburg police. She had been allowed a kind of sitting
room, with dirty yellow curtains hanging at the windows, a few
pieces of furniture placed awkwardly, and even an upright piano
in one corner that waited for her to begin playing. So it was not

one of the frightful dungeons known to political prisoners but, all the same, a prison.

For her sole entertainment Fanny had a view of the street. At the hour of the promenade, she opened the window and looked out at the carriages going by. She was overcome by the uncertainty of her fate. The babushka, who was not so nasty, understood her dismay. To distract her, she told saucy anecdotes, taken from her long years in the secret police, and she had seen a lot! Like all the old women in Russia, she was a bit of a clairvoyant, so she took out of her pockets a deck of grimy tarot cards and began drawing cards for Fanny, predicting a glorious future.

Finally a door opened and a tall, distinguished-looking man came in; his cold, calculating blue eyes were fixed on Fanny. He introduced himself as the messenger of Count Shuvalov, chief of the secret police. He greeted the prisoner courteously and seemed almost embarrassed to see her in such a place.

"You have many precious jewels, letters, and precious papers."

"And so?"

"Madam, I must have them."

"Sir, that's impossible."

"In that case, madam, I'll leave you alone to give you time to think."

Fanny heard the key turn in the lock.

The same man returned the next day to request that Fanny hand him the papers and jewels he had mentioned.

"It's impossible," she replied, "since they were left off at the United States embassy. But if you want to go there, you can and inspect anything you please."

Shuvalov's envoy assumed a haughty expression. It was beneath the dignity of a Russian civil servant to go seeking the cooperation of a foreign diplomatic mission. What, he insisted, had she left off at the American embassy?

"Letters, an acknowledgment of a hundred thousand rubles signed by the grand duke Nicholas, and his imperial highness's will . . ."

With a nasty look, the visitor withdrew. Fanny understood that she was suspected of leaving off more at the embassy than she had said.

Night was falling and the jailers brought in kerosene lamps. The old babushka, who once again saw a worried Fanny, sat down at the piano to play. It was out of tune, and she played badly.

In fact, Fanny didn't need to worry, for her friend Ambassador Jewell was taking steps in her favor. Panicked by the policemen's intrusion, the chambermaid Joséphine had not, however, lost her mind. They had scarcely taken Fanny away than Joséphine rushed to the American embassy, and Mr. Jewell immediately took the affair in hand. He wrote an appalled letter to General Trepov. What? An American citizen had been arrested without any explanation being officially given? The ambassador of the United States thus asked the chief of police in St. Petersburg to give the explanation straightaway! No reply.

An hour later Jewell sent a second, threatening letter. This time, Trepov did reply. The ambassador's protégée had been brought to the central building of the police with all the care and attention owed to one of her rank. . . . She lacked for nothing, was in good health, and in the best of dispositions.

Jewell had a feeling he was not being taken seriously. This time he wrote to Count Shuvalov, demanding explanations. Still no reply. Then he rushed to the representatives of the other great powers and shortly managed to make the arrest of Fanny Lear an affair of state! What were things coming to if in the Russian Empire the police could arrest a citizen of a foreign country without giving a reason, with no justification, without informing the diplomats concerned? Ministers and ambassadors spoke with one voice against this unprecedented abuse of rights. Reassured of their support, Jewell again took up his pen. From then on he wrote in the name of the entire diplomatic corps. At that point Trepov did not delay. They should definitely not be worried; the American citizen was in no way guilty and would shortly be freed. . . .

Nicholas must be insane, Alexander II repeated, opening the meeting of the family council that was to decide his nephew's fate. It was the only possible explanation. Nicholas was insane, had announced the family physician, Dr. Havrowitz, who always guessed which way the wind was blowing.

"Nicholas is insane," declared his relieved father the grand duke on leaving this council.

"The question is: what to do with my son?" he wrote in his diary. "After long deliberation, we have decided to await the medical report, but independent of its conclusions, to declare that he is suffering from a mental illness, which will satisfy the public.

"At the end of the council," continued Constantine, "I personally thanked God. For however painful and hard this can be, I am the father of a helpless and mentally disturbed child. To be the father of a publicly denounced criminal would be unbearable and ruin my whole future. . . ."

The emperor was just as relieved, observed the minister Miliutin during his daily audience. Alexander II had brought up the subject of the affair of Nicholas Konstantinovich. The day before, three psychiatrists brought in by Dr. Bablinski had examined the accused. Their conclusion was that in his speech as in his acts, he appeared out of his mind. He was told that he would lose his rank in the army, that he would be deprived of the honors he had received at birth, and that he would remain arrested indefinitely. He did not appear contrite but, on the contrary, began joking! He even went as far as being sarcastic about his accusers, about his family. Unquestionably, these were signs of madness!

The decision had thus been made the evening before to recognize the grand duke as mentally ill. The emperor added that his American mistress would shortly be freed and extradited from Russia with an ample financial compensation sufficient to keep her quiet.

"That's the only way to preserve the dynasty from shame and scandal," concluded the minister. "Recognizing the madness is the only way to find the grand duke Nicholas innocent in a certain way and thus his family innocent as well."

Things were thus restored to order.

Returned from Germany, the grand duchess Alexandra went back to the Marble Palace. She did not visit her son, who was shut up elsewhere in the same palace. On the other hand, she summoned her other sons to her boudoir, the corner room with a wide view of the Neva and in the distance the gilded spire of the Peter and Paul Fortress. She had decided to speak to them in order to prevent their believing the rumors. "My children, do you know about Nicky?"

Constantine, the eldest of the three, answered in the affirmative, and added, "I'm sure that Nicholas's crime can be explained only by his insanity."

The grand duchess nodded in agreement. "Unfortunately, he has been quite deranged recently; he has stopped going to the chapel and praying, he makes fun of everything and everyone."

Then she went back to the stolen diamonds. She also mentioned other objects that had vanished. She couldn't stop talking. The petrified boys huddled together. The emotion was too strong; suddenly Constantine started to cry. His mother didn't notice it, carried away as she was by her rage against Nicholas.

In the meantime Alexander II changed his mind. He lacked
the courage to declare publicly the insanity of Nicholas, who would
continue to be held in secret.

Fanny still was unaware of the steps being taken in her favor by Ambassador Jewell as well as the promise elicited from General Trepov
to free her immediately.

Five days had gone by since her arrest when she had another
visit by Shuvalov's messenger, whose name she never learned.
Going on the offensive, she demanded to see, or least communicate
with, the representative of the United States. All right, replied the
visitor, but not until he had gotten back the documents left off at
the embassy.

"I'll do nothing of the kind!" exclaimed Fanny.

She and the policeman looked at each other sideways and sized
each other up. In the end, the man uttered the key words, "How
much?"

He didn't ask this quite so baldly, but it came to the same thing.
She was no longer suspected of concealing compromising documents in the embassy. Nor were they pursuing the jewels that
Nicholas had given her; she had a feeling they were willing to let
her go. On the other hand, the police wanted at any cost to get back
the will and the grand duke's promise concerning the hundred thousand rubles and, to achieve this, would accept sacrifices. The hard
bargaining lasted more than twenty-four hours until Fanny proved
ready to give in. No one could take from her what she had left at
the embassy but, in remaining inflexible, wasn't she going to compromise Nicholas? Perhaps in showing herself to be conciliatory,
she was making these monsters more indulgent with him. They
compromised on fifty thousand rubles, but she would give them the
documents only when she had returned home.

That very evening Fanny recovered her freedom, her faithful Joséphine, and her apartment on the square of the Michael Palace in the disorder left behind by the police, with the doors of the wardrobes open and the drawers thrown on the floor. Her blotting papers, her writing tables, her albums, her papers, and even the books had been taken away as well as her personal objects. The rooms were swarming with police in plainclothes determined to camp there in order to keep her under surveillance. The babushka, who had followed Fanny, was bearable, but the police!

Fanny wrote to Ambassador Jewell, who wrote once again to General Trepov, who then ordered his men to leave the apartment and post themselves on the ground floor or in the street. They were assigned to dog Fanny's every move. Before he disappeared, one of the police warned Fanny that the next day, a Sunday, she would have a visit from Count Levasher. Levasher! He was a member of what she called the "silver-plated elderly." The idea of receiving this old and fervent admirer relieved her.

However, when he came the next day, she scarcely recognized him. This drunkard was sober for once, and he had put on a uniform to indicate that he had come on official business. He began by deploring everything that had happened. If he had known . . . Fanny was annoyed by this honeyed tone.

"Now it's too late, it's a pity that you didn't know sooner what you had to do!"

Imperturbable, Count Levasher went on. The emperor in person was looking into Fanny's fate. He was very touched by her conduct and had been very impressed by her. He was even grateful that she had tolerated Nicholas and his whims for so long. . . . He is well intentioned concerning her, but he would like to know her plans. . . .

To sell everything and leave Russia as soon as possible!

"And when will this departure take place?" asked the count in a casual tone.

"I need at least two or three weeks to put all my things in order."

Levasher pounced. "Impossible, you must leave quickly! For the longer you stay here, the more the scandal will grow. It will die down only if you leave." Then he dropped his urbane tone and hurled at her peremptorily, "You have until the end of the week to leave! In the meantime, no appearing in public or going to any theater, tavern, or restaurant."

Fanny laughed in his face. Given the situation in which she and Nicholas found themselves, she would hardly go out and have fun in public places.

He then asked her a very surprising question. "On your word, do you think that the grand duke Nicholas has lost his reason?"

"No more than you have!"

One last question. "What has become of the documents you left at the United States embassy?"

"I gave them to those concerned."

That is, to the messenger of Shuvalov . . . Again that lack of coordination and this rivalry between the police forces, Fanny noticed. What she was very careful not to say to her visitor was that she was keeping in her possession most of the letters, notes, and telegrams that Nicholas had sent her, still carefully hidden in the secret drawer in the living room table.

At which point Joséphine informed her that a certain Dr. Bablinski was in the antechamber and asking to be received. She was never left alone in peace! But who was this doctor and what did he want? With a gesture Fanny indicated to her chambermaid to introduce the new visitor.

Pale, thin, and weasel-faced, Bablinski had deep-set eyes that ferreted around everywhere. "I am a psychiatrist, madam."

"Why have you come here? I'm not crazy, as far as I know!"

"No, but the grand duke Nicholas is. In any case that's my diagnosis."

"I assure you he is as sound of mind as you and I are!"

Obviously the psychiatrist didn't believe her and fired questions at her about Nicholas's mental state. Fanny could only protest. A few eccentricities perhaps, but who doesn't have them? The psychiatrist appeared to reflect before asking a question that seemed to her peculiar. "What is the source of your influence over him? He clamors for you day and night. . . ."

"I don't know. No doubt he knows me so well that he trusts me, and besides I've done everything to be nice to him."

Without much conviction, Bablinski still tried to get Fanny to talk, then he withdrew, clearly disappointed.

So Nicholas clamored for her . . . Fanny was deeply moved by this. What wouldn't she give so that he would be with her at this moment, in the apartment in which calm and silence again prevailed. Suddenly the service door opened revealing Saviolov, who had kept a key to it. But it was a transformed Saviolov. He had always seemed old to Fanny, but also alert. Now the weight of the years was weighing him down. He hesitantly stepped forward, his back bent, his eyes red.

He came to get the slippers that Nicholas had left in the apartment. Fanny eagerly questioned him about the prisoner.

In a droning voice Saviolov confided that Nicholas would remain under arrest in the Marble Palace until his insanity was announced. Then he would be taken back to his own place on Gatchina Street, still under arrest. At the Marble Palace the aides-de-camp of the grand duke the father were in the antechamber, but a madman could prove dangerous, so his jailers installed themselves in his bedroom and didn't take their eyes off him for a minute, day and night. There were also physicians, Dr. Havrowitz, the psychiatrist Dr. Bablinski, and their assistants. And when Nicholas was rebellious, ranted and raved, shouted, broke an object, immediately the male nurses flung themselves on him and put him in a straitjacket. For the slightest misbehavior, they gave him icy showers; several times they even beat him.

It just couldn't be that Nicholas was being treated this way, Fanny said to herself, pale with horror. And how was he reacting?

He had a sudden high temperature and had to be put to bed. He remained there very ill for four or five days. Fanny would have liked to fly to his bedside. At no time had their fate seemed to her more cruel.

The next day Saviolov once again slipped into the apartment: Nicholas was demanding a vest and a scarf. Hadn't he brought a letter or at least a note? No, his imperial highness can't slip him anything. Besides, Saviolov himself was thoroughly searched both when leaving and coming back to the palace.

Every day he presented himself to ask for this or that piece of clothing, or a familiar object his master had left at Fanny's. He came to ask for Nicholas's pillow, embroidered with his initials. Fanny would hand the object to Saviolov, who the next day told her that Nicholas had felt it, seeking whether it might have a letter from Fanny inside. Not finding anything, he had had tears in his eyes and threw the pillow on the floor.

Fanny was disconsolate about her own stupidity. She hadn't understood that these scattered demands for clothes and objects were a line thrown so that they could communicate secretly. It wasn't too late to do some good. Tomorrow she would slip a letter in the object that Saviolov came to demand of her.

But the next day that faithful manservant brought sad news. Awakened very early, Nicholas had gotten up and dressed as if everything were perfectly normal. Dr. Bablinski came to pay his daily visit.

"You're claiming that I am insane?"

"Yes, your imperial highness."

"Well, so be it; one ought to give in to the fantasies of the insane, don't you think? Let me be given my Fanny, my dear little mistress; if not, I'll be completely insane until my wish is fulfilled!"

The psychiatrist shrugged, examined his patient as usual, and left him, determined to not take account of Nicholas's request. On the other hand, the latter kept his promise. Since Fanny was not brought to him, he methodically set about destroying every piece of furniture in his room, smashing the paneling, the windowpanes, the mirrors, tearing curtains and cushions. Thanks to his impressive strength increased by rage, he managed to smash everything to pieces while fighting off his jailers.

As a result the measures against him were toughened, including a prohibition on bringing him anything whatever from the outside. The means he had imagined for communicating with Fanny were stillborn. She wept with disappointment, with grief.

"I recognize that I am a criminal and at the same time I am ill. Consequently, on the one hand I have been ordered to remain under arrest, and on the other, physicians have been sent to take care of me."

Nicholas was shut up in his bathroom and hastily scribbled these notes, which he later hid in a closet:

> If I had an everyday illness, if I suffered in a leg, or arms, these doctors could relieve or cure me, but my trouble is very different and the soldiers guarding me who blindly follow orders add to my ordeal. I ask them: What are you doing to me? They answer: You are being healed. . . . Then why not put me to bed and make me swallow many medicines? I think the doctors could change my situation radically. For example, they could claim that the care was insufficient to cure me as long as I was not granted a certain freedom, and as long as it

was impossible for me to see the persons I love, and also as long as I was condemned to inaction.

Thanks to the doctors who have declared that I was ill, I have been spared Siberia and hard labor.

And yet I don't think Siberia could be any worse than what I experienced for seven years under Baron Mirbach's supervision. It won't be difficult for the doctors to complete his good work. They could listen to my confession, examine my nerves. Why wouldn't they end up sending a telegram to whom it may concern, saying, "The grand duke Nicholas is so deranged that we cannot guarantee that he has not completely lost his mind. Only one thing could cure him: Sending him on an expedition far away following our orders and having him accompanied by a doctor given precise instructions."

They claim to be looking for an effective treatment for me, but they refuse to let me take part in the expedition in Amu Darya for which I spent six months preparing. Isn't that a cause for really going crazy? . . .

To entertain me, they brought me the parrot I love so much. It would be a shame not to love such an exquisite creature. When I am sad and melancholy, he makes fun of me, which almost makes me merry, with his jokes and sleights of hand. He's a clown! I gaze at him and find his fate very similar to my own. He bears a strong resemblance to a man who has been under arrest for a week. He may make others gay, but his pink crest flops over instead of standing straight up. It must be said that previously he was free in the garden. One morning a gardener noticed with horror that he had perched on the highest palm tree and eaten two fine leaves. Now these leaves were extremely rare and it had taken two years to make them grow. The parrot was put back in his place, he was tied with a chain around his foot.

Today they have withdrawn from my bedroom the informers in charge of my surveillance. They have also taken away the chain on the parrot's foot. We are both seated facing each other with our heads resting on our chests. It is not easy to get over such a shock. . . .

Nevertheless, it is easier to survive it when one knows that someone suffers just as much, such as my parrot. . . . You could maintain that this feeling is selfish and bad, and I would agree with you. . . .

My thoughts grow muddled, my hand weak, I must get some rest and also swallow my medicines. . . .

During her last days in St. Petersburg, Fanny feverishly packed up her things. The day before her departure, she went to the Peter and Paul Fortress to pray at the tomb of Peter the Great, at the very place where Nicholas had given her his baptismal cross. She went to bid farewell to Ambassador Jewell, then she had the audacity to visit General Trepov in order to thank him.

Trepov expressed his regrets that they had not let him manage this affair. He would have surrounded it with the most total discretion, and then, especially, neither she nor Nicholas would have had to suffer what had been imposed on them. When she was leaving him, this worthy civil servant was so moved that he threw his arms around her and kissed her.

The next day the babushka, who hadn't let Fanny out of her sight, accompanied her to the train station. She even followed her into the coach. There Fanny found a man already settled who, in her sight, gave her a penetrating look. She immediately guessed his identity and murmured, "It's a policeman in plainclothes. . . ."

The man heard this and blushed crimson. He rose and greeted her with the greatest politeness. Fanny and the babushka, who were almost friends, effusively said their good-byes. The babushka wept hot tears. She'd miss her little madam, and she must remember the marvelous future she had predicted for her with the tarot cards.

The train started moving. In Fanny, the relief of leaving the Russia she now detested fought against her chagrin in abandoning Nicholas and her bitterness at her inability to help him. Would they at least have a chance to see each other again someday?

14

Nicholas's fate continued to be a state secret, his name vanished from the official court communiqués, but the whole city talked of nothing else! The police could censor what was printed, but it couldn't censor what was spoken. Precisely fueled by the official silence, rumors spread, swelled, agreed with one another, or conflicted.

Most of them were surprisingly accurate; the people were clearly well informed. Many of the rumors were about the theft of the diamonds, with some disagreements owing to confusion between the two burglaries. The icon was not in the grand duchess's bedroom, but in the chapel of the Marble Palace. . . . Worse, it seems a servant had been accused, whom Nicholas, the real guilty one, left to be sentenced and sent to Siberia! This thesis was upheld by the ever-benevolent family and was to be accredited by the Romanovs up to the present day.

"You don't have it straight," asserted a well-informed countess. "It was not the diamonds set in the icons he stole, but a diamond choker belonging to his mother. He gave it to his American lady, who displayed it at a gala at the Opéra, where of course our imperial family immediately recognized it!"

"I have information," claimed a baroness also well connected, "according to which the grand duke Nicholas, in a crisis of insanity, killed one of his valets!"

"Fortunately, he was put away!" the majority concluded, for at least he no longer presented the frightful spectacle of his mental deterioration.

Quite a different story came from Stephanie Dolgoruki. She came from one of the grandest families in Russia and was a distant cousin of Katia, the emperor's all-powerful mistress. Like everyone, she had heard of the scandal, but she had her own information sources that enabled her many years later in writing her *Memoirs* to assert: "The very broad-minded grand duke Nicholas was suspected of having socialist ideas. But as it was difficult to exile a member of the imperial family for this reason alone, the authorities concocted a story of precious stones that disappeared from an icon in the Marble Palace. . . ."

This claim was confirmed by a completely unexpected figure, Pobiedonostev. Before becoming the inspirer of the empire's most reactionary politics, he had already been the pillar of Russian conservatism. Hating everything closely or even distantly connected with the liberals, he was in no doubt that the grand duke had in fact been sent off because of his liberal opinions.

Stephanie Dolgoruki's cousin Sofka Skipwith, who was married to an Englishman, went even further. She was certain that, driven by leftist ideas, Nicholas had entered into a revolutionary conspiracy.

"The grand duke's American lady" constantly cropped up in these rumors and counterrumors. And the newest development in the scandal was abundantly interpreted: the imperial government did not at all appreciate the zeal displayed by Ambassador Jewell in favor of Fanny Lear. So he had been disgraced and his recall had been demanded. In order not to offend Russia, Washington complied in a way that was downright insulting to Fanny's admirer.

On the other hand, not a single word about Savine!

And "the grand duke's American lady" in all this? Cradled by the North Express, she had left Russia and, just over the border, began weeping without being able to stop. She was impatient to arrive in Paris and finally to find there the peace and quiet she craved. She was greeted by a storm! Upon her arrival at the Grand Hotel near the Opéra, where she had reserved a suite, she was assailed by French, English, and American journalists who all requested an interview, who all, when she refused them, reported anything whatever in the editorials that spread daily on the front pages. Fanny Lear had been the accomplice of the grand duke. . . . She had drugged him. . . . She had wanted to marry him!

The scandal had overflowed Russia's borders, and the democratic countries had no means of muzzling the press. A thieving grand duke! Newspaper readers feasted with delight on the more or less invented details of the affair. The great personalities of the time commented on it with hypocritical horror.

"These terrible stories about the son of the grand duke Constantine that have been published in the English newspapers . . . I have heard it said that he had stolen his mother's jewels! What really happened?" asked Queen Victoria of her daughter, the heiress princess of Prussia, who answered in the same spirit:

"The affair of the son of the grand duke Constantine is frightful! I haven't spoken to you about it, but since you refer to it, I shall tell you what I know. He stole the jewels on the icons of his mother's chapel and took them to a moneylender. He wanted money to pay the debts he had incurred with an American woman of a shady reputation. That is where such acquaintances lead weak young persons!"

In Paris, Fanny could no longer go out. Everywhere, she was recognized, and immediately there was whispering; fingers were pointed at her, and faces of people she knew turned away rather than greeting her.

Certain ones, the boldest among them, bowed before her and wildly flattered her; others repeated horrors behind her back, so much that her only solution was to remain shut up in her suite. Her one bitter occupation consisted of cutting out articles about her in the newspapers and gluing them into large albums. Nicholas's photo was constantly present, and the impossibility of communicating with him only increased her sadness.

And Savine? Was she still thinking of him? In any case she didn't know anything about his fate. In fact, the handsome artilleryman had been sentenced to a penal colony. On what charge, after what confessions, by what authority? No one knew. His destination was the town of Tomsk in Siberia, where upon his arrival he was confined to a camp. A slow death awaited him, the most dreadful, the most unbearable for a young man full of life, for a pleasure-seeker full of appetites. But one fine day he disappeared literally under the nose of well-armed squads. So inexplicable was this feat that his prison guards pathetically wrote that "he faded into thin air." Then they reassured themselves, for they knew that one day or another, Siberia would catch up with the escapee, dead or alive.

Some forty miles southeast of St. Petersburg sat a pretty estate named Ielizavetina, belonging to Prince Tchernishev. The Neva lazily crossed its stretches of meadows. In the middle of the woods of birches stood a small neoclassical château. The colonnade, the dome, the symmetrical pavilions—everything was painted white.

Not far from it stood a model farm provided with the most modern comforts and the latest agricultural inventions, where the humans lived as pleasantly as the pigs, for there the people were devoted to the raising of pigs.

The park of Ielizavetina was rightly celebrated for its poetic charm. People extolled the pure and healthy air of the region. The proof, this young man coming out of the farm's central building, who was the very image of health. He wore peasant clothes easily, but everything about him proclaimed that he belonged to a higher social rank than that of the peasants. He was surrounded by men, some in white smocks, others in uniform, who all seemed anxious to assist him and satisfy his every desire. Followed by his cortege, he went into the pigsty. There, he gave food to the residents; he did not seem at all bothered by the mud and refuse in which he was walking, by the filth around him, and the usual stench in these places did not seem to reach his nostrils. Then he sat down at a table and went over the accounts at length, verified the sums spent. He worked out to the last penny the product of the previous sales, then he drew up his daily report about the smooth running of the farm.

Despite the banality of its subject, the report was that very day on the desk of the emperor of all the Russias. For the pig farmer was none other than his nephew! Alexander II congratulated himself for having transferred him to the country, was delighted at knowing him completely settled down and perfectly integrated in his new simple, rustic, and balanced existence.

With the report under his arm, the emperor went to the Marble Palace to have the grand duchess Alexandra read it. The specialists had forbidden Nicholas any visit and any communication with his parents, brothers, sisters, and they, despite their grief, accepted this, for they knew that this measure had been taken only for the good of the dear absent man. So they had news of him only from the emperor. At every one of these meetings with his sister-in-law, the tsar repeated the psychiatrists' conclusion, which was that there was no doubt Nicholas had been insane when he committed the crime. The man is not a thief, he insisted, he is a demented person. Each time the grand duchess had tears in her eyes, and then her face took on an expression of profound serenity.

The truth about the grand duke's "sojourn" at Ielizavetina was, alas, very different. Just after he arrived there, all the servants Nicholas had known since childhood were dismissed, starting with Saviolov, and replaced by real brutes. Moreover, they were changed every two or three days so he didn't have the time or the possibility to win them over to his side. These men — doctors, nurses, members of the secret police — were paid enormous salaries to guard the grand duke. So they had every interest in prolonging the situation and they didn't give him a moment's peace. Night and day they watched over him, forced him to put on the most rustic clothing to humiliate him, constrained him to do the roughest work. They obliged him to saw wood all day long. As soon as he opened his mouth to state a wish or a mere opinion, they yelled, "Sir, be quiet! Imperial highness, you're crazy!" When he demanded a book or some object, they brought him toys for a very young child.

Worse yet, they displayed him. . . . Indeed, one of his former regiments was camped not far from the estate. Officers he had known well went by on horseback in their finest uniforms, joking and caracoling. When they saw their former comrade in arms reduced to serfdom and on display by his guards, they stopped to look at him insolently and to snigger. The most precise information about the harshness and even cruelty of the treatment suffered by Nicholas reached his horrified friends, who repeated it.

"All that is only made up, lies spread by evil tongues!" retorted the imperial family. "My son is perfectly happy in his new life," declared the grand duchess Alexandra. "The emperor has the goodness to inform me almost daily of his progress." Now, the emperor is the truth!

"Am I a madman or a criminal? If I am a criminal, let me stand trial and sentence me. If I am a madman, let me have treatment, but, in either case, give me some hope that I can one day recover life and liberty! What you're making me suffer is cruel and inhuman. . . ."

Upon reading this note that Nicholas had managed to send and that was handed to her after her husband had read it, Alexandra gave up her serenity and frowned. For having written such insanity, Nicholas must be even more insane than one had thought! The doctors must have done their work very badly; the proof of it is that they don't stop bickering.

Indeed, specialists and psychiatrists had still not given a diagnosis of the exact nature of Nicholas's illness and about the proper treatment. Nearly every day they went to Ielizavetina to examine him. And while their patient was sent back to the pigsty under the surveillance of the guards, the specialists, in the beautiful columned living room of the main house, while drinking their tea and wolfing down sandwiches and cakes, got lost in a tangle of contradictions.

Some of the patient's actions could be considered those of a madman. . . . However, this madness was far from being continuous. Most of the time the patient expressed himself with the clarity and perspicacity of an exceptionally intelligent person. His mood changed rapidly, going from nervous excitation to a profound depression. "His imperial highness mixes excellent and bad qualities, good and bad desires in the most complete disorder."

On the one hand, the patient "is profoundly loyal to the emperor, the empire, very attached to military discipline and to his duties as an officer"; on the other hand, he still cherishes the insane idea of escaping to a foreign country and going to America. . . . He is capable of the most delicate kindness and also of unexpected hate. Havrowitz, who had a great knowledge of the family, told of a nervous weakness marked by visions and hallucinations inherited from his mother. The good doctor proposed "a plan for psychological and hygienic cure" marked by absolute solitude, frequent icy showers, and other treatments already tried on Nicholas. There existed, principally in Germany, "specialized institutes," in plain language "madhouses," where he would be perfectly taken care of.

Professor Bablinski absolutely did not agree. He detected no basic depravity in the patient, and his state would not justify his internment in any case. On the contrary, it is necessary to lessen the severity of the treatment and, for example, withdraw the secret policemen who never take their eyes off him. But above all, said the psychiatrist, "Sending his imperial highness abroad will only cause a new and completely undesirable flood of remarks and rumors."

He signed his report and sent it along with that of Dr. Havrowitz. Now it was up to the emperor to decide.

On December 11, 1874, Alexander II signed a ukase announcing to the whole world that his imperial highness the grand duke Nicholas Konstantinovich was suffering from a grave illness that necessitated a special treatment.

Nine months had gone by since the scandal burst forth. Nine months during which Nicholas's official state remained in the dark. Indeed, a madman hadn't the right to be mad as long as the tsar, "the Lord's anointed," hadn't decided it.

Attached to the report of the psychiatrists was an unsigned note explaining that the site of Ielizavetina had a major disadvantage: the estate was close to the Schlussburg road, which led to a small port from which it would be easy for the grand duke to escape

and go abroad. . . . On the emperor's order, Nicholas was transferred to the other end of the empire, the Crimea.

For the well-to-do of the empire who were able to go there
every winter, Crimea was a paradise. Around the Livadia Palace, a
vacation spot for the emperor, villas, more or less huge palaces, rose
in tiers up the steep hills amidst cypresses, olive trees, and orange
and lemon trees that ran down the slopes to the sparkling sea.

The weather was always fine in Crimea. Legends flourished
in this blessed land and poets found inspiration in it. White yachts
dropped anchor in the crystalline waters at the foot of terraces made
fragrant by jasmines and roses.

The opinion of Bablinski prevailed. Nicholas was placed in an
enchanting setting, Oreandra, his parents' splendid estate. Finished
were the hard labor at the farm and the ill treatment. Nicholas
was treated with decency and consideration. This change of the
rules obviously appeased him. Over the weeks his conduct became
exemplary.

Prince Utomsky, his father's aide-de-camp, had been named
his great chamberlain—protocol required it—in other words, his
chief guard. Reassured by the grand duke's apparent docility, he
took liberties with the rules and allowed him to receive the rare in-
dividuals living all year in the surrounding area, in particular the
charming Alexandra Demidova, née Abaza, worthy mother of a
family, above any suspicion.

Alexandra was twenty, strikingly beautiful, with a fine and
melancholy face, starry-eyed with large dark eyes, and a mass of
black hair. She seemed, not without reason, the very picture of
unhappiness. Her husband had mistreated her and so she was
seeking refuge in Crimea with her two small children. Nevertheless, she did not want to get a divorce, for she remained faithful
to her torturer to whom the sacred vows of marriage connected
her.

Touched by her fate, Prince Utomsky invited her more and more often to have tea with his imperial highness. One afternoon he even relaxed his surveillance to take a nap, leaving them to a tea set for two. The sunlight was streaming through the large windows, with the aromas of the sea and the perfume of flowers. In the air was all the sensuality of the south. Nicholas and Alexandra threw themselves at each other and, in an instant, the tea of good form foreseen by Prince Utomsky turned into an extremely sensual clinch.

When Prince Utomsky, emerging from his afternoon nap, returned to the living room, he found the grand duke and the mistreated wife seated at some distance from each other and chatting about eminently serious subjects. With the blessing of the great chamberlain, the teas for two occurred again and again — as well as their erotic supplements. Alexandra was not the type for Nicholas, who loved only voluptuous blondes, as Fanny knew very well! But since leaving the Marble Palace, he had had no news of her. He very much suspected that her letters were being intercepted, and he hoped that she was thinking of him while wondering if she was being faithful to him. Could he demand it, for that matter?

He had no more contact with his family, and though his fate had improved, his future remained uncertain and was filled with darkness. So this diversion, the first Nicholas had experienced since his internment and, moreover, a diversion of a high standard, was welcome. Alexandra was instantly crazy about him and he himself became fond of her.

One day Prince Utomsky discovered what was going on. The reports he sent to the court show his utter dismay. First he accused himself; he was the one responsible, it was he who had presented Alexandra Demidova to the prisoner. But how could he know that she was a schemer of the worst kind? This woman was motivated by self-interest to the point where it could well be that she would try to blackmail the imperial family! In response, the court ordered the elimination of all visits to Oreandra.

Too late, for Alexandra was expecting a child by Nicholas! The emperor was furious when he learned of this situation. When he was informed, Nicholas burst out laughing; he had had a good trick on "them."

To put the greatest distance possible between the lovers, the grand duke was immediately sent in August 1875 to the Ukraine with his "chamberlain" and his retinue and put under house arrest in Uman, more than 150 miles from Kiev, a flat countryside where eddies of fine black dust rose at the least breath of wind. There were fields as far as the eye could see, large villages grouped around an onion-domed church, and nothing else. No château, no society, no beautiful women. There Nicholas could only remain peaceful, and it would be a clever Alexandra who could find him there.

Meanwhile, Alexandra had bombarded the imperial family with incendiary letters. She imperatively asked to be reunited with Nicholas in order to take care of him, she demanded that the child of his she was expecting be declared legitimate, and finally proclaimed that he was innocent of the theft he was accused of!

Nevertheless, in the depths of his impregnable Ukrainian retreat, Nicholas had a visitor. Professor Bablinski, his psychiatrist, came to check on the progress of his illustrious patient and to give him the present he had brought, the memoirs of Fanny, which had just been published in Brussels.

Before letting him read the book, he spared him no detail about the publication of all his letters and telegrams, the secrets he had entrusted to Fanny about his education, his family, and the emperor himself. Everything that she laid out in her book, the psychiatrist, without constraint, repeated to Nicholas, whose first reaction was to be, quite simply, terrified. This publication could only make his already thorny situation worse.

In fact, the good Bablinski had used this pretext to root out any trace of the man's passion for Fanny and to show his patient the dangers of similar love affairs, for example, the one he had had with Alexandra. All the same, the grand duke was much stronger than the psychiatrist believed, if only for resisting this therapy. He regained his composure and plunged into the reading of *Romance of an American.*

What skill in argumentation, and then too the book was well written, which made it even more convincing. Fanny enlarged on her love for Nicholas, and also depicted with a note of sincerity Nicholas's love for her. In fact, Nicholas's only great and most serious fault was his kleptomania, the source of the whole drama. . . . On page after page she described the obsessive mania for piling up art objects irrespective of their value or authenticity. Besides, he had even swiped many of her little jewels that she would still be missing if she hadn't demanded that he give them back to her. The theft of the icons in the chapel of the Marble Palace? A fit of kleptomania! The disappearance of the diamonds from the star, for of course he was the guilty party, Nicholas would never have committed such a theft if he hadn't been a kleptomaniac! She well recalled the final days before his arrest, when the precious stones fell out of his pockets.

But not a word about Nicholas's contacts with the revolutionaries, nothing about his promise to marry her, nor about his invitation to leave for Paris to get married in secret there. And not a word about Savine, who wasn't even mentioned!

Upon finishing his reading, Nicholas had that strange smile and that gaze vacantly into space so characteristic of him. After all, Fanny was depicting him in the most attractive colors. And then her memoirs were an attack, perhaps veiled but all the same delectable, on the imperial family, the court, and the police and their techniques.

"So is everything she has written thus true, imperial highness?"

Bablinski did not leave off repeating this question to his patient. Nicholas shrugged. What could he answer? That he was not the thief of the diamonds? He still loved Fanny too much to even attempt to heap abuse on her. Bablinski guessed that Nicholas was hesitating and, thinking he was ramming the point home, gave him news that he had not asked for.

"First she wanted to publish her memoirs in France, but the imperial government, once alerted, managed to get the French Republic to confiscate the book and deport its author. That is why the book was published in Belgium, where she had to seek refuge."

"So she's become a pariah like me." Nicholas didn't mention Fanny anymore, but allowed himself a few confidential remarks: "Ah, women, my dear Bablinski, all the same. Never trust them with a secret. Take that poor Alexandra Demidova . . ."

Nicholas admitted it, he had felt a deep fondness for her at the beginning of his incarceration. It was a time when everyone turned their backs on him, and she alone showed some compassion for him. Then she pursued him determinedly, bombarded him with letters as she had flooded the imperial family with requests. Thank God, he was rid of her. Thank God, he was cured of women!

Utomsky complained under his breath. His health adapted badly to the harsh Ukrainian climate. And then the boredom of being cut off from the capital, from his friends, his usual life, was eating away at him. In fact, it was he who was the prisoner. . . . But what wouldn't he give for his beloved master, the grand duke Constantine, who had given him the responsibility for his terrible son!

All the same, the sense of duty had its limits! Fortunately, he could say to himself that he had won, that he had in the end managed to separate the grand duke from the diabolical Demidova. Besides, his imperial highness was much too busy to think of that schemer! And the "grand chamberlain" proudly reported that Nicholas was daily looking into the fate of the peasants, was interested in this or that case, intervening to provide assistance here and there, studying local agricultural problems. Thus, no need to worry any longer!

Until the day when the employees of the small police station of Uman came to inform Prince Utomsky that a stranger, a woman from somewhere else, had arrived in the village and rented a beautiful house there. Shortly afterward she fetched the local midwife and gave birth to a beautiful boy. She gave him the first name Nicholas. Nicholas! The prince's attention was aroused.

"And what was the name of this beautiful unknown woman?"

"Mrs. Alexandra Demidova," replied the police sergeant, and he added that the grand duke Nicholas had paid several visits and gone as far as congratulating her for the birth of her son.

"Of their son," gloomily replied the "grand chamberlain."

Once again Nicholas was separated from Alexandra. He was sent back to Oreandra, in Crimea.

He scribbled a telegram to Bablinski, begging him to give him back Alexandra if he didn't want his patient to go completely mad. He handed the telegram to one of the valets guarding him, one named Gregorieff, who refused to take it. Then Nicholas in a sudden fit of rage savagely struck him. Every day similar scenes of violence recurred. To everyone he proclaimed that they hadn't yet seen what he was capable of. So let him be put under arrest, let them hand him over to the police!

The psychiatrist and the police unrestrainedly blamed this madman in their reports, forgetting that in Oreandra there was also a disinterested and hence impartial observer. He was the administrator of the estate, Count Grabe.

The count didn't give a damn whom he pleased or displeased, and he told Nicholas's family a totally different story that the eldest brother reported in his diary. Grabe was horrified at the treatment imposed on Nicholas. The doctors, he said, proved to be extremely brutal, and it would be downright better to kill a man rather than keep guard over him, shut up this way, without allowing him any freedom of movement and while treating him so roughly! More-over, Grabe had heard the doctors announce that they were ready to give up and send the grand duke abroad, to Germany, to a specialized establishment. Once again Nicholas was being threat-ened with being shut up in one of those madhouses, whose fright-ful description, long passed over in silence, now makes people shudder with horror.

On that evening in February 1876, it was late when Nicholas accepted his supper. Served by the lone Gregorieff, he ate and drank a great deal, then wrote a letter that he handed to the valet with instructions to take it downstairs to Prince Utomsky. The valet did what he was told and left him alone. Nicholas took advantage of this and locked himself in.

In the dining room on the ground floor, the "grand chamber-lain" was finishing his dinner with members of the staff. He began reading the letter brought to him by Gregorieff and grew pale: Nicholas announced that he could no longer stand the conditions being imposed on him, so he preferred to commit suicide. Not hav-ing any poison, he would swallow the phosphorus of many matches he had carefully stripped. And let no one administer an antidote! If anyone tried to force one down his throat, he would stab himself with a knife he had hidden in his pocket.

Utomsky lost his head. Nicholas alive caused only problems for him, but Nicholas dead would be a catastrophe! His staff members were agitated, in the grip of the same panic, all except "his imperial highness's controller of finances," Keppen, originally German. While the others discussed and exclaimed without moving, Keppen ran to the floor above and repeatedly knocked on Nicholas's door.

Nicholas finally opened up for him. With one hand he made the gesture of cramming the matches into his mouth, in the other he was holding a dagger. . . .

Keppen did not let himself be upset and set about reasoning with him. He succeeded without too much difficulty, for Nicholas had already grasped the absurdity of his gesture. Finally there was an incredible scene, Nicholas thanking Keppen for saving his life.

Seven months later the secret police assigned to follow the comings and going of Alexandra Demidova reported that the latter, after staying in Odessa on the road to Crimea, had left for parts unknown. Resigned, the tsar, in his small slanted handwriting, noted on the back of the telegram that the "parts unknown" were probably the city of Tirov, south of Moscow, where, on his orders, his nephew had been detained for he had taken the most drastic measures.

Prince Utomsky, who had given up, was replaced by another old hand of the grand duke Constantine's house, General Witkovski, and thousands of miles were supposed to isolate Nicholas. It was as if all the policemen in the most policed empire in the world could do nothing against a woman who was determined!

For his part Nicholas seemed to take no interest in the flower-speckled grasslands that rolled to the horizon, the immense forests swarming with game. He was shut up at his own place, deep in books on Central Asia, the dream that was never far from his mind.

On the alert, the Tirov police reported no suspect presence. On the other hand, as the weeks passed, General Witkovski's reports on the conduct of the illustrious "patient" became more and more surprising. For some time he had been getting up only at two in the afternoon, retiring after midnight. He frequently returned to his bedroom with the excuse of headaches. He increasingly had his breakfast, lunch, and dinner served in that room. In the bookstore of the small town where he was allowed to go, he bought the novels of Alexandre Dumas and other casual reading for which he had previously shown only scorn.

Witkovski brought together his imperial highness's doctors and other members of the household staff to discuss the best ways to handle these incongruities. Once more it was Keppen who found an explanation. Taking advantage of Nicholas's absence owing to a visit in the town, he went into his bedroom, searched through his drawers, looked under his bed, opened his closet . . . and came upon a ravishing young woman! He had her step out to scrutinize her. She was as graceful, fragile, and tremulous as Odette when the prince charming stares at her hungrily in *Swan Lake.* It was Alexandra Demidova! How had she found out where Nicholas was? How had she gotten into a house that was guarded night and day? This young woman who looked so melancholy must be a she-devil!

That was indeed what General Witkovski believed. Following the example of his predecessor Utomsky, he condemned Alexandra in his reports. Not only had she broken the laws of propriety, but also the law period. The grand duke was not responsible; it was she who was the nightmare! She must have the faculties of a ghost, for she was continually there, day and night, without anyone's being able to lay a hand on her, not giving Nicholas's entourage a moment's peace and preventing Witkovski from shutting an eye. To cap it all, she was once again pregnant by the grand duke. Finally, she threatened to go to St. Petersburg to meet with the members of the imperial family and set forth her case.

Witkovski no longer knew what to do except throw up his hands and beg to be relieved of his post. The emperor granted his request and what's more named him senator to reward him for services he had not rendered.

15

Orenburg is on the other side of the Ural Mountains, at the gateway to Asia. It was one of those cities that the Russian Empire had founded not so much earlier, since it had begun a process of indefinite expansion. The city was populated for the most part by Germans, who had been imported in massive numbers, and was given a German name. It is an administrative city, laid out in straight lines, with straight streets and very similar buildings row upon row; it oozes boredom.

Nicholas arrived there in the early summer of 1877 under the guard of General Rostopsov. His new supervisor had more the brutal firmness and irrevocable decisiveness of a noncommissioned officer than the suppleness and half measures of a man of the court.

He knew to act so quickly to separate Nicholas and Alexandra that the grand duke was not present at the birth of his daughter Olga, and the two lovers would never see each other again.

Rostopsov, who had had the idea of going even further than his predecessors and who, with the tsar's enthusiastic approval, had chosen the borders of Siberia to conceal the incorrigible prisoner, blandly agreed that the authorities of the small city could organize a reception in honor of the grand duke. With Demidova far away forever, Nicholas wouldn't find anyone to replace her in the families of narrow-minded and zealous minor civil servants!

It was the first time in three years that his imperial highness the grand duke Nicholas Konstantinovich was to reappear in public. Orenburg's tiny society was consumed with curiosity about him.

For three years he had been repeatedly taken from one place to another, thousands of miles apart, obliging him to adapt to places, new environments. The policemen let him rot in destabilizing ambiguities, now treating him like a madman, now like a grand duke, now like the worst of criminals. Alternating dangerous liberties and pointless cruelties. Nicholas could have come out of the nightmare prematurely aged, trembling in every limb, his eyes frightened, his hair white, but he was a prince, handsomer, more arrogant, more attractive than the elite of Orenburg had ever seen. He greeted the officials with majestic grace, kissed the hands of their wives, clapped the backs of their sons, and cast an incendiary gaze at their daughters, who blushed with pleasure. He raised his glass filled with warm champagne to propose innumerable toasts to the sound of *oompahs* from a military band that was awkwardly attempting a waltz; he even agreed to open the ball on the arm of a fearfully ugly woman, the wife of the region's governor, General Krivanovski. By the time he left the dance, everyone there had fallen for his charm and eagerly awaited an occasion to see him again. He, on the other hand, swore to himself never to do anything like that again.

Rather than enduring such a tedious party, he preferred to explore the area surrounding the city and immerse himself in exciting nature. Grasslands stretching as far as the eye could see mingled with fertile plains of vineyards and plowed fields, and in the distance, covered with dense forests, were huge mountains with snowcapped peaks. All this verdure abruptly ceased and gave way to deserts of sand where barely submissive tribes roamed: the entrance to Asia.

Nicholas observed the nomads with slanting eyes who came from there, these Kirghiz whom the imperial administration was trying to Russify by teaching their children the Russian language as well as the Kirghiz language, the Gospels as well as the Koran.

His fellow-feeling extended to the Uralian Cossacks, who were a majority in the region of Orenburg, men with broad shoulders and slim waists, women with admirable eyes, dressed in picturesque clothes. The Cossacks were perhaps sly, but they proved loyal, hospitable, and above all they displayed clearly democratic leanings that attracted Nicholas. So he didn't hesitate to set off with them in an expedition, watched over by the henchmen of Count Rostopsov.

Following their example, he was capable of going without stopping for fifty or sixty miles by horse or sleigh, taking with him food for himself and his horse. When his provisions were used up, he was obliged, like his companions, to slit his horse's throat and feed on its raw flesh while weeping over its death.

Nicholas's preference was to accompany them on their fishing expeditions. All summer long the sturgeons swam back up the nearby river. When the cold suddenly arrived, it was then too late for them to go back down toward the sea, so they settled for hibernating in a deep spot under the ice, forming whole sleeping shoals. When the ice was sufficiently solid, Nicholas and his friends crawled out on the surface, which was so transparent that they could see the sturgeons, which could then be gathered up. The winter's first fishing expedition lasted only a day; it was called "fishing for father," for local custom had it that the fish caught in that take was sent to the tsar.

Count Rostopsov could congratulate himself. Orenburg was not the pleasantest town he knew, far from it, but at least it was far enough from civilization to avoid bad company and scandals. The choice of that place couldn't have been more judicious; as for the cure, its benefits were plain for all to see. The grand duke was only studying the indigenous behavior of the Kirghiz and fishing with the Cossacks.

On a morning in 1878, the caressing breeze, the smell of flowers, the merry buzzing of insects coming in the window of the "grand chamberlain's" office announced the arrival of spring and prompted him to put off writing his reports. He began delightfully daydreaming . . . only to be interrupted by his chief henchman. "Count, his imperial highness has been secretly married!"

Rostopsov nearly fell out of his armchair. "But to whom?"

"He married Nadedja von Dreyer."

"What? The daughter of the chief of police of Orenburg, General Alexander von Dreyer?"

"The very one, your excellence. His imperial highness must have met her at the reception of the civil servants that was arranged for his arrival."

How did this romantic idyll come about? How did this love grow under his nose without his noticing it? All the horror of his situation flashed before his eyes. Quite involuntarily he was responsible for this outrageous marriage. What was the emperor going to say? A grand duke who was a thief or a madman was already too much, but a grand duke married to a commoner was an indelible stain!

A zealous employee, he began by ordering an inquiry. His subordinates went hunting, and it didn't take them long to report their wealth of information. Questioning the members of the von Dreyer family, they came upon a first cousin of Nadedja. Not only had he been present at the wedding, he had been its official witness! One thing leading to another, they went to the priest who had solemnized the union, a priest from the little village of Berda, near the city. He suspected nothing, for the bridal couple declared their names as Nadedja von Dreyer and Lieutenant Nicholas Volynski. Volynski?

Count Rostopsov searched his memory. Of course, that was the name of the grand duke's favorite regiment, the one to which not so long ago he gave all his attention! Perhaps a marriage under a phony name isn't valid. . . .

Rostopsov started hoping again. Bucked up, he went to find General Krivanovski, the region's governor, and accused him of negligence. After all, he was responsible for what happened in the area entrusted to his administration.

"Me, responsible? But Count, it was you who were assigned to the surveillance of the grand duke, not I!"

The governor-general and the count "guardian" separated, each one hurrying to his office to write page after page in his report accusing the other of inexcusable negligence.

Rostopsov recovered a semblance of composure and went to question Nicholas. The latter welcomed him with a burst of laughter.

"You were indeed wrong in presenting the local society to me! For in the middle of the pimply young virgins with tousled hair, there was a hidden treasure. Had you noticed, you would have certainly avoided setting her before my eyes. She had the goodness to respond to my advances. I had time to hone my skills. Surely you know that I am a past master in the art of doing exactly what I want in the knowledge and sight of my kindly guards. So my Nadedja and I are living a great romance. . . ."

For once, Rostopsov was clever enough to take a joking tone with him. "Your imperial highness's reputation is no longer to be made; people ascribe hundreds of mistresses to you, and that you unearthed one even in this godforsaken hole proves your talent and your obstinacy. That you went to bed with the daughter of the chief of police is consistent with your prior activities. But why the devil marry her?"

Kind and smiling, Nicholas had no trouble explaining it to him. "I wanted to burn all the bridges."

Indeed, he couldn't fulfill any of the responsibilities of a grand duke and, quite obviously, what the future held in store for him wouldn't change that. So he had wanted by this marriage to cut himself off from the dynasty and become a citizen like any other . . . with the rights of any citizen, which for the time being were denied him. This marriage, for Nicholas, represented freedom.

"That is understandable," retorted Rostopsov, "but why Nadedja von Dreyer?"

Because she was different from the others. . . . She was neither an adventuress attracted by his position or what remained of it, nor a madwoman passionately in love with Nicholas's charms. She was extremely mature for her young age, reflective and reserved, endowed with an innate dignity and profound humanity. She loved Nicholas for himself and hesitated for a long time before marrying him. Though she finally accepted, it was with the absolute conviction that she could bring him a great deal in transforming and curing him.

After all, that is not a bad solution, a fairly persuaded Rostopsov said to himself. The grand duke isolated from the dynasty by an unequal marriage and made docile by a woman who suited him, the couple would disappear in the profound obscurity of a provincial and bourgeois life and the too-visible Nicholas would so utterly melt into the crowd that no one would pay him any attention. Wasn't that the goal sought by the court? And Rostopsov persuaded himself that the emperor and the family would see matters as he did.

So he wasn't at all prepared for the icy shower of displeasure of his august master.

On August 17, 1878, in the *Official Paper of the Empire* there appeared a ukase by which his imperial highness the grand duke Nicholas Konstantinovich ceased to be the colonel-in-chief of the Volynski Regiment, of the 84th Regiment of the Shirvan Infantry, of the Ismailovsky Regiment of Guards, of the 4th Battalion of Rifleman Guards, of the horseback guards, and of the crew of the Navy Guards. He no longer had a rank in the army, to which he no longer belonged. He also lost all the honors and privileges of his rank. The emperor even thought of taking away his rights to the throne, but that was legally impossible. . . . The disgrace was infamous and public. The theft, the insanity were muffled by a secret decision. The morganatic marriage was pilloried.

As a result, Nicholas, who had almost disappeared from people's memories, became once again a subject of conversations in St. Petersburg, so much so that some people wondered if the emperor hadn't chosen this pretext as retribution for old or even new grievances.

People pricked up their ears to rumors coming from Orenburg; people repeated the contents of the reports of the police responsible for guarding the exiled grand duke. Lately, it seemed, he was making increasingly seditious remarks against the emperor and the system of government. At a dinner in the presence of the Orenburg city authorities, he cried out, "I shall go among the people wearing all my decorations and the people will rise up to defend me!"

Nicholas protested in writing. He denounced his guards, who never gave him a moment's peace, read his correspondence, interfered with his private life, and, to justify their high salaries, spread frightful rumors about him. If they would just leave him in peace with Nadedja Alexandrovna, all would be well.

In response, the court decided that the marriage ceremony as it had been performed was not valid. Moreover, to be wed, every member of the imperial family had to receive the emperor's prior consent. The Holy Synod, the highest authority of the Orthodox Church, was to be the judge.

Soon, Count Oldenburg, minister of the imperial court, was triumphantly able to announce that the church had declared the marriage annulled. Was Nicholas to be transferred for the ump-teenth time? For once, they acted intelligently. Since his arrival in Orenburg, Nicholas had gone on dreaming of Central Asia, not as a utopist but as a realistic pioneer. Through his readings, he was studying the region in depth and conceived the plan of establish-ing a railway line linking Mother Russia to Turkestan.

A show was made of approving his idea and consequently he was allowed to mount a first expedition of reconnaissance. Setting out to explore the desert, traveling into Central Asia—that was indeed what Nicholas had been demanding even before his arrest! It was the dream of his life. So he accepted without a second's hesi-tation. His dear Nadedja encouraged him in it. For, Holy Synod or not, they considered themselves still married and lived under the same roof.

"Don't worry, I'll be gone only a few weeks, for the season is already far gone. Soon, very soon, we'll be together again, and on my next expedition, you'll accompany me."

To accompany him Nicholas chose two railway engineers, a topographer, and a professor at the University of Kazan, a re-nowned botanist but exiled like him. During the expedition Nicho-las accomplished the work of an experienced technician and a competent person in charge. He was in his element. The hard life of the camp did not discourage him; on the contrary. He was aware of intelligently working hard and putting his faculties into the ser-vice of a grandiose plan.

He collected a mass of unpublished and vital information about the areas he was passing through that would be needed for Russian implantation. This process completed, and with winter approaching, he ordered an about-turn.

"We'll go back to Orenburg."

"No, not to Orenburg, imperial highness, but to Samara."

"Why Samara?"

"Orders from higher up."

Samara was a city built along the Volga, hundreds of miles from Orenburg. A few decades earlier the region had been nearly uninhabited, but the river, despite the devastating floods it caused, amounted to a source of wealth that stimulated colonization.

On arrival, Nicholas asked for his wife. Nadedja was to stay in Orenburg. Orders from higher up! This was an implementation of the annulment decided by the Holy Synod. Nicholas appeared to be resigned. He found some consolation in preparing for his next expedition. He spent his days deep in reference books, maps, statistics. He didn't go out and didn't seek to have fun. Besides, the winter was dismal, with torrential rains that turned the streets into bogs and made the Volga overflow.

At the start of the summer of 1879, Nicholas left again, this time for more than a month. His companions of the preceding year were joined by other scholars, men of science, but also artists assigned to make paintings of the regions traversed, altogether about fifty people, plus the horses and camels. They were to travel by land and also by water on the Amu Darya.

Leaving straight toward the southwest, they reached Samarkand. The city was no more than a shadow of what it had been in the Middle Ages. The sumptuous and gigantic monuments built by Tamerlane and his dynasty had gone to ruin, but they still proudly bore witness to a glorious past. They continued to Bukhara and then Khiva.

Nicholas met the emirs and their court, bearded and turbaned characters dressed in embroidered caftans. Theoretically, friendship treaties linked these kinglets to Russia. In fact, they had become vassals and had no voice in the matter. With his natural courtesy, Nicholas soothed their bad temper and became friends with these princes scarcely out of the bloody Middle Ages. He even appreciated their vast palaces of dried mud and wood where barbaric sumptuousness was neighbor to primitivism. He was far away from everything, he worked hard, he was coming close to happiness. He came back at the end of ten weeks, tanned, in glowing good health.

The members of the expedition received decorations and awards, all except him. He couldn't care less. He wrote articles on the most varied subjects that had interested him during his journey and sent them to St. Petersburg. The court's orders were strict. Nothing of what he had written must be published. Still, his articles were so perspicacious, so revelatory, so useful that several magazines insisted on publishing them. The court gave in. The articles were to appear, but without the writer's name! Which didn't prevent Nicholas from receiving unanimous praise for his remarkable work, and in particular for his study about the possibilities of irrigating the desert.

Filled with his success, he asked once again to be reunited with Nadedja. Once again he was refused.

Having tasted the freedom of the great open spaces, Nicholas could not bear the thought of returning to his cage without even the mellowing influence that his "wife" would bring him. All the more so as his jailer Rostopsov, still terrified of having brought the emperor's displeasure upon himself, proved more petty and tyrannical than ever. So Nicholas went to war against him and stated in no uncertain terms that he would no longer obey his instructions. The panicked court dispatched Professor Bablinski there. A new "medical" examination of the "patient" was the panacea!

Bablinski was neither bad nor stupid and went to the trouble of listening. In his reports he first remarked that Nicholas had lost all faith in equity and justice because of the behavior of his guardians. He consequently recommended eliminating the position of guard-general held by Rostopsov and replacing it with that of a special tutor who would not be continually on the back of the "illustrious patient"—in short, he advised lightening up on the regimen to which Nicholas was being subjected.

So Rostopsov was dismissed and Nicholas was brought back to the area around St. Petersburg. He was settled in the aristocratic property of the Pustynka, a large, graceless barn of a place overlooking a garden in the French style that had become fashionable in the seventeenth century. All around it, a wooden fence with pointed ends had been hastily built to cut off the château's occupant from the rest of the world. He was forbidden to see Nadedja, and his healthful activity of explorer was replaced by idleness.

He was placed so close to the capital that he almost inhaled its temptations, but he didn't have permission to set foot in it. His family was quite close by, yet not one member came to see him because the psychiatrists were still warning that getting together again could cause a dangerous nervous excitation in the patient. Visits were not absolutely forbidden, but simply had to be screened. But no one came. Not his childhood friends, nor his army comrades, nor holiday companions, nor pretty women—no one dared come near the man with the plague.

No one except Saviolov. He was now retired and living in Pavlovsk in the dacha once given by Nicholas to Fanny. Despite his age and his rheumatism, he hadn't hesitated to make the tiring trip to see his young master once again. He showed up at the gate of Pustynka and was admitted. Nicholas had him enter the living room and received him as though he were the greatest lord at court. The two men embraced; the elderly one let his tears run onto his white mustache and Nicholas himself had misty eyes. Saviolov had brought vodka, piroshki, cakes and other sweets, and that liqueur made with mare's milk that Fanny had found revolting and Nicholas really enjoyed. Knowing the fatherly tenderness Saviolov felt for him, Nicholas freely discussed his family and the recent events with him.

The empress Maria Alexandrovna had died, her consumption finally overcoming her valiant struggle. The emperor hadn't even waited for the period of mourning to end before marrying his mistress, the imperious and magnificent Katia. He immediately granted her and their illegitimate children royal titles. The scandal was tremendous! The whole outraged family had risen up against its head.

"Except my father, I bet!"

Indeed. But though Constantine had given his blessing to the remarriage of his elder brother, it was to further his political influence over him. And to further his own most original, most audacious plan . . .

"My mother hasn't come. I've never had any message from her. Does she still hate me?"

"You're mistaken, imperial highness, it's your father she's angry at, even through you."

"And if my brothers and sisters haven't come to see me, is it because they're afraid of Mama, afraid of the emperor?"

"They love you, they're constantly asking about your news, they cry because you're not there."

"And my father, does he love me? And if he doesn't come see me, is it because he's afraid of his wife?"

Saviolov thought the reality was more complex. In fact, Nicholas was his mother's weapon against his father. If the father came to see his son, Alexandra would complain to the tsar, who would be obliged to order his own brother to stay away. If he protested the tsar's severity, the conservative forces would take advantage of this to create some distance between the two brothers.

"So my father is sacrificing me for his politics!"

Constantine had had a hand in getting Count Loris Melikov appointed as prime minister—"An Armenian, just think," sighed the people of St. Petersburg. With his support and with the emperor's accord, Constantine was polishing up a Western-style constitution.

Saviolov remained skeptical. These innovations meant nothing much to him. Nicholas explained to him what a Russia with a constitution would be like: equality perhaps, but above all freedom, no more oppression, no more arbitrariness, no more secret police, no more fear.

"You realize, your grandchildren could get an education."

"They're good the way they are! But since my young master says that the constitution is a good thing, he's right."

"The history of our country is at a crucial turning point. Obviously, the conservatives must be wildly against it, determined to do everything to prevent the birth of a constitution. Just like the revolutionaries. If Russia made such a leap forward, the carpet would be pulled out from under their feet; they'd be unemployed! If a constitution is officially announced, they'll have no reason for being." And he murmured, "I wonder what Sophia the revolutionary thinks and what she and her friends are cooking up."

On March 1, 1881, the emperor was coming back from a military review. His carriage was taking the street that ran along the vast park of the Winter Palace, very close to Fanny's old apartment. There, several members of the secret police and a few uniformed regular policemen were his only assurance of safety. Suddenly there was an explosion. Someone had thrown a bomb and the carriage was in pieces! Miraculously, Alexander II came out of it unharmed.

"Nothing's happened to me, don't worry."

Immediately, there was a second explosion. There hadn't been one but two armed terrorists. The second one hit home, and the emperor lay in a pool of blood. They managed to bring the dying man to the Winter Palace. They took his mutilated body up to his apartments, leaving long reddish rivulets along the large marble steps of the stairway. The whole family was called to his bedside. Even his morganatic wife Katia was permitted to see him. She threw herself on him and held his inert body, her lace negligee covered with bloodstains. Alexander II was dead.

Nicholas learned the news that very day from one of the court messengers responsible for informing every member of the imperial family. He received the news with mixed emotions. The very first feeling was one of horror. Russia had had massacres, assassinations, but up to then never an attack of this kind. After all, it was his uncle, his sovereign to whom Nicholas had long ago vowed fidelity, an irrepressible devotion. Yet the emperor, called the liberating tsar, had betrayed him. Even recently, when his brothers and sisters had asked for permission to visit him in Pustynka, Alexander II had curtly refused.

Nevertheless, he was obsessed by the idea of this man he loved lying lifeless and torn to bits in a pool of blood. Who could have committed such a well-planned crime? In the face of this unprecedented tragedy, Nicholas had never felt so strong a need to be reunited with his family, but he knew that this was impossible. Then he decided to go into mourning, and dress in black from head to foot.

The new emperor was Sasha the Bear, now Alexander III. He had a thoroughly happy married life, but he had suffered much from his older brothers. So the scandals of immorality were over: Katia, who the day before had been all-powerful, was requested to move immediately with her little bastards. Also over were the attempts at democratization; we saw where that leads! Uncle Constantine, who wanted his constitution, shall not have it. Alexander III detested him, for the grand duke repeated to anyone willing to listen to him that his nephew was a more or less idiotic nitwit. Then

Constantine, until further order, was to remain in the countryside at his Pavlovsk estate, and he was strongly advised to never set foot in town. Members of the foreign press were having the time of their lives! The grand duke Constantine had been seen in Paris, where he settled down after abandoning his two wives, the legitimate one and the other. . . .

Seated under a tree in the park of Pustynka, Nicholas was getting ready to have his breakfast when his attention was caught by the headline spread out in large type in his daily paper: THE ASSASSINS OF HIS IMPERIAL MAJESTY THE LATE EMPEROR ALEXANDER II HAVE BEEN ARRESTED.

He began reading avidly, and the male nurses assigned to oversee him, who were some distance away, saw him stand up and reel as if he had been shot. He seemed crazed, ready to collapse. Then he straightened up and, walking like a robot, headed for the estate's little chapel in the park. The worried nurses followed him. They noticed he was still holding a crumpled sheet of the paper in his hand. He went into the tiny sanctuary and noisily closed its door. The nurses approached but didn't dare enter. They pricked up their ears and heard groans, sobs, incoherent words. Inside, Nicholas, squatting in a corner, was rereading the article.

The police had made haste and didn't take long to find the trail of the tsar's assassins. They had effected a surprise raid on their den, had found irrefutable evidence of the assassination attempt and its preparations. The guilty parties were arrested, all of them belonging to one of the numerous small revolutionary groups under police surveillance for quite some time. Among them, a woman, "a female monster who did not hesitate to ride roughshod over the modesty of her sex to bring death." Her name, Sophia Perovskaïa. With what money did she and her accomplices launch this assassination?

The hours went by. Nicholas remained despondent, hunched up in the chapel. Then a semblance of calm came back to him, accompanied by a touch of common sense. Knowing Savine, he knew that he would certainly have held on to the million rubles meant for the revolutionaries, or at least the largest part of it. And even if he had turned over the money from the theft of the icons to Sophia Perovskaïa and her revolutionaries, seven years had gone by during which they would have had a hundred chances to spend it! But even if one chance in a thousand or ten thousand remained . . . The idealists whom he had believed in had turned into assassins. The need for them to act violently before the promulgation of a constitution excused nothing. Whether he wished it or not, he was their accomplice. His sense of guilt both overwhelmed him and spurred him to react.

"My lord, I am expressing only one wish, to bow before the remains of my beloved uncle to ask him from the paradise where he is to pardon me. I will even make this pilgrimage in chains. But may your imperial majesty, out of his immense goodness, allow me to come back for a few hours to St. Petersburg."

Once this note was written, Nicholas wondered who would plead his case before Alexander III.

Only one person could do it: his mother! Despite everything he had thought up to provoke and shock her, he continued to love her, all the more so as she had turned him out of her heart. And what if this attitude was merely an appearance, if his mother, in her heart of hearts, still loved him? He wrote to her asking her to intercede on his behalf with Alexander III.

Curiously, she accepted.

Because the police were bent on protecting him from the terrorists, but especially because he loathed society life, the new tsar settled in the country, in the gigantic château-barracks of Gatchina built by Paul I. Relinquishing the too-formal large apartment, he and his family set up their quarters in the mezzanine.

It was there that the grand duchess Alexandra was received. To avoid the splendor of eighteenth-century interior decoration, which was thought uncomfortable, they sought a "cozy" feeling, filling the rooms with plush, green plants and a whole fashionable hodgepodge of bric-a-brac. The ceilings were so low that Alexander III, a giant, almost touched them while his wife, the grand duchess's favorite niece, Mini, looked quite petite. Having become the *tsarina,* she had kept her warm simplicity and welcomed her aunt with that radiant smile that attracted all friendly feelings. Then she withdrew. The grand duchess sat up straight on a small gilded chair while the tsar read Nicholas's note.

Sitting in his heavy mahogany armchair, he took his time before responding.

"Nicholas is not worthy of paying his last respects before the ashes of my father, whom he so cruelly saddened. Don't forget, Aunt Sannie, that he has brought shame upon us all. So, he won't see St. Petersburg as long as I live."

Despite herself, the grand duchess burst into tears. Alexander III stood up, approached her, sat on a flimsy chair that threatened to give way under his weight, and took her hands. "Dear Aunt Sannie, you think me very harsh, I know, but you don't know for whom you're interceding. It's mainly because of his behavior toward you that I bear Nicholas a grudge."

Flabbergasted, Alexandra questioned her nephew. After a silence, he revealed that, according to recent reports of his guards, Nicholas had said some really shameful things about his mother. She didn't want to know any more about it. She made a deep curtsy, and withdrew, letting her moiré train rustle. The first lie to come along, discovered in a malicious report, enabled Alexander III to shift his hatred of the father to the son and also stir up that of the mother.

And, once again, Nicholas had to move. He was sent to Pavlovsk, not of course to his parents' palace, but to the fortress built at the forest's edge by Paul I — his favorite ancestor — who from there could watch over the daily maneuvers of his regiments and engage in his favorite occupation, playing war games with his soldiers. Since then, the building had been abandoned.

Thanks to the extreme cruelty of Alexander III, Nicholas could see the palace where he grew up through the windows of the fortress in which he was confined, but there was no question of going anywhere near that paradise; the orders of the tsar were pitiless: strict and constant surveillance of grand duke Nicholas. Visits prohibited. Promenades allowed but only on foot. Approaching the château or any of the pavilions where his family might meet him — prohibited. In brief, he is interned close to home and family without being able to see them.

This sadism so typical of his cousin didn't frighten him. He had found it hard to accept his father's disfavor and he would have given anything to be able to keep him company, possibly console him. Now there was the execution of Sophia, which he learned about from the newspapers. Certainly she was guilty, like her companions sentenced along with her. Certainly she had helped in planning and organizing a man's assassination and she had blood on her hands. But she had acted in the name of her convictions. But she loved . . . Arrested with her lover, executed with him, it had been he she thought of on her way to the scaffold, it was he for whom she wept when she asked for her shackles to be loosened.

"Loosen them a little, they're hurting me. . . ."

"Soon you're going to hurt even worse!" replied the police officer.

Nevertheless, she was not firm on her feet when she mounted the wooden steps.

Nicholas suffered imagining the frail young woman whom he had known hanged in front of hundreds of gaping onlookers who'd rushed to see the death of a member of the weaker sex. Her skirt had to be tied around her ankles, it was said, to prevent the onlookers from satisfying their basest curiosity. All the same, Alexander III, at the dawn of his reign, could have pardoned her; because of his inflexibility, she became the first woman to be hanged in Russia, that is, a heroine.

Against this narrow-minded tyrant, Nicholas employed the only weapon at his disposal, scoffing. "The young tsar has proved to be very cruel. He persecutes his cousins and hangs young women. Not surprising in a murderer!"

"Alexander III a murderer?"

"What, you don't know history?"

He had an elder brother who was meant to come to the throne upon the death of his father, Alexander II. Warm, intelligent, and open, the brother bore the hopes of a whole people. He was even engaged to a Danish princess with whom he was very much in love. She was named Maria Feodorovna, Mini to the family. Now, one day it happened that Alexander feigned a boxing match with his brother. While boxing for the fun of it, they rolled on the grass. And then the elder brother lay there inert, he had injured himself. No one realized the gravity of his condition. He died several months later. As a result, Alexander became heir to the throne, and very soon he married his brother's former fiancée.

"Shakespeare must have passed that way," observed Nicholas with a carnassial smile.

His words, immediately reported to Alexander III, infuriated the sovereign. Because of this, he remarked, as if by chance, that many people had vacation residences in Pavlovsk, many people could catch a glimpse of the interned grand duke, perhaps even have some contact with him, many people ran the risk of hearing his siren song and standing up for him.

The cleaver fell in April 1881. Nicholas was exiled to Tashkent, at the far end of Central Asia. It was far away, so far away that people never heard of it, even when making an effort. According to the emperor's orders, he would be subject to rules nearly like those for criminals, treated not like a member of the imperial family but like any other prison inmate. At the slightest protest he would be arrested and incarcerated. As a consolation, his imperial highness would have the right to be accompanied by Nadedja Alexandrovna von Dreyer.

However, the marriage had been annulled! Perhaps, but since their separation, she had conducted herself with such dignity and discretion, in sharp contrast to the outbursts of Fanny Lear and the demands of a Demidova, that the emperor decided she might have a good influence on the infernal Nicholas. So once again this man and this woman were officially reunited, they who in the eyes of the church were merely living together.

16

It *had been just over ten years* since Russia had conquered Tashkent. Central Asia, with its sandy deserts and rocky peaks, however, had been since prehistory a place of transit and of civilizations. Kingdoms and empires were born there, then vanished under the assault of invaders. How many dead cities slept under the dunes of sand! Then, little by little, governments lost interest in it and kinglets and emirs took over. In its very recent push toward nationalism, Russia deposed one after another. Thus in 1865 it snatched Tashkent from its sovereign, the khan of Kokand. After the victorious campaign of Khiva, in which Nicholas had taken part, the immense territory had become a mere province of Russia with Tashkent as its administrative center.

All the same, the country had changed since Nicholas had fought
there eight years before. A road had replaced the half-obliterated
tracks. Dunes and rocks no longer concealed enemy horsemen waiting in ambush; on the other hand, convoys were threatened by bandits, and the escorts assigned to them served a purpose.

This blistering austerity pleased Nicholas, who revisited with
pleasure those landscapes to which his thoughts had turned again
and again. He repeatedly found a pretext for getting down from
the carriage and mounting a horse to breathe great lungfuls of fresh
air. The excessive heat did not irritate him; on the contrary, it stimulated him. During the day, allowing himself to be led by the pace
of his mount, during the night stretched out under his tent while
sleepless, he let his thoughts sweep over him. The face of Sophia
Perovskaïa constantly forced itself into his recollections. He had
met her only once, but she had made an indelible impression on him.
And he was haunted by the image of that young woman hanged at
the end of a rope.

Then he thought again of his mother. He saw himself once running to her, to kiss her while she pushed him aside. A new memory
emerged, an entrancing figure, Fanny Lear, so cheerful! He even
heard her laughter and relived the nights spent with her, all that
seemed so far away . . . Suddenly he sensed that he was being
watched; he met the anxious gaze of Nadedja. In reuniting her with
him, had they wanted to humiliate him?

He'd had many women in his life, some of them had even
counted or counted still, but Fanny would remain forever the one.
Never could he have denounced her for the theft of which he was
accused. And the haunting question returned: was he responsible for
the emperor's assassination? To break free of this torture, he would
like the journey never to end; he would like to wander the earth
forever.

With the temperature continually rising, Nicholas and the

people accompanying him had to travel from nightfall to dawn. They dozed on horseback and in carriages under the starry sky and collapsed on their beds in the morning, soaked with sweat.

They reached Tashkent in the height of summer. According to custom, the well-to-do left the overheated city to retire to the lush suburbs in their *kibitka*, their summer villas. The most beautiful one was made available to Nicholas and Nadedja. They entered a large house of dried mud extended by an immense tent from Bukhara that had multicolored sections, which served as a living room. In the moonlight they crossed a vast garden made fragrant by roses and mock oranges, where the paper lanterns that hung on the pomegranate trees were reflected in pools of water. Poplars and elms delineated areas of shadow on the moon-silvered ground.

The next morning the newcomers entered Tashkent. They first visited the Russian city, a workplace in full swing, filled with public buildings still under construction. On the straight, dusty streets flanked by two rows of trees, low whitewashed houses of earth were lined up with small gardens in front of them protected by wooden fences. Everywhere freshwater ran along canals. Here and there in the center of squares, which were much too large and nearly empty, stood large, brand-new churches. Several thousand colonists lived in the Russian city together with at least twice that number of soldiers from the garrison. The vast majority of the population, Muslims of the Asiatic race, was jammed into the native city, a maze of narrow streets that wound among the mosques, the bazaars, and the crumbling palaces.

These natives, whom the Russians scornfully called "Sarts," actually belonged to tribes that dated back to the start of recorded history. Born on horseback, they rarely went anywhere on foot and even took their steed to go a distance of a few hundred yards. Nicholas stopped one of them and asked him how old he was when he had learned to mount a horse.

"I wasn't taught to mount a horse, you simply get on."

A city of pioneers, Tashkent was worthy of the American far West. Adventurers, men without faith or law, and crooks swarmed in the city. Colonists who were disappointed by this reality, which they had imagined to be quite otherwise, and soldiers who had been ground down by too many months in the garrison did as they pleased. The main occupation of these inhabitants was drinking. There were many casinos, brothels, brawls, gunshots, and amidst this general loss of moral fiber, corruption was flourishing,

But there were also incorruptibles, men of enthusiasm and energy who applied themselves to the development of Central Asia. The huge volumes of the *Albums of Turkestan* were published year after year, newspapers were started, libraries created, one expedition after another left in search of the unknown nooks and crannies of the province.

And these expeditions set Nicholas to thinking. Ever since he had tried them, he had been intoxicated by them. To leave for the unknown, to plunge into virgin lands was to attain that freedom that he so needed. He had gotten the blessing of the imperial government for his earlier expeditions and he had learned from those experiences. He knew that his articles, his reports, the information he provided were an essential basis for knowing the region.

Despite the instructions of Alexander III, he was not received as a mere nobody. His title too deeply impressed these provincial officials for them to be able to forget it because of the sovereign's stroke of a pen. They welcomed Nicholas with a certain discomfort, an almost visible embarrassment, and they didn't forget any of the honors due his station.

On his arrival he proposed to the authorities to set up an expedition at his own expense. They were effusive in their thanks, they congratulated him on his patriotism, they promised to respond as quickly as possible, the time it took to telegraph St. Petersburg.

Days and weeks went by, and Nicholas started to get impatient. If they were to mount an expedition before winter, there wasn't a minute to lose! Of course, his imperial highness was right, still a few days and everything will be all set. The possibilities of leaving in time dwindled to the point of disappearing. . . .

The winter proved to be terribly harsh. A wind seemingly composed of razor blades blew with no letup. At night the frost was so severe that one morning Nicholas and Nadedja awoke to an awful sight. All the pack donkeys, leashed to the trees in the square, had died of the cold. Then the ice was followed by torrential rains; they turned the canals into muddy rivers overflowing at the slightest chance, the streets becoming open sewers.

When the wind howled in the chimneys and the rainstorms furiously beat on the windows, Nicholas stayed inside with Nadedja. Her sweetness and intelligence helped him resign himself to inaction. He finally understood that owing to orders from higher up, there would be no expedition for him. So then what to do? In any case, the season's poor weather prohibited any movement. He profited from this by indulging in his favorite pleasure, reading. He dove into history, into stories, into the region's legends. He was almost able to be happy.

When good weather returned, he went riding in the surrounding countryside. He crossed the beltway of orchards around the city, took the roads shaded by mulberry trees, rode along the cotton fields, which stopped at the irrigation canals. Next to them began the stretches of sand. He came upon some native villages surrounded by trees and fields with crops. Scattered here and there were only rare tamarisks in the way of vegetation, and then the oases, which became less and less frequent, smaller and smaller. Succeeding them were dunes as far as the eye could see, heaps of rocks, cliffs hollowed out by caves. On the horizon was a line of peaks of the Alai Mountains. Sand and stone, and nothing else. All along the track, warning signs grew more numerous: skeletons of camels, donkeys, horses, and sometimes humans, the remains of caravans that for thousands of years had attempted to cross this fatal region.

Nevertheless, Nicholas was irresistibly attracted to what was justly named the "starving steppe." Sometimes the temperature became so scorching that he was forced to shade himself from the sun in the first refuge he came across. So it was when one day he found a seemingly abandoned caravansary. As he approached the inn, he heard the marvelously melodic song of a nightingale that belonged to the very old custodian of the premises, forgotten there by the management. He was a native, a Sart. He lived all alone in this bleakness, with this bird his only company. Carried away, Nicholas proposed to the old man to buy the feathered creature.

"But it's my life that would go off with it!"

Yet he gave way at the number of gold rubles that the grand duke forked out. The delighted Nicholas set off again, with the bird and its cage, which he hung from the branch of an orange tree in the winter garden. The next morning just after he woke up, he took up station before the cage to hear the nightingale sing. No luck. While Nicholas waited all day, the nightingale remained mute in the corner of its cage.

Then Nicholas understood. He took the cage and brought it back to the desert to the old custodian of the abandoned caravansary. The latter ventured no commentary, but set the cage back in its place and held out the gold rubles for Nicholas, who refused to take them.

Nicholas's rides often took him back to the caravansary. He listened to the old man talk about the past, for he knew all the region's legends. He evoked the distant time when in this very desert his slant-eyed forefathers farmed a rich earth and reaped abundant harvests. "For before becoming a hell, these lands were a paradise. . . ."

The old custodian's stories had Nicholas remembering things he had read. Many centuries earlier the natives had known how to irrigate the region, but the Mongolian invaders, wiping out everything in their way, had left it a desert. Why not bring prosperity back to the "starving steppe" the way he had brought the nightingale to the caravansary so it would sing again. He had noticed that the yellowish dust that blinds the traveler at the slightest breath of wind consisted of loess, a fertile soil that just needed water for everything to grow.

Nicholas began by going back to the grid of the dried-up old canals. He would bring water from the Amu Darya over a huge distance. To do this he would need a sizable workforce. He steered clear of the trap of asking the local officials, who would have seized on every pretext for refusing him. It occurred to him to go find the new khan of Khiva, the son of the one he had helped conquer. The son had been left with a shaky throne, a palace full of cracks, and a highly limited autonomy, but he still had prestige and influence.

Nicholas employed his charm and natural courtesy to win over this sovereign of whom the Russians were so contemptuous. The khan had only to make a gesture: workers would rush by the thousands to get jobs on construction sites! As for money, it wasn't the government that would allocate the funds; the grand duke offered nearly all the two hundred thousand rubles he received each year from the imperial prerogative.

He was there every day overseeing the work. He carried out the plans and had a giant canal dug. He didn't feel the heat, nor fatigue, nor thirst. . . . The undertaking lasted for months — nothing stopped it, not the cold, the wind, or the rain. When the canal was finished, Nicholas gave it the name Iskander, the local dialect's name for Alexander the Great, the mythic hero who had come into these regions and been the first to foresee its irrigation.

The water flowed! But the natives preferred living in poverty, filth, and epidemics rather than farming the fields Nicholas offered them. They distrusted every initiative taken by the Russians, which they saw as ways of more effectively enslaving them.

Too bad for the natives, Nicholas will appeal to the Cossacks to occupy the land he had made fertile. They were originally from the Ural Mountains, but several revolts had led to their exile in this area. They too were outcasts and most of them belonged to a religious sect dating back to ancient times and named the "old believers." So they were treated like lepers by the Russians and detested by the natives, their hereditary enemies. They rebelled at any hint of regimentation, for the government went about it maladroitly and brutally. Nicholas himself treated them humanely and without disdain. Very quickly the Cossacks inhabited the seven villages that Nicholas had had constructed, "the grand duke's villages" they were called in the region. *"Babush, babush!"* "Holy Father!" shouted the Cossacks catching sight of him; they would die for him.

Nicholas settled in the place to which he had given his name, Nikolski. He almost never went back to the city, and Nadedja courageously followed him. At the start of the work, they lived in a yurt, a tent made of skins. Then they moved into a house made of clay, quite simple, but surrounded by a magnificent orchard they had planted.

"In Russia," Nicholas explained to Nadedja, "it would take ten years to make our garden productive. Here one year is plenty!"

They were not taking account of the region's traditional plague, the locusts! Both of them suddenly heard a sort of rumbling and nature appeared immobilized, the cattle and the dogs behaving as if mad with anxiety. As the rumbling grew louder, the natives in the village ran in all directions. Some of them reappeared armed and fired shots in the air. Others came out of their houses with saucepans on which they began furious banging. Nicholas observed that the racket organized to block the invasion was absolutely ineffective. The Cossacks themselves hastily dug trenches in an attempt to collect insects in them before setting them on fire with oil. Two days later, the trees once sagging from fruit were only bare branches and the lush pastures gave way to scorched earth. Everything had to be started all over again!

Nevertheless, Nicholas lost none of his spirit, his optimism, his energy; he took up the work again and encouraged the others to do likewise. The abundance came back quickly, so much so that the once cursed region attracted other natives, the Kirghiz who built their own village and farmed their own fields. Also arriving were descendants of the German colonists brought several centuries ago to the area of Orenburg and some of whom had proceeded as far as Tashkent. Lured by the new possibilities of the "starving steppe," they settled here with their bicycles and the Lutheranism that they had never abandoned.

Bicycles in the desert; the region's old people rubbed their eyes thinking it was a mirage! The Cossacks still on horseback, the Kirghiz wearing embroidered caftans in their two-wheeled carts, and the Germans on their bicycles got on well and agreed to offer the most cordial hospitality to visitors. There, where the desert had stretched out as far as the eye could see, populated only by the skeletons of its victims, there henceforth reigned a checkerboard of green, yellow, and white fields where cotton, sorghum, and winter barley grew side by side. Well-maintained roads replaced the dusty tracks, and herds of cows peacefully grazed in the meadows.

Pleased with his unexpected success, Nicholas decided it was high time to take care of Nadedja, his lucky star. They'd already had a son, Artemi, and would soon have a second one, Alexander. This new family had to have a roof a bit sturdier than that of the villa put at their disposal.

He chose a vast plot at the center of the Russian city and there had erected a small palace in an incredibly affected rococo style. In the surrounding park he planted trees and flowering bushes that he had imported at great expense. For the first time, the inhabitants of Tashkent saw oaks! He set up a zoo in a corner of the park. On fine days the cages were taken to its center so that the neighbors could come and admire the wild animals. Another spot in the park was to contain kennels whose residents would accompany the grand duke in his hunting.

He spent without restraint to furnish his palace, ordered some furniture and curtains from Paris, china from Limoges, glasses from Baccarat. He would have loved to get back some of the marvels he had collected before the dramatic turn of events, but his palace in St. Petersburg had been emptied, as he ironically noted. "My dear family, because they love me so, has taken all my collections in memory of me. My mother has even snatched the statue of my mistress that I ordered in Italy."

Fortunately, an ambassador took on the task of enlightening the grand duchess about the identity of the model. "But it's Fanny Lear, the American woman!" The grand duchess didn't stand in the way of sending the sculpture to Tashkent.

When the workers opened the box in his garden, Nicholas gazed a long time at the scandalous nude, then ordered that it be placed in the center of the palace foyer, in the place of honor. Immediately he rushed to the bazaar right in the center of the eastern city and headed straight for the tiniest of shops, run by an Armenian jeweler he knew well. He dug in the display window where some magnificent gems were in a disorderly heap, and spread out the most beautiful ones on the velvet rug, particularly some diamond earrings in the form of hands each holding a cascade of other huge diamonds. Back home, he lovingly adorned the statue of Fanny, attaching a necklace of rubies to her neck, diamond bracelets to her wrists, the fabulous pair of earrings to her ears, and a diadem of emeralds to her marble chignon. "There you are, decked out as you deserve, my little grand duchess!"

In a small bedroom of a modest house in Nice, Fanny wanted to keep the window open to enjoy the air as long as possible. On that evening in May, the day was slowly fading away on the Côte d'Azur. She was stretched out on her chaise longue. On a whim, she wanted to change her dress and replace its somber look for something else, in bright colors. The faithful Joséphine, though protesting this pointless task, had to comply and help her. They talked at length about the past, Joséphine leaning toward her mistress so Fanny would find it less effortful to express herself. Then seeing her eyes close, the maid tiptoed out of the room.

After Brussels, where she had published her memoirs, Fanny had left for Italy. She had resumed her first profession and her original name, for money slipped through her fingers. The first opportunity that came along was a good-looking young man, rich and also noble since he was an illegitimate son of the king Victor Emmanuel. He reminded her a bit of Nicholas. One day the police had shown up at her hotel to notify her of a deportation order, as the king did not wish to see his little bastard involved in a scandal like the one that had shaken the imperial family of Russia! Fanny had gone back to her mother in Philadelphia, and then on to New York.

Eventually, because she felt lonely and tired, she had returned to Paris, her favorite city. She had hoped to get news of Nicholas but hadn't had any, and the papers didn't mention him anymore. She had no more money and had rented a modest room.

She was still beautiful, but no longer young enough to attract a clientele from the upper classes. One day she'd begun coughing up blood. The neighborhood doctor she went to see had not hidden the truth from her. She was suffering from consumption and required healthy foods like eggs and milk, and above all sun. Had she family, friends? She had only a single one, her former maid, now long retired to her native Brittany.

Fanny had written her, and Joséphine hurried to her side. Madam shouldn't have any worries! Madam had once been very generous. No question of salary. As for living in the sun, Joséphine arranged it, with the savings that Madam had made possible for her. The two women had thus left for the Côte d'Azur and settled in Nice.

Slowly, Fanny's room became dark and she felt herself plunging into total darkness. An hour later Joséphine came in, holding in one hand a kerosene lamp and in the other a glass of some opaque liquid. "Madam, it's time to take your medicine. Madam, oh Madam . . ."

Then, to the sound of waves coming in the open window, Joséphine began silently weeping.

Fanny's death was the subject of a few lines in a small number of newspapers, one of which made its way to the fertilized steppes of Central Asia. "On May 7, 1886," read the obituary notice, "Hattie Blackford, known as Fanny Lear, passed away in Nice, in oblivion and poverty."

For Nicholas this news rekindled the past. He saw again with an extraordinary intensity their first meeting at the opera ball, their turbulent passion, their laughter, their travels, their quarrels, their adventures, and their separation. As the memories came to him, he once again imagined St. Petersburg, and he was filled with a great tenderness. With this certainty: Fanny had betrayed him, but she loved only him. And he had cheated on her, but he loved only her, to the point of sacrificing for her his honor and his freedom.

❊   ❊   ❊

From one past to the other, it was now his younger brother Constantine who sent his best regards. The newspapers announced his coming to the region for a military inspection.

After being separated from his family for more than ten years, the prospect of seeing him plunged Nicholas into an extraordinary agitation. His brothers and sisters had permission to send him news, but how could he respond to the younger ones who'd certainly heard only terrible things about him? Nevertheless, the imminent arrival of Constantine made him less shy and gave him the courage to write.

"Dear Kostia, Several times I put off writing you, thinking that very soon I would see you in the flesh. In any case, I'm sure that you didn't think you'd ever get a letter from me. . . ."

And Nicholas went on to describe a peaceful, busy life. He was at the irrigation work site all day long, and in the evening he studied, took notes about future undertakings. Or he read recently published novels. This stay-at-home life would almost certainly have turned him into an old man; fortunately, the first set of projects is finished and "once again I feel young and motivated."

Too long condemned to silence, Nicholas confided in this brother, who perhaps mightn't have understood him, but who had always shown a profound attachment to him. He also talked of having learned about the engagement of Frederika von Hannover, the princess who had refused his hand in marriage. Finally he had the explanation for that incomprehensible attitude. She had always been in love with her father's secretary, and after so many years she finally had the courage to ride roughshod over the taboos to marry him. This scandalous union horrified all the monarchies, and Nicholas couldn't help feeling deeply nostalgic about it. He asked his brother Constantine to send him the princess's most recent photo; probably she was radiant, for, he added, "She has that face that typically becomes even more beautiful with the years."

He added this mysterious sentence. "When I see you, I will tell you of the strong and deep influence that my brief contact with her had on my life." His fate might have been different if Frederika had said yes to him. . . .

He wrote further. "Please let me know if I have any hope of seeing Mama. I want so much to kiss her hands and talk to her sincerely and openly. . . ."

He knew, however, that this was impossible, for he had been denied permission to leave Tashkent, even for a short absence. As for his brother, "Kostia is extremely tenderhearted. When he came here for the military inspection, I decided to go see him. But he, Constantine, because he loves me so, because he is so tenderhearted, could not bring himself to leave his special train to meet up with me. So I didn't see him at all. . . ." A missed opportunity.

Meanwhile, Constantine had married a princess of Saxony Altenburg, a niece of the grand duchess Alexandra. Not at all a beauty, Nicholas had judged by the photos, but a person of merit, a tolerant, open, and courageous soul. They had a son John. He was the first great-grandson of the emperor to be born in this dynasty.

Not wishing to see the grand dukes proliferate, Alexander III decided to limit their number: that title would belong only to the sons and grandsons of the emperors! This reform led the old grand duke Constantine to come out of his retirement. As liberal as he was, he was beside himself at the idea that his grandchildren would not be grand dukes. Another blow from Sasha the Bear, who was fierce in his hatred! The old man bombarded the nitwit with furious letters to oblige him to do away with this family-based reform. Without any success.

At this, the grand duke was the victim of a stroke that left him partially paralyzed and unable to articulate a single word. For Alexandra the moment of revenge had come. Without Constantine being able to protest, she expelled her husband's mistress Kuznetsova and his bastards from their homes in Pavlovsk and Crimea.

In 1892 he was at death's door. He tried to make it understood that he didn't want any visitors around his bed. In response, his wife increased them. A stream of relatives and friends came one after another. Knowing perfectly well that she was countermanding her husband's last wish, the vengeful Alexandra repeated, "It's the price he must pay!" Nevertheless, as the end was approaching, she let down her guard. A loyal aide-de-camp let the former ballerina and her children enter, giving them a chance to see for the last time the man who had so loved them.

His father's death didn't come as a great blow to Nicholas. Although he was close to him politically, it was his mother whom he had loved passionately. His father had shown toward him if not comprehension, at least indulgence, and in the beginning had defended him. But he had sided with the accusers and had done nothing to make his son's fate any easier. Since then he had never sought any contact, and the years had further loosened the ties between them.

On the other hand, Nicholas was counting on his inheritance to enable him to increase his good works. And as nothing came to him, he wrote to the minister of the imperial house a long letter intended for the eyes of the emperor. He recalled that for a long time he had been the heir of Pavlovsk, that his father had considered him such, and for this reason had allowed him to invest considerable sums for improvements to the estate and for its regular maintenance. Nicholas included the receipts, whose total came close to a million rubles. With Pavlovsk having come to his brother Constantine, Nicholas asked what capital would be given him.

After receiving this letter, the minister of the imperial house consulted the grand duchess Alexandra, who replied through the director of her own house. Alexandra didn't think it was possible to give her eldest son the sums he demanded. . . . First, it was not a million, but barely a quarter of that sum, for which, moreover, he had already been reimbursed! On the other hand, the upkeep of Pavlovsk, a national monument, was so costly and brought in so little income that it was impossible to take away the least sum from it. . . . To this letter was appended a note, also from the director of her house, dictated by the grand duchess.

"Very clearly, the doctors at the time had declared that the insanity of his imperial highness required strict supervision of his every action. . . . Now in Turkestan the grand duke had much too much freedom of action. His friends and the choice of the persons around him are no longer under supervision."

In short, the grand duke's presence in Central Asia was leading to a catastrophe that called for measures. They will begin by critically investigating his work on irrigation. The persons in his entourage will gradually be taken away and replaced by "trustworthy servants." The amount and utilization of the sums possessed by him and his wife Nadedja are to be audited and their accounts placed under the control of a guardian. Of course, the undertakings of his imperial highness are excellent, but "they must not be expanded beyond the modest works undertaken by a private company, far from the extent that they already had." These measures were to be applied gradually, "for changes that are too great and too immediate would not be adequate in connection with a mentally ill person."

Nicholas had made a great error in speaking of an inheritance. As a result, on the order of the court, they went after that perfectly legal fortune that belonged to him, they drove out the few friends that this disgraced person had been able to keep in order to create a vacuum around him, they attacked the lone occupation that he had at heart without hesitating to destroy the admirable work he was accomplishing. All this with all the sanctimonious and syrupy hypocrisy of which the era was capable.

17

Not long after this, Alexander III died prematurely, indirectly a victim of the terrorists he had ruthlessly pursued. The terrorists had managed to derail the imperial train. The tsar, seeing the roof of the coach where his family was sitting start to cave in, had held it up with his arms and, thanks to his Herculean strength, had succeeded in keeping it from crushing his wife and children. But this left him with a lumbar weakness that turned into kidney disease. He died just after turning fifty.

Nicholas had always known that he could expect nothing from him, particularly not an easing of his fate. But it was very different with the new emperor, his cousin Nicholas II. When Nicholas had been exiled, his cousin was only six. Everyone praised his

sweetness, goodness, and generosity. Prompted by the best of intentions, this young man sincerely wanted the best for Russia and
the Russians.

Nicholas began by throwing a sounding line: his second son,
Alexander, had recently fallen ill and could be operated on only in
St. Petersburg. So Nicholas wrote to the new emperor to ask for
permission to send his son there, and he received it. He entrusted
the child to a doctor and gave him a letter for his brother Constantine,
who welcomed the child. Encouraged by this good omen, Nicholas
wrote the tsar once again asking him to grant his wife Nadedja and
their two sons an aristocratic patronymic. Nicholas II hastened
to please him and by ukase decreed that Nicholas's family would
henceforth bear the magnificent name of Iskander, which called to
mind Alexander the Great.

After this success Nicholas began to have hope. He had so
often had the leisure to mull over the events of his past that he had
succeeded in making the guilt disappear. So he contemplated seeing his exile come to an end and starting his life again from scratch.
"I constantly think of you all," he wrote his brother Constantine.
"More and more I regret not having the happiness of seeing my
mother and you after such a long separation." He referred increasingly often to the leniency that Nicholas II could show in his favor.
He was unaware of the pitiless instructions that his mother had
spelled out at court after the story of the inheritance. He was unaware just as much that the gentle, shy, and weak Nicholas II had
decided to follow step-by-step his father's policy in all its severity
and that, disappointing from the outset a great part of his people,
he didn't grant any pardons to those who had hoped for one.

Nicholas was to remain stuck in Central Asia!

A cholera epidemic came to distract him from his glum thoughts.
This endemic illness regularly struck the region, and this time it
spread with stunning speed, particularly in the poorest neighbor-

hoods, those of the Muslim old town. The Russian authorities required the whole population to undergo a medical checkup. The Muslims rebelled: impossible for the Russian doctors to examine their wives! Then these same authorities decided to bury the dead without a ceremony in order to prevent contagion. The natives protested and went on burying their dead by night as they had done in the past. Those who violated the sanitary measures were arrested. Then there was a revolt.

In actual fact, the revolt was several years in the hatching. The natives were finding it harder and harder to put up with the Russian presence. Then, helped along by the cholera, rioting broke out in Tashkent. The crowd seized the city commander, pummeled him, and manhandled the head Muslim of the old town, who was accused of collaborating with the Russian occupier. The governor-general Vrevski ordered the arrest of the most important merchants and the city's religious chiefs. Tashkent was sinking into fear.

Nicholas knew that the natives wouldn't lay a finger on him; he'd shown that he considered them his equals and not members of an inferior race only good for being subjugated. To combat the epidemic he had doctors come from St. Petersburg and turned part of his palace into a hospital. He and Nadedja made sacrifices without counting the cost, making daily visits to the ill, seeing to their comfort, and helping the exhausted nurses. Terrified by the riot, the Russians shut themselves up in their homes. Nicholas kept his great doors open. That is how he welcomed the natives injured in the riots and looked after them, just like the ones ill with cholera.

But his old demons had been awakened. On arriving in Tashkent, he thought he was fulfilling his dream. But there, memories of his former life came flooding back. His family, the court, St. Petersburg were infusing temptations in him he thought he had forgotten. Disappointment and bitterness plunged him into the alcohol from which Fanny had once rescued him. In their reports the specialists who looked after him spoke of a "real obsession" for alcoholic drinks. That he got drunk and turned violent . . .

He had already drunk a lot before dinner, but he was not staggering and walked straight into the dining room. The only things that betrayed his state were his flushed complexion and feverish eyes. He sat down at the head of the table. Nadedja arrived in turn. He rose laboriously from his chair and greeted her respectfully. She sat next to him with their two sons. The others—the doctors, the officers who saw after his safety—took seats a little distance away. He barely touched the dishes but constantly refilled his glasses of wine and vodka. To fill in the silences that were becoming increasingly awkward, Nadedja uttered a few commonplaces. Suddenly he pounded his fist on the table so hard that the plates and glasses clinked. "But you talk only nonsense!"

And immediately he hurled insults at her. Gently, without raising her voice, she tried to protest. Then, with the back of his hand, he hit her. Everyone sat there, transfixed, and Nicholas started shouting. "It's because of you that I'm an outcast from my family, it's because I married you . . ."

He didn't finish his sentence and fell into a morose reverie. Nadedja rose with dignity, took the hands of Artemi and Alexander, and left the dining room. Nicholas didn't have the strength to get up.

The sun had just risen and its oblique rays were setting fire to the plain. Having risen very early, the party was already on horseback. Nicholas was on his favorite brown stallion, Karaghese. Following him were Boris, his hunting master, and a Kirghiz who was holding a reserve horse bearing provisions, a bag of oats, and bunches of fresh alfalfa. Each horseman had two bags hanging from the sides of his saddle that contained rice, wheat, vegetables, and biscuits. They knew the Cossacks would offer them their hospitality, that their houses were always open to visitors and particularly to their benefactor. Even so, they didn't want to take undue advantage of it.

Loaded down as they were, they took their time to go across the plain, enjoying the morning coolness. Arriving at the base of the mountain, they took a stony path and entered into a narrow valley that the rays of the sun had yet to reach. The slope became steeper. The sun caught up with them, forcing them to blink. In front of them they heard the rumbling of a torrent whose waters hurtled down the slopes between huge rocks.

The horsemen came out onto a rather vast plateau. Suddenly their mounts halted, pawing the ground, pricking up their ears. Before them, in the middle of the road, a horse skeleton was the prey of foxes, crows, and vultures that scattered at the sight of them. All three of the riders saw at the same instant a vague mass move in the tall grass. A large brown bear stood up. He spotted them and, instead of running away as other members of his species would have done, he sat down. Then he got up again and approached, waddling and emitting friendly growls.

Boris, the head of the hunt, seized his rifle and aimed it at the beast.

"Stop! Don't you see he has a collar around his neck?" shouted Nicholas. "This must be a tame bear."

Nicholas threw it some lumps of sugar that he always carried. The bear skillfully caught them and began crunching them with great pleasure. To express his thanks, he showed the tricks he knew: he stretched out on the ground and rolled around with delight, walked on his front paws, and, having finished his act, he "passed the hat."

Once again Nicholas threw him some candy. At that moment a strikingly beautiful teenage girl emerged from behind a bush. Her features still had something of the child about them, but her body was already that of a woman. Her dark, mistrustful eyes turned to the bear. She called, and the animal immediately obeyed and came to her side, both of them disappearing in the shade of the thickets.

The scene had been so quick that the three men wondered if they hadn't seen an apparition.

By midafternoon, the hunt over, Nicholas and his companions rejoined his Cossack friends in one of the villages he had had built for them. He was welcomed with their customary warmth. They sat at the table. Nicholas was indeed among friends, but he sensed they were worried. The head of the village waited to be asked several times before disclosing the reason.

A marriage had been arranged between two families. At the last minute the woman's family wanted to cheat the future husband's family and give them a less sizable dowry than they had promised. To break one's word this way was a deadly sin for the Cossacks! The fiancé's family didn't want the marriage anymore.

For the woman's family it was a dishonor, and for the fiancée herself it meant the absolute impossibility of finding another husband. The head of the village implored Nicholas to arbitrate the affair. Everyone had eaten and drunk considerably when the members of the two parties were summoned to appear. The door was opened and, rather roughly pushed by her parents, the fiancée appeared.

Nicholas instantly recognized the keeper of the tame bear. She was named Daria Eliseievna Tchassvitine. She was only sixteen and didn't look at all frightened. While the two parties yelled and heaped insults on each other, she stood planted in front of him staring at him with a certain insolence. Nicholas searched her face, her shapely figure, and let himself be impregnated by the adolescent's sensuality. He wanted to take her, that very minute, in front of everyone. . . . In a hoarse voice he ordered that she be brought to him the next day in his palace so that he could have a chance to be better informed about the affair.

"I won't come without Nicholas!" Daria expressed herself loudly.

"But who's Nicholas? A fiancé?"

"No, it's the bear."

"The more Nicholases, the merrier! She may bring the bear," ordered the grand duke.

The next day, Nicholas, hidden behind his window, waited impatiently and saw them cross the square. The father, long and tapering white mustaches, astrakhan hat, silver dagger through his belt, rode a magnificent black horse. The daughter, wrapped in her caftan and veils, appeared to be as expert a rider as her father. Placidly seated in a cart, the bear followed her. Father and daughter were immediately shown into Nicholas's office. Nicholas proffered a man's purse. "This is for the inconvenience to you. I shall have your daughter taken back."

The father weighed the purse in his hands and withdrew. Nicholas approached Daria, slowly removed her veils, her caftan. Then, one after another, he took away all her clothes. The light of the dying day entering through the window lit up the body of the teenager, who was now wearing only a thick necklace of gold coins and red leather ankle boots embroidered with gold. Without a word being uttered, with the greatest gentleness, Nicholas led her to the sofa.

That night the illiterate but diabolically voluptuous little Cossack Daria didn't leave the palace of the grand duke Nicholas. Not for the next few nights, either. As for the bear, he was housed in a large cage and immediately became the main attraction in the palace's private zoo.

The treatment Nicholas was made to suffer by his family and the court freed him from the obligation to maintain propriety and moderation. He no longer had to contain himself. Far from hiding Daria, he showed her off in his open carriage through the city's most crowded streets, brought her into his box at the theater, had a pretty villa built for her in the outskirts of the city. He expressed the loudest joy when she became pregnant. And soon he divided his day between his two families. During the day he remained with Nadedja and their two sons, took care of his business, and saw to a thousand affairs. In the evening he went to Daria's villa. Nadedja submitted without opening her mouth. It wasn't in her nature to complain.

She was indeed the only one not to talk of her husband's escapades, for the whole town did so for her, with the customary exaggerations and inventions that were regularly collected by the secret police and that sprinkled the reports sent to St. Petersburg. Since Nicholas had mistreated Nadedja in front of witnesses, they didn't fail to embroider on the subject. . . .

"Recently his imperial highness tried to push Mrs. Nadedja Alexandrovna von Dreyer into the arms of Plovtzev, a rich merchant of the city. His imperial highness had intended to surprise the lovers and demand a large sum of money from the guilty party. After Mrs. Nadedja Alexandrovna von Dreyer refused, the grand duke made increasingly frightful threats against her, to the point that Mrs. von Dreyer went to find his excellence, the governor-general of Turkestan, to ask for his aid and protection. . . ."

From the office of the minister of the imperial court in St. Petersburg the report flew to that of the grand duchess Alexandra, who had it read to her by her cousin, the prince of Saxony Altenburg, who was visiting Russia and who repeated his horrifying story to all his relatives.

One report followed another, all with the names of women. For Nadedja and the young Cossack Daria were not enough for Nicholas. The secret police cited Mrs. Sesjarghina, the wife of an unpretentious member of the administration "whom his highness met at the Military Club . . . ," a brief affair with Mrs. Nina

Ivanovna Stakoff, the wife of an archaeologist, was followed by the birth of a son. . . . In any event, his imperial highness wasn't a racist since there was a veritable harem of native women whom he kept in his palace!

After informing the family, the minister of the imperial court judged that the grand duke was going too far and sent the governor-general of Turkestan a request for an explanation. "A bedtime story!" replied Vrevski. The court, but especially Nicholas's royal family, was annoyed at reading this dismissal. Vrevski was easily taken in! He was displaying the guiltiest laxity. He must be replaced and a man much firmer and less gullible must be named instead. The grand duchess demanded it. . . . In the prevailing opinion, Nicholas was just a dangerous sex maniac capable of doing anything to satisfy his impulses. And, following the well-tested recipe, a new team of psychiatrists was dispatched to Tashkent.

Without a break these men subjected the patient to examinations, interrogations, treatments, and instructions, and they concluded, "We firmly deny the effects on the imperial highness's brain of a case of syphilis contracted more than twenty years ago. On the other hand, the symptoms of a psychological illness remain highly significant. To put an end to the disorderly behavior recorded in the reports, his imperial highness's energy must be channeled and to do this we have concluded that the best way would be to encourage him to pursue his work on irrigation. . . ."

The good practitioners were unaware that the grand duchess and the court had sent precise instructions to slow down and even halt this work. They were just as unaware of the jealousies that Nicholas's successes had given rise to. The imperial government and the local administration were both furious for not having thought before he did of fertilizing the "starving steppe." So they had decided to follow his example. This time a much larger area would be fertilized!

They sent engineers to get training abroad; they wrote whole volumes of plans that came and went between St. Petersburg and Tashkent; as an appetizer, they leveled whole mountains; on preparations alone they spent ten times more than Nicholas had spent to complete his work! Then, slowly, the governmental project that was to compete with his own drowned in the bottomless depths of the imperial administration.

Nicholas made great fun of the psychiatrists' recommendations, the obstacles raised by his family, and the jealousies of the administration. Without asking anything of anyone, he undertook a second series of works, much larger than the first one. Enormous dams collected water from the rivers and cataracts. The new canal he had dug was over sixty miles long; he gave it his grandfather's name, Nicholas I. He had villages for the colonists spring up like mushrooms, and hundreds of thousands of acres were converted to agriculture and animal rearing. Nicholas planned these works so judiciously and carried them out so carefully that they have never been surpassed; their benefit is felt up to the present day, and he himself is rightly considered the principal driving force in the economic development of Uzbekistan.

At the same time, on the land that he had reclaimed from the desert, he kept two vast properties for himself, the Golden Horde and the Iskander. Then he introduced the cultivation of American cotton and built factories for processing it on the spot. These developments yielded enormous sums for him. More than a million rubles of income from just one of these properties!

Since the money for his work had been cut off, he earned money himself. He went into business. He bought and resold plots of land and houses. Soon real estate speculation had no secrets from him. As a precaution he put many of his possessions in the name of Daria the Cossack. He also opened a bakery whose specialty was the rolls favored by the inhabitants of St. Petersburg! Immediately, the city's Sanitary Commission decreed that this commodity didn't conform to manufacturing standards. An order came to close the bakery. Nicholas complied and the next day opened a new shop exactly facing the one just closed. "My bakery," he proclaimed, "is like the Phoenix, it's reborn from its ashes!"

He was also interested in the public good and paved the streets of Tashkent at his own expense. He had a club built, and then a theater. He created the city's first cinema, which he called the Khiva. An outdoor cinema, the Summer Khiva, was to follow. Much more discreetly, he was the backer of a brothel, the Old Woman, which was set up on Samarkand Street. Nor did he forget the poor people, and bestowed considerable sums on charity organizations that he had founded and that he personally looked after.

His prestige was growing along with his popularity. Then, since that popularity proved unassailable, Nicholas was surrounded with increased surveillance. The officers charged with his so-called security were joined by a horde of secret police agents in civilian clothes who followed him everywhere, even in his home. The slightest gestures, the slightest words were the subjects of enormous reports sent to the capital. Oppressed with his constant, silent surveillance, he came to suspect everyone. He reacted with his usual method, provocation.

In those final years of the century, some ten young people freshly graduated from the School of Administration in St. Petersburg were appointed to a post in Tashkent, their first job. The journey by train to Orenburg was fairly comfortable, but next the interminable trip by road, in the heat and dust, seemed to them indeed tough going. They already missed the Russian heartland but, they reasoned, Tashkent was the first rung of that ladder that everyone dreams of climbing to the top.

Once at their destination they were put up with families, and what they discovered surprised them. Expecting the Middle Ages, they found a standard of comfort more or less equivalent to what they'd left behind! Before receiving their posting they took a tour of the city conducted by a very old official who, never being promoted, had been fossilizing for decades. Each morning he fetched the young graduates to take them exploring. On the main street they were dumbfounded to see the stores, the theaters, and other public places.

"To whom does this brand-new theater belong, sir?"

"To him whose name must not be uttered. . . ."

"And this candy store that's so well stocked?"

"The same person."

"And this nice restaurant?"

"To the same person, but don't repeat it!"

"And this hotel? Does it belong to him, too?"

"You've said it . . ."

"So he owns the whole city!"

"Shut up, there are things it's better not to say here."

They arrived in front of the palace of the governor-general of Turkestan, a vast white barn of a place with colonnades, as boring as the countless other buildings constructed by the administration throughout the empire. But what did these young people see that made them rub their eyes that way? Some twenty young women entirely naked, wearing only huge hats surmounted by a mass of flowers. Streetwalkers? Certainly not; they didn't have that look about them. Peasants rather. But what were they doing in that getup right under the governor-general's windows? The old official told them, speaking in a lowered tone.

"It's him. He is furious about the new fashion in large hats coming from the West. He finds them unbecoming. So from one of the villages he had built he summoned these women who are devoted to him body and soul, and had them parade to express his displeasure. . . ."

Suddenly the attention of the curious onlookers was drawn away from the peasant women clothed like Eve. The young graduates felt a tremor in the crowd on this sunny late morning along the shopping street, the Novoi Prospekt. A barouche approached at high speed.

"It's him!" exclaimed the old official.

A sparkling carriage approached at high speed drawn by four magnificent horses and followed by a pack of perfectly trained pedigreed dogs. The livery of the coach driver and the grooms, the harnesses, and the shirt of the man sitting in the rear seat were all red.

The young graduates had eyes only for "the one whose name is not to be uttered." To them he seemed enormously tall and very thin. The extraordinarily handsome face had kept all its youthfulness despite the beginning of baldness. He responded to the greetings with inimitable grace. A woman was seated next to him, very straight and very dignified, modestly but elegantly dressed. Facing the couple, two boys were seated. One was almost an adolescent, the other still a child. The coach had already passed the young graduates, who ignored the order of the old official and long followed it with their eyes.

They saw the coach again that very evening. Despite his age, their guide was so full of energy that theirs eventually flagged. Exhausted, they were on the point of separating to go back to their quarters when, once again, they saw the carriage arrive right in front of them. "He whose name must not be uttered" was recognizable from a distance by his scarlet shirt. Kind and magnificent, he went on greeting well-wishers like a debonair sovereign. But, oh surprise! Another woman was seated next to him, much younger than the one in the morning, a wild beauty, dazzling, laughing, dressed in many-colored silks and covered with glittering diamonds. Facing the couple were three little and very young children.

"He has two families," explained the old official. "This morning it was his official family, the good Nadedja Alexandrova, may God bless and protect her! That, now, is his whore of a Cossack with her bastards. . . ."

The young graduates separated and went home. They avidly questioned their landlords and landladies. The men were sometimes reticent about answering, but the women, and even more the native servants, showed no hesitation in speaking. And to the young graduates there appeared a very different image from that drawn by the old official.

Everyone adored him. He was so generous, so simple! He was always ready to come to people's aid, but all the same, his private life, his two families, his mistresses, his bastards . . . The men took on an admiring look, the women, dreamy, smiled. He was not merely a king for modern times, he was a sultan in the old tales, brave and gallant, throwing gold coins to the crowd and honoring all the women.

The next day the old official abruptly announced that they were invited by the grand duke to dinner that very evening. The young graduates found it hard to believe in an honor like this, but their mentor humbled their vanity. "He's bored . . . so he invites all the newcomers. He spotted you yesterday in the street during his ride."

The young graduates were not listening to him; they had only one idea in mind, that they were going to meet the fabulous sultan of Turkestan. But before the party they had to attend a gathering of learned civil servants, who overwhelmed them with advice.

"Treat your host with respect, but remember he is not considered a member of the imperial family. Take his words with the greatest caution. Don't forget that he's mentally ill! Hold on to his every word, if need be write it on your cuffs and report it to us exactly."

Surprised by this deliberate tactic of intimidation, anxious at the idea of meeting this character who was both fawned upon and despised, they arrived at Nicholas's palace well ahead of time. They went through a rococo iron gate and entered an enchanting park. The scent of roses was so powerful they were almost intoxicated by it. They climbed the marble steps guarded by two stone lions and entered a very large entrance hall. They had eyes only for the statue adorning the center of the room, a nude woman of extraordinary beauty in polished white marble covered with jewels.

Footmen liveried entirely in red from collar to shoes led them through several sitting rooms. Mouths open, they admired right and left the heavily framed paintings from the Italian and Flemish schools, the opulent hangings, the French furniture of marquetry and bronze that seemed to them of tremendous value.

Shown into a huge library stuffed to the ceiling with books and filled with the odor of cigars, they were asked to wait.

A door opened, a curtain of red velvet parted, and he was before them. He was even taller than it had seemed, his face much more youthful, with that penetrating gaze, that inviting smile. He was in civilian clothes, dressed entirely in black. He came up to them and held out his hand to each one. Some of them bowed deeply in an overdone greeting, others, reviving the old custom, reached for the hand to kiss it.

"No, no, we're here as friends, no salute, no hand-kissing, please!"

At the table the young graduates stuffed themselves from dishes exquisitely prepared by the French chef; drank more than they were accustomed to of the wines, which were also French; and admired the Sèvres china, the Baccarat glasses, and the English silverware marked with the monogram NK surmounted by the imperial crown. The duke's savoir faire and the waves of champagne took away their shyness.

Nicholas questioned them at length about their families, their studies, and gradually about their aspirations and opinions.

"Have you read this book?" he asked, laying a volume on the table.

The young graduates were startled; it was Kropotkin's *Memoirs of a Revolutionist*! Although they had shown themselves to be model students, some of them had inquired as discreetly as possible about liberalism and had attended cells and lodges where this book was discussed. Its author had been arrested, but he managed to flee Russia and find refuge in Switzerland, where he published an anarchist magazine. Of course, his book was banned throughout the empire, on the penalty of imprisonment.

"Imagine, I knew the author a long time ago when he had the title prince and was a page at court."

And the dinner went on, which soon degenerated into a drinking binge. At a signal from Nicholas, the footmen withdrew. He recommended his guests serve themselves. He himself increased the libations and banged his glass on the table so heartily it broke.

"Tell me frankly. Wouldn't I be better on the imperial throne than Nicholas II, who with his two tiny feet tries to put on the great boots of our ancestors?"

The young graduates froze in silence, both horrified and thrilled by such a sacrilege. Out of his pocket Nicholas took two revolvers that he threw on the table.

"If you don't answer me, I'll use them. Is it yes or no. Can I legitimately claim the throne?"

A few murmurs were heard, some shy "yeses" mixed with "I don't knows."

Nicholas rose and grasped a bottle of champagne. "Stronger or I'll break this over your head!" He looked threatening, crazy. The young graduates were terrified. At their expression, Nicholas burst out laughing. He took his chair and sat down again.

"Well, finish your drinking and go home to bed. I suppose you have to get up early tomorrow."

He saw them out himself, had them go through the sleeping palace, and closed the door after them.

The young people were still too shocked to discuss the evening. They were in a hurry to leave, but at the same time each in the secrecy of his soul had become an unreserved supporter of the great sultan of Turkestan. Which didn't prevent them the next day from repeating to their superiors what their host had said, word for word. And their superiors hastily filled out page after page: his imperial highness claims he is a pretender to the throne. His imperial highness is seeking supporters with the intention of overthrowing his majesty and taking his place.

18

"*I am very touched* by your prayers, dear Mama, you are very good to ask God to grant your dear Nicholas good health and wish him to begin his second fifty years under the best of conditions."

With the coming of the twentieth century, Nicholas had his fiftieth birthday, and for the first time since his arrest twenty-six years before, his mother showed him some tenderness and sent him her best wishes. Despite this gesture, Nicholas guessed that she bore him a grudge. So he added, "It is impossible to reproach me for what I don't deserve. I have always tried to behave well, in spite of humiliations. . . ."

Alas, his provoking words during the dinner given for the young graduates unleashed new anger. On orders from higher up, his irrigation project was halted. And he was notified of a prohibition against undertaking others. This time it was impossible to disregard the commands; he was indeed condemned to idleness. Moreover, he ended up alone. The two sons he had had by Nadedja, Artemi and Alexander, had been authorized, at his request, to pursue their studies in St. Petersburg, a pretext for their mother to go increasingly often to the capital. There, at least she could forget his boorishness and was no longer condemned to seeing her rival the Cossack enthroned next to him every evening! What she didn't know was that Nicholas was in the process of breaking away from his "second wife." He was fifty, he was discouraged, and he felt he had wasted his life.

And at this beginning of 1900, the special unit of the police, otherwise known as the spies assigned to keep the grand duke under surveillance, arrested a country priest. They interrogated him, worked him over with methods that had earned them their reputation, and managed to wring the following deposition from him.

"My name is Alexis Suridof. I am a priest in the village of Kaufmanovsky in the Tashkent area. I am thirty years old. On 27 or 28 February, I was visited by a stranger, a very tall man in the service of his imperial highness, who said to me with no explanation that they were waiting for my visit at the palace.

"Excuse me, I made a mistake. . . . I didn't receive this visit February 28 but rather two or three days earlier. The 28th, then, I went on horseback to Tashkent.

"In a corner of the palace, the same servant was waiting for me. He had me enter and accompanied me to the second floor. There were many icons on the walls. His imperial highness was alone. He asked me to take a seat, then began by telling me that for years he had not been living with his wife and that he wanted to bring happiness to a young woman named Valeria Shmelinskaia. . . .

"It was time for dinner. His imperial highness had cognac served and also mutton. Next, he asked me if I could consecrate his marriage to Valeria. I refused, arguing that I could not conduct such a sacrament without the permission of the tsar.

"Then he asked if I could at least bless them. . . . I accepted. He went to fetch Miss Valeria Shmelinskaia, who came in with her mother. The rings were ready. I told his imperial highness and his fiancée that they could exchange them and I would bless them by saying 'God bless you.' I read no prayer during this ceremony.

"A week after this engagement, it was a Saturday, I received in the village a visit by a certain Paul Petrovitch Melinovski. He attempted to convince me to consecrate the marriage of his imperial highness. If I accepted, he promised me in the name of the grand duke to get a much larger parish for me. Then he invited me to share his meal and, to speak frankly, I became quite intoxicated.

"Two days later, a Monday, I went once again to the city, in the evening. I met Mr. Melinovski and we entered the palace by the main door. His imperial highness led us through the winter garden to a room apart where a table had been prepared. Waiting for us there were Miss Shmelinskaia, dressed all in white, and her mother.

"I hadn't taken anything with me, no vestments, no nuptial crowns, no cross. His imperial highness looked annoyed, and I immediately wrote a note to a colleague, Father Peter, asking him to send me this and that religious object, explaining that it was a matter of helping a dying man. Mr. Melinovski went himself to Father Peter, and a short time later returned with the items asked for. He laid them on the table that was to serve as an altar, I put on the vestments, we lit the candles, and I began the ceremony.

"I recited the sacramental prayers. I took the couple's hands in mine and had them go round the altar three times. I gave them communion in the chalice. After the ceremony, champagne was served and we drank the couple's health. Then, Mrs. Shmelinskaia, Mr. Melinovski, and I left. Valeria remained with the grand duke in the palace.

"Thinking about what I had done, I did not feel good. The principal act of marriage consists in those three walks the bride and groom make around the table wearing the nuptial crowns. Now we didn't have any crown and so I cannot affirm that I consecrated the marriage in a canonical way. I conducted this ceremony like a play to please his imperial highness, whose request I couldn't refuse.

"I must also confess that, before the aforementioned ceremony, Mr. Melinovski had asked me to follow him to another room where he gave me several glasses of cognac, with the result that my head wasn't very clear. In addition, I had noticed that his imperial highness threatened me by placing two loaded revolvers on the altar. When was the act of marriage signed? I don't remember very well, and I can't be sure that I put my signature on any document whatever. I think that I was so drunk at the moment that I don't remember anything."

Valeria Shmelinskaia was a high school student of fifteen. Her father, a recognized alcoholic, had abandoned his wife and children. Her mother was the daughter of a Jewish school principal in Minsk. Living in a modest apartment outside of Tashkent, she raised her three daughters all by herself. Despite her youthfulness, Valeria, the eldest of them, was already known to be an accomplished beauty. Blond, with large blue eyes lighting up a mischievous face, a body in its prime with springlike grace, she bore some resemblance to Fanny Lear . . . Having noticed her in the street, Nicholas immediately sent a reliable man to her mother to get her permission, in return for hard cash, to meet her daughter in private.

The good priest didn't mention that he had been promised thirty thousand rubles. The bride herself received a note for one hundred thousand rubles that she could cash on reaching her majority. The haggling had been hard with the mother; she asked for a lot. They had compromised on fifty thousand rubles for her.

Well before the secret police, the whole city was in the know and buzzed with rumors. The most excited were obviously the bride's classmates, and these innocent girls spread the sauciest stories. Apparently the grand duke was equally in love with a sister of Valeria's and couldn't decide which of them he wanted to marry. So he demanded to see them both naked and Mrs. Shmelinskaia agreed to show off her two daughters in the simplest possible trappings!

Having chosen Valeria, the grand duke required that she no longer go to school. The mother protested. The grand duke himself had had to write a letter to the school's principal. He also wanted Valeria's brother to quit school because he had been a witness at the marriage. Faced with the hubbub unleashed by this affair, the Shmelinskaia tribe took things philosophically, repeating, "He's a grand duke and he promised us fifty thousand rubles!" As for Nicholas, he was overwhelmed with happiness. No more problem with being in his fifties. Valeria filled all his days and all his nights; he was in love like a kid.

At the Winter Palace the emperor Nicholas II was holding an exceptional family council in the presence of the minister of the imperial court, Baron Frederiks, and of the minister of the interior. It was quite unlike that time when Alexander III had made everyone keep silent with his powerful voice and his fist banging on the table. Henceforth, among the brothers of the late emperor, whoever shouted loudest imposed his will on their weak nephew, the tsar. Uncle Vladimir with the immense sideburns, Uncle Sergei thin as a rail, Uncle Alexei, fat and high-strung—all of them demanded an exemplary punishment for their cousin.

"Never has our family had such a scandal! Bigamy!"

It was also very unlike the time when Nicholas's father, the grand duke Constantine, with his stentorian voice and obscene vocabulary, blocked his opponents. His second son, Constantine

Konstantinovich, was an artist, a poet . . . He didn't hold his own in the face of his raging cousins, and his protests were not listened to.

"But he's not a bigamist, since the family itself obtained the annulment of his marriage."

"That's been forgotten! Since then, in the eyes of the world he's been the husband of Nadedja von Dreyer."

Shyly, Nicholas II proposed sending a trusted personality to take a look at the situation on the spot. That would prove to be Admiral Koznakov, assigned by grand duke Vladimir. Constantine managed to persuade his cousins and nephews to add to the admiral at least two psychiatrists renowned for their tolerance, the professors Harding and Rosebush.

The committee took eleven days to reach Tashkent. Admiral Koznakov moved in with the governor-general and began conducting his inquiry by questioning the local authorities without letup, also members of the secret police, the guards, and the doctors.

The two psychiatrists preferred to meet the "patient" first, so they went to Nicholas's palace. Both of them were struck not only by the luxury of the residence that had so impressed the young graduates, but by the artistic quality of the furniture, the art objects, the paintings, and the sculptures. In the red living room they came to a halt before an extraordinary series of porcelains from China, and then in the gallery before some Roman antiquities. So they were struck by the contrast between the value of the collections and the setting where the "patient" chose to receive them.

The latter was in a small bedroom without furniture, a low ceiling, situated under the palace's attic. Nor was there a bed, and the psychiatrists found his imperial highness stretched out on a narrow mattress right on the floor. As he himself informed them, he spent most of his days there. Besides, he hadn't gone to the trouble to get dressed and received them wearing only his underwear. Next to

the mattress, cigarette butts and burnt matches were strewn on the
floor. Half-full glasses were lying about here and there around a
large bottle of cognac. They didn't know where to put their feet,
for eight dogs lived there with their master and stayed there most
of the time stretched out next to him.

The psychiatrists noticed that the grand duke had had his
head, chest, arms, and legs shaved. To their surprise, Nicholas explained that this was a custom acquired in the steppe, as hair on
the body becomes matted with dust. Why did his imperial highness remain stretched out on his mattress most of the time without doing anything?

"Quite simply, gentlemen, because I've been henceforth forbidden to get on with my irrigation work."

The psychiatrists decided that, before coming to a decision,
they would observe the grand duke in his spare time. They asked
for permission to come back.

The next day they were shown into the library. They found
Nicholas freshly shaved, sweet-smelling, elegantly dressed in a red
shirt and boots, with black pants. Playing the fine gentleman, he
offered them fruit, tea, wine, he himself being content with a few
caraway cookies and two or three glasses of champagne. In the
course of numerous interviews they were to have with him, the psychiatrists were to see him sometimes replace the champagne with
tea laced with rum. "We must emphasize that we have never seen
the grand duke drunk. Or very rarely when the evening dragged
on, he tended to drink a little too much and the next day to excuse
himself sending someone to say that he could not receive us because
he was not feeling well."

Nicholas sometimes received them as a tramp in his hovel,
sometimes as a grand duke in his library. The psychiatrists began
by having him recall the most various subjects. On the geography
and history of Turkestan, Russian domestic politics, and the inter-

national situation he demonstrated extraordinary knowledge and expressed opinions of dazzling intelligence.

As for his hobbyhorse, irrigation, the psychiatrists noticed that he was certainly the greatest expert on the topic in the whole empire: particularly on the irrigation of Central Asia, he was ten times better informed than all the ministers of agriculture! Nicholas took them to areas he had made fertile, the villages he had created, and the two psychiatrists pointed out in their reports: "Working and living in the steppe, his imperial highness has gotten very close to the workers, immigrants, and in general the most simple of peoples. He has established privileged links with them. He knows how to treat them, he has built them houses, given them their lands. They have nicknamed him 'the tsar of the starving steppe' and he is extremely popular with them."

Spending as much time as possible with their "patient," they noted a certain regularity in the irregularity of his life. Late in the evening the grand duke left his palace to go look for Valeria Shmelinskaia, whom he kept in his hovel until morning. In the meantime, Nadedja Alexandrovna von Dreyer Iskander had returned from St. Petersburg; she lived in the palace but saw her "husband" only after dinner. Finally there was also Daria Eliseievna, whom Nicholas customarily invited in the afternoon for a brief visit.

The psychiatrists plucked up the courage to question Nicholas about Valeria and he answered them straight out. "There is nothing bad about having an affair with a new woman. I inherited this quality." Nicholas gave a faint smile, his most charming—"Or rather I inherited this problem from my ancestors. It has been a widespread practice for centuries among the princes of the whole world."

"But, imperial highness, there is Nadedja Alexandrovna . . ."

"Obviously she doesn't want to be the old wife when there is a young one in the role!"

"Wouldn't the best thing be for Nadedja Alexandrova to leave Tashkent and move to another town?"

"Actually, why not help me leave with Nadedja and go abroad for a long trip, to France, to Egypt, possibly to America? I would be far away from here, time for the rumors and agitation to die down, and later I would be delighted to come back to Tashkent."

"Your imperial highness could take advantage of it to study new systems of irrigation. They say much good of the ones the Americans have perfected."

Nicholas sensed the trap and answered in an irrevocable tone, "I would like very much to go abroad with Nadedja, but Valeria must not be deported from Tashkent for any reason. She's here, and she must stay here until she dies."

As the days went by, the two psychiatrists felt a growing liking for Nicholas, whom they ended up, despite his eccentricities, not finding as crazy as all that. Thus they were torn between the need to take care of their future (the powers want Nicholas to be insane, so he must be) and their desire to avoid excessively cruel measures with a man who did not deserve them.

Their conclusion betrays this ambiguity. "His imperial highness is affected by a permanent mental insanity that can be likened to a case of madness. Because of this illness, the grand duke cannot enjoy total freedom. However, it is preferable for him to continue living in Turkestan and he should be allowed to carry on his work on irrigation."

That was forgetting the head of the mission, Admiral Koznakov, who, without taking the trouble to listen to Nicholas, built up a very different opinion. He had already had the priest fired who, between a bottle of cognac and two revolvers, gave the nuptial blessing. And at dawn one morning, at his instructions, the secret police, profiting from the fact that Valeria hadn't spent the night at Nicholas's palace, came to arrest her at her mother's where she lived. They gave her barely enough time to get dressed and pick up some things before putting her under guard on a train. She was sent off to Tbilisi in Georgia, with an absolute ban on setting foot again in Tashkent.

Then Koznakov named a new guard, or jailer it would be more appropriate to say, for Nicholas, General Gestov, whom he chose for his "firmness." The latter got things off to a good start. He bribed half of Nicholas's servants to spy on him, had him trailed in the streets by two soldiers, and forbade him to leave Tashkent.

"I feel like a circus animal that people are allowed to poke fun at," concluded Nicholas, who invented a new way of counterattacking. He wrote to the emperor Nicholas II and asked him to relieve him of the title grand duke. He no longer wished to belong to the imperial family, and thus would be able to live as a simple citizen and do what he wanted. Nicholas II didn't take the trouble to reply.

As a last resort he wrote to his brother Constantine.

"I indeed had a right to marry Valeria, since my marriage to Nadedja was not recognized as legal by the Holy Synod. Valeria risked her reputation for me. Despite my love for her, I didn't think I had the moral right to marry her out of respect for Nadedja. So I was content to make a commitment to her by oath before a priest. That was enough for me, however, to consider her my wife. I ask you to help me get her back as quickly as possible, for she has problems, pains in her chest, possibly consumption, and I'm afraid that the severe climate of Tbilisi is not good for her. Besides, she is pregnant by me. . . . "

But the grand duke Constantine could do nothing for him.

As the weeks went by, Nicholas came out of his voluntary seclusion. General Gestov noted that he went more and more often to the city club, the theater, the restaurants, but above all he recorded with intense relief that Daria the Cossack was invited once again to Nicholas's palace and that she spent several nights there. Gestov was reassured that Valeria would be soon forgotten.

In Tbilisi, thousands of miles away, Valeria, whose mother and sisters had caught up with her, was guarded night and day by the secret police in a small apartment on Kadiaski Street, yet the lovers managed to correspond. On the way to her exile, Valeria had traveled with a sailor named Libidif, who was touched by her fate and the brutality of her guards. He took it upon himself to carry her letters. For his part, Nicholas had some loyal friends, including a certain Ivan Afamassiv, who accepted to convey his secret correspondence. The two love messengers used the good offices of the Kaskas and Mercouri Maritime Company, which transported the letters from one coast to another of the Caspian Sea.

"My whole life belongs to you only," Nicholas wrote Valeria, "and my sole wish is to be able to tell you that nothing shall make me back away from you. I shall jump over every hurdle, my very dear princess, so as never to be separated from you again. And however serious may be these obstacles created by my guardians, the doctors, and other rats, we shall be reunited. . . . I love you, I adore you more than anyone else and I cannot live without you. . . . Your doctor Nicholas."

One fine day Afamassiv arrived in Tbilisi and had the national costume of a Georgian woman brought to Valeria. The first thought had been to disguise her as a young boy, but Nicholas feared she would be too conspicuous. So Valeria put on the clothing and darkened her blond hair with the dye Afamassiv had brought. On Nicholas's written advice, she added glasses with tinted lenses and a large checked handkerchief that she held to her cheeks, as if she had a toothache. All was set. Valeria's mother and sister left the apartment. Two secret police agents followed close behind. A short while later Valeria came out on the street.

She took a carriage to the train station, where she was to find Afamassiv. Inexplicably he wasn't there. Trembling with fear, she took the train for Baku by herself. Reaching the port, she managed to find the *Alexei,* the ship where the sailor Libidif was waiting for her. But scarcely had the ship left the shore than her savior, dead drunk, tried to assault her sexually. Despite appearances, she was strong enough to resist. They reached the other shore of the Caspian Sea at the port of Krisnavosk.

As they were disembarking, Libidif spotted some policemen on the quay and told Valeria not to move. He went down to the bazaar to buy her a Tartar woman's costume. He found at the back of the ship a small door used by the crew and had her come belowdecks. He helped her get past the police cordons disguised this way and put her on the train for Tashkent. For hours on end the train advanced over the monotonous plain and then made an unexpected stop at the Samarkand station. The platform was swarming with men in civilian clothes who were rushing in every direction and looking intently in the interiors of the coaches.

Thus it happened that the policeman Anisiniakovlev came into the coach, entered the compartment, and asked Valeria for her passport. The passport was made out to Elisabeth Shmelinskaia, age forty-five. The slip of a girl in front of the policeman had certainly not reached that age! He gave the alert. Valeria's true identity was soon discovered and she was arrested.

At Samarkand itself she was made to undergo a complete medical examination. The doctor didn't take long to recognize that she was neither pregnant nor suffering from tuberculosis. She was brought back to Tbilisi and restored to her apartment-prison. Specially appointed investigators came to interrogate her incessantly about her flight and her accomplices. They forced her to hand over the marriage certificate, legal or not, that united her with Nicholas as well as the promise signed by him to pay her a hundred thousand rubles when she reached her majority. A short time later other policemen showed up in the apartment on Kadiaski Street and took Valeria, her mother, and her sisters off to parts unknown. From that day on Nicholas was never to have any news of her—with no police document recording her transfer, all trace of Valeria was lost for good.

After Valeria's attempted flight, Nicholas's relations with Gestov became distinctly cold. The "overseeing general" continued to live at the palace to keep him under better surveillance.

That night the general was sleeping the sleep of the just when the door of his room burst open. The plainly drunk grand duke loomed forth. With his hand on his pocket, he showed that it contained a revolver.

"Either you leave Tashkent on the first train or I shall kill myself right in front of you. . . . Answer right now!" shouted Nicholas, getting out his gun.

Gestov, scarcely awake, leaped out of bed, took Nicholas's hands in his own, and asked him to calm down and accept the tsar's will.

"I do not accept the tsar's will!" bellowed Nicholas, even louder.

Gestov admonished him as gently as he could. Tomorrow he would regret his words, he would even blush at them. Suddenly Nicholas seemed to calm down, his agitation subsided.

"You're right, the person of the tsar is sacred. From now on I won't speak of him." His words were still muddled. "You've decided to be the guardian of the Iron Mask! You do your duty as demanded in high places!"

And then with a drunkard's tiresome repetition, he went over and over his story, his marriages, his recriminations, with his speech having only one aim, one name, one conclusion: Valeria.

"Give her back to me, for Christ's sake!"

He must have gone on drinking for the rest of the night, for in the morning he was still not sobered up.

Every day the park and the entrance hall of his palace were filled with his clientele: Cossacks, natives, colonists with whom he

had populated his villages. They came bringing him modest presents, to appeal for his intervention, to ask for his help, or simply to
greet him. That morning they were more numerous than usual.
Nicholas appeared, and from high up on the marble steps outside
the building, he harangued his followers with a voice that sounded
groggy but carried far. "Let us march on the capital and overthrow
the tsar!"

He was proposing nothing less than recruiting them, and
their thousands of comrades, and with them the young civil servants, the soldiers who were disgusted by tyranny. Did Nicholas
take himself for a Pugachev, the peasant who claimed to be the
tsar Peter III, miraculously resuscitated, and who roused half
of Russia against Catherine II? Those heroic times were long
gone. Cossacks and natives hung their heads, turned away from
the speaker, and slowly dispersed. But the speech had not gone
unnoticed.

Nicholas was immediately put under arrest and forbidden to
communicate with anyone. Gestov was even thinking of transfer-
ring him to the other end of the empire, to Courland in the Baltic
states, but meanwhile he was sent in haste to Tver, an important
center northwest of Moscow on the road connecting the two capi-
tals. He was temporarily housed in the governor's palace.

Shortly after being arrested, he fell ill. He was struck down
by headaches and a burning fever and, in his delirium, he repeated
Valeria's name. He was so sick that they chose a more benevolent
climate for him for the time being. Were they going to start all over
again, carting him around from one place to another over thousands
of miles by train, coach, or boat? For three years he had been made
to wander from one end of the empire to another, but he was twenty-
five then and now he was twice as old. . . .

It was a very sick man who arrived in Crimea. This time he
was not allowed to live on one of the family properties; he was put

under house arrest in Baklava, a market town near Sebastopol made famous by the battle that had taken place there a half century earlier between the Russians and the allies. He was the compulsory guest of a certain Swingman, who had some property there.

A year went by in silence and total solitude. But at least he was left in peace, and it might be hoped that the Mediterranean climate of Crimea would do him some good.

At the end of this time, Nadedja was authorized to join him. In the meantime she herself had been alone, had reflected, and had forgiven. The Cossack and her three little bastards, Valeria and her furious passion, the others who were more episodic in his life and less well known, they were all forgotten.

In rejoining him she expected to find a sick man with diminished faculties or a raving maniac. To her surprise, Nicholas seemed to her perfectly calm, very much the master of himself, and Nadedja told the guards and other spies repeatedly that he seemed to her more mentally healthy than he had ever been. But she knew, she sensed that he was a broken man and that he would not recover easily from the sudden separation from Valeria. Then, with all her self-denial, she set about working to restore his spirits.

She decided to keep him occupied. Every evening they were authorized to go out in the carriage after dinner. She began by getting him to notice one or two scrawny dogs wandering by the side of the road. Nicholas threw them some food, with a resultant increase in the number of dogs each day. Soon the provisions taken along were no longer sufficient and the dogs followed the carriage back to the house. Nicholas instructed his cooks to prepare meals for them. Very quickly, it was a whole refuge for homeless dogs that he was supporting!

From there Nadedja went on to homeless children. They were even more numerous than the starving canines. Legions of them begged around the churches in the villages. Nadedja encouraged

Nicholas to open a soup kitchen. It had immediate success. The little paupers swelled in number to the point that the secret police stepped in to close the welcome center. Too popular! Nadedja spent her time writing to bring about its reopening or some lightening of Nicholas's regime.

However, the main aim was achieved; she and Nicholas had finally come closer. It was not happiness, far from it, but despite the constraints shackling them, Nicholas appreciated Nadedja's sweetness, which he thought he'd never see again.

19

On that afternoon of June 1903 both of them had left to go for a ride. The carriage went up and down amidst the vineyards of the countryside, the sky dotted with fleecy clouds. They went through wide orchards with green fruit alternating with fields of flowers that would soon be cut and leave by train for St. Petersburg.

When the carriage went along the cliff overlooking the sea, Nicholas had it stop. He got down and, standing before the gulf, looked at length at the Black Sea, so calm at that moment, but sudden and unpredictable storms could make it terrifying. Nadedja came to his side but, respecting his silence, left him lost in his thoughts.

A point grew on the horizon, came nearer, and proved to be a white ship with fine and slender lines

"Certainly a private yacht. Let me imagine, Nadedja, it's coming to look for us, it's going to anchor at the bottom of the cliff. A sloop will be untied from it, and we'll get on to be ferried to the ship. Immediately the yacht will raise anchor and take us away, far away, you and me. . . . We shall cross the Bosporus, we'll sail the Mediterranean, perhaps we'll push on to South America or we'll go around Africa! We'll go where fate has decided and where freedom awaits us."

Meanwhile the white yacht had disappeared behind the cape in the direction of Sebastopol.

Nicholas and Nadedja melancholically made their way back. Soon they got back to the villa where the psychiatrists, guards, and spies were waiting for them.

That evening they lingered later than usual on the veranda surrounding the house, waiting for the close of day. Their attention was caught by a little cloud of dust on the road, growing steadily as it approached. A carriage was coming in their direction. To their surprise, it crossed through the gates and drew closer to the villa. So who could come without being announced when all visits were prohibited?

The carriage stopped in front of the veranda. Out came a woman dressed in traveling clothes. The astonishment, the emotion, transfixed Nicholas to his spot for an instant. It was his sister, Olga, the queen of Greece! He rushed into her arms and they embraced. He stood away from her and gazed at her, unable to say a word. It was the first member of his family he'd seen after thirty years of separation . . . And it was Olga.

She was now a grandmother, but the years had taken away nothing of the slimness of her figure and the elegance of her appearance. Her face had perhaps thickened and a few fine lines had appeared, but the warm, radiant gaze, the large eyes were unchanged. Nicholas saw tenderness and love in them.

Olga took out of her purse a tortoiseshell lorgnette inlaid with her diamond monogram and through its very thick lenses in turn stared at her brother.

"You've become nearsighted, Olga, like our father!"

He took Nadedja's hand and presented her to his sister, who bid her rise from her curtsy and pressed her to her breast. Straightaway Olga demonstrated that she considered Nadedja her brother's legitimate wife.

In turn, she presented a tall teenager in a sailor's outfit who was standing behind her. "This is Christo, my youngest child."

"But your grandchildren, his nephews, must be almost as old as he is!" Nicholas said.

The queen blushed.

"He arrived when we were not expecting any more. . . ."

"Do you mean that you and your husband were still making love more than twenty years after your marriage?"

"Hush, Nicky, you're as impossible as ever!"

And both of them burst out laughing.

"But how did you get here?"

"My husband's yacht brought me from Piraeus."

"So that was the large white ship we saw passing a while ago."

"At Sebastopol, I gave the slip to the men in charge of our security. I said nothing to the police about what I intended to do. I took Christo, who was dying to meet his uncle, and it wasn't hard to find your villa."

"Can you at least spend the night here?"

"Unfortunately, not this time, for the emperor sent me his train, which is waiting to take us to St. Petersburg."

They settled in the villa's large living room. Nadedja had tea, cakes, and fruit brought in. Queen Olga questioned her at length about their sons. Artemi, the elder one, was going on twenty. . . .

"And Alexander, my godson? I was so happy that you chose me to be his godmother. I've seen him several times at our brother Constantine's. He looks at lot like you, Nicky!"

Alexander was already fourteen. Thanks to the emperor's kindliness, and certainly thanks to the intervention of his godmother, he had received the authorization to prepare for the military school where his brother would soon graduate.

Nadedja rose and took Christo's hand. "I'm going to show Nicholas's nephew the house and the garden."

She wanted simply to give the brother and sister some time alone together.

Olga went up to Nicholas, sat down beside him, and put her hand on his. She questioned him about the present and the past. And he, the doubter, the hypersensitive one, felt so much solicitude, so much desire of comprehension, that he spoke.

Ill treatment, yes, he had been subjected to it, but that was not the worst. "If you, Olga, managed to slip through the police cordons to come see me, it's because you're the queen of Greece. . . . But it's because I'm a grand duke that I was separated from Valeria, that my marriage to Nadedja was annulled, that we were forced nevertheless to live together to keep up appearances and respectability! As for my work, the administration has done everything in its power to keep me from getting on with it. . . . Either I am a member of the imperial family and am treated as such, or I am a citizen like any other Russian and left free to do what he wants! Or I am crazy and am treated as a madman must be, or I am a criminal and let me be tried! But anything instead of this ambiguity that has been gnawing at me for thirty years. . . . Do you know whatever became of Alexandra Demidova?"

"She ended up getting a divorce and remarried a count, Sumarokov Elston. She died some twelve years ago, of consumption. Her husband, a very good fellow, adopted the children that . . . that she . . ."

"You mean my children? I'm delighted for them."

Nicholas inclined his head and, without looking at his sister, asked in a muted voice, "And Valeria? Any news?"

"None. No one seems to know where she is."

Olga saw a tear running down her brother's cheek. She held him in her arms. He gently pushed her aside and straightened up, his grief belonging only to him.

The silence stretched on, the silence that predominated in the house, making it seem deserted, the silence that prevailed in the surrounding countryside while the daylight died away. In a tremulous voice, Olga asked the question that had obsessed her for so long. "Tell me, Nicky, were you guilty of the theft of Mama's diamonds?"

"I call that 'the accident of the star' . . ."

He hesitated for a long moment, then his eyes looked into hers. "Yes, I stole."

Could Nicholas explain to his sister that he was guilty of another theft, that of the icons . . . ? Could he confess to her that he might have been responsible for an assassination, that of the emperor their uncle? He was believed guilty of the theft of the diamonds from the star for so long that it had become a reality. So many years, so many events, so many habits had covered up the past with so many layers that it was better not to stir it all up. He loved his sister too much to shock her with the truth. She would certainly have tried to understand, but he would have had to talk to her over days and nights, he would have had to tell her his whole life story. Now she was going to leave.

She leaned over him and kissed him.

"From the bottom of my heart I thank you, Nicky, for your sincerity and your confidence. I had pardoned you a long time ago. But today I love you even more."

She couldn't stay any longer, for she mustn't keep the imperial train waiting.

But she promised to come back.

Olga never came back to Crimea because, thanks to her intervention, Nicholas was taken back to Tashkent. Never would she have been able to get the tsar's consent to Nicholas's return to St. Petersburg, but she understood that her brother would feel better in the setting where he had lived for so many years, and his nephew Nicholas II graciously granted the authorization she requested.

Nicholas, accompanied by Nadedja and their cortege of doctors and guards, thus returned to the rococo palace he had taken so much pleasure in building. And Tashkent thus recovered its "sultan."

Progress had reached even Central Asia; a railway line henceforth connected Tashkent with the rest of the empire. The travelers, the tourists, Russians or foreigners, multiplied. For everyone the main curiosity of the city was the scandalous, perverse, and thieving grand duke. Everyone asked to be received by him, and everyone was fascinated. First of all, by his appearance. His marked thinness made him seem even taller. He sported a monocle and, winter and summer, he jammed a fur hat on his shaven skull. Red continued to be his favorite color; his clothes, his servants' livery, and his horses' harnesses were red. All the visitors were won over by his manner, his refined courtesy, his brilliant conversation, his immense culture, his irresistible witticisms, and then what a will, what energy! However, some noted eccentricities, sarcasm at the expense of the imperial family, which was embarrassing. Provocative, totally unpredictable, Nicholas continued to give rise to the most incredible rumors. Full of verve, he succeeded in putting people off the track. In reality the surveillance around him increased, the espionage intensified, his financial tutelage had become total, and if he wanted to make some purchases in a store, a "guard" accompanied him to pay.

His imperial highness decided to make a gesture for the village of Kaufmanovski whose priest, Father Suridof, had been dismissed for having "married" him to Valeria. Since then the villagers felt themselves to be orphans and their brand-new church of which they were so proud seemed to them as sad as a tomb. To console them, Nicholas announced that he would give them the most beautiful icon of the Virgin. He summoned a monk who painted holy images, installed him in his palace, and gave him the most detailed instructions for realizing his order as he wished. The monk complied and, under the grand duke's daily surveillance, created a masterpiece.

On the day of the solemn delivery of the holy image, the whole village gathered in the church. Some priests from the surrounding area had been found who sprinkled the villagers with holy water and filled the sanctuary with incense. A choir sang. The grand duke was present with his whole entourage and the authorities. The villagers were deliriously happy. The icon was brought in; it weighed a good deal, for it was very tall, and it was set on a console, where it could be seen by the whole congregation. The priests took off the brocade covering the Virgin and revealed her to the believers.

Despite the sanctity of the place, the villagers couldn't hold back their cries of wonderment! The painter-monk had not skimped on the gold nor on the colors. The most sumptuous fabrics and the most magnificent jewels adorned the Mother of God, whose delicate face was rendered with striking realism. The priests, who were usually frowning, had the expressions of delighted children. The village of Kaufmanovski henceforth had the most beautiful icon in the region!

Sitting in the first row, the chief of the Tashkent police stared wide-eyed, as if he had seen an apparition that was not divine, but satanic. He muttered, made disordered gestures, pointed at the holy image, and managed to utter, "But ... it's ... Sophia Perovskaïa!"

It was indeed the terrorist who had been hanged for her part in the assassination of Alexander II and whose features Nicholas had never forgotten! At the time the chief of police had been a mere cop in St. Petersburg, He had taken part in the pursuit of the assassins, and it had been his squad that had hunted out Sophia. He too had never forgotten her face.

The priests pronounced a vague blessing, then hastily took refuge behind the iconostasis. The authorities withdrew, outraged; only the villagers saw the grand duke Nicholas out with many demonstrations of respect, and an absolutely delighted Nicholas started off again in his barouche.

Nevertheless, the villagers didn't want trouble, especially with the police. That very evening a delegation took the icon to Nicholas's palace and gave it back to him without saying a word. Nicholas hung it in his bedroom and gazed for a long time at the terrorist who had been sanctified through his efforts.

To her alone could he ask the question that had bothered him for more than thirty years: had she or had she not received the money from the stolen icons? Could he consider himself the financier of his uncle's assassination? It seemed to him that Sophia's lips gave a faintly ironic smile.

He no longer budged from Tashkent, for he was certain that the emperor would never pardon him. And he would die without having solved the mystery of his own secret. He felt discouraged once again. He told himself that nothing would ever make progress, not in the empire, and not in Tashkent. He himself, with his marriages, his scandals, his flashes of genius, and his provocations, would not change. He was wondering if he wouldn't do better to resign himself when history suddenly erupted.

First the Russo-Japanese War broke out. . . . The Russians enthusiastically rushed into it, persuaded that they would make short work of these wretched little yellow men! They suffered the most complete, the most humiliating of defeats. Much as Nicholas could be considered a revolutionary, he was also a patriot, a Romanov who had Russia in his blood. He suffered but could do nothing.

The defeat was followed by revolutionary movements that broke out everywhere in the country. Strikes, uprisings, assassination attempts, peasants' revolts; the proud empire saw itself paralyzed and humiliated by its people. In St. Petersburg, people were persuaded that the revolution so often announced had finally arrived. Outside the city the situation remained much calmer, as usual, but there were a lot of agitators, demonstrations, and strikes. For a time the railway workers managed to halt all railroad traffic in the region.

Nicholas felt implicated in this revolution, unlike the war. He convened the striking railway workers, showered them with pleasantries, and had them construct at his expense a small train that would go around his property. The strikers joyfully complied, delighted to satisfy their beloved grand duke. And when this masterpiece was finished, he had them paint it red. Wasn't that his favorite color?

The revolution of 1905 ended as quickly and mysteriously as it had flared up, without anyone being able to say why. And life resumed. The empire seemed indestructible, at least to those who wanted to go on believing in it.

Although the court had become very dull under an emperor who preferred the bourgeois and family life to the splendor of power, the glamour of the imperial family remained intact, as in the emblematic figure of the grand duchess Alexandra. Forgotten was the slightly mad young wife surrounded by seers and quacks; she had turned herself into a sublime old woman. She was adored by her grandchildren, whom she showered with gifts; her favorite was Christo, queen Olga's youngest son, who had been taken to see Nicholas in Crimea. He was full of praise for the tenderness and generosity of this lady who had a soft spot for her grandchildren.

Although in her eighties, she still held herself very straight. Crowned with white hair, dressed with the last word in elegance, still slim-waisted, she trained her diamond-inlaid lorgnette at those who approached her. At court ceremonies she seemed to have stepped out of an old portrait. Dressed in silvery moiré, flooded with diamonds, followed by an endless train whose weight she didn't seem to register, she could stand immobile for hours on end. She symbolized the solidity of the empire, and no one could imagine that one day she would pass away.

That, however, is what she did in 1911, after a very brief illness. She was not to see again the man who had been her favorite son. And yet Nicholas had several times begged her to agree to a meeting. She had never replied.

Upon her death, her other children felt much freer toward the reprobate. His brother Constantine finally agreed to see him. A military tour of inspection was taking him to Tashkent. In the special train headed for the heart of Central Asia, he feared the welcome he would receive from Nicholas. The train stopped in the middle of the countryside to allow the governor of Turkestan as well as the "guards" to get on in order to bring him up to date on his elder brother's state of mind.

The train entered the Tashkent station at 9 P.M., still full daylight on that October evening. As Constantine noted, the sky was a light yellow but the air was rather cool. The guard of honor, the national anthem, presentation of arms, then Constantine was immediately taken to Nicholas's palace.

"I was profoundly nervous before this interview but, possibly because of the presence of Nadedja, Nicholas's wife, our meeting was very friendly and sincere. We spent the whole evening pleasantly chatting."

Pleasantly, nothing more. For Nicholas was far from feeling for Constantine the intimacy and love that he felt for their sister Olga. And the younger brother, despite his kindness, his open-mindedness, his tolerance, had always been impressed by this strange character, who vanished while he was still very young and whose horrific acts people discussed endlessly. Nevertheless, Nicholas respected in Constantine the artist and the poet whose translations and writings had earned him an immense reputation in Russia.

Constantine did not stay with Nicholas, but they saw each other every day. The two brothers breakfasted together and Nicholas had him visit his palace. Constantine in turn invited him to a large dinner offered in his honor by the governor of Turkestan, but Nicholas declined, explaining very frankly that in his modest civilian suit, he felt out of place among all those uniforms. On the other hand, Constantine easily convinced Nadedja to be present at the dinner, for he was quickly attracted to this beautiful, modest, dignified woman who had borne so much at Nicholas's hands and continued to bear so much with courage and patience.

Nicholas visited Constantine, who presented to him the members of his retinue. Nicholas proved amiable and gracious with each of them, and greeted one by one the cadets who formed a line on the stairway. For the last day, a Te Deum was sung in the cathedral followed by another military inspection. Constantine agreed to visit with great pomp and ceremony the old people's home that Nicholas had created in town. Up to the last minute both of them avoided any tricky subject and were content to exchange commonplaces under the anxious eyes of the officials. In the evening, Constantine left Tashkent.

A short time later the First World War broke out, almost by surprise. One of Constantine's sons, Prince Oleg, age twenty-two, was seriously wounded in a cavalry charge he had courageously led against the enemy. His father, despite faltering health, and his mother rushed to Vilna, where he had been taken. Constantine pinned to his son's chest the Cross of St. George, the medal for bravery. It was the final joy of the young man, who died in his father's arms. He was the only member of the imperial family to be killed in the war. His father did not recover from it. He continued to deteriorate and passed away a few months later.

Tashkent was far away and the war was hardly felt there at all. There were, however, restrictions, requisitioning, new taxes, fixed prices imposed on farmers — measures that irritated the population. The war was apparent primarily through the thousands of German prisoners sent as far from the front as possible, in Central Asia, to be interned in makeshift camps. They were an embarrassment, a burden, and their presence also irritated the natives.

As usual, the most pernicious rumors about the grand duke were spread in the town's sitting rooms, where it was said that he played at being a spy for the Germans, delivering state secrets to them. . . . Once more his "guards" were zealous, so much so that the minister of the interior, on reading their report, was perturbed and ordered a further investigation. Once more the governor-general of Turkestan, like his predecessors, denied these absurd accusations. Nicholas's opponents would never stop, for a character so disconcerting always gives rise to truths mixed up inextricably with falsehoods.

The winter and the war forced Tashkent to hunker down. The winter brought freezing wind and torrents of rain, forcing the inhabitants to lie low at home. The war interrupted communications, drying up the flow of visitors and tourists. The war also made it increasingly difficult to supply the city and helped the black market flourish.

Suffering from myocarditis and chronic bronchitis accompanied by emphysema, Nicholas was bedridden for weeks. Nadedja looked after him devotedly, not leaving his bedside. But no sooner was he back on his feet than she was off to St. Petersburg — renamed Petrograd out of an anti-German reaction — for the wife of their son Alexander was about to give birth and she wanted to be present for it.

The still-convalescing Nicholas no longer went out. He was glum. He had always needed a public and now felt abandoned. Artemi and Alexander had enlisted. Daria the Cossack no longer interested him, nor the two little boys they had had together. Only the daughter, little Daria, still had his affection. She was now a tall, powerfully built teenager. Her real gift for music drew her father's attention, and he hired someone to teach her to play the violin. Taking advantage of Nadedja's absence — she took a very dim view of the Cossack's brood — he had Daria come often to the palace and asked her to play for him the old sonatas that enlivened his solitude.

The dramatic events of the war were going on so far away that in Tashkent they seemed an abstraction, a fictional story read in the newspapers that had no connection to the reality of Central Asia. Nevertheless, at the start of 1917, Nicholas noted a kind of restrained agitation. In Petrograd, strikes and demonstrations were increasing. Tashkent didn't budge, but people discussed, formed groups, and held forth more and more loudly.

On the afternoon of March 2, Nicholas, who had recently taken to going out again, was taking his daily ride in a barouche. He suddenly saw people running in every direction, waving newspapers about, yelling things he couldn't make out. He sent his daughter Daria, who was with him, to buy a paper. Since the war had begun the newspapers were only thin sheets of poor-quality paper badly printed. He adjusted his monocle and read in large type: ABDICATION OF THE TSAR! He pored over the details. There, at headquarters, Nicholas II, under pressure from generals and politicians, had abandoned the throne in favor of his brother, the grand duke Michael.

Nicholas ordered the coach driver to make a U-turn and return immediately. All evening long, visitors came and went to discuss the news, to get his opinion. The people were worried. "What will tomorrow have in store for us?" they repeated with an anxiety that arose from their eventful history, filled with bloody tragedies, which had taught them to beware of changes. They waited anxiously for the next day.

The telegraph brought the news: the grand duke Michael had declined the throne! With the monarchy overthrown, a provisional government was formed.

Then, everywhere there was an outburst of spontaneous joy! Among the natives, because for them the empire was colonialism. Among the Russian colonists, because the empire was the police, censorship, and the nitpicking, heavy-handed, tyrannical administration. Among the civil servants, because the empire was the egotistical, obnoxious little dictator who made their lives miserable. Everyone went out into the streets! There was laughter, singing, applause. The "Marseillaise" rang out for the first time in Tashkent's history! The refrain, hitherto prohibited as revolutionary, was taken up by tens of thousands of voices.

Nicholas shared intensely the natural, sincere, and general joy. For him the empire's fall meant freedom. No more tsar; that meant no more exile, no more prison! He was no longer grand duke, but how many times had he begged to have that title taken away from him! He was a citizen like any other, which was what he'd always wanted to be. No more guards, no more spies, no more restrictions, no more prohibitions! After forty-one years of internment without bars, he was free to go where he wanted, to do, to say, and to think what he wanted.

The joyful fever overran his palace. The latest news was brought to him, the true along with the false. He was told who the members of the provisional government were, but he didn't know any of the names. Wait, he had heard the name Kerenski. Kerenski, of course! He was the general inspector of instruction in Turkestan. The provisional government's newly named minister of the interior must be his son. He had attended high school in Tashkent. Many of the city's inhabitants remembered the boy. Not a good student but a "fine talker," yes. In fact, an old acquaintance! Nicholas decided to send him a congratulatory telegram. A few days later the document was published in every newspaper in the country. Imagine! A grand duke delighted by the founding of a republic! Thus, even after the empire's fall, Nicholas was pursued by his title like a ghost filled with reproaches.

There was a freedom celebration in Tashkent, on March 10. Although spring had not yet officially arrived, it was a marvelously fine day and almost warm. The long winter that had for centuries weighed Russia down was over. Everyone took part, paraded, everyone applauded—the soldiers of the garrison, the worker delegations, the schoolchildren, and the Asians in their velvet and brocade caftans. The policing was done by volunteers. Everywhere there were red flags, banners, cockades, red ribbons.

In the Russian style, one speech followed another, numerous and interminable, spoken by generals, heads of workers' delegations, and even by the governor-general of Turkestan, Kuropatkin, a leftover from the empire. He finished with the yell repeated by thousands of voices: "Long live great Russia free!"

Nicholas was present, very much in the public eye, with his red shirt, red carriage, red livery, and red harnesses. After all, he had called for the revolution with all his heart. With amazement he looked at the enthusiasm of the crowd, but also at its maturity, which was apparent in the perfect orderliness of the parades. He had a feeling that he was seeing the people for the first time.

In a few days the top civil servants, the officers, the ranks of the police faded into the background, just like the imperial coats of arms, the crowns, and other emblems. The representatives and symbols of authority had been obliterated as if miraculously. The government no longer existed, and yet there was no disorder, no anarchy, and no violence. On the contrary, all over there was good fellowship, goodwill, mutual aid, and smiles. The city also seemed transformed. How it had changed from the time when Nicholas had first arrived there! It was now a great built-up area of more than two hundred thousand residents. The avenues had been made longer, and buildings were multiplied. The native town that once took up three-quarters of the city's surface area was now only one neighborhood among others. Tashkent was a modern city, a city of the future.

Everyone spoke of "the future." Everyone, beginning with Nicholas, smiled at the future. The republic would enable him to realize the dream he'd been cherishing for decades, seeing the capital again, his city, the one that in his heart would always be St. Petersburg, even if it was now named Petrograd.

Happy and all alone, he took the train without asking anything of anyone, but—what a difference!—no more sitting rooms reserved for important persons, no more sentinels presenting arms, no more employees in the sleeping cars to open the doors, and above all no more special compartment. It was for Nicholas the first real experience of mingling with the people, an ordeal for a great lord of sixty-seven hitherto accustomed to seeing the working classes at a distance.

Nevertheless, the joy of experiencing his freedom made him forget these circumstances, for example, the lateness of the trains.

It would take him more than a week to reach Petrograd! The train stopped at every station, sometimes for hours. It also made many stops in the open countryside to let trains pass that were taking new recruits to the front or taking the wounded behind the lines. No more dining cars; food could be bought only in the miserable shops in the stations. Nicholas got to know the greasy papers, the dirty bottles, the slugs of vodka passed from hand to hand. Impossible to sleep when people are squeezed ten and twelve to a compartment. Only exhaustion got the better of this lack of comfort and gave him a few hours of restless half sleep.

20

Finally the train entered the Petrograd station. Nicholas hadn't been able to let anyone know about his arrival as the mail worked poorly and telegrams, save for those of the government, didn't reach their destination. No one was waiting for him; he had to fight just to find an old carriage. His route to reach his family's apartment took him through just about the whole city.

He lowered the carriage's dusty window and eagerly looked outside. Of course he recognized the buildings and the monuments, but it was the atmosphere that had changed. No more elegant strollers on the Nevsky Prospekt; most of the luxury stores had their window curtains closed. No more imperial coats of arms on the pediments of his family's palaces. Their sentry boxes abandoned, their shutters closed, they seemed deserted. Yet Nicholas happily inhaled the air of his city.

The carriage moved slowly forward. It arrived, finally, far behind the Peter and Paul Fortress, at the corner of the Kammenosstroski Prospekt and Bolshoi Street. He had to carry his suitcases up the stairs. He rang, and it was Nadedja who opened the door for him. Her instinct told her he might come.

He met Alexander's wife, then their first child, little Kyrill, who was going on two. Last, they led him to the cradle where a baby was sleeping, barely a few weeks old, and he leaned over his grand-daughter. They had reserved for him the apartment's finest bed-room. Nicholas was surrounded, celebrated, fed, toasted, and right away his daughter-in-law asked him to be the godfather of her newborn daughter.

The Orthodox Church usually baptized several months after birth, but under the circumstances, the baptism of Nicholas's god-daughter took place a few days later. The neighborhood church was poorly lit and more or less empty. Only a few old women came and went, knelt down, and lit a candle. The priest seemed hurried, in-different; when the godfather had given his name to be written in the register, Nicholas Romanov, he did not flinch. Only the family attended the ceremony, which lasted a short fifteen minutes. When the baby was undressed to dip her in the baptismal font, she began screaming more vigorously than anyone expected.

"She will have character," murmured her grandfather.

As customary, the priest asked him what name he was plan-ning on giving his goddaughter.

"I baptize thee Natalya . . ."

In the next few days Nicholas became reacquainted with his city. From morning to evening he walked the streets and along the canals. The familiar places, his former palace, the balconies of Fanny's apartment didn't stir up any nostalgia in him. He didn't want any of the past, for it had been too painful. He convinced himself that he had succeeded in sweeping it away and could look at the world with a fresh eye.

Once more he fell in love with this city that he rightly considered the most beautiful in the world. He had always found it easy to meet people; he went into cafés, tearooms, he chatted with strangers. There was indeed an atmosphere of freedom that hadn't existed previously. People could breathe again, relieved at being no longer under surveillance and the threat of a denunciation. But in other respects the city was in bad shape. Public transportation practically no longer existed and lines of people stretched in front of food stores. Strikes broke out at the drop of a hat; every day bellowing demonstrators paraded, red flags in the lead.

Nicholas avoided getting in touch with people again. He distrusted the welcome he would receive but also feared compromising people he had known. He realized that supporters of the ancien régime would henceforth be suspect and that the least visit could weigh down their dossier.

The emperor, the empress, and their children were prisoners in the palace Alexander of Tsarskoie Selo. The other members of the imperial family hid away in their palaces or vacation homes, appalled at having seen their world crumble, and terrified as well. Everyone lived a meager existence, most of the time by their wits, selling their jewels by weight. For their subsistence they had depended on income paid by the imperial privileges, which vanished with the revolution. Only Nicholas, who had built up a personal fortune through his investments, could go on living well. He had money but could buy nothing with it. The war and then the revolution had brought ruin to the country.

As the days went by, Nicholas felt his discomfort growing. However, he went to Pavlovsk, where his close relatives had taken refuge. He well recognized the palace, but everything was so changed.

No more guards, no more manservants, no one to welcome him, the formerly raked footpaths overrun by weeds and the gardens changed into vegetable plots.

He made the acquaintance of his brother's widow, the grand duchess Elisabeth Mavrikievna. But above all he found his sister Olga, who was also a widow, her husband King George having been assassinated in a street in Salonika four years earlier. Thin, sad, dressed all in black, she had lost all that innocence, that gaiety that had made her radiant.

At the start of the war she had come to Pavlovsk to set up a military hospital there. She devoted herself to the wounded without regard for herself and was respected and adored by all. Despite his refusal to live in the past, Nicholas was horrified to find the palace of his childhood all topsy-turvy. The furniture, the paintings, the precious knickknacks had been put in crates while hospital beds were lined up in the sitting rooms and galleries. He found the war wounded even on the landings. The new administration had requisitioned the family apartments to set up offices there. Queen Olga and his sister-in-law had been relegated to the servants' rooms on the third floor.

The windows on a level with the ground admitted scant light. Nicholas, Olga, and his brother's widow sat around a heavy mahogany table. The sole servant was a young peasant girl of the area, Niusha. She brought a relic of the past, a silver tea set stamped with the two-headed eagle. But the tea was no longer imported from London; it was made from herbs of the region. No more succulent sandwiches, no more petits fours. Some black bread and a rather rancid oil.

"That's all we have, poor Nicky, there's no more sugar or butter."

Olga described the situation as her brother avoided seeing it, for this eminently sweet woman also knew how to be clear-sighted.

The war went on, every day soaking up more lives and Russian reserves. Daily existence became increasingly precarious, with its restrictions, its shortages. Starvation laid siege to the cities more effectively than the Germans. The provisional government was hanging by a thread. Kerenski had little trouble waging war on all fronts; he was threatened mainly by the Bolsheviks. The whole country was swept with uncertainty about the future, and every day it slid a bit closer to anarchy, that old Russian demon that appeared at every crisis.

Nicholas realized he was out of place in Petrograd, where he would definitely be torn between the ancien régime to which he belonged in everyone's eyes even if he didn't want to, and the new regime about which his doubts were growing and in which he couldn't serve, even if he wanted to, without compromising himself. So he would leave, taking his immediate family with him. In Central Asia they would be at peace and have time to anticipate coming events.

For their part, the queen Olga and his sister-in-law knew that they could be thrown out of Pavlovsk at any moment. So, when Nicholas and his sister embraced before separating, they wondered deep in their hearts when they would see each other again, even whether they would ever see each other again.

Nicholas was relieved to be returning to his former place of exile, now his chosen place of residence. Nadedja followed him together with their daughter-in-law, Alexander's wife, and their infant grandchildren, Kyrill and little Natalya.

He noticed changes. The provisional government arrested the leaders named by the empire, even General Kuropatkin, the governor-general who had presided so blithely at the freedom celebration. Kerenski's men had been named to important posts. Even if he detested them, Nicholas had lived among the authorities not long ago, and they knew one another. Now he knew no one. It was the dictatorship of the anonymous.

The prisoners of war, surviving under atrocious conditions, had been freed but their rations had been cut off. Then these thousands of Austrians, Czechs, and Germans overran the city. They tried to find odd jobs, some moved in with women from the region, but above all they burglarized, attacking people if need be.

For their part the soviets of workers and peasants proved increasingly noisy, arrogant, and demanding. At summer's end they caused unrest. The provisional government dispatched an expeditionary body that, by dint of exhortations and arrests, pacified the province. The calm, however, remained precarious.

Despite everything, life went on, the revolution making itself felt less than in Petrograd or Moscow. Cars were requisitioned. Trees along the avenues were cut down because of a fuel shortage. Farming and cotton-producing industries, having been snatched away from their owners and given to the workers, functioned poorly. Moreover, Moscow demanded larger and larger allotments. Food began to be scarce. Nicholas, who was able to hold on to his carriage and horses, would go to have a drink at the Regina Hotel, where he would meet the few consuls still at their jobs, the war correspondents, adventurers of all kinds, and a good many spies from all nations. Nicholas could tell himself that nothing had changed, except for the freedom that he had found. . . .

One day in autumn the representatives of the authorities came to Nicholas's palace. They brought back to him the hunting guns, revolvers, and other weapons they had confiscated a few months earlier.

"We fear a bad surprise. Hold on to these weapons to defend yourself."

"Defend myself against whom?"

"Against anyone who wants to disturb good order . . ."

That's to say, the Bolsheviks, Nicholas realized.

One morning not long after, gunfire broke out. The Bolsheviks were attacking. For four days Tashkent was turned into a battlefield, four days during which Nicholas and his family lived cut off in their residence. He took the precaution of moving the women and children to the rear of the palace, which didn't prevent stray bullets from breaking the windowpanes. One of them came very close to his head while he was imperturbably reading in the library; it didn't distract him even for a minute from his reading.

The Bolsheviks won. Nicholas understood this when he saw soldiers passing his window dressed in every imaginable outfit. The civil servants of the provisional government and officers of the regular army had been taken prisoner, their hands tied behind their backs. That night Nicholas stayed up very late reading, and he heard, carried by the silence, salvos and even cries muffled in the distance. He understood that the conquerors were executing their prisoners without restraint. He only hoped the women were deeply asleep and heard nothing.

Soon the newspapers told him that the Bolsheviks, the masters of Russia, had arrested all the members of the imperial family they could lay hands on. They were thrown in prison, waiting to be sentenced. Every day the people living in the palaces waited for the visit of a commissar, which, they knew, meant arrest, probably torture, and death.

Nicholas had taken his precautions. He knew that it was principally he whom the new regime would go after. He arranged it that as soon as the forerunners of misfortune arrived to take him, the servants were to lead the women and children out through the garden to seek shelter among his loyal Cossacks. Nevertheless, as the days went by, nothing happened. No police, no arrest. The representatives of the new order became invisible for Nicholas. He kept his residence, his personnel, and above all his freedom.

He was indeed the only one among the ancien régime to enjoy these privileges, for every day arrests and executions increased in an atmosphere of growing terror.

When one day Nicholas saw employees from his estates, factories, and businesses being hauled off to prison, he decided to react. He jammed his fur hat on his head, got into his carriage with the red harnesses, and ordered his coach driver to take him to the governor's palace. He didn't need to introduce himself; every door was opened for him as if by magic. He went into the large office where, for decades, he had visited a succession of governors-general.

The commissar Constantine Bravin now occupied it. This man, very tall, very stocky, with a big round face crisscrossed with wrinkles, skin pockmarked from smallpox, and small squinty eyes behind large glasses, jovially welcomed his visitor. He had wine and cakes brought in and spouted commonplaces, avoiding as much as he could using Nicholas's former title and calling him "Citizen Romanov." Cutting these pleasantries short, Nicholas asked for the release of his employees.

"They are enemies of the people!" the commissar spit out.

And he launched a tirade the like of which Nicholas could read every day in the newspapers. He made an unsuccessful attempt to argue. Commissar Bravin made a speech worthy of a public meeting. Despite his rage and disappointment, Nicholas stifled a yawn, then when the other man had stopped, he asked him in a gentle voice, "Why haven't you arrested me so far? Am I not a member of the former imperial family?"

"You have performed the most courageous, most generous aid to our predecessors."

Nicholas turned pale. "How do you know?"

"You're a living legend among the revolutionaries!"

Nicholas detected the irony in the tone of the commissar, who went on, "You are the most illustrious victim of the recent tyranny! We have freed you from the yoke and we honor you."

Returning home, Nicholas told himself that he wasn't at all sure he appreciated that kind of honor.

A few weeks later he saw some Kirghiz, Turkomans, and other Sarts hurrying past his windows. These natives were hoping that the revolution would grant them independence, instead of which they had to suffer constraints that were much more burdensome than under the ancien régime. Disappointed, they decided to protest. Nicholas came out on his front steps to watch them parade by. Recognizing him, many of them lowered the fists they had raised and stopped shouting slogans in order to cast him a smile and wave.

Nicholas came onto the square and joined them. Out of the corner of his eye he saw at the end of the square Bolshevik soldiers massing, barring the streets, and setting up machine guns. Panicked, he forced his way through the crowd that was trying to hold him back, and he shouted, "Don't do that! For heaven's sake, don't do that!" He was shouting so loudly that everyone stopped, the soldiers who were arming the machine guns and the demonstrating natives. He heard the harsh voice of a Bolshevik officer, "Lead the citizen back with all the honors that are due him!"

Two noncommissioned officers came up to him, each took an arm, and they pulled him toward his palace. Suddenly the air was full of staccato firing, followed by a cloud of smoke. Nicholas heard the screams of the wounded and the moans of the dying. The two officers who had unceremoniously thrown him into the entrance hall of his palace had slammed the door and were outside on the steps.

Nicholas was ill once again and had difficulty breathing. His chest hurt but above all, for the first time in his life, he found he had no appetite, no energy, no desire. He was too weak to get up, so he remained all day stretched out on the ottoman in his library.

Nadedja had managed to find a doctor. All the well-known ones had died as "enemies of the people." One of the few who'd stayed in Tashkent was an intern who hadn't even had the time to get his diploma. It didn't take a lot of experience, however, to diagnose a case of pneumonia. He shook his head while making out his report.

Nicholas couldn't care less; he had no desire to live. The revolution he had called for with all his heart, and that he may have fostered with a contribution nearly forty years earlier, had proven to be the worst nightmare. It was blind malice, cruelty, sadism, but above all mediocrity. The rats had climbed out of the sewer and were now governing.

He couldn't stand anyone around him save for Daria, the daughter of the Cossack. He had her come to him almost daily to hear her play. His German upbringing influenced him anew, and he preferred Bach and Mozart to Russian music.

One afternoon he felt so weak, so bad, that he sent for Father Théophile, an old, almost illiterate priest who had a parish in one of the villages that Nicholas had founded. He appreciated this simple, humane man. The two men remained cooped up for a long while. Then Nicholas had Daria come in.

He had to make an effort to turn his head, and he looked at length at the large icon hanging on the wall, where the Virgin had taken on the features of Sophia Perovskaïa. Then he ordered Daria to open all the doors. She understood when she reached the entrance hall, for, from the sofa where he was stretched out, Nicholas had a straight-line view of the statue of Fanny. The cold light of the setting winter sun seemed to bathe the white marble nude with a golden veil and made the jewels she was wearing glimmer faintly. With his gaze fixed on the image of that woman he had so much loved, he died, between his daughter and his confessor, between the bastard of a Cossack and a humble village priest.

"Fortunately, God has called him back to Him. They were preparing to arrest him tomorrow," murmured the old, bent, bearded priest.

"How do you know?" asked the surprised Daria.

"My sister's granddaughter is the chambermaid of Commissar Bravin. She heard everything."

"But why my father?"

The holy man straightened up, stared at the girl with the mature figure, and, in a stentorian voice that one wouldn't have expected of him, declared, "Because he was the greatest benefactor that Turkestan has ever known."

It was cold, but the sun was shining in Tashkent. In the St. George Cathedral, the priests brought out from their hiding places their vestments of pale blue, pink, and gold brocade, and their diamond-studded miters. Too bad if the police arrested them, it's not every day that a member of the imperial family is buried. They had even unearthed a large flag embossed with the two-headed eagle, with which they had covered the casket.

Nicholas's two families were seated near his remains. On the one side Nadedja, her sister-in-law, and her grandchildren, and on the other, Daria Eliseievna and her children.

The church was packed on that February morning of 1918. All the candles had been lit, lending sparkle to the gold of the icons and the clergy's jewels. Clouds of incense rose toward the cupola from which a large Pantocrator blessed the gathering. At the solemn sound of the voices of the magnificent choir, the Orthodox liturgy, now outlawed, unfurled its hymns and its splendors. Then the casket was carried out of the sanctuary.

On the square the communist authorities were all waiting, with Commissar Bravin at their head and all the soldiers from the garrison gathered to honor one last time the most illustrious victim of tsarism. Behind the row of officials, the vast square was teeming with people. Hundreds of thousands of them had come, from the outskirts of the city, but also from all the villages in what was once called the "starving steppe," and even from the distant mountains. They were all there, Cossacks, colonists, natives whom Nicholas had made prosperous, the humble, the needy to whom he'd given alms, the old people, the orphans, the sick persons whom he'd welcomed in the hospices he'd created. The crowd was so large, so jammed, that the casket had to slide on a carpet of shoulders to reach the place of burial.

The solemn moment approached. The civilians, the commissar, the ranks of the Soviet secret police, the judges who daily sent the survivors of the ancien régime to the firing squad froze while the military band performed Beethoven's funeral march. On an order from the officers, the red-cockaded soldiers presented arms, and flags with the hammer and sickle were inclined.

The casket was slowly lowered into the grave dug at the place where a monument to the deceased was to be erected. Innumerable men and women were weeping. One last time they shouted, "*Babush! Babush! . . .*"

In Tobolsk, in Siberia, the winter had been especially harsh — the temperature had fallen to minus 11 degrees Fahrenheit — but when the end of February came, the temperature became milder. Yet it was cold, very cold, but not in the villa of the town's governor.

It was a rather small palace, which looked like all the administrative buildings constructed throughout the empire. It was very well heated and equipped with every modern comfort, with hot- and cold-water bathrooms. Exceptionally in these uncertain times, the domestic staff was on the job. Because the war had just come to an end and restrictions became more severe daily, food was not plentiful, but people were far from going hungry. Every day two or three dishes were on the cook's menu, written out on cards engraved with the two-headed eagle.

For the house of the governor of Tobolsk had become the prison where the emperor Nicholas II, the empress, and their five children were locked up. They lived in a kind of luxury that for months had been forgotten by the Russians, but the conditions of their detention were gradually deteriorating. Excursions were prohibited and promenades were limited to walks in the garden, around which a fence had been erected. Of course, they couldn't receive any visitors, and to get the news they had only the local rag.

Did they know or suspect what fate had in store for them? The courage they displayed made it impossible to guess their feelings. Every day the guards became more unpleasant. The emperor and his family were in the most absolute solitary confinement and yet they mysteriously continued to send and receive letters to and from relatives and friends. They discussed current events, exchanged news in a measured, courteous, and elegant style that didn't give a hint of their cruel situation.

On February 26, 1918, the grand duchess Tatiana Nicolaïevna, the tsar's second daughter, wrote her Aunt Xenia, who had sought refuge in Crimea, "In her letter Aunt Olga tells us Uncle Nicholas died of pneumonia. . . ."

This sentence, which is lost in the long letter by a daughter of Nicholas II, is the only family announcement of the death of a man who in his youth made so much commotion. A few weeks later Tatiana and her family were taken from Tobolsk to points farther east. They went deeper into Siberia to the town of Yekaterinburg and were locked up in the residence of a rich storekeeper of the town, the Ipatiev house, which had been requisitioned and sinisterly rebaptized "the special-purpose house."

Weeks later still, one night in July, the family were abruptly roused from their sleep. The guard ordered them to get dressed hurriedly, for they had to be moved at once. They were taken to the cellar and asked to wait. Then under the supervision of their jailer, a few drunken soldiers with guns in hand entered that small room and shot them at point-blank range. They finished off with bayonets the ones who were still breathing. A few minutes were all that was needed to kill the emperor, the empress, their five children, and the few men and women who had agreed to follow them and share their fate.

The slaughter was the signal for the extermination of the other Romanovs. Michael, the younger brother of Nicholas II, was killed with a revolver. Other grand dukes were shot. Assassins threw the grand duchess Elisabeth and several of her close relatives into a pit and tossed grenades in after them to finish them off. There was now no living Romanov in the territory of the Soviet Union.

Except, however, in far-off Tashkent, where a little boy and little girl barely of an age to walk were living peacefully. They were authentic Romanovs, the grandchildren of the grand duke Nicholas Konstantinovich. Every day their grandmother Nadedja took them to observe the construction of their grandfather's tomb, for the Bolsheviks, with their bureaucratic state of mind, were completing what they had promised. Elsewhere they were throwing the corpses of the emperor, grand dukes, and grand duchesses into common graves or into deserted mine pits; here they were erecting a monument to the glory of the least well known of the Romanovs.

One fine day in 1919 there arrived in Tashkent an English officer, Colonel Bailey. Described as a liaison officer, he was above all a distinguished spy from the no less distinguished Intelligence Service. He quickly struck up a friendship with the commissar Bravin. The latter, to honor his guest, was eager to show him the pride of the city, the brand-new museum. The two men entered the large rococo building. The well-informed Englishman knew that this was the former residence, now very recently nationalized, of the late grand duke Nicholas.

In the entrance hall he was nearly knocked down by a little girl who, while running, hadn't noticed him. She stopped, looked at him, then directed her large blue eyes to a white marble statue of a naked woman. She looked at her with a kind of adoration. As for Bailey, he had heard descriptions of her and recognized the effigy of Fanny Lear. The museum attendant appeared, a woman who was tall, thin, and with drawn features. Looking sullen, she bade them visit the building.

Bravin explained to the Englishman that the museum had been opened to show how, in the old decadent times, the bourgeois — which he pronounced "boorzhooy" — lived, including all the ruling classes. Bailey admired the paintings and the sculptures. He understood that these works of art had been assembled by a man of culture and taste.

The two men met up before a display cabinet where the Bolshevik noticed an Indian dagger with a hilt set with precious stones.

"Open," he ordered the museum attendant, "and give it to me."

The attendant refused. She didn't have the right to lay hands on the slightest object in the museum. Bravin was annoyed and let her understand that she was taking a big risk in opposing a Bolshevik order. Bailey nudged him with his elbow and tried to make him back off. Bailey didn't understand, Bravin insisted, and he turned threatening. Then Bailey pulled him to one side. "Shut up, it's the princess . . ."

"What princess?"

"The princess Iskander, the grand duke's widow."

Bravin had seen too little of her to recognize her. He seemed impressed, so true was it that the titles of the ancien régime impressed the Reds, but he didn't want to lose face. He proposed giving the "lady attendant" a receipt for the dagger. Nadedja Alexandrovna, for it was she, shrugged her shoulders and accepted it grumblingly. She set the piece of paper in the display cabinet in the place of the dagger that she had been forced to hand over to the commissar.

In truth, despite the events that were speeding up history, despite the disruptions shaking Russia, Nicholas was not forgotten. Even beyond the grave he continued to benefit from complicities among the masters of the day, who furthermore had named his widow an attendant at their old residence to enable her to go on living there.

"I never loved my grandmother, she made me afraid. She forbid us from treating her as a grandmother. We had to call her Aunt Vava. And then she was very ugly . . ."

Cousin Talya was recalling memories of her childhood. This was in September 1999 and I was in her tiny apartment in a Moscow suburb.

Talya's affection didn't extend to Nadedja Alexandrovna, but did extend to the tamed bear that Daria the Cossack had brought with her to the palace. He was let out of his cage to entertain the public, and Talya never tired of seeing him do his act.

"One day an onlooker threw a brick at him and the furious bear rushed at him. The guards had to put him down. I can still see his bloody body on the marble steps in front of the palace. . . ."

The civil war broke out. The Bolsheviks, threatened on all fronts, almost lost Central Asia. But they ended up regaining the advantage and unleashed the real Red Terror on a scale that was monstrous and previously unimaginable.

Nadedja was abruptly driven out of the palace and was allowed only to live in a hovel at the bottom of what had been her park.

"She lived alone," Talya remembered, "surrounded by many dogs, in a poverty that became more abject each day, too weak to get up and go to the market. On awakening, she found either a banknote slipped under her door or a plate of rice on the threshold, which she owed to the generosity of the Cossacks or some natives whom her husband had helped. One day one of her dogs, suffering from rabies, bit her. My grandmother died all alone in horrible pain. A very short time later my mother and my brother and I left Tashkent to go to Moscow. . . ."

Talya was silent. The dying light of the afternoon was streaming into the tiny living room and bedroom, barely filtered by the leaves of the apartment's lime trees. All were silent: Andrei and Yuri who had accompanied me; Lisa, the young and strikingly beautiful journalist who'd become Talya's friend; the children who stuck their heads through the half-open door; and even Malesh, the dog.

I was watching the petals of a half-faded rose fall from the vase on the oilcloth covering the table when Talya turned her magnificent eyes toward me. Then, in the voice of a *tsarina* used to command, she exclaimed, "He was innocent!"

She expressed this conviction with a cry of suffering. Then I understood. After more than a century, the grand duke remained stricken from the list of the Romanovs because he stole some diamonds on his mother's icon, because he was still considered a thief. For no one knew that story I had just heard. The fall of the Iron Curtain had certainly restored to Talya her true identity; she was henceforth in everyone's eyes the princess Natalya Alexandrovna Iskander Romanov, but she remained the granddaughter of a thief and had not been admitted by the imperial family, or what was left of it.

The time for my departure was drawing near. Talya was bent on accompanying me to the door of her block of public housing. On the steps outside, grandmothers and children came running and

formed a circle. As we drove off in the taxi I turned and saw, domi-
nating the little group, the tall and lonely figure of an authentic
Romanov.

After the summer vacation, I wanted to get back in touch with
Talya. Lisa the journalist responded to my fax. Talya had left for
the home of some friends in the countryside. She liked arranging
this sort of surprise and would temporarily disappear without leaving an address.

Time passed and Talya didn't put in an appearance. Lisa was
worried and phoned left and right; no one had seen her. Lisa informed the hospitals and the police. She ended up finding her again.
Talya had had a stroke while walking in the street. Taken to the
emergency room, she had survived but she was paralyzèd. Incapable of speaking, she couldn't state her identity or give the names
of her relatives.

Lisa went to see her on her hospital bed. Talya could no longer
speak. Only her blue eyes retained their intensity, which tried to
convey a legacy, a request, or an order.

She died the next day, alone, as she had lived. She had hardly
received me, the first member of her dynastic kinship to come to
pay her a visit; she had hardly spoken and told me what she had
kept for so long in her heart, and then she passed away.

I understood. Immediately I began writing the biography of
the forgotten grand duke.

Descendants of
the Grand Duke
Nicholas Konstantinovich

In 1925 the exiled head of the imperial House of Russia, the grand duke Kyrill Wladimirovich, granted the surviving descendants of the grand duke Nicholas Konstantinovich the title of prince Romanovsky Iskander, which Talya, her brother Kyrill, and their father, Alexander, could then bear.

Kyrill died in 1992. Since childhood, his sister and he had never gotten along.

The mother of Cousin Talya, Olga Iosifovna Rogovsk, belonged to the Polish gentry. She died in Moscow in 1962. Divorced from Talya's father, she had been remarried to Nicholas Androssof, who died in Moscow in 1936.

Alexander Romanovsky Iskander, the second son of grand duke Nicholas Konstantinovich and Nadedja Alexandrovna von

Dreyer, born in 1889 in Tashkent, had during the Russian civil war enlisted in the army of General Wrangel. He fought in Crimea, where he distinguished himself by his courage. Later he was moved to Gallipoli in Turkey and ended up in France. In 1920 he went for a visit in Greece to see his aunt and godmother, the dowager queen Olga of Greece. He never wanted to accept a penny from her. He worked in all professions — chauffeur, night watchman, cook, but also foreign correspondent. In 1930 he was married for the second time in Paris, this time to Natalya Konstantinovna Khanykov. He died in Grasse in 1957, as did his second wife in Nice in 1982.

Artemi, Alexander's elder brother, had adopted the mystico-philosophico-religious theories of Mrs. Blavatsky and became a follower of Theosophy. He signed up to join the ranks of the Bolsheviks and took part in the Red crackdown during the civil war and died of typhus in Tashkent in 1919.

Alexandra Abaza, the divorced Demidova, died of tuberculosis in 1894. The two children she had by the grand duke Nicholas Konstantinovich eventually received from the emperor Alexander III the patronymic Volynski, the name of their father's favorite regiment, and were recognized by an imperial ukase as belonging to the hereditary nobility.

Her daughter Olga died insane in 1910.

Her son Nicholas, an officer in various regiments, died, like his mother, of tuberculosis, in 1913.

As for Alexandra's second husband, who had adopted the two children, the count Paul Felixovich Sumarokov Elston was a first cousin of the famous Prince Yussupov. He died in Nice in 1938.

The Cossack Daria Eliseievna married and then went to live in Moscow. The date of her death is not known. On the other hand, a little is known about the fate of the three children she had by the grand duke Nicholas.

Stanislas, the elder son, died (probably shot to death) in Tashkent in 1919, a victim of the Red Terror.

Nicholas, the second son, enlisted in the Red Army. He died in 1922, either from a drug overdose or from an accidental asphyxia while visiting his mother.

Daria, the daughter, couldn't continue her study of music because of the death of her father and the civil war. She became a bookseller, then moved to Moscow and worked as a secretary in various organizations, and became an assistant of the writer Mariette Shaginyan. Like her half brother she was very interested in the theories of Mrs. Blavatsky and became a follower of her successor, the priest of anthropotheosophy, Rudolf Steiner. She died in Moscow in 1966.

As for Valeria Shmelinskaia, it is impossible to learn what became of her after she disappeared from Tbilisi in 1901.

Finally, Nicholas Savine, after successfully escaping from Siberia, had extraordinary adventures on several continents accurately reported by the American journalist and writer Stella Benson. He died in the 1930s in an asylum in Hong Kong.

Acknowledgments

First of all I thank my cousin Nicholas of Russia, who generously passed on information to me and opened his archives. He and his wife, Sveva, have never ceased encouraging me in this project.

Thanks to Andrei Maylunas and Liza Kuzalenkhova.

I also thank Misha Orloff, Iouri Kanski, my cousin Irina Bagration, director of the archives of the Mironemko Russian Foundation, Meg O'Rourke, Olga Bobrinsky-Pichon, and Olivier Nouvel.

Pierre André Hélène, Jean Riollot, Alexandre Khanykoff de Berwick, nephew by marriage of the prince Alexandre Iskander, Mrs. Andrée Savine.

Bernard Fixot.

Anne Gallimard, Caroline Lépée, Chantal Théolas, Patrick Odile de Crépy.

And of course, as always, Marina.